ONCE UPON THE RIVER PLATTE

ALSO BY TIMOTHY J. KLOBERDANZ

One Day on the River Red

Sundogs and Sunflowers: Folklore and Folk Art of the Northern Great Plains (co-editor)

We Remember: Stories of the Germans from Russia (co-editor)

Thunder on the Steppe: Volga German Folklife in a Changing Russia (co-author)

Readings in Introductory Anthropology (co-editor)

Plains Folk: North Dakota's Ethnic History (co-author)

Iron Spirits (essayist)

As High as the Eagle Flies

The Tragedy at Summit Springs

ONCE UPON THE RIVER PLATTE

a novel by

Timothy J. Kloberdanz

★ **Legendary Rivers of the American West Series** ★

CLOVIS HOUSE
Fargo, North Dakota

Clovis House
P.O. Box 1957
Fargo, North Dakota 58107-1957
www.clovishouse.com

Cover photo: Sunrise above the Platte River, Nebraska/iStockphoto.com
Cover and interior design: Jenay
Cover graphics: Cassie Ward
Author photo: Clovis House

ISBN 978-0-9993712-0-6 (paperback)
ISBN 978-0-9993712-1-3 (e-book)
LCCN 2017914138

A portion of the profits from the sale of this book will go toward Pawnee language and culture programs that are aimed at youth and are sponsored by the Pawnee Nation of Oklahoma.

FIRST EDITION

PRINTED IN THE UNITED STATES OF AMERICA

For Rosalinda
who always believed in this book
and whose fascination with the Platte
compels her to return again and again

CONTENTS

RUNNING

There is the darkness that allows for strange shapes and faint slivers of light. And then there is the unrelenting darkness, the kind that devours any semblance of light.

The man ran in unrelenting darkness. Although the ground was uneven, he managed to keep his footing. He clenched his fists and drew his arms close to his chest as he ran.

Zephaniah was naked and awash in his own perspiration. Sweat dripped from his neck and back, forming two little rivers that raced down the valley of his spine. Every part of his body was in motion and every single muscle felt the strain.

Despite the unrelenting darkness, he knew he was being watched. He could feel their eyes on him. They were all around him and the combined gaze of them felt like a barrage of red-hot laser points.

Suddenly, his feet left the ground. His whole body twisted and turned until he was upside down. Zephaniah closed his eyes and braced himself for the impact. For a few moments, he was suspended in the air but he did not cry out or even groan.

With a muffled splash, Zephaniah fell into a deep body of water and he began to sink to the bottom. The water was warm and mucky. He held his breath and quickly swam to the top. When he broke through the surface and opened his eyes, he could see nothing. Again, there was only the unrelenting darkness. He took another deep breath and kept swimming. He closed his eyes so tightly that his nose and his eyelids hurt.

Zephaniah thought he was swimming in swamp water but he slowly realized it was not warm water at all. It smelled and tasted of blood.

He kept his eyes closed but he knew. Each time he kicked or put out his arms to propel himself forward, he felt the blood that was all around him. It clung to him like a second skin.

The minutes passed. Zephaniah sensed there was something else in the pool. He felt an object brush against the side of his head and then he felt others.

Chunks of ice were falling into the pool and they became so numerous that the blood in the pool turned incredibly cold. Zephaniah grabbed at the ice until he was able to take hold of one of the chunks. It seemed heavy and yet when he let go of it, the chunk floated in the pool of thickening blood. And there were more pieces of ice all around him. This was a strange mixture. Blood and ice.

Zephaniah took a deep breath and kept swimming. He was determined that nothing would stop him. Not the blood. Not the ice. Not even a whole ocean of blood and ice. Nothing.

PART ONE

HEAT-CRAZY

"*Sha-ya-loh.*" *The Great Flat Water makes this sound even when the world grows so dark that not a single star can be seen. It is at such times that the mighty river rests. But the river never rests for long. Soon it stirs and once again the river can be heard. "Sha-ya-loh."*

On other nights, when the stars do come out, the brightness of those stars is reflected up and down the length of the Great Flat Water. It is as if the river suddenly sprouts thousands of tiny eyes that blink in the darkness. The eyes ride the waters of the river, gently bobbing up and down, and sometimes their nighttime journey lasts for hours. They dance and they shimmer until the first light of dawn. Then, one by one, the eyes of the river disappear so quietly that they seem to slip beneath the surface of the water and become a part of the river itself.

The Great Flat Water is a true prairie river, but its origins lie in the Shining Blue Mountains to the west. The river is unlike all other rivers because of its unusual birth. It came into the world as twins.

The birth was not an easy one. Yet the difficulties that surrounded the double birth only made the newborns stronger and more independent. When the Twins emerged from the womb of the Shining Blue Mountains, each one went its own way. The male twin headed north and the female twin traveled south.

Their separate journeys took the Twins through the Shining Blue Mountains and onto a huge expanse of prairie. While North Twin and South Twin took completely different paths, they eventually found themselves heading eastward toward the land of the rising sun and the lush tall grasses.

Like two runners in a race, North Twin and South Twin ran side by side for a great distance. They were often very close, but they did not touch or even acknowledge each other. It was their stubbornness that kept them apart for so long. Finally, the two exhausted runners abandoned their independence when they reached the Mound Where the Burrowing Owls Turned to Stone. There, at this ancient place on the prairie, North Twin and South Twin slowly approached each other. When they embraced, they were reborn. The Twins became one river, the Great Flat Water.

Because of its unusual birth and its age, the Great Flat Water was respected by those who were nourished by its waters. All of the surrounding rock and plant and bird and animal nations recognized the primacy of the river.

Among the oldest of the animal nations was the Star Singer Nation of First Prophetess. When the rocks and plants and birds and other animals rested, there were always a few scouts from the Star Singer Nation of First Prophetess who roamed the nearby hills and prairies. Sometimes these scouts would raise their voices in nighttime song and their singing echoed throughout the land of the Great Flat Water.

The Star Singer Nation of First Prophetess included many astute and stout-hearted individuals. Among them was a young female with amber-colored eyes who was known as Ahwa. Her birth name was "Awakened by the Thunder," but it was a name that was so special it was rarely used. Like most of her family members, Ahwa had become a renowned hunter. She also had learned many of the old secret ways from one of her grandmothers.

For more generations than anyone could remember, the ancestors of Ahwa had crept up to the edge of the Great Flat Water. They were early risers, so they usually did this well before sunrise. They moved cautiously, looking all around to make sure it was safe. When it was not, they would hide in the tall grass or the willows along the river. Sometimes, they had to conceal themselves for a long time and their tongues would ache and curl with thirst.

This morning, as Ahwa neared the river, she did not approach so timidly. She did not even pause and look behind her as was the Star Singer custom. She looked straight ahead and moved with confidence and great speed.

"Kai-yoht!" That is what the Two-Leggeds called out whenever they saw Ahwa. She knew their scent well, for it was a strong and unusual one. She also knew that she should remain out of sight, but it was no longer her way. She did not want to hide or suffer any kind of humiliation ever again. The previous night had been a hot and muggy one. Ahwa was thirsty and she yearned to drink from the Great Flat Water. No other river or stream seemed to satisfy her so completely.

As Ahwa hurried toward the Great Flat Water, she remembered the many family members she had lost. The Two-Leggeds had hunted down and killed most of them. Nearly always, the Two-Leggeds carried away the bodies but Ahwa did not know why.

Once, during the past winter, Ahwa heard the frantic cries of her youngest sister. Ahwa searched for her and found that she was caught in one of the jagged-toothed traps of the Two-Leggeds. The two sisters bit and gnawed at the metal trap for more than two days, but it was of no use. Ahwa's sister died in that trap and Ahwa could still taste its metal in her mouth. The name of Ahwa's youngest sister was Yellow Light Shining. And it was in the fading light of a golden winter evening that she had breathed her last. The tragic death of her sister weighed heavy on Ahwa and for a long time she grieved. Ahwa began to question the existence of the Gods of the Wild. Where were they? Why were they so silent? Did they even care?

Now Ahwa charged toward the Great Flat Water as a warrior— and the most dreaded kind of all. She was a warrior who could not forget. And she was a warrior with nothing left to lose.

"Sha-ya-loh." Awakened by the Thunder could hear the Great Flat Water rousing from its short sleep. Ahwa's heart was beating fast. But her heart was strong. Today she was unafraid and she was ready. "Sha-ya-loh."

CHAPTER
1

He slowed down and parked his pickup truck about thirty feet from the river bridge. He pretended not to see the "NO MOTOR VEHI-CLES ON SHOULDER" sign that was posted alongside the road. It was just before sunrise and there were not many cars on the highway.

The old man got out of his pickup and went to the back of his truck, where he lifted out a black plastic bag that was tied shut with bright red drawstrings. He looked around and then carried the bulging bag down to the river. The man walked briskly and kept passing the heavy bag from one big freckled hand to the other.

When he reached the water's edge, the old man quickly tore open the bag and emptied its smelly contents into the river. A huge mass of tangled fish heads and entrails did a downward somersault into the slow-moving water. The old man then took the empty plastic bag and stuffed it into some weeds along the river. His task completed, the old man bent down to wash off his hands.

At about the same time that the old man felt the water touch his hands, he sensed something behind him. As he turned to see what it was, an animal faced him. At first, due to the animal's boldness, the old man thought it was a wolf. But then he saw the animal's pointed ears, long narrow snout, and its yellowish-brown fur. He also noticed its amber-colored eyes.

"Hah! A coyote!" the old man laughed. "A coyote!"

The man waved both his arms and tried to scare off the animal. He repeatedly shook the water off his hands as if he were trying to repel the wild animal with drops of holy water.

"Git the hell outta here! Git! Git outta here!"

But the coyote did not move. She stared into the man's eyes with defiance. Her tail was upraised and it seemed to expand to twice its size.

The old man advanced forward. As he did so, he screamed and waved his arms up and down like an excited bird flapping its wings. But the coyote growled and stood her ground. The old man jumped back in surprise.

As the man slowly inched backwards, he did not take his eyes off the coyote for even a moment. He kept stepping back until he could feel himself at the water's edge. His eyes were wide open and he was breathing fast.

Suddenly the coyote leapt forward and struck the man hard, with the full force of her extended front legs. The old man fell backwards into the water, causing a loud splash that could be heard up and down the river. But the coyote kept her balance and landed on the edge of the riverbank. She watched the man as he thrashed about in the waist-deep water. The man was cursing and hitting at the water with the pink palms of his hands.

The coyote watched the old man and did not let him approach the water's edge. Each time the man came closer and tried to get to shore, the coyote let out a deep and prolonged growling sound.

After a few minutes, the man waded downriver. But when he tried to come ashore, the coyote was waiting for him and would not let him get any closer. The old man remained in the water and appeared frustrated and confused.

As the man in the water watched, the coyote went up to the river's edge and drank. She kept her eyes on the old man as she lapped up mouthfuls of water. She drank slowly and for a long time. When she was done, the coyote hunched down on all fours, got into a relaxed position, and simply watched the man.

The old man remained in the river and waited several more minutes. Each time he tried to come ashore, the coyote would get up, growl, and refuse him access.

As the sun rose higher in the sky, an occasional car could be seen speeding across the nearby river bridge. Each time a car went by, the old man waved his arms, trying to get someone's attention. Several times, he yelled out: "Help me! Help! Somebody help me!"

Eventually, the driver of a cement truck saw the man in the river and stopped to investigate. He called out to ask what was wrong. By now, other motorists were stopping on the bridge as well. The old man in the river had become hoarse and his voice hardly could be heard. But he kept calling out nonetheless, and he waved his arms to signal that he was indeed in trouble. At times he flattened his right hand and rapidly tapped it on the center of his chest, as if he were having chest pains.

As the truck driver made his way to the river, the coyote turned away and looked back for a few seconds. Then the animal disappeared into the weeds. By the time the old man had been rescued, he could utter only one word.

"Coyote," the old man whispered, as if he were afraid that by saying the word too loud it might make the amber-eyed creature suddenly return.

CHAPTER
2

They milled about, talking and taking pictures. Most of them were retired people in their seventies and eighties and they belonged to a bus group that was going to an Indian casino near the Nebraska-Iowa border. En route to their destination, the travelers stopped at Buffalo Spring, a new tourist center south of Columbus, Nebraska. The bus driver assured them that here they would find clean restrooms and plenty of snacks and cold drinks.

After several of the older bus passengers had visited the gift shop, they stood in the shade of the bus and talked among themselves. It was extremely hot and the people were anxious to get back into the air-conditioned bus.

The shop owner appeared outside, smiling and carrying a clear plastic container in his hands that resembled a fish bowl.

"Okay, everyone!" the shop owner shouted, trying to be heard above the sound of so many conversations going on at once. "Gather 'round. I want to let you in on something. Some of you are going to get mighty lucky at the casino today. Now how do I know that? Well, listen up. Nebraska is one of only two states in the whole union that is roughly 77,000 square miles in size. So there are lucky sevens in that figure. And you all know what happens when you get sevens at a casino? You hit a jackpot! So you're standing in a lucky state and you're getting closer and closer to your El Dorado. Now before you go and feed all those hungry slot machines, I want to give you a little treat. It's a piece of our very own beef jerky, and it's not too spicy. You gotta try it. So come on!"

Several of those in the bus group crowded around the shop owner. He held out the plastic container and let everyone help themselves to a two-inch strip of reddish-brown meat.

"Awfully nice of you," one woman said, as she reached into the jar and took one of the last remaining pieces. "And awfully salty," she said, as she tasted the jerky. "You're not giving us these samples so we get thirsty and have to buy more sodas, are you?"

Instead of professing his innocence, the shop owner just shook his head and laughed out loud. "With the drought we've been having, beverage sales are at an all-time high," the man said. "So just enjoy our house specialty. And don't look a gift horse—or a gift cow—in the mouth."

Many of those in the crowd laughed, but a few made their way back to the gift shop to buy some of the beef jerky and more soft drinks.

A square-faced bus driver who was sweating heavily and fanning himself with his cap stepped forward. "We leave in ten minutes, so please be ready to go by then. Ten minutes!"

About half of the group had gathered in front of a small pasture and artificial spring that were adjacent to the gift shop. An eight-foot wire fence had been erected around the enclosure. Within it were three buffalo, including a large bull.

The buffalo bull stood directly behind the fence and seemed to be unaware of all the people who stood watching on the other side. Some of the bus passengers were still gnawing on their strips of jerky. Others were taking pictures or staring at the buffalo.

Suddenly, the buffalo bull shook its enormous head and began pawing at the hard-packed ground with its front hooves. As it did so, bits of dust and dirt flew in all directions.

"Bet he's doing that to keep away the flies," a man wearing a blue and white golf cap said. "I doubt if anyone goes in there to swat all those flies on his hind end."

The buffalo bull continued tearing at the ground with its front legs, doing so in a rapid, relentless fashion. Soon the animal seemed to be at the center of its very own dust storm.

The dust began to drift over the fence, bothering many of the assembled tourists. Several coughed and started to head back toward the bus. But those with upraised cell phones remained and were intent on recording the strange event.

Just as the square-faced bus driver called for the others to board the bus, the dust-covered bull charged forward and rammed its head into the wires of the fence. It pushed against the wire with all its might. The wires grew taut, groaned under the pressure, and then began to snap, one by one.

As the buffalo bull broke free, the tourists screamed and ran in all directions. Most hurried for the open door of the waiting bus. But a few others ran toward the gift shop.

Several of the individuals who were running for the bus were pushed down and trampled by the frightened crowd. Seeing this, the bus driver rushed to help them up and to get them on the bus. But as he did so, the buffalo charged through the dust and butted the driver so hard that his shirt ripped open and his cap went spinning into the air.

The buffalo now turned and faced the bus. The bull lowered his massive head and charged full speed at the huge metal vehicle. Soon the whole bus shook from the ferocity and force of the attack. Everyone on the bus screamed and those watching from inside the gift shop screamed as well.

The bull repeatedly backed up, snorted, and charged the metal sides of the bus. At times, the vehicle shook so violently that those sitting inside feared it might topple over. Each time the buffalo charged and made contact with the bus, those inside the gift shop screamed. The shop owner tried to quiet them down so that he could call for help.

As all of this was going on, the buffalo cow and calf approached the opening in the fence. The cow hesitated a moment and then darted through the opening and the calf followed close behind. The two animals headed downhill, toward the river.

When the buffalo bull saw the other buffalo heading off, it backed away from the battered bus and faced the glass doors of the gift shop. As it did so, anguished and ever-increasing screams arose inside the shop. The shop owner and a number of others in the store quickly propped wooden tables and chairs against the glass doors to make a crude barricade.

The buffalo bull snorted loudly and lowered its shaggy head. Thin threads of mucus hung from the animal's nostrils and dangled in the air like cobwebs. The bull gave another loud snort and then charged the front doors of the gift shop.

Upon impact, huge sheets of plate glass came crashing down on the animal. Some of the large glass fragments flew into the store and shattered. Two elderly travelers inside the shop dropped, as if struck by shrapnel.

A security alarm also was set off at the moment of impact and this startled the buffalo. The animal shook off the broken pieces of glass and it tossed its head back and forth repeatedly.

Suddenly, the bull lunged forward and the makeshift barricade of tables and chairs crumbled. The people in the shop screamed so loudly that at times their cries were more deafening than the non-stop whine of the security alarm. The passengers on the bus also cried out and an old woman with tousled hair stood near the driver's seat and slammed hard on the horn with both hands, as if she were doing CPR on the injured vehicle.

The buffalo bull was now inside the shop. The animal looked all around, baffled by the incessant noise of the security alarm. Then the bull slowly backed up until it was completely outside.

Instead of charging again, the buffalo shook its head and tore at the ground with all its might. Soon, it created another dust storm. The dust became so thick that the bull barely could be seen.

When the dust finally cleared, the buffalo bull was gone.

Within fifteen minutes, several ambulances and police cars had made their way to the tourist center. A television news crew also was on the scene. After the police had taken pictures, a female reporter stood directly in front of the battered bus.

When the signal was given, the reporter removed her sunglasses and raised a small, pencil-thin microphone so that it was only a few inches from her mouth. Facing the television camera, she gripped the mike and began her report:

> "The past few days have seen unexplained attacks by wild animals in several parts of eastern Nebraska. Here, south of the town of Columbus, a small herd of buffalo broke through a fence and charged a bus and a gift shop filled with elderly tourists. Several individuals were fatally injured and a number of other people were rushed to a nearby hospital. The full extent of their injuries remains unknown.
>
> "As you can see by the badly damaged condition of the tour bus behind me, the buffalo rammed into this bus repeatedly. Law enforcement officials are urging everyone to remain calm and to keep their distance from wild animals of all kinds. Officials also are asking that unusual animal activity be reported immediately, especially any aggressive behavior.
>
> "Reporting live from south of Columbus, Nebraska, this is Marcella Ramón of Premiere Plus News."

CHAPTER
3

Zephaniah sat and stared out his office window. Although he had an impressive view of the Washington, D.C., skyline, his mind was elsewhere. He did not even hear his boss, Douglas Kerrington, enter the office and tap his fingers on Zephaniah's desk.

"Knock, knock," Kerrington whispered, as he moved a large chair closer to the desk. The oak chair made a slight squeaking sound as he pulled it across the carpet.

Ever so slowly, Zephaniah turned around and nodded. Kerrington nodded back and scooted the big chair even closer. Both men were silent and simply stared at each other.

Zephaniah Pike was an agent who worked for the FSPD, the Federal Special Projects Division. He took pride in both his adaptability and his many professional accomplishments. Although he was in his mid-forties, he retained the look of a seasoned athlete. Yet his physical build was not the result of genetics, but of early morning workouts in which Zephaniah Pike drove himself to near exhaustion. The agent had intensely dark, guileless eyes that made strangers either want to get to know him better or to avoid him completely. He impressed people as being someone who was totally comfortable with himself and his surroundings. But today Zephaniah Pike felt strangely detached and even physically uncomfortable. When he first came into his office, he sat down and scanned the city skyline to see if he could find anything out there that seemed as out of place as himself. Try as he might, he could not.

Douglas Kerrington was the Director of the FSPD. He was in his early sixties, and his round, wire-rim glasses seemed to complement both his baldness and his rotundness. He decided to speak first. As he did so, he firmly clasped both of his hands together, as if he were about to wrestle with himself.

"Zeph, I'm really glad to have you back. You've been through a lot and if you feel you need more time, I certainly would understand. You only had a couple of months."

Kerrington waited for an answer, but Zephaniah simply looked at him and hoped his boss would not detect how completely out of place he felt.

"No," Zephaniah finally said. "I needed to come back. I spent most of my time out on Assateague Island. Did a lot of running, swimming, and thinking. Now it's time for me to get back to work. But it's a lot harder than I expected. I feel like only part of me is here."

Kerrington nodded to indicate he understood. He was used to talking fast, but he tried his hardest to speak more slowly.

"How is it with you and Darla? Are things any better?"

"Not really," Zephaniah answered. "We're still separated. We even talked about a divorce. But we've agreed to take more time and to think over everything. Darla still gets pretty emotional whenever I'm around."

"And what about Twila?" Kerrington asked. "Are you able to see her much?"

Zephaniah looked away from his boss's gaze before responding.

"Not as much as I'd like. But Darla will let me take her to a park or a restaurant once in a while. I'm waiting for a chance for the three of us to sit down as a family again. Just not sure if that'll ever happen."

Douglas Kerrington freed his clenched hands and let out a deep sigh.

"Give it time, Zeph. I'm sure it'll work out. These things can't be rushed. Remember, time heals all wounds."

"Yeah," Zephaniah answered. "Time heals all wounds. Some old fool who lived more than a hundred years must have come up with that one."

Kerrington chuckled. "Now don't go questioning the proverbial wisdom of the ages. Or the pithy sayings of old men like myself."

Zephaniah Pike forced a smile. He felt incredibly torn. He wanted to talk about his problems, but he also wanted to put them behind him, to forget them, and to move on.

"I know this is your first day back," Kerrington said. "And I can see you've got a ton of files piled up on your desk. There's probably even more e-mail and voice messages that you need to sort through. But I do want you to take a close look at that report out of our Omaha office. I made sure your assistant put it at the top of your stack of files. Have you had a chance to look at it yet?"

"I did indeed," Zephaniah Pike answered with a grin. "At first I wondered if you or someone around here wasn't pulling my leg. Have I been demoted to chasing after animals in the backwoods?"

"You haven't been demoted," Kerrington said in a very serious tone of voice. "When I considered all the possibilities, this assignment seemed like the logical one for you at this time. You've been away and so you need to ease back into things. I don't think you're ready to be thrust into a pressure cooker in Los Angeles or Miami right now. The Nebraska thing is on the level and it's important. We need to find out what's going on out there."

Zephaniah Pike nodded but rolled his eyes a little. "Yeah. The Nebraska thing. Sounds like something best left to the fish and wildlife officials. Not quite sure how it even concerns us."

Douglas Kerrington rose from his chair and went over to the window. He studied the Washington, D.C., skyline and tried to take it all in as he spoke.

"I'm not sure yet to what extent we'll be involved. But we do need to check it out—as soon as possible. A couple of the places out in Nebraska where these attacks occurred are on federal lands. And a growing number of human fatalities and serious injuries are being reported. I'm also concerned about what the local reaction will be. If groups of armed citizens and environmental extremists lock horns or start to take things into their own hands, we could have some mighty big problems."

Zephaniah Pike got up from his desk and joined Douglas Kerrington at the window. But instead of studying the skyline as he spoke, he looked at his boss.

"Chances are," Zephaniah said, "we're dealing with an anomaly of some kind. We've seen this sort of thing before. Something a little out of the ordinary happens and people overreact. Our very presence may cause undue concern."

"Well," Kerrington countered, "the folks out west already are concerned. And the whole thing is starting to get a lot of press, even here in D.C. The governor of Nebraska has asked the Secretary of the Interior to send in special agents to help them contain this thing. That's where the FSPD comes in."

"Yes," Zephaniah agreed. "That's where the FSPD always comes in. But it still sounds like something the local fish and wildlife officials should be handling."

"They are involved and they will be assisting us," Kerrington responded. "But first we do need to check this matter out for ourselves. Our Omaha office is looking for more expertise and more direction."

Kerrington took his eyes off the skyline and finally faced Zephaniah Pike.

"Zeph, I know you've been through a lot lately, but I want you to go to Nebraska and check out this thing firsthand. Do you think you can do that? Are you up to it?"

"I didn't come back here to spend all my time pushing paper and answering mail," Zephaniah replied. "Maybe a little time in the great outdoors of Nebraska will do me some good."

"Are you familiar with Nebraska?" Kerrington asked.

Zephaniah frowned.

"No, not really. It's always been flyover country for me. All I know about Nebraska is that it usually has a strong football team and last year the team's defensive starters were very impressive. The capitol of the state is Lincoln. And Nebraska is smack-dab in the middle of the country. Otherwise, the place is pretty much a blank slate."

Kerrington winked and patted Zephaniah on the back. The director reached into his suit pocket with the other hand and took out a small piece of folded paper. It was no larger than the ribbon of paper found in a fortune cookie. Douglas Kerrington handed the piece of paper to the agent. He did so in a slow and deliberate manner, as if the two men were being closely watched.

Zephaniah Pike unfolded the piece of paper, read the words, and nodded. He committed to memory the secret code name and number of this latest project: "Fire Diamond 8-2-0." To help him remember, the agent visualized a large diamond surrounded by orange and red flames. Then he formed the strip of edible paper into a small ball and threw it into the back of his mouth.

Douglas Kerrington watched the agent chew and swallow the tiny object. In an age of hyper-technology and virtual worlds, the little paper ritual seemed like an anachronism. But it was one of the rituals that bound the men and women of the tightly knit FSPD together. Due to the past intrusions of international computer hackers and cyber terrorists, the agency had reverted to a paper-based system for the bulk of its internal communication and record-keeping. Paper files were now a necessary part of daily life in the FSPD, much like computerized data banks, surveillance drones, and biometric scannings.

"Our Nebraska agents will cooperate with you fully," Douglas Kerrington said. "Just keep me posted on your progress and your whereabouts, Zeph. Have a safe trip and good luck to you."

The two men shook hands, but it was Zephaniah who pulled away first and faced the window. "I'll see what I can find out," he assured his boss. "I should be in Omaha before you sit down to watch the evening news."

As Douglas Kerrington walked toward the door, he glanced back and saw Zephaniah Pike still standing at the window. Kerrington studied the agent's silhouette and noticed how it was framed by an immense window of excruciatingly bright sunlight. The director felt compelled to say something more. But he decided to leave things as they were.

CHAPTER
4

Two men in dark blue suits and nearly identical maroon ties met Zephaniah Pike as he stepped off the plane at Eppley Airfield on the northeastern edge of Omaha. The men, who worked out of the Nebraska FSPD Office, identified themselves as Agents Jake Vogel and William Simmons. They escorted Zephaniah Pike to a secured meeting room at the airport. Inside the windowless room was a long rectangular table and six chairs. There were also bottles of fruit juice and spring water, several tall drinking glasses, and a large plastic container of ice cubes on the table.

A small computer was set up and the three men went to work without any small talk. Agent William Simmons projected a multi-colored map of eastern Nebraska onto the wall before he sat down. He was dark-haired and had a habit of putting his tongue in his lower right cheek so that it made his face look as if he had a small swelling.

Agent Jake Vogel directed everyone's attention to the map. He was in his early forties and had eyes that were light blue-gray in color. His blond hair was clipped short and it looked as if he had sat down for a close haircut only minutes before. Before Vogel began to speak, he unloosened his tie a little and took a quick sip of water.

"Thus far, there have been more than sixty reports of wild animal attacks and animal-related incidents in eastern Nebraska. The red arrows indicate where all of these have occurred. The first attack took place near the town of Clarks on the morning of July 22. The most recent incident occurred only a few hours ago near Central City, Nebraska. A small plane went off the runway at the municipal airport west of the city there. The pilot reported seeing a coyote running toward the plane. The pilot was afraid that if he hit the animal head-on, the impact might damage the nose landing gear. So he tried to avoid hitting the coyote, and in doing so lost control of the plane. No one was killed, but a couple of people were injured. Among those on board was the Nebraska lieutenant governor and also a state legislator. With this latest incident, the media coverage has intensified and the news reports are being picked up nationally and internationally. Not surprisingly, the Nebraska governor has taken renewed interest in these incidents. He seems determined to do something. The Central City plane mishap is now number sixty-seven on our list."

"Sixty-seven separate incidents?" Zephaniah Pike asked incredulously. "All at different times and in different locations? And all in a period of less than three weeks?"

The two agents looked at each other, then at the map, and nodded.

"Sometimes," Agent Simmons explained, "a number of animals are involved, but more often the attack is made by a single animal. The incidents include a red hawk that swooped down and attacked a motorcyclist and his girlfriend. The motorcyclist died as a result of his injuries and the girl is still in intensive care. There was also a ranch family that was attacked by a large bobcat. The family lived along the river and they were attacked in their own backyard. Their youngest son was critically injured."

Agent Simmons cleared his throat before continuing.

"We've also had reports of white-tailed deer behaving strangely and causing cars and trucks to go off the road. There was a van full of people that tried to dodge a couple of deer. It went off the highway by Duncan, Nebraska, and nearly all of the occupants were killed or sustained serious injuries. Then there was that incident with the buffalo south of Columbus. Seven people died as a result of that encounter. Several other attacks have occurred at night, but the animals responsible for those attacks have not always been identified with any certainty. So we've got quite a mixed bag here."

Pike squinted and studied the map for a long time before responding.

"Okay. From reading the preliminary report, I know that buffalo, coyotes, foxes, hawks, and deer have been prominent. Are there any other wild animals that have been involved?"

"This is the current breakdown," Agent Vogel said as he flashed a list on the wall. "These are the various animals that have been identified and the number of separate attacks by each type." He read aloud each of the entries, but refrained from trying to pronounce the scientific names for each species:

Badger *(Taxidea taxus)*	4
Bison *(Bison bison)*	1
Bobcat *(Lynx rufus)*	3
Coyote *(Canis latrans)*	9
Great Horned Owl *(Bubo virginianus)*	1
Red Fox *(Vulpes vulpes)*	8
Red-Tailed Hawk *(Buteo jamaicensis)*	9
Rough-Legged Hawk *(Buteo lagopus)*	7
Striped Skunk *(Mephitis mephitis)*	5
Swainson's Hawk *(Buteo swainsoni)*	4
White-Tailed Deer *(Odocoileus virginianus)*	8
Unknown	8

"Looks like a bunch of sports scores," Zephaniah Pike remarked. "And the coyotes and the red-tailed hawks are leading!"

Everyone laughed. Agents Vogel and Simmons relaxed a bit more in their chairs. They looked at each other and seemed relieved that Agent Pike could find something to joke about.

"Weren't buffalo involved as well?" Pike asked.

"They were indeed," Agent Vogel answered. "But Dr. Hotaru informed us that the correct name for buffalo is 'bison.' In fact, she corrected us on that one a couple of times. She also reminded us that there are differences between red-tailed hawks and red-shouldered hawks, striped skunks and spotted skunks, great horned owls and screech owls. That sort of thing. Dr. Hotaru insists on complete and accurate identification of each of the wild animals. That's why we always try to include their scientific names in all our reports."

"Dr. Hotaru?" Pike inquired.

"Yes," Agent Vogel explained. "She has been helping us the past few days. Dr. Hotaru is a professor of wildlife biology at the University of Nebraska in Lincoln. She's an expert on Great Plains animals and animal diseases. And she comes to us with high recommendations from nearly everyone."

"Okay," Pike said, still looking at the list of animals that was projected on the wall. "What do all of these animals have in common?"

"Well," Agent Vogel answered, "with the exception of the buffalo—or bison—all of these animals are wild. I hesitate to describe the bison as domestic, but they were confined at the time of the attack. They were not living in the wild when the incident occurred. But they escaped and have yet to be found."

"Go back to the map you first showed me," directed Agent Pike. "Most of these attacks have occurred along a river, right? Which river is that?"

"The Platte," Jake Vogel responded. "There are a lot of trees and other vegetation all along the Platte, so most of the wildlife tend to stay close to the river. The animals have plenty of cover there and, of course, water. There's been a drought in that portion of the state, so the Platte is now one of the few places where wild animals can still find water. And in some places, there's not even much water in the Platte itself."

Zephaniah Pike stood up and walked over to the wall so that he could study the image of the map even more closely.

"According to what I see here," he said, "the animal attacks are rather spread out, but they do fall somewhere between the towns of Grand Island and Fremont, Nebraska. The town of Columbus seems to be pretty much at the center of everything that is happening. How big is Columbus?"

"Not sure exactly," Agent Simmons answered. "Probably around twenty or twenty-five thousand people."

As the Washington, D.C. agent studied the map, he noticed that Columbus actually was situated on the Loup River, which emptied into the Platte only a short distance southeast of the city.

Zephaniah Pike placed his finger on a black dot on the map.

"There's our bull's-eye. Right there—the town of Columbus. And from the looks of it, this area appears to be the eye of the storm."

The agent slowly repeated the phrase to indicate he found it to be an apt one: "the eye of the storm." Then he returned to his chair at the table to view the map from farther away.

"Okay, due to its location and size, Columbus will be the FSPD base of operations for this project. I think it best that we work out of a large hotel there. Get us as many hotel rooms and meeting rooms as you can. That's where we'll stay. Oh, be sure to reserve a good-sized room that is wired for computers and large screens and as much auxiliary equipment as is possible. And double check to make sure the hotel has a decent exercise room and a swimming pool. The FSPD wants its agents to stay physically fit and I wholly support that."

The two younger agents looked at each other and began packing up the computer gear.

"Just a couple more things," Pike said. "I want you to take me to Columbus tonight. I'll spend the evening going through all the reports concerning the animal attacks. And let's not rule out the human element. I want to see some background information about all the radical environmentalists, animal rights advocates, and other known extremists from this part of the country. Get an updated list to me just as quickly as you can. By the way, you should know that in keeping with our new security measures, I prefer paper copies of a lot of things. It's way too easy to miss something when all the information starts to back up and then we're merely scrolling through lengthy reports on the computer screen. And we can't afford to miss anything. Understood?"

Vogel and Simmons nodded, but they realized Zephaniah Pike still had something on his mind.

"What was the name of that scientist we're working with?" he asked.

"Hotaru," Jake Vogel answered. "Dr. Susan Hotaru."

Zephaniah Pike looked at his wristwatch and seemed to be calculating the difference in time zones.

"Go ahead and set up a breakfast meeting for me with Dr. Hotaru at the hotel in Columbus. Ask her to be there at eight sharp. Tell her I'm looking forward to meeting her. Oh, and one more thing: Let her know I personally prefer the word 'buff-a-lo.' "

Agent Vogel smiled and unlocked the door. He and Simmons escorted Pike out of the air terminal and walked him to their vehicle in the short-term parking lot. Even though the sun was going down, the heat was so intense that the pavement seemed to grow soft under their feet as they walked.

While leaving the airport in Omaha, Pike noticed a small lake that was adjacent to Eppley Airfield. Homes of various sizes and multi-colored docks could be seen on the opposite side of the lake. Pike also could see skyscrapers to the southwest, but they seemed a few miles away. His eyes returned to the lake and he scanned the many houses that lined its shores.

"That's Carter Lake," Jake Vogel said, noticing Zephaniah Pike's interest. "I have a friend who's a pilot and who flies out of here all the time. The guy never drives to work. Just takes a boat across the lake and then walks in the rest of the way. He's really got it made."

"Nice," Pike agreed. "Very nice indeed."

"Well," Vogel said with a grin, "be sure to feast your eyes on the bright blue color of Carter Lake. Things are gonna look a whole lot different in an hour or two. When we get into that eye of the storm that you mentioned, it may seem like we're in something more like a big dust storm or even a firestorm. Columbus will be mighty, mighty dry."

As the three agents headed west out of Omaha, Zephaniah Pike sat in the back seat and looked out the side windows. Even after they were many miles outside of the city, he was surprised by the large number of cars and trucks whizzing by at breakneck speed on the highway. But as he surveyed the surrounding Nebraska countryside, he found it rather drab and unremarkable.

Agent Pike's special assignments had taken him all over the United States and even to other parts of the world. He had tracked down and arrested an arms trafficker in Kotzebue, Alaska, and helped dismantle a terrorist cell in Puerto Rico. "I've seen it all," he liked to tell people, and he truly believed that he had. But what if there were still a place somewhere that did hold some real surprises for him? And if such a place even existed, the agent mused, what were the chances that it would be Nebraska?

Zephaniah Pike gazed out at what seemed like endless cornfields stretching out on both sides of the highway. He noticed that there were hardly any clouds in the sky. But a few streaks of red and traces of a peach-golden color could be seen on the distant western horizon.

CHAPTER
5

As reports of unusual animal encounters made their way across eastern Nebraska, many radio stations were flooded with calls from anxious listeners.

In Omaha, Nebraska, the popular radio host Charlie Morgen canceled his interviews with two entertainers on his "Morning with Morgen" program. Instead, he urged callers to share their thoughts and concerns about the reported animal attacks.

Charlie Morgen: "In case you just tuned in, we're talking about the latest rash of animal encounters here in eastern Nebraska—most recently, that incident that involved our lieutenant governor over in Central City and those buffalo that went berserk near Columbus. Caller, you are on the air. Good morning!"

Caller #1 (younger female): "Hey, I just want to say that I don't think you should have canceled the other show. You have to be pretty hard up to devote so much time to all this stuff. I mean, come on, a dog growls at a mailman nearly every day of the year. Since when—"

Charlie Morgen: "Excuse me, caller, but we're not talking about an occasional barking dog here. We're discussing wild animals that have attacked and killed people. If that's not newsworthy, one can only wonder what is."

Caller #1: "I just think you should have kept to your original schedule. I took the morning off so that I could—"

Charlie Morgen: "Sorry about that, caller. We do have another call. Go ahead, you are on the air."

Caller #2 (younger male): "Good morning, Charlie. I do agree with you that these animal encounters deserve news coverage. But let's not leave Holy Scripture out of all this. I want to share something from the Book of Jeremiah, where it warns that there are wild animals waiting outside our cities to—"

Charlie Morgen: "Thank you, caller. Those who are interested can look it up and judge for themselves. We have another call. Caller, you are on the air. . . . Caller, are you there? Caller?"

Caller #3 (older male): "Maybe the chickens are coming home to roost."

Charlie Morgen: "The chickens are coming home to roost? What are you getting at? Caller, are you still there?"

Caller #3: "The chickens are coming home to roost. That's all I have to say."

Charlie Morgen: "Alright then, we have someone else who is on the line. This caller is from Fremont. Go ahead, please."

Caller #4 (older male): "Good morning, Charlie. I think you're doing the right thing by focusing more attention on these animal attacks. My wife and I were involved in one just a few days ago."

Charlie Morgen: "Really, caller? Please tell us more."

Caller #4: "Emily and I were driving on Highway 30 over by Ames, Nebraska. Ames is only a little ways west of Fremont. The weird thing is we had just purchased a new car and so we decided to take it on the highway to see how it would do. Suddenly these two big deer darted right out in front of us. I honked and honked but they didn't run away. They leapt right toward us! One hit the hood of the car and the other went right through our front windshield."

Charlie Morgen: "Were you and your wife injured?"

Caller #4: "No, thank God. Our air bags were deployed and I think they saved us. When those air bags inflated, they hit us like a ton of bricks. Luckily, we just had a few cuts and bruises. But we were pretty shaken up and our brand-new car was totaled."

Charlie Morgen: "I'm glad it wasn't worse. But tell us, did those deer seem to be acting different or behaving abnormally?"

Caller #4: "Oh yeah. They both stared right at us before they leapt at the car. Those big eyes of theirs were full of hate. It seemed as if they wanted to kill us and they didn't care what it cost them. The one deer landed right between Emily and me and it was pretty cut up. It stared at us even as it lay there bleeding to death in our new car."

Charlie Morgen: "Did you report this incident to the state patrol?"

Caller #4: "Of course. They said it was just one of a whole bunch of deer-related accidents that have occurred recently. They told us we were real lucky. Other people have not been so fortunate. But I tell you, Charlie, the eyes of those deer were really something. They just didn't look normal. They were so full of hate."

Charlie Morgen: "Thank you, caller, for sharing what must have been a horrific experience. Thank you so much. Looks like we have a call from way out in Calico Creek. Good morning, caller."

Caller #5 (older male): "Good morning, Mr. Morgen. You know, it's been a very hot summer. A lot of people are on edge. But it hasn't been easy for the animals, either. Many of them are thirsty and just plain scared. They don't know where to go. People need to give them some space and to be more understanding. And we all need to cool off. When people get heat-crazy and their blood starts boiling, they can't think clearly."

Charlie Morgen: "Heat-crazy, you say? Heat-crazy? Well, Calico Creek, it sure sounds like you are taking the animals' side in this discussion. Are you?"

Caller #5: "Mr. Morgen, this isn't about taking sides. It's about the need to just cool off and try to be fair-minded."

Charlie Morgen: "Wow, it seems Calico Creek is more 'way out' than I had thought. I see our next caller hails from right here in Greater Omaha. Please enlighten us, Omaha."

Caller #6 (younger female): "I agree with that man from Calico Creek. All of this talk about wild animals becoming vicious and attacking people really concerns me. We shouldn't jump to conclusions. That's not like us. I'm proud to live in this state and to call myself a Nebraskan. Real proud. So folks, let's try to have an open mind and to keep things in perspective. Thanks, Charlie, for letting me vent a little and express my opinion."

Charlie Morgen: "We have a listener from Beechwood standing by. Caller, what's on your mind?"

Caller #7 (older female): "Charlie, I listen to your show every morning and I wouldn't miss a single one. It makes my day complete."

Charlie Morgen: "Thank you, caller. Do you have something to contribute?"

Caller #7: "Yes, it's about my Chihuahua. Her name is Pipsqueak."

Charlie Morgen (laughing): "Pipsqueak? Now there's a name. It must strike fear in all the dogs of the neighborhood. Pipsqueak the Terrible!"

Caller #7: "When I first got Pipsqueak, she was so tiny she could practically curl up in the palm of my hand. I've had her for about five years now. But lately she's been acting funny. I tried to give Pipsqueak a bath the other day and she snapped at me. She's never done that before. I just wonder if Pipsqueak—"

Charlie Morgen: "Maybe Pipsqueak just wants a new name. I'm sure she's alright. Good luck with her! We have another call. Caller, you are on the air."

Caller #8 (older male): "I want to respond to that fellow who called in earlier and said that 'the chickens are coming home to roost.' When I was a kid, I spent a lot of time on my grandparents' farm out on the Big Blue near Stromsburg. Well, there were a couple of chickens that would chase us kids all around the yard. My grandma didn't stand for it. She got out the hatchet and waved it at the culprits. As she sharpened that hatchet, she told us something in a tone of voice I'll never forget: 'Feisty chickens today, feathers in the wind tomorrow.' And then she went to work with her hatchet. So just let the chickens come home to roost. We can handle 'em."

Charlie Morgen: "Thank you, caller. Not sure how we've drifted to this talk about feisty chickens and the sad plight of a little dog out there named Pipsqueak. But at least you're listening and letting us know what's on your mind. Hey, I think we have another call. . . ."

CHAPTER
6

Zephaniah Pike sat at a table in the hotel restaurant in Columbus and studied several files that had been given him earlier that morning. Every so often he looked up and noticed the people who came into the restaurant. Several of the customers wore bright red caps and T-shirts that proclaimed their pride in the University of Nebraska's football team. One older man, who looked like a former linebacker himself, sported a frayed black jersey over his red T-shirt. The jersey was emblazoned with a skull and crossbones. Pike made mental notes of even the smallest details: a scar on the thumb, a copper bracelet, the shape and size of a handbag. The agent was accustomed to observing people and noticing many different things at once, ranging from the obvious to the minuscule.

But this morning nearly everyone in the hotel restaurant was checking out Agent Pike as well. When he picked up a spoon and stirred his coffee, heads turned. When he scooted his chair closer to the table, the waitress looked over in his direction. When he inquired about the availability of bagels and lox-flavored cream cheese, the whole restaurant grew quiet. He was clearly the center of everyone's attention.

The agent also studied his physical surroundings closely. The tan-colored, high-backed chairs in the hotel restaurant looked new, but the tables were a few years older and were completely covered by odd-fitting white and blue tablecloths. Even though it was August, not a single fresh flower could be seen anywhere in the restaurant. Small arrangements of artificial red and yellow flowers stood in white vases on every table. Instead of pictures showing local landmarks, there were framed prints showing mountains and forests and ocean-side towns. There was nothing visible in the restaurant that reminded him he was in one of the prairie states.

Earlier that morning, after Zephaniah Pike swam a few laps in the hotel swimming pool, he noticed an unusual mural as he toweled himself dry. The pool-side painting showed three large ships with square-shaped sails and ornate crimson crosses. The ships were sailing in single file on an amazingly calm and level body of water. The ocean in the mural was so intensely blue that it matched the color of the swimming pool. Beneath the mural was a familiar verse in gothic lettering: "In fourteen hundred and ninety-two, Columbus sailed the ocean blue."

Later, after the agent had shaved and dressed, he walked around the Christopher Columbus Hotel and Convention Center to orient himself. The hotel complex was a fairly new one, built on the south side of the Platte River and close to Highway 81. Throughout the hotel, the agent saw even more examples of the Christopher Columbus theme. To one side of the large banquet room, there were three boat-shaped buffet tables. Each "ship" had a different but familiar name emblazoned on its hull: the Santa Maria, the Niña, and the Pinta.

Still later, as Zephaniah Pike stood in the main lobby of the hotel before going into the restaurant, he studied a life-size painting of Christopher Columbus. An elaborate gold frame gave the painting an antiquated, almost classic look. As the agent moved closer to inspect the picture, he realized it was an original painting, even though it bore no artist's name. Yet the scene in the painting was unmistakable. Christopher Columbus stood on the shore of a newly discovered land, with a sword in one hand and an unfurled banner in the other. The flag was tipped with a gleaming gold cross. Despite the upraised conqueror's sword, the agent noticed that the hands of the great European explorer looked very pale and delicate. Rays of light streamed down on Columbus and his gray eyes gazed heavenward. In the background of the picture, barely visible, were dark-skinned figures with long black hair. They were naked and they were well outside the bright light that enveloped Christopher Columbus. The eyes of the mysterious figures mirrored a strange mixture of awe and apprehension. But it was hard to see the figures clearly, for they were crouching in fear and darkness.

Zephaniah Pike stared at the large painting for a long time. Something drew him into the painting and seemed to hold him. When he finally pulled himself away, he glanced back, yet it was not the eyes of Christopher Columbus that were following his own.

★ ★ ★ ★

"Excuse me. Are you Agent Pike?" asked an Asian-looking woman. "Are you Agent Pike?" she repeated.

Zephaniah Pike gripped the edges of the restaurant table, rose to his feet, and nodded.

The woman carried a small, dark computer case and a purse that matched the color of her pants suit. She wore little jewelry except for some gold earrings that resembled miniature ladybugs. The woman seemed nervous but she stared directly at the agent and did not smile. She was very attractive, but there was a faraway look and what seemed to be a strange sadness in her eyes.

"I'm Dr. Susan Hotaru. I believe you're expecting me."

The agent nodded again and extended his hand. After shaking hands, he gestured for the scientist to take a seat at the table.

"Yes. I'm Agent Pike and it's a privilege to meet you. Maybe you can join me for some breakfast? They have an extensive menu here. Lots and lots of meat and potato dishes. I even skimmed the lunch menu and they make something here called a 'kraut burger.' Listen to this: 'an oven-baked turnover filled with seasoned hamburger, chopped onions, and cooked cabbage.' Doesn't sound like your typical burger, does it?"

"I'll just have a cup of tea," Dr. Hotaru said. "I take it this is your first visit to Nebraska?"

"It's the first time I'm not just passing through on the way to someplace else. I flew into Omaha last night from Washington, D.C. The drive to Columbus was very interesting. Highway 30 seems to be as choked with traffic as some of our major highways back east. The trucks seemed to fly past us at ninety miles an hour. And the Nebraska countryside is a lot more settled than I had imagined."

Dr. Hotaru raised her eyes and feigned a slight frown.

"You were expecting to find sod houses and lots of open prairie?"

Zephaniah Pike raised his own eyes and pretended to be disappointed.

"Well, I did expect to see at least one herd of buff-a-lo. Maybe it was getting too dark, but I just couldn't spot any buff-a-lo at all. No buff-a-lo at all."

Dr. Hotaru nodded to show she understood what the agent was doing.

"I've already been made aware of your fondness for misnomers."

"Misnomers?" Agent Pike answered with a big grin. "Now I may be just a little old-fashioned, but somehow the name 'Buffalo Bill' rings a whole lot truer than 'Bison William.' And 'bison appendages' just don't sound nearly as appetizing as 'buffalo wings.' "

"Using the term 'bison' has nothing to do with political correctness," Dr. Hotaru countered. "It has more to do with accuracy. Many of the animals of the Great Plains were given incorrect names by the early European explorers and settlers. Bison are not 'buffalo.' Pronghorn antelope are not really antelope. Prairie dogs are not—"

"Dr. Hotaru," Pike interrupted with a smile, "I get it. And I trust your professional training and judgment. If you are a stickler for the facts—and nothing but the facts—I'm firmly on your side. You're a scientist who deals with facts and I'm a federal agent who constantly tries to get at the facts. So in terms of how we both do our work, I think you may soon learn that we share a lot in common."

As they talked, both the agent and the scientist suddenly realized how quiet everyone in the restaurant had become.

"I think we share something else in common," Pike whispered. "We are both at the center of some mighty serious staring and eavesdropping."

When the waitress appeared before them, Agent Pike ordered one of their breakfast specials. Dr. Hotaru asked about what kinds of herbal teas they had available and finally settled for a cup of regular black tea. The people in the restaurant grew even quieter as the two placed their order. After the waitress left, the noise level around them picked up a bit.

"I think it best to talk about business after we get out of here," Agent Pike said quietly. "From now on, I think we'll have breakfast in one of the meeting rooms we've reserved."

"You can't blame people for being curious," Dr. Hotaru explained. "This is a fairly small town and people often wonder about strangers. They're just curious."

Zephaniah Pike grinned.

"Somehow, I think all of this intense interest is about more than just curiosity and small towns," he said. "But enough about those around us. How about you? Have you lived in Nebraska long?"

"Yes, about ten years now. I was born and raised in the Seattle area but studied at the University of California in Berkeley. Living in Seattle, I guess I took rain for granted. But I became intrigued by semi-arid regions and especially by the animals of the Great Plains. So when a job opened at the University of Nebraska, I decided to take it. I've grown to appreciate this region, its wildlife, and yes, even its people. But I have to admit, I don't get out as much as I would like. I spend most of my time on campus, teaching and doing research."

"Do you have family?" Pike asked.

"If you are asking if I'm married, the answer is 'no.' But I do consider the academic community my family. And my research projects and my publications are my offspring. I watch each of them grow and develop. And I take a bit of pride in that. So yes, I'm surrounded by what I would consider a family."

"Just curious," Pike responded. "I'm trying to get in the spirit of Small Town America. I admire the value of family, I really do. So I'm not making fun."

The serious expression on Dr. Hotaru's face changed to one that was becoming more open and more relaxed.

"And you, Agent Pike. Do you have family?"

Zephaniah Pike looked away for a few seconds before beginning to respond to Dr. Hotaru's question. The waitress appeared and brought their order, but the agent did not seem to have much of an appetite. He sampled each of the breakfast items and nodded as he tried each one.

"Yes," he finally answered. As he spoke it seemed as if he were suddenly in an echo chamber. "But my wife Darla and I are separated. We have a daughter. She's seventeen. Her name is Twila."

Everyone in the restaurant seemed to grow quiet again. Dr. Hotaru felt the silence as well and tried to counter it with the sound of her own voice. But she spoke very softly.

"Twila? That's a beautiful name."

Agent Pike's eyes looked distant and incredibly sad.

"Yes," he readily agreed. "And the name fits. She's a beautiful girl and she lights up our lives."

"I'm sure," the scientist said, as she faced the agent and smiled. "And she must be very proud of her father. I remember reading about you when you were at UCLA and training for the Olympics. We were all rooting for you. I even remember what everyone called you—'The Zephyr.' "

"Yeah," Zephaniah Pike said in a half-whisper. "That was me alright—'The Zephyr.' I trained for a lot of years and then, only a month before the Olympics, I had that knee injury. And then there were a couple of surgeries after that. It all kinda took the wind right out of my sails."

"But you won a lot of other competitions," Dr. Hotaru said. "We all knew you were one of this country's finest track stars. And if you had been able to compete in the Olympics that year, we know you would have made us proud and brought home the gold."

"Maybe," the agent answered. "But we'll never know for sure, will we? So in some ways I guess I got off the hook. But I'd be lying if I said I didn't think about it at times. Then again, that's all in the past. 'The Zephyr' hung up his running shoes many years ago and he's long forgotten."

"Not entirely," Dr. Hotaru said. As she spoke, she nodded toward some of the people in the restaurant who were staring at Zephaniah Pike.

"Ah, come on," the agent protested. "You mean to tell me they're looking at me because they recognize me? Not likely. I'm probably one of the first African-Americans they've ever seen in these parts. That's why they're staring."

"Don't be so sure. This is a part of the country that idolizes sports figures. And people around here have a good memory. They don't forget outstanding athletes."

Zephaniah Pike seemed to grow uncomfortable as the scientist talked. He looked around the restaurant until he got the attention of their waitress. The woman totaled the bill as she walked toward them. The agent signed for it and then gathered his things and prepared to leave.

"Could we get two half-ices to go?" Dr. Hotaru inquired of the waitress.

"Half-ices?" the agent asked. "First it was 'kraut burgers' and now it's 'half-ices.' I suddenly feel like I'm on another planet."

The waitress returned with two plastic bottles of spring water, the bottom halves of which were clouded and frozen solid.

"That'll be sixteen dollars," said the waitress.

Dr. Hotaru paid the waitress and handed one of the "half-ices" to

Agent Pike.

"You'll appreciate this when it gets even hotter today," she said. "Keep it handy so you don't become dehydrated. A 'half-ice' has become a regular summer item here the last couple of years. And you'll get to like them."

"At eight bucks a bottle, I'd better like them," the agent laughed. "Man, oh man. Eight bucks for a half-frozen bottle of plain water. And I always thought the cost of living was high in D.C."

CHAPTER
7

After they left the restaurant, Agent Pike and Dr. Hotaru made their way to a small park that was sandwiched between the hotel complex and the Platte River. The summer sun already felt so hot that the two individuals sat down at a picnic table in the shade of a large cotton-wood tree.

"Well," the agent began, "you've been involved in this investigation for a few days now. So what do you think is going on?"

The scientist took a pair of sunglasses out of her purse and put them on before answering.

"To be honest, as I become more involved I become more and more baffled. It's extremely frustrating. I haven't seen anything quite like this before. And my colleagues at the university concur. Until we're able to take a really close look at some of the animals or birds that are at the center of these violent encounters, we won't know much. We need to observe them firsthand. We need to run tests. We need lab analyses of various kinds. Until then, there's not much that I can tell you."

"Have you examined the carcasses of any of the animals involved in the attacks?"

"Only a few," Dr. Hotaru admitted. "But they were so badly shot up it was difficult to ascertain anything. The deer that were killed when cars or trucks hit them have yielded very little information. More than a million deer are hit by motorists every year, so trying to determine which deer are 'abnormal' or unusually aggressive is problematic. And we have gone over all the reports, as well as the video footage of that widely publicized bison incident. We also have several photos of a hawk attack taken by a motorist. But none of this gives us much to go on."

"What about the victims?" Agent Pike asked. "What do the medical exams and autopsies show?"

"Thus far, there have been twenty-three fatalities," Dr. Hotaru explained. "Seven people died when the bison bull attacked, but many of the injuries were the result of other people who panicked and knocked them down in their attempt to flee. Another individual who was killed was a young motorcyclist. He was attacked by a red-tailed hawk, but his wounds were fairly superficial. During the attack, he crashed his motorcycle and that's what killed him. We've also examined the bodies of a number of the other victims, but so far we have nothing definite."

Zephaniah Pike shook his head before he even asked the next question.

"This kind of aggressive animal behavior must be caused by something. So help me out here. What are the things that might be causing all of this?"

"That's the problem, Agent Pike. The possibilities are almost infinite at this point. We're not sure where to look or exactly what to look for. We need more to go on. I'm sure you can understand that. One thing that I do know is that eastern Nebraska is not the only area of the country in which there is unusual animal activity. In the Dakotas and Minnesota, large numbers of migratory birds appear to be confused and disoriented. In parts of Kansas and Missouri, squirrels are abandoning the trees and burrowing in the ground. And many of the deer and elk at Yellowstone are leaving the confines of the park and going elsewhere, in numbers that are increasing daily. But when it comes to so many cases of animal aggression, well, this problem seems to be confined to eastern Nebraska. At least for now."

"Is animal aggression like this something that has been documented before? Is there any kind of parallel or precedent?"

"Of course we have documented cases of animal aggression," Dr. Hotaru answered. "We've seen cases all around the world. Animals, like humans, suddenly will become aggressive and strike out for a wide variety of reasons—when their young are threatened, when their territory is invaded, or when food resources become scarce. All of these responses are to be expected. But why so much of this is going on all at once—in the space of only a few days here in the Platte Valley of eastern Nebraska—that's the real mystery. The Platte River represents the merging of the North Platte and the South Platte Rivers. Those two rivers originate hundreds of miles away in the Rocky Mountains of Colorado. But the animal attacks are confined only to the Lower Platte River area in this part of Nebraska. It's very strange. Yet the fact that these incidents appear to be limited to a certain area and a short time span actually may help us generate some answers."

"Yes," Zephaniah Pike agreed. "It would seem so. Maybe there's a particular set of circumstances that has given rise to these animal attacks. Might the drought you are experiencing here in the Midwest be a factor? The newspapers are filled with articles about record-breaking temperatures, prairie fires, and water shortages." The agent held up the half-ice in his hand as if he really wanted to make a point.

"Drought may indeed be a factor," Dr. Hotaru said. "It is August and this is usually the month when it gets the hottest. The last couple of years, we've been having drought-like conditions, which is very unusual for eastern Nebraska. In fact, we had flooding problems just a few years back. Droughts are more common in the western portion of the state. This area usually gets about thirty inches of rain a year. But the amount of precipitation this year and last is way, way below average. People around here have tried just about everything to make it rain. They've been seeding the clouds up and down the valley, but that has been expensive, with rather poor results. Yet still they fly their planes and they keep trying. Last July Fourth, a lot of little communities around here had bigger fireworks displays than ever before. Some demonstrations went as long as two or three hours. They seemed to think that the more they shook things up in the sky, the more they might loosen something and make it rain. But some of those nighttime shows only made matters worse by causing a number of grassland fires. Religious groups have held prayer vigils and there have been processions into the fields. There are even a few towns that have hired professional rainmakers. The people are desperate and it is hard to fault them for trying just about everything.

"So, yes, the drought here is very unusual due to its intensity and its duration. There are even places here in the valley where the Platte River has no water at all. Not even a drop. So I'm afraid you're not seeing this part of Nebraska at its best. This is the tall grass prairie part of the state and it's usually very fertile and rather beautiful."

"Maybe," Zephaniah Pike wondered aloud, "this part of Nebraska is a particularly sensitive area that is suffering from the effects of what many government scientists have been warning about, things like 'lethal heat' and 'climatic crisis.' I might be dating myself, but I still remember when 'climate change' and 'global warming' were the hot topics of the day."

The scientist shrugged her shoulders in a way that indicated anything was possible. "In light of the record temperatures we've been having, I wonder why my senior colleagues ever used the term 'global warming.' Here in this little part of the world, we're well past the warming stage. It's more like 'global melting.'

"Things have gotten so bad," Dr. Hotaru continued, "the locals now claim that drought is a four-letter word."

Agent Pike crimped his right eyebrow a bit to show he did not quite understand.

"'Drought' is now a four-letter word? Is this some kind of Nebraska riddle? Okay then, let an outsider from the East Coast give it a try."

The agent looked all around him and even down at his shoes before he began.

"Dust? Heat? Wind? Dirt? Sand? Grit? Zero."

"Zero?"

"Zero," the agent repeated. "I'm already out of four-letter words that might apply. So go ahead, Professor, you tell me. What's this new four-letter word for 'drought'?"

"H-e-l-l."

"Hell?" Zephaniah Pike flashed a big smile. "Then 'hell' it is."

"There's more," Dr. Hotaru continued. "I read somewhere that back in the 1800s, one of the early promoters of this city claimed Columbus was at the center of the universe. And as such, the Columbus area was equidistant from both heaven and hell. Well, it's not every day you get to position yourself at the center of the whole universe. Now is it?"

"Whew!" the agent exclaimed. "I suspected Columbus might be at the center of everything. Sure enough, it sounds like it is. Whew-eee!"

Zephaniah Pike threw back his head and laughed for a long time. Then he fanned his face with both hands as if to revive himself and get more air. Dr. Hotaru was amused by his antics and laughed as well.

As the agent and the scientist talked, they saw Vogel and Simmons running toward them.

"Agent Pike!" Vogel shouted. "Those runaway buffalo have been located. They were spotted a few miles southeast of here, out near Isabella."

"Dr. Hotaru, this may be the break we've been waiting for," Pike said. "Let's get out there right away."

Agent Pike motioned for the other two agents to bring the car.

Within minutes, everyone was in the vehicle.

"Let's go!" Zephaniah Pike shouted. "Let's go see some buff-a-lo!"

The FSPD agent grinned and rubbed his fingers in the air as if to erase one of the words that he had just said. But Dr. Hotaru did not pay the gesture any undue attention.

CHAPTER
8

The three agents and Dr. Hotaru sped from Columbus toward the little town of Isabella. Agent Pike and Dr. Hotaru sat in the back seat of the sedan and periodically checked their cell phones for new messages and updates. Everyone in the car seemed unusually quiet.

"Is this your first time working with the government?" Agent Pike asked, breaking the silence. He stopped looking out the window and stared directly at Dr. Hotaru.

The scientist opened her eyes wide and took a deep breath. It was obvious she wanted to choose her words carefully.

"Well, this is my first FSPD project. As you know, things have been rather strained between the scientific community and the government in recent years. A certain president and his administration were anti-science, and we've been paying for that debacle ever since. I'm not sure if we can undo all the environmental damage and neglect that resulted back then. But right now, our country is facing some extremely serious problems that affect not only wildlife but also human life. So I felt I had no choice but to heed the call and maybe be of some help."

"I'm glad you're here," Agent Pike said. "And I want you to know that not everyone in our government supported the anti-science agenda of the past. A good deal of courageous maneuvering and even personal sacrifice went on behind the scenes. You should know that."

Agent Vogel turned off the highway and took an unpaved road that went east along the Platte River. Several pickup trucks and vans now came into view and they also were hurrying in the same direction. The unpaved road was dusty and it became increasingly rough and bumpy. At times the three agents and Dr. Hotaru felt themselves lifted off their seats with such force that they all had to laugh a little. Their heads hit the top of the vehicle repeatedly.

"Vogel!" Agent Pike shouted. "Take it easy! You trying to give us brain concussions?"

"Sorry, Sir. This is what they call a corduroy road and it's designed for pickup trucks, not cars. But I think we're almost there."

Within minutes, they reached their destination but were surprised by the number of vehicles and people they encountered. Cars and pickup trucks and vans were parked in a huge circle. Two sheriff's vehicles had their lights flashing. Men dressed in hunting gear seemed to be everywhere. Nearly everyone carried a hunting rifle, except for a TV news team that carried camera equipment.

The FSPD agents and Dr. Hotaru got out of the car and surveyed the scene. When they spotted the sheriff, they made their way to his side. He was talking on a cell phone and was just finishing as Agent Pike approached. The sheriff wore a tan cowboy hat and large sunglasses that were so dark his eyes hardly could be seen.

"Good morning, Sheriff," Zephaniah began. "I'm Agent Pike and I'm with the FSPD out of Washington, D.C. With me are two special agents from our Omaha office and also a wildlife specialist."

The sheriff stepped back a bit and stared at the four individuals. "I'm Sheriff Wells and I was told the FSPD might get involved. You should have been here a couple of minutes ago. That's when we had a little action."

The sheriff pointed toward the center of the huge, makeshift circle of cars and trucks.

"Those buffalo started acting up and we had to stop them before they hurt any more people," the sheriff said. He seemed to realize he was well within range of the news reporters and the TV camera. "We're just waiting to see if that old bull is going to get up again. We're not letting anyone get too close to these animals until we know they're dead. Good and dead."

Dr. Hotaru looked at Agent Pike, hoping he would protest. But then she decided to speak for herself.

"Sheriff Wells," she said, her voice rising sharply. "I'm sure you were instructed by your superiors not to harm these animals. There are reasons we needed these animals alive. Don't you realize—"

Agent Pike stopped her and faced the sheriff squarely. The agent spoke in a very soft tone of voice, so soft that none of the reporters could hear him.

"Dr. Hotaru needed to observe these animals alive," Agent Pike said in a near-whisper. He stood only inches away and looked directly into the sheriff's sunglasses. "Alive, not dead."

The sheriff did not whisper back but instead spoke loudly so that everyone could hear.

"We tried our best to contain these wild animals. But that old buffalo bull got the others excited and they went crazy. We did what had to be done. The safety of this area's citizens is our number one concern. We're here to protect the people. Last I heard, that was supposed to be the role of the FSPD as well."

A number of individuals who stood nearby nodded in approval and a couple of them held their rifles high.

Agent Pike continued to stare at the sheriff. The sheriff cleared his throat and turned toward a group of reporters who wanted to ask him questions.

Dr. Hotaru shielded her eyes from the sun with her hand and tried to see the bison. They were lying in the high grass and she could see only two of the animals.

"I'm going out there to get a closer look," Dr. Hotaru told Agent Pike. He looked at her for a few moments and then motioned for

Agents Vogel and Simmons to get three assault rifles from the trunk of their vehicle.

"Okay," Agent Pike said. "But you're not going out there without the three of us at your side. You do your job, but we have to do our job as well. Understood?"

Dr. Hotaru nodded and waited for the three agents to arm themselves. Meanwhile, she put on some plastic gloves and a small white mask that covered her nose and mouth.

The sheriff and the other people who stood in little groups behind the ring of trucks and cars grew silent. They watched as the three FSPD agents and Dr. Hotaru headed into the clearing.

The first animal they came across was the bison cow. She lay sprawled out on her side, her long tongue sticking out of her mouth. She had been shot repeatedly and the grass around her was dark and bloody.

Not far away, Dr. Hotaru and the three agents found the bison bull. He was crouched down in a position with his front legs extended. It almost seemed like he intended to get up again. His massive head had sustained numerous wounds and his left eye and a portion of one of his horns had been blown away. Dr. Hotaru studied the animal, especially its nose and mouth. She then inspected the entire body to see if she could find any evidence of prior injuries or wounds. The scientist noticed several lacerations on the bull's back, but then she remembered reading how the same animal had crashed through the glass doors of a gift shop.

Agent Pike also studied the animal but with a different kind of interest. He had never seen a real bison close up before and he marveled at the beast's huge size. He also noticed how it had a wild, shaggy look and seemed to blend in with the tall prairie grass. The agent bent down even closer to look at the bull's right eye. It remained wide open and Zephaniah Pike briefly saw a distorted reflection of himself in the shiny darkness of that one great eye.

When Agent Pike and Dr. Hotaru stood up, they noticed a couple of people trying to get their attention. They were pointing at something in the grass about twenty-five feet ahead of them.

Agent Pike and Dr. Hotaru and the other two agents soon came upon the body of the bison calf. It's color was much lighter than that of the adult animals. Like its mother, it also lay on its side. It had sustained only a couple of shots. But as Dr. Hotaru bent down and inspected the body she discovered that the calf was dead as well. After she completed her investigation, she placed her hand on the calf's body and kept it there for a long time. Even through the plastic gloves she could feel the heat of the calf's body.

When Dr. Hotaru stood up again, she faced Agent Pike. "I don't see anything out of the ordinary, but it's hard to tell now that they're all dead. We'll need to run lab tests and we need to do so right away. Could you arrange to have these animals taken to a lab as soon as possible?"

"Yes," Agent Pike answered. "We'll get on it immediately." As he spoke, he noticed Sheriff Wells and a couple of his deputies approaching. Suddenly they stopped, as if the sight of Dr. Hotaru in her mask and gloves gave them reason to hesitate going any further.

"Hey!" the sheriff called out. "Maybe you FSPDs don't like seeing these dead buffalo. But I suspect these aren't the only bodies you'll be seeing today."

Zephaniah Pike looked surprised. He and his two agents and Dr. Hotaru walked toward the sheriff and his deputies. They could see a couple of the cars driving off at great speed and raising a cloud of dust.

"I just got word that a man was found dead over by the town of Ferdinand. From the looks of it, he was killed by animals. I'm told they even chewed on him." As the sheriff said this, he seemed to be chewing on his every word as well.

Agent Pike motioned for his group to head back to their car. But Sheriff Wells walked directly in front of them so as to block their way.

"Guess this latest development puts a different spin on things," the sheriff continued. "Now tell me, if we should come across any of the animals that killed that poor man, should we just cuddle up to 'em and talk real sweet? Maybe give 'em a little saucer of milk or something? Or do we do what we have to in order to protect ourselves and other good folks so that no one else gets hurt?"

Agent Pike did not answer. He simply stared at Sheriff Wells in a way that seemed to draw the passing seconds into minutes. Everyone, especially the sheriff, expected Agent Pike to speak. But Zephaniah Pike did not. He wanted to have the final word, but something stopped him. While staring at the sheriff, Agent Pike saw the full length of himself reflected in the curved lens of the sheriff's dark sunglasses. The image reminded him of what he had seen when he peered into the eye of the dead beast.

CHAPTER
9

"How far to Ferdinand?" Agent Pike asked Jake Vogel as they headed west on a country road.

"Looks like it's about twenty miles," Vogel replied. As he spoke, a map appeared on the screen of a small FSPD location monitor that was inside the vehicle. Within seconds, the multi-colored map showed where they were and the precise location of where they were heading.

"Let's make a quick stop at the hotel in Columbus before going to Ferdinand," Agent Pike instructed. "I want to see what else may have come in for me. Might as well get some work done as we keep driving back and forth between all these places. Everything here in Nebraska seems so far apart."

Dr. Hotaru was already at work in the back seat of the car. Despite the bumpy ride, she was typing on her computer. Her disappointment at the outcome of the bison discovery was evident to everyone. But instead of venting her anger with verbal outbursts, she turned her attention to her notes and typed furiously.

When the group reached the south edge of Columbus, Agent Simmons ran into the hotel that served as their base of operations. Within only a couple of minutes, he returned to the car with a handful of files for Agent Pike.

As they drove toward the town of Ferdinand, Agent Pike thumbed through the files and some other papers. One of the items was a confidential report he had requested only a few hours previously. It was a listing of animal rights advocates and other activists in eastern Nebraska. The list included more than seventy names, along with addresses and biographical notes. Agent Pike perused the list and committed to memory about a dozen names.

When the investigative team reached the town of Ferdinand, they drove south to a bridge that spanned the river. There a small crowd had gathered. Besides several cars and pickup trucks, an ambulance also could be seen.

As Zephaniah and the others approached, Agent Pike was surprised to see Sheriff Wells standing under the bridge, close to the water's edge. But when Pike got closer, he realized that although this county official also wore a tan cowboy hat and sunglasses, the man was not Sheriff Wells.

Agent Pike was relieved to discover that this sheriff was a bit friendlier as well. He immediately extended his hand to Agent Pike.

"You must be the agent with the FSPD," the sheriff said. "I'm Horace Jones, the local sheriff. I was told you might be stopping by for a look-see."

Agent Pike nodded. "What do we have here?"

Sheriff Jones directed Agent Pike and his group to a dark place under the bridge close to the river's edge. The sound of buzzing flies filled the air. Hundreds of round swallow nests could be seen all along the underside of the concrete bridge.

"The body is that of a Caucasian male in his sixties," Sheriff Jones began. "Looks like he's been dead a day or two. His face and hands show signs of some kind of bite or claw marks."

"Any evidence of a struggle?" Agent Pike asked as he looked down at the bloated body.

"Hard to tell," the sheriff answered. "But we found lots of small two-inch tracks in the mud all around the body. Most of the tracks have five digits and look like little human handprints. Take a look for yourself."

"Raccoon tracks," Dr. Hotaru stated, as she bent down to inspect them more closely. She was wearing her plastic gloves and mask. The sight of her in the mask and gloves obviously made the sheriff nervous. He took a few steps back and allowed Dr. Hotaru more room.

"Yes," the sheriff said. "Those tracks do look like raccoon tracks alright. But I don't believe I ever heard of raccoons attacking a man. Then again, I don't believe in little people who live under bridges and who attack folks either."

"Any identification yet?" Agent Pike asked.

The sheriff was quiet for a few moments. "We did find an old social security card on him that was awful worn and faded. We could hardly make out the name, but it looks like 'Robert A. Perkins.' So we're pretty certain the guy was 'Muskie' Perkins. He was a homeless type who trudged up and down this river like the mountain men of old. I reckon people called him 'Muskie' since he used to trap muskrats years ago. Or maybe it was because of the way he smelled. He got drunk a lot and often wound up in jail. Probably did that so he would get a soft bed and a hot meal every once in a while."

The official bent down and directed everyone's attention to the dead man's hiking boots.

"Just look at that; the soles are completely smooth and full of holes. He must have walked thousands of miles in his life. Even though he was usually on foot, we sometimes saw him in a rowboat going up and down the river. He probably sold that boat or stashed it somewhere. Hard to tell.

"He sure didn't have much," the sheriff continued. "In one pocket he had a couple of dollars and some loose change. In the other, he had an old pocket knife. In his back pockets, we found some odds and ends, mostly pieces of paper and such. We found no driver's license or any other type of identification besides that old social security card. And we found this."

The sheriff directed one of his assistants to retrieve a small brown object that was in a plastic bag.

Agent Pike inspected the object closely. He passed it to Dr. Hotaru and his two agents.

"It's a wood carving of a muskrat," Dr. Hotaru said, as she examined the object. "It's very detailed. Even has a tail that's flat on the sides. The muskrat's chewing on one of its front legs. Muskrats do that when they're nervous or caught in a trap. They'll even chew off a leg in order to free themselves."

"Yes," Sheriff Jones agreed. "Muskrats do that alright. And ol' Muskie liked his freedom, too. Every time he got out of jail, he'd hightail it to the river. Guess he valued his freedom, such as it was. 'Til the coons got him. Poor bastard."

"When was the last time you saw him alive?" Agent Pike asked.

"Some weeks back," the sheriff answered. "Didn't see him as often in the summer as we would in the winter. He'd be in town quite a bit during the cold months."

As the sheriff talked, Agent Pike walked over to one of the large cement columns that supported the bridge. The words "MISERERE NOBIS" were visible at eye level. They had been written on the column in a brownish color that looked like dried blood.

"Has that been there for a long time?" Agent Pike asked the sheriff.

The official shrugged his shoulders as if to indicate it did not seem important.

"Not even sure what the hell those words mean. Probably just some Mexican graffiti or some gang slang."

Zephaniah Pike motioned for Agent Vogel to write down the two words.

"Call our linguistics expert in the D.C. office," Agent Pike instructed. "And tell them to get back to me as soon as possible with an interpretation."

Agent Vogel nodded and turned to make the call on his cell phone.

Zephaniah Pike walked back to where the body was and looked down at it for a long time.

"Did the deceased have any family members or close friends?" Agent Pike inquired as he inspected the worn soles of the dead man's boots.

"Not really," Sheriff Jones said. "Muskie kept to himself and was quite the loner."

"What about Old Man Elk?" said a gruff-voiced man standing to the side of the sheriff. The man also wore a tan cowboy hat, as well as a neatly-pressed shirt and a shiny deputy's badge. He was sweating profusely and there were huge sweat stains under both his arms.

"Yes, that's right," the sheriff agreed. "Muskie did hang around that old Indian at times."

"Is there an Indian reservation in this area?" Agent Pike asked.

"There are a couple," the sheriff answered. "They're northeast of here. One of them is that of the Winnebago. But Old Man Elk lives over by Calico Creek and keeps to himself. He's some kind of artist. Makes and sells things, you know. He probably whittled that little muskrat we found on the body. Every once in awhile, we'd see him and Muskie in a boat. They would go up and down the river. They always went real slow."

"The Indian's name is 'Old Man Elk'?" Agent Pike asked.

"Yeah, that's what folks around here call him. He doesn't seem to mind. After all, he's a fairly old fellow by now. But he also goes by the name of just 'Elk.' Guess he figures he's like Picasso or something. Just goes by 'Elk'."

"How far away is Calico Creek?" Agent Pike asked the sheriff.

"About ten miles west. There are two little towns named for creeks, Calico Creek and Silver Creek. Calico Creek will be the first one you come to. But don't you dare blink or sneeze—or you'll miss it for sure."

"Have you spoken to Mr. Elk about finding this man's body?" Agent Pike inquired.

"No," the sheriff replied. "No, hadn't thought about it really. You thinking that old Indian might know something important about

Muskie Perkins?"

"Maybe," Agent Pike replied. "It's worth a try. How about my agents and I stop by his place and talk to him?"

"That's fine with me," Sheriff Jones agreed. "We have a lot of other leads to run down and it seems our office is getting more calls than we can handle these days. We're hoping you federal types can help us figure out what is going on around here. We like to think we can take care of things ourselves, but this animal crap is getting way out of hand. This might well be a bona fide 'conundrum.' People are getting scared and I don't think I need to tell you what happens when people get real scared and they start feeling we've failed them. You need to solve this conundrum. And you need to do it damn quick."

Agent Pike nodded and turned to go just as Dr. Hotaru stepped forward. She was still wearing her mask and gloves. Seeing the look on the sheriff's face, she pulled her mask down so that it rested just under her chin.

"Sheriff Jones," she said, "please keep in close touch with us. Once you remove the body, be sure to keep it in isolation. There needs to be an autopsy and a full run of tests."

"Are you saying that we're dealing with something contagious here?" the sheriff asked. He took off his sunglasses so that Dr. Hotaru could see the concern in his eyes.

"At this point, we don't know," Dr. Hotaru explained. "Maybe I'm being overly careful, but until we know something for certain I think we need to consider every possibility. And that includes a highly contagious disease."

Sheriff Jones did not say anything in response. He just put his sunglasses back on and shook his head.

CHAPTER
10

Agent Pike and the three others were quiet as they traveled north toward the main highway. Simmons now took his turn driving and Vogel was on his cell phone getting updates.

Zephaniah Pike and Dr. Hotaru sat in the back seat and looked at each other. Dr. Hotaru could tell he was uneasy and wanted to say something.

"Pull to the side of the road and stop," Agent Pike ordered. Simmons immediately slowed down and parked.

Agent Pike faced Dr. Hotaru and put up his hand as if trying to calm her before she became excited by what he was going to say.

"You're upset with me," the scientist guessed. "You think the mask and gloves may be causing undue alarm."

"Yes," Agent Pike admitted. "I think the sight of such things does cause concern, but I can put up with that. At least for the time being."

From Agent Pike's facial expression and other body language, Dr. Hotaru could tell there was more that he wanted to say. Agents Vogel and Simmons sat in the front seat, staring ahead, acting as if there were a soundproof screen that separated them and the two individuals in the back seat.

"What really bothers me," Agent Pike began, "is this nagging feeling that you're not telling me everything. Do you think we're dealing with some kind of contagious disease, a disease that can spread from raccoons and buffalo to humans? Is such a thing even possible?"

"Possible?" Dr. Hotaru repeated back the word in a way that clearly betrayed her belief that it was.

"Just consider some of the most deadly diseases in human history that have been passed on by insects and animals," Dr. Hotaru began. "Bubonic plague, malaria, yellow fever—"

Again, Agent Pike put up his hand and interrupted her. "We don't have time for a lecture, Dr. Hotaru. We just need to know if we should all be wearing gloves and masks. Is there any hard evidence for your concern?"

Dr. Hotaru thought for a moment before answering. "At this point in time, there's no hard evidence. But I have been checking health reports for this stretch of the Platte Valley. In the past two weeks, more than two hundred and fifty people have been hospitalized or treated for what doctors have been calling 'heat hyperpyrexia.' That's another name for heatstroke. Many of the patients complained of extremely high temperatures, confusion, irritability, and even convulsions. Those things are symptomatic of heat hyperpyrexia, but they also could be early indications of something more serious.

"One of the reports that really got my attention is what several of those hospitalized told the examining physicians. When asked to describe how they felt, the patients kept saying 'the world's topsy-turvy and things just aren't the same.' So there was not only obvious confusion, there was severe disorientation as well. This seems to be a very unusual type of heatstroke, if indeed it is heatstroke at all."

"But wouldn't you expect to see cases of heatstroke during a prolonged drought?" Agent Pike asked.

Dr. Hotaru nodded. "Yes, of course. But it's the idiosyncratic nature of the heatstroke symptoms and the large number of cases that has me concerned. And we're seeing a high incidence of heat hyperpyrexia in the very same geographical area where we also find so many wild animal attacks. The animals that are attacking may be confused and disoriented as well. I can't rule out the possibility that there is a link between unusually aggressive animals and so many ill people who are complaining of confusion and a strange, topsy-turvy feeling."

Agent Pike flexed his fingers and looked down at them as he spoke. "So you are saying it is quite possible for certain diseases to pass from wild animals to humans?"

Dr. Hotaru answered even as the agent was finishing his question.

"The great flu epidemic of 1918-1919 killed tens of millions of people worldwide. As far as we can tell, that disease was passed from wild fowl to domesticated animals and then to humans. And there's one theory that the disease originated right here in the Great Plains, in the nation's heartland."

Instead of looking shocked, Agent Pike smiled. Dr. Hotaru knew why. The scientist was trying to answer his questions, but she found herself delving into history again.

"I'm sorry," Dr. Hotaru said. "I didn't mean to drone on and on."

"Actually," Agent Pike said, "it's rather refreshing to listen to someone who has such passion. I respect that. But right now, I need answers."

"So do I," Dr. Hotaru responded. "But to get at the answers, I have to ask the right questions. And one of the questions I have been asking myself the last couple of days is this: Are we dealing with the big one?"

"The big one?" Agent Pike asked.

Dr. Hotaru was silent and everyone in the car grew completely quiet as well.

It was Agent Pike who finally broke the silence. "Don't leave us hanging, Doctor. What's this big one you're talking about?"

Dr. Hotaru looked at Agent Pike and then looked ahead at Agents Vogel and Simmons, who had both turned their heads slightly to hear her answer.

"The Jumper," Dr. Hotaru answered.

Again, everyone in the car remained very quiet.

"That's our name for it," Dr. Hotaru explained. "A disease agent that can quickly mutate and jump from one completely different species to another. If it can do that, it can jump just as easily to humans. For the first time in my career, I've been thinking about it a lot the last few days."

"The Jumper," Agent Pike said, echoing the scientist's words. "Actually, I'm a little relieved. When you said 'The Jumper,' I envisioned this really big, floppy-eared rabbit hopping and jumping around, crushing cars and houses and everything in its path."

Everyone in the car laughed, even Dr. Hotaru.

Agent Pike's cell phone rang and he took the call. The smile on his face slowly disappeared as he held the phone in his left hand and wrote down some notes on a pad of paper with his right.

"Okay, thanks," Zephaniah Pike said as he finished the call.

"That was our linguist in D.C. The words 'MISERERE NOBIS' are Latin. There's supposed to be an accent mark over the second 'e.' The words translate to something like 'Have mercy on us' or 'Take pity on us.' The linguist said the phrase was used in the old-style Roman Catholic Mass."

Everyone in the car was quiet.

"So," Agent Pike finally said, "it all seems kind of fitting. We apparently find ourselves in 'Topsy-Turvy Land.' According to Dr. Hotaru here, we're also in a place that is equidistant from both heaven and hell. And now we have a dead man with bite marks and nearby are some words from a dead language. The plot thickens."

Zephaniah Pike tapped the car seat in front of him. Agent Simmons knew it was a signal to get back on the highway.

"Let's find something to eat in the mighty metropolis of Calico Creek," Agent Pike suggested. "And then we'll pay this Mr. Elk a little visit."

Dr. Hotaru looked at Agent Pike and seemed perplexed. "Why not let the local authorities ask Mr. Elk about the body we saw under the bridge? I'm not sure I understand why you feel you need to do this."

Agent Pike looked through his files and then pulled out the FSPD list of political activists in the region.

"It may only be coincidence," Agent Pike said. "But as you know, Mr. Elk is linked to that dead man we just saw. Mr. Elk also happens to appear on my list of animal rights advocates and radical environmentalists. And now it turns out that this same individual just happens to live a few miles away. These are the kinds of things that cluster up and just beg for further investigation. That's where the FSPD and I come in."

Zephaniah Pike stared out the window at the rolling Nebraska countryside. Dry, sun-baked weeds lined the roadside, and the corn stalks in the fields looked just as pale and lifeless.

"Maybe Calico Creek will provide some answers. At this point, even a few good clues would suffice. The sooner we get to the bottom of this Nebraska thing, the better for you and me. And the better for everyone."

PART TWO

CALICO CREEK

She ran briskly through the trees that lined the Great Flat Water and then she turned north. As she passed a large corn field, several blackbirds flew up and called out in loud surprise. Their cry had an unusually sharp and scolding tone. She stopped and looked at the blackbirds until they scattered and flew away.

Ahwa continued going north. The sun was hot and the intense heat of the day made it look like there were glistening pools of water in the far distance. But she knew these glistening pools were only the stuff of daytime dreams. She trusted more the things that she encountered in the realms of moonlight and starlight. She was, she knew, a creature of the night. But today she wanted to explore places she had never dared to go before, even if it meant traveling in the brightness of midday.

As she ran, she felt energized, as if the burning sun and the overarching blue sky were fueling her.

Suddenly, Ahwa stopped. She felt something shaking the packed earth beneath her feet. She was on hard soil that was devoid of grass and weeds of any kind. But she could feel the ground trembling beneath her.

Ahead of her, something was coming at great speed, and as it moved closer, a huge cloud of dust followed directly behind it.

The sound and look of it were hideous. But Ahwa did not run away or hide in the tall weeds that lined both sides of the hard-packed ground on which she stood.

The strange thing that was moving toward her suddenly stopped. As it did so, the trailing cloud of dust behind it became smaller and smaller.

She faced the strange thing, staring into a set of huge unblinking eyes. Ahwa could smell the strange thing and it had a bad smell, so vile that she had to squint as she inhaled the awful odor.

Then the strange thing cried out, with a high piercing sound that hurt her ears. But the cry was more pathetic than terrifying.

Instead of running away, Ahwa leapt onto the strange thing. The feel of it was slippery and very hot, hotter than anything she had ever felt before. The undersides of her feet burned with pain.

Ahwa peered into the strange thing and she saw within it more eyes, smaller eyes, eyes similar to those she had looked into before. These were eyes that stared back at her. These were eyes that beheld her. These were eyes that feared her.

CHAPTER
11

The town of Calico Creek turned out to be so small that the only food readily available was in a roadside tavern. After ordering some club sandwiches and half-ices in Calico Creek, Zephaniah Pike and his two agents and Dr. Hotaru headed west on Highway 30.

Everyone in the car was still chuckling over Pike's reaction in the tavern after he inquired about the "Rocky Mountain Oyster Special" and was told the "oysters" were deep-fried beef testicles served on a hamburger bun with a tangy sauce.

Zephaniah Pike and Dr. Hotaru sat in the back seat of the car and Pike continued to shake his head in disbelief. Vogel was driving and Simmons was operating the location monitor in the vehicle.

They crossed over a bone-dry creek with low, multi-colored clay banks. "Not much of a stream," Pike murmured. "But from the looks of it, I'm guessing it was the inspiration for the name Calico Creek."

Soon they turned south and went down a narrow country road with corn fields and tall weeds on both sides. The road was a bit rough and dusty, and they could hear pieces of loose gravel hitting the metal underside of the car.

"You sure this is the right turnoff?" Vogel asked Simmons. The agent, who had his eyes on the monitor, nodded affirmatively.

"There should be a house on the left side of the road about a half mile ahead," Simmons said. He looked up and tried to get a glimpse of a distant building. But the tall weeds and corn fields all along the road made it difficult to see very far.

As Zephaniah Pike stared out the window, something caught his eye. He asked Vogel to slow down.

"Are those weeds over there what I think they are? Those tall ones to my left. Look!" Agent Pike pointed to some dust-covered plants that were about four feet in height and had distinctive-looking, jagged leaves.

"Looks like marijuana alright," Simmons confirmed. "And there's another bunch a little ways up the road."

"Now don't get too excited," Dr. Hotaru cautioned. "Hemp used to be cultivated in this part of the country by the early settlers. They used it for textiles and for oil. I doubt very much if what we're seeing is the psychoactive variety. More likely, it's the old industrial type. But if you want to get out and take a few samples, I'm sure it would be alright. Look, there's some more hemp over to the right. It seems to be growing wild all along this road."

"Well," Zephaniah Pike muttered, "I guess after the folks around here have gotten their fill of deep-fried cow nuts and 'kraut burgers,' they sit back and roll themselves a big fat joint. From the looks of it, there's enough here to get all of Nebraska high."

"I'm sure *that* hemp is not the psychoactive type," Dr. Hotaru repeated. "And so it's fairly harmless. The only thing you probably would get from it would be a bad headache."

Agent Vogel continued to drive slow enough that everyone could examine the plants growing in clumps all along both sides of the road. Then he picked up speed again. But as he stepped on the gas, Vogel seemed to change his mind as he quickly shifted his right foot from the gas pedal to the brake.

The agent brought the car to a sudden and complete stop. Everyone felt the jolt of being thrust forward in their seats, but Vogel made no apology.

When the dust cleared, everyone in the car could see an animal in the middle of the road. At first, they thought it was a farm dog, but the animal wasn't barking. It had large pointed ears, a long narrow muzzle, thin legs, and buff-colored fur. The animal simply stared at them.

Vogel honked the car horn, but as he did so, Dr. Hotaru reached forward and gripped his shoulder firmly. He knew that meant to remove his hand from the horn immediately.

"Just sit tight," Dr. Hotaru whispered. Everyone in the car stared ahead, but no one with the intensity of Dr. Hotaru.

"There it is," she continued to whisper. "*Canis latrans,* the prairie coyote. But this is very, very odd behavior for a coyote. It's out during daytime and does not seem to be frightened at all."

"Does it appear healthy?" Agent Pike asked in a slow and restrained tone.

As he said this, the coyote jumped on the hood of the vehicle and peered through the front windshield. The full length of the coyote's body could be seen by everyone in the car.

"Yes," Dr. Hotaru whispered, "there's no visible sign of mange— no hair loss or scabbing. This coyote is a bit skinny but otherwise looks okay. Its behavior is very strange. Incredible, in fact. It sees us, but it is not afraid.

"For decades, this country has been waging a war against coyotes. That's one reason why they usually avoid us and keep their distance. More than half a million coyotes are killed each year. Yet their numbers keep growing and growing. We now find them nearly everywhere, even in our largest cities. Coyotes have given the word 'resilience' a whole new meaning.

"So take a close look, gentlemen. This creature is really checking us out, and it is only inches away. An encounter like this is more than just a bit unusual. It's downright incredible."

The coyote continued to look into the car with such boldness that even Agent Pike and Dr. Hotaru, who were in the back seat, could see the bright amber color of its eyes. Then the animal suddenly changed the position of its four feet and rocked its body back and forth.

"You want us to shoot it or something?" Agent Simmons asked.

"Only if you have a tranquilizer gun," Dr. Hotaru answered, still whispering.

"Not a bad idea," Agent Pike said. "But we don't have one with us."

The coyote jumped on the roof of the car and everyone inside could hear the animal circling the top of the vehicle. It sounded like it was doing a strange little dance.

"The car's hot," Dr. Hotaru said with a smile. "I don't think the coyote will be up there too much longer."

Within seconds, the animal moved to the back of the car and then leapt off the trunk.

Everyone in the vehicle turned completely around and watched as the coyote ran down the road, its bushy tail moving back and forth in a mocking sort of way.

At a distance of about fifty feet behind the car, the coyote stopped in the middle of the road. It turned its head to the side and looked back, but only briefly. Then it was once again on its way.

CHAPTER
12

After the encounter with the coyote, Agent Vogel continued driving south on the narrow country road toward the home of Old Man Elk. But the agent drove much more slowly, as if he were uncertain of what to expect.

To the right of the road, a hand-lettered sign came into view. It hadn't been painted in a while, but there was no mistaking its warning: "NO TRESPASSING."

A few feet beyond this sign was another sign: "NO HUNTING." And directly behind it was still another sign: "NO SOLICITING." Everyone in the car chuckled when they saw the fourth wooden sign: "NO PROSELYTIZING."

"Anyone know what the word PROSELYTIZING means?" Agent Pike asked wryly. "We just might have to call our linguistic expert again."

They continued on and saw a much larger sign, with its message spelled out in even bigger and bolder letters: "ABSOLUTELY NO VISITORS WITHOUT PRIOR APPOINTMENT. CALL FIRST."

Agent Pike read the message on the fifth sign out loud. "This fellow sure knows how to roll out the Nebraska welcome mat. At least we know what kind of artist he is. He spends all his time painting signs."

A sixth sign now could be seen that identified the site as "CALICO CREEK ART STUDIO." The silhouette of a big-antlered animal was painted in a corner of the sign.

"We must be in the right place," Agent Pike said, as he looked at Dr. Hotaru to confirm that the animal logo was indeed that of an elk.

Upon entering the yard, they could see a large, unpainted farm house. A sienna-colored pickup truck was parked to one side of the building. Various sheds and other outbuildings also could be seen.

As the agents and Dr. Hotaru got out of the car, they heard the non-stop barking of dogs. Everyone remained close to their car doors. But no dogs ran toward them. The barking grew louder and seemed to come from inside the house.

"Okay, Simmons," Agent Pike instructed, "go see if anybody's home."

Agent Simmons looked a bit apprehensive, but he slowly walked toward the front door of the farmhouse. The barking of the dogs grew even louder and more intense.

The agent paused for a few seconds before going up the steps that led to the main entrance.

As he put his foot on the first step, Agent Simmons suddenly pulled out his gun and fired twice toward the front door of the house. The sound of a glass window could be heard shattering from the force of the gunshots. Large fragments of glass fell upon the steps and splintered into even more pieces.

Agent Vogel dropped to the ground and pulled out his firearm as well. Agent Pike ran to the other side of the car and forced Dr. Hotaru down. Both of them crouched behind the vehicle as Zephaniah Pike pulled out his own handgun.

"Simmons!" Agent Pike cried out. "What's going on? Simmons!"

The dogs were still barking and they could be heard running back and forth inside the house.

"He's got a rifle!" Simmons yelled. "He came at me with a rifle!"

"Stop firing until we know what's going on!" Agent Pike shouted.

"You hear me, Simmons?"

"Yes, Sir!" the agent answered, but he continued to aim his gun at the broken window in the front door of the house.

Agent Pike motioned for Dr. Hotaru to remain behind the car. He ran over by Agent Simmons with his other hand outstretched and bent down as far as he could.

"Mr. Elk!" Agent Pike called out. "Mr. Elk! Are you there? Mr. Elk!"

The moments passed. Finally they heard a voice coming from inside the house.

"What you guys want?"

Agent Pike breathed a sigh of relief. "We're federal agents from the FSPD!" he shouted. "We just want to talk."

"You guys ever hear of phones? You're supposed to call first, like the sign said."

"I'm sorry," Agent Pike answered. "But we're already here. So can we talk now?"

"You need to call first," the man inside the house said.

Agent Pike rolled his eyes. He put his gun away and took out his cell phone. He dialed for directory assistance. He briefly talked on the phone but spent most of the time waiting.

"I'm not able to get your number!" Agent Pike called out. "There is no listing for a 'Mr. Elk.' Makes it a little hard to schedule an appointment."

"Not really," the man inside said. "Try 'Calico Creek Art Studio.' "

Agent Pike again dialed for directory assistance. After a couple of minutes, he dialed the number of the Calico Creek Art Studio.

"I can't get through!" Agent Pike yelled out again. "I keep getting a busy signal. Is your phone off the hook?"

"No."

"Mr. Elk!" Agent Pike shouted. "I keep getting a busy signal."

But there was only silence.

"Hey!" Zephaniah Pike called out again. "Would you please check your phone?"

"It should be okay now," the man in the house said. "I was on the phone with the sheriff's office."

"The sheriff's office?" Agent Pike cried out.

"Yes," the man inside said, his voice barely audible. "When strangers come into my yard and start shooting up my home, I call the law. They should be here in a few minutes. We'll just wait 'til they get here."

"We're federal agents from the FSPD," Agent Pike repeated, his voice sounding angry. "And we've already spoken to two sheriffs this morning. We would have gladly shown you our identification badges, but you never gave us a chance. You came to the door with a rifle."

"A rifle?" the man inside asked. His voice sounded surprisingly calm. The dogs had quieted down a bit, so it was not as difficult to hear the old man's voice. "My front door sticks. I push it open with a piece of lead pipe. So there was no rifle. That was just my door opener."

Agent Pike looked at Simmons to see if the man inside the house might be telling the truth. Simmons shrugged his shoulders as if to indicate he was uncertain.

Zephaniah Pike took his cell phone and dialed the number again. Soon he heard a phone ringing inside the house.

"Hello," someone answered. "Calico Creek Art Studio."

"Cute," Agent Pike muttered into the phone. "Real cute. Let me try again. We're federal agents with the FSPD. We just want to talk to you. You are Mr. Elk, right?"

"Yeah," the man answered. "This is Elk. But you should have called first. If I'd have known there would be so many of you stopping by, I'd have baked an angel-food cake and set out my good china. That's the civilized way, isn't it?"

Agent Pike's tone turned apologetic. "Listen, I'm sorry. But I think we'd all feel better if you put away your lead pipe or whatever that thing is. Just come out here with your hands raised in the air so we can talk face-to-face. We just want to talk."

"Ah," Elk answered. "I'm supposed to come out there with my hands up after you've shot into my home? No, thank you. I think it's best we wait until the sheriff gets here."

"Now just hold on," Agent Pike said. "Don't hang up. The reason we came by is to talk to you about Muskie Perkins. I understand Muskie was a friend of yours?"

"Yes," Elk said. "But I wonder why you're speaking of him in the past tense."

Zephaniah Pike closed his eyes and grimaced.

"I'm sorry. His body was found near Ferdinand this morning. Down by the river."

Elk was silent and did not say anything. The dogs also grew silent.

"I'm sorry to have to tell you about Muskie this way," Agent Pike said. "Sheriff Jones told us that you and Muskie were friends."

"Yes," Elk said, very quietly.

In the distance, sirens could be heard. As the sound grew closer, the dogs inside the house started up again. But instead of barking, they howled in unison, as if to drown out the high, piercing sounds of the approaching sirens.

CHAPTER
13

When the two cars with sheriff's deputies pulled into Mr. Elk's yard, Agents Vogel and Simmons remained crouched down with their guns, but both men held up their badge identifications with their free hands. So did Agent Pike. Dr. Hotaru remained in a half-sitting position behind the car.

Agent Pike approached the four deputies with his upraised badge and they talked briefly. Then Zephaniah Pike called for Mr. Elk to come out and show himself. The dogs inside the house were still barking, but Pike could hear someone telling them to be quiet. At times the language did not sound like anything that resembled English.

The front door of the old farmhouse opened very slowly, for it seemed to be stuck. An old man emerged, with two large dogs close on his heels. They were whining and trying to get out of the door at the same time. But he called to the dogs to remain inside.

The old man had long gray hair that was tied in back and hung down to his waist. He was wearing a long-sleeved work shirt and faded jeans. He was in his stocking feet and his arms were at his sides.

"Hands in the air!" Agent Pike ordered. "Up in the air!"

The old Indian slowly raised his arms. As he did so, Agent Pike noticed that the old man had numbers tattooed on each of his fingers, directly beneath each knuckle.

"Are you Mr. Elk?" Agent Pike asked.

"Yeah," the old man answered. "I am Elk."

"Is there anyone else in the house?" Agent Pike continued.

"Only Apollo and Artemis. They're my two dogs," the old man replied. "They're scared. They want to come out. You shook 'em up real bad."

"Come down the stairs, but do so very slowly," Agent Pike ordered. "And watch out for the broken glass."

The old Indian walked down the steps and then stood facing the agents, his arms still raised in the air.

Agents Vogel and Simmons approached and frisked the old man. Then Agent Vogel stood back and signaled to Agent Pike that Mr. Elk was unarmed. The four sheriff's deputies watched everything, but they did not draw their guns or appear apprehensive. The lights on their cars continued to blink and revolve, casting an eerie red glow on the old Indian's dark and wrinkled face.

"Do you want me to call and get a search warrant so we can look in the house?" Agent Simmons asked. "I swear he came at me with a rifle."

Agent Pike did not answer. He walked closer to the old Indian and looked directly into his eyes. The agent noticed that the old man's dark eyes looked surprisingly young. They almost seemed out of place in such a worn and wrinkled face. The old man's eyelids were especially thick, but they could not conceal or detract from the intensity of his eyes.

"Like I said," the old Indian repeated, "it was just a piece of pipe. You can look for yourself. It's inside, lying on the floor right where I dropped it when your man shot at me."

Zephaniah Pike motioned for the two agents to investigate. The dogs inside were growling, so the agents approached very slowly. Elk called out to Apollo and Artemis to quiet down and to remain inside. Agent Vogel stuck his head through the broken glass window to get a closer look. But he did so very slowly and carefully, as if he were inspecting a guillotine.

"There's a long piece of lead pipe lying on the floor," Agent Vogel said.

Agent Simmons went to the broken window and briefly peered inside the house. Looking very surprised, he nodded in agreement.

"Mr. Elk," Agent Pike said, putting his gun back in his holster. "You have my sincere apology for this misunderstanding. We'll take care of the damage just as soon as we can."

The old man said nothing. He looked at Agent Pike as if there were something more he expected the agent to say.

"Well, can I put my hands down?" Elk finally asked.

"Of course," Agent Pike said. "But you sure gave us quite a scare."

"I gave you quite a scare? *You?*" the old man asked, sounding very surprised. He looked at each of the three agents and the four armed deputies.

"I'm Special Agent Zephaniah Pike from the FSPD Office in Washington, D.C." He slowly removed a long, black leather wallet from the inside pocket of his suit jacket. He opened it so that the old man could see the large, oval-shaped badge that identified the agent as a member of the Federal Special Projects Division.

"The FSPD—Fizz Pidd," Elk said as he studied the badge. "Like I said before, you should have called first. I'm not into formality, but I have my work to do. And I don't like to be disturbed when I'm working."

"Again," Agent Pike responded in a forceful yet contrite tone of voice. "I'm truly sorry for the misunderstanding."

Dr. Hotaru, who came walking from behind the agents' car, approached now as well.

"Mr. Elk," Agent Pike said. "This is Dr. Hotaru. She's not an agent, but she is working with us. She's a scientist from the University of Nebraska who studies wildlife."

Dr. Hotaru nodded as she was introduced and the old Indian nodded back.

"And these are Agents Jake Vogel and William Simmons," Zephaniah Pike said.

"We've met," the old Indian said. Even though the comment sounded humorous, Elk did not smile.

Agent Pike looked at the four deputies who were standing at a distance, listening and watching.

"You guys can head back into town," Agent Pike said. "Thanks for your help."

"I'd prefer they stick around until you're through questioning me," Elk said, loud enough so that everyone in the yard could hear.

"Alright," Agent Pike agreed. "Alright. Can we talk inside?"

"No," Elk said. "My place is a mess. Lots of broken glass, bullet holes, frightened dogs. We'd best talk here in the yard."

"Again," Agent Pike said. "I'm sorry about the misunderstanding."

The old man stiffened. "Mis-un-der-stand-ing?" He sounded out the word slowly and sarcastically. "Guess I need a few more signs. Maybe 'NO SHOOTING,' 'NO ARMED FEDERAL AGENTS,' 'NO UNPROVOKED ATTACKS.'"

Agent Pike looked at Elk and then raised his right forefinger and shook it slightly as if to signal he would apologize only one last time.

"Mr. Elk," he began, "you're a little angry with us and I understand that. I do. You've got good reason to be. I'm sorry not only about the events of today; I'm also sorry about your friend Muskie. That's why we came here, to ask about Muskie. His body was found under the river bridge, near the town of Ferdinand. We're not sure exactly how or when he died."

Elk listened. The dogs inside his house were starting up again, but the old Indian did not yell for them to be quiet.

"When was the last time you saw Muskie?" Agent Pike asked.

The old man thought for a few seconds before answering. "Sometime last week. Not sure which day. He stopped here and we talked a bit. He was very weak. I told him he should go to a hospital. I even offered to drive him to the one in Columbus. But he said he wanted to die outdoors. He said he was ready."

"He seemed to be that bad?" Agent Pike asked.

"Yes."

Surprised, Dr. Hotaru stepped forward. "What kind of symptoms did he exhibit?"

Elk looked at her incredulously. "He was very ill and spitting up blood. He would get real confused and his hands would shake. Cirrhosis does that, you know."

"Cirrhosis?" Dr. Hotaru asked.

"Yes," Elk answered. "Muskie was told he had cirrhosis years ago. But he never stopped drinking. He always wanted me to drink with him. But I wouldn't. I told him alcohol would kill him if he didn't stop drinking."

"We're not sure that's what Muskie died from," Agent Pike interjected. "When his body was found early this morning, there were bite marks on his hands and face and raccoon tracks all around him."

"You saying raccoons killed Muskie?" Elk asked in a disbelieving tone.

"It's a possibility," Agent Pike asserted. "He may have been ill with cirrhosis, but it may have been wild animals that killed him."

"I doubt that," Elk answered. "During all the time I knew him, Muskie had no problem with animals. He used to do some trapping when he was younger. But he gave up that business many, many years ago. Muskie drank and he had his faults. But he had a heart of gold. He could get along with anyone, human and animal alike. Once, when the two of us were in a boat out on the river, Muskie extended his right arm. He just held it there. Soon some big monarch butterflies landed on his arm. More and more kept coming. They were all over his hat and they clung to the back of his shirt. In no time at all, it looked like he was wearing an orange and black robe of fluttering butterfly wings. It was a sight to behold. Monarch butterflies do not do that for just anyone. They are very fussy. And they are good judges of character."

"That may be," Agent Pike answered. "I'm glad you have some

fond memories of Muskie. But surely you've heard of all the animal attacks that have been occurring here in the Platte Valley?"

The old Indian was silent.

"Surely you've heard," Agent Pike repeated.

"I don't have a television or a computer," Elk said. "But I have a radio and yes, I have heard some of the reports you speak of. But Muskie was not attacked and killed by raccoons. He was very ill and close to death when I saw him last week. Muskie wanted to die outdoors and it sounds like he got his wish. So I don't believe he was killed by raccoons."

"What makes you so sure?" Agent Pike asked.

"I'm not sure of very much," Elk admitted, "and that is a sad thing for an old man like myself to say. But I know raccoons. They are very curious and like to leave their mark everywhere. That is why you find their tracks in the mud of nearly every riverbank. And they like to chew and nibble on things that they come across. That's their way. They mean no real harm. Raccoons would not have killed Muskie. If they nibbled on him after he died, that is simply their way."

"So you're telling us those marks on his body were little love bites?" Agent Simmons asked in a mocking tone of voice.

Agent Pike looked at the old man in a way that seemed to apologize for Simmons' boldness. Pike thought for a few more moments before speaking again.

"Mr. Elk," he began. "Have you noticed any strange behavior on the part of wild animals during the past few days? Any strange behavior at all?"

"Depends on what you call strange," the old man answered. "Raccoon behavior seems very strange to you. But it doesn't seem so strange to me."

"What if I were to tell you," Agent Pike continued, "that while we were driving here today we saw a coyote in the middle of the road that leads right up to your house? We honked, but the animal did not run away. In fact, it jumped on our vehicle and did a little dance number on the roof of the car."

"That I would have liked to have seen," Elk said, grinning. "A coyote dancing on top of a car filled with federal agents! Yes, that sounds just like Coyote."

"Such animal behavior does not strike you as strange?" Dr. Hotaru asked.

"No," the old Indian said, still smiling. "Not when it comes to Coyote. Years ago, I saw a coyote climb way up into a tree. Another time, I remember when he stopped a nighttime baseball game by running off with third base. And when I was a boy, I came across a coyote that was in my uncle's outhouse. Coyote was inside going through an old catalog. But I never found out what he wanted to order. I've often wondered, what would a coyote order out of a catalog?"

"Very amusing," Agent Pike said. "But the situation we're dealing with is quite serious. We've seen dead animals and a dead man today. And there have been confirmed reports of other deaths and wild animal attacks. Regardless of what you seem to think, we have a mighty big problem on our hands."

"Yes," Elk agreed. "If you think you have a mighty big problem, then you do. But do not expect everyone to think the same way that you do."

"My concern is people," Agent Pike countered in an exasperated tone of voice. "People want to be able to walk outdoors and not have to worry about some crazed animal suddenly attacking them. Our real concern is not raccoons or coyotes, it's people."

"Maybe that's the problem," the old Indian answered. "If your sole concern is with people, then that blinds you to other possibilities. But what about the animals? When you get back on the highway, you may see a dead porcupine lying on the roadside. You may also see the rotting body of a white-tailed deer lying in the ditch beside the beer cans and other garbage. And if you look real hard, you'll see the shell of a turtle, broken and smashed to bits. These creatures simply are trying to go where they and their ancestors have gone for thousands of years.

What about them? How can you ignore their worth and their losses?"

As Elk spoke, Zephaniah Pike suddenly realized why the old Indian's name appeared on the agent's list of activists and animal rights advocates. Pike did not agree with the old man, but the agent was struck by the old man's forthrightness and choice of words.

Dr. Hotaru seemed impressed as well, but she remained silent and appeared to be deep in thought.

"What about hunting?" Agent Simmons asked. "Do you disapprove of hunting?"

"No," Elk answered. "In my youth, I was a hunter. And I know many good people who are hunters. Hunting is an honorable thing. But like all good things, hunting can be abused and turned into something very shameful. When I come across animals that have been shot and killed for no reason, it makes me angry. True hunters don't engage in such senseless killing and they despise the actions of those who do. Such hunters are cowards and they give all hunters a bad name."

"I think that'll be all for today," Agent Pike said. "Someone will come out and repair the damage to your home as soon as we can arrange it. We'll take care of the expense."

"Make sure they call first and make an appointment," Elk replied. "I'm a busy man and have quite a few projects to finish. There are animals in the wood who are calling for me to free them."

As everyone turned to leave, the old Indian stopped before going into his house and looked down at all the broken glass on the steps. Then he called out to Agent Pike.

"Maybe Coyote will dance on your car again," the old Indian said, smiling. "Just be sure to turn up the radio so he can keep time to the music. He'll like that."

CHAPTER
14

As the agents and Dr. Hotaru headed down the road, everyone looked out the car's windows as if searching for some sign of the coyote.

"Where to next?" asked Agent Vogel. He was driving and trying to look ahead, as well as to his right and left.

"Let's get back to Columbus," Zephaniah Pike answered. "We've got a lot to do."

Dr. Hotaru turned her eyes from the window and looked at Agent Pike.

"So what do you think of Mr. Elk?" she asked.

Agent Pike smiled. "He's an interesting old man. But some of what he says sounds a little crazy. We need to check him out and I plan to do just that."

"But he sounds very informed about the animals in this portion of the state," Dr. Hotaru argued. "He may have insights that could prove helpful to us. Maybe we should talk to him again and share some of what we know."

"Tell you what," Agent Pike proposed, "if the autopsy report on Muskie Perkins indicates that he died of natural causes and was not the victim of a raccoon attack, we'll pay Mr. Elk another visit. We'll soon find out how much he really knows about animals—and people."

Agent Pike thought for a few moments, looking perplexed. "Were my ears deceiving me, or did Mr. Elk say something about 'animals in the wood' calling to him to be released?"

"That's what he said," Agent Simmons said. "Sounded like the old man is demented or something."

Dr. Hotaru let out an audible sigh. "Sounds more like he's an artist who carves things out of wood. What he said didn't hint of senility. I think he was talking about his art in a metaphorical sort of way."

"What was the name of that tribe the sheriff said lives around here?" Agent Pike asked. "Winnebago? Anyone here know anything about the Winnebago Indians?"

Everyone in the car fell silent.

"My area of specialization is wildlife biology," Dr. Hotaru finally said. "I took an anthropology class many years ago in college, but I never learned anything about the Winnebago Indians. For some reason, I don't think of Indians when I hear the word 'Winnebago.' I doubt if many people do."

Agent Pike's cell phone rang and he deftly took it out of his pocket and answered. It was his boss, Douglas Kerrington, calling from the main office in Washington, D.C. Dr. Hotaru, who was sitting beside Agent Pike in the back seat, could hear nearly every word spoken by the caller.

"We've had quite a full day, Douglas," Agent Pike said, speaking very softly. He began summarizing the day's events but suddenly was interrupted.

"Zeph," Douglas Kerrington said, in an excited tone of voice. "People are really putting a lot of pressure on us to do something. Environmental organizations are sending people into the area there. And groups of hunters are mobilizing and they're talking about going after wild animals or anyone who stands in the way. Some pretty disturbing footage of those buffalo that were killed earlier today has been televised nationwide. The whole thing is starting to get out of hand. But we can't let that happen. Now can we, Zeph?"

"No, Sir," Agent Pike answered.

"I hope you can manage things and get me some answers as soon as possible. The FSPD needs to put a tight lid on this Nebraska thing or the whole damn mess will boil over. So just try to contain it and do it quick. Can you do that, Zeph?"

"I'm doing my best, Sir."

"Alright. Keep in touch. And be careful."

* * * *

That evening, Zephaniah Pike sat at a desk in his hotel room. He was dressed in only a T-shirt and boxers. The television and air conditioner were on, as well as his computer. The air conditioner was bulky and loud, yet it managed to circulate some cool air into the room. Agent Pike stared into the computer screen and skimmed his e-mail. Then he did a search until he found a number of sites, including one devoted to the Winnebago Indians. He jotted down some notes as he scanned the pages of the rather extensive site.

He rubbed his eyes and looked at the stack of paper files that he had picked up that same evening. For a long time, he stared at the telephone in his room and then he took out a special phone card from his wallet. The agent did not want to use his cell phone since the mobile phone was FSPD property. He dialed several numbers and waited. The telephone at the other end of the line rang for a long time before someone finally picked up.

"Hello."

"Hi, Darla. It's Zeph."

"What time is it? Is everything alright?"

"Yes, everything's okay. I'm sorry it's so late."

"Where are you?"

"Columbus, Nebraska."

"Where?"

"I'm in eastern Nebraska. I'm on that case investigating those wild animal attacks."

"Those what?"

"Thought maybe you heard about it."

"No. No, I haven't."

"Darla, is Twila there?"

"Yes, but she's sleeping."

"I didn't realize it was so late. Guess I forgot about the time change."

"You always do."

"Just wanted to see how Twila was."

"She's fine. But it's awful late. We need to keep this short." There was a long pause. "Good night, Zeph."

"Yeah, okay. Good night."

Zephaniah Pike slowly put down the receiver. He stared at his computer screen. Then he turned to the television and watched it for a few minutes. A late night talk show host was laughing as a man demonstrated how his pet terrier could climb up the steps of a plastic slide for children. Once at the top, the dog then spread out its legs and nervously coasted down the slide.

When Zephaniah finally went to bed, he closed his eyes, but the face of the coyote that he had seen earlier that day came to mind. He opened and closed his eyes. Then he saw the coyote's face again and the animal's amber-colored eyes. The scene changed slowly and he saw a yellowish-brown coyote running on a road. The animal suddenly turned and began climbing a leafless tree. The coyote went from one branch to another, in a rapid zigzag fashion.

CHAPTER
15

Dr. Hotaru walked down the long hallway of the hotel. She had awakened early, yet it seemed there were always agents and other people milling about, no matter what time of the day it was.

She passed by several rooms that had been converted into temporary offices. They were filled with computers and large tables cluttered with maps and stacks of files. Finally, she spotted Agent Pike sitting at a desk and talking to Agent Simmons. Agent Pike had taken off his suit jacket and the sleeves of his white shirt were rolled up. He looked as if he had been working for some time. She politely waited until he was free.

"Good morning, Agent Pike," Dr. Hotaru said. Although he looked very tired, he nodded and smiled. He pointed to a chair in front of his desk and beckoned for her to sit.

Agent Pike leaned toward the scientist and spoke very softly.

"There's a big meeting this afternoon and a number of officials will be there. Not sure what will come out of it. But people are clamoring that something be done and real soon. The meeting is set for two p.m. in the conference room of this hotel. You'll be there?"

"Of course, Agent Pike," Dr. Hotaru answered.

"You know," he said, again speaking very softly, "we spend an awful lot of our time addressing each other with titles. From now on, just call me Zeph."

"Zeph? As in 'The Zephyr'?"

"No. Zeph, as in Zephaniah Pike. But that's a mouthful for most people. So 'Zeph' is just fine."

Dr. Hotaru smiled. "Okay, 'Zeph' it is. My first name is Susan. I guess it's something of a nickname as well. My real name is Tsuya, but that was always hard for most people to say or spell correctly. So I go by Susan."

"Susan Hotaru," Zeph repeated to himself, smiling. "Susan Hotaru. Sounds like the name of a prize-winning scientist."

As Agent Pike spoke, he reached for a file that was stamped "CONFIDENTIAL" and handed it to Hotaru. "We just got a preliminary autopsy report on the body that was found down by the river yesterday morning. Take a look."

Susan Hotaru opened the classified file and quickly turned each page. She seemed puzzled.

"Are you sure this is the right file?" the scientist asked. "Every single page is blank."

"Sorry about that," the agent replied as he gestured for the file's return.

"It's one of our new security measures. Now that our agency is back in the 'Paper Age' again, we need to ensure that the wrong people can't read our documents." The agent opened the file and lightly touched his right thumb to the lower center of each page. Within seconds, the full text came into view.

"Here you go," Zephaniah Pike said as he handed back the classified file. "But you'll have to read it fast. In a few minutes, the print will begin to fade and then completely disappear."

"I see the FSPD is making efficient use of the latest advances in biometrics," Dr. Hotaru said as she read through the report. "I assume you're using a combination of personal thumbprints and recognizable DNA to safeguard your paper documents?"

Zephaniah Pike nodded. "It's a bit more complicated than that. But

I really can't say more."

The scientist studied the autopsy report as the agent continued talking.

"It's preliminary. But as you can see, it appears that the man died of massive internal bleeding. That's consistent with late-stage cirrhosis."

"And the bite marks," Hotaru commented, "occurred after he died. So maybe he wasn't attacked and killed by wild animals after all."

Pike nodded, lightly drumming the top of the desk with his fingers. "The blood work and other lab tests you wanted run are being done, but they will take a while longer. Same for the three dead bison. We'll have to wait for those lab reports as well."

"So this new information means it might be wise to pay Mr. Elk another visit?"

"Yes. I already called him this morning. He didn't seem too excited about talking to us again. But he said if we felt we had to, he would talk. But he asked that only you and I come this time."

"Will it be possible for only the two of us to go?" Hotaru asked.

"I don't see why not. Simmons will be returning to Omaha. Vogel will stay on. I told Mr. Elk that you and I would be at his place around eight-thirty. So we should leave in a few minutes."

The scientist looked at her wristwatch and nodded.

"I did some web searches last night," Agent Pike continued, "and I found a number of things we were wondering about. Came across a site about the Winnebago tribe. And I even found a whole website devoted to Mr. Elk. It was done by an international art critic who seemed pretty impressed with his work. He had a lot of praise for Mr. Elk's intimate knowledge of wildlife. Did you know that several of his carvings have sold for a good deal of money in places like Paris and Munich?"

"No, I didn't," Hotaru admitted. "But this wouldn't be the first time a talented artist was ignored by the locals. Maybe it's better for him this way. He doesn't get bothered so much."

"There wasn't any biographical information about Mr. Elk on that website. He seems to be something of an enigma. He wrote several letters to newspapers years ago about environmental issues and Native American stuff. That probably explains why his name appeared on my list of 'activists.' I'll be getting the full scoop on him shortly."

Agent Pike slipped on his suit jacket and called out to Jake Vogel, who was standing nearby, for the car keys.

"Vogel," he said, "you'll look into those things we talked about?"

The blond-haired agent nodded and held out a ring of car keys.

"And did you put that piece in the car?"

"It's in the trunk," Vogel answered.

Hearing this, Hotaru's mood suddenly shifted. She gave Agent Vogel a puzzled look and hoped he would say something more.

"Let's go," Pike said.

As Susan Hotaru prepared to leave, she looked again at Agent Vogel. She gave him another chance to say something, perhaps something that might reassure her. But he simply raised the forefinger and middle finger of his right hand. Then he spread his two fingers apart and flashed a "V" sign. The scientist wasn't sure if the gesture signified peace, victory, or the first letter of Vogel's last name. He smiled broadly and seemed to revel in the uncertainty.

CHAPTER
16

The drive from Columbus to Calico Creek was only about a dozen miles, but it was too long a stretch to fill with small talk.

"Zeph," Hotaru finally asked. "Are you expecting any trouble today?"

"No more than usual," Agent Pike replied. "In my line of work, anything and everything can happen. One takes it as it comes."

As he turned onto the dusty country road that led to the home of Elk, the agent slowed down considerably. Clumps of tall hemp plants again could be seen.

"Do you think Mr. Elk might be dangerous?" Hotaru asked.

"Not sure yet. If you are wondering if I suspect he might be an environmental terrorist, I don't think so. But he is an eccentric. And he does appear to have some beliefs that might be described as radical or even extreme."

"Surely that doesn't make one dangerous."

"No," Agent Pike admitted. "But deeply held beliefs that are decidedly different from those of the mainstream sometimes go hand in hand with terrorism. Mr. Elk may be just an old Indian who has some pretty antiquated ideas. Then again, he may be peppering sites all along the river with something that makes certain wild animals go berserk. One never knows. I've seen it all. Believe me, I've seen it all."

Agent Pike stopped the car in the middle of the road and looked all around. "This is the spot where we saw that coyote yesterday, isn't it? Well, if we see it again, this time I'm prepared."

Hotaru now realized what Agent Vogel had alluded to back at the hotel.

"You have a tranquilizer gun with you?" she asked.

"Uh-huh," Pike responded. "You asked if we had one in the car yesterday. Well, today we do."

"I doubt we'll see the same coyote in the same place," Dr. Hotaru said. "Coyotes are not that predictable. If they were, they'd be extinct by now."

Nonetheless, Agent Pike studied the area closely. He even got out of the car to survey the entire countryside. Then he got back into the dust-covered car and drove on.

"Catching one of these strange-acting animals might be just what the doctor ordered," he said with a big smile.

"I appreciate the effort," Dr. Hotaru remarked. "But I think Mr. Elk wanted us to give that coyote a taste of rock 'n' roll, not a tranquilizer."

The hand-painted signs along the road came into view and both Agent Pike and Dr. Hotaru looked at their watches. It was eight-thirty.

As they turned into the yard, two large dogs came running toward the car. One was a black Belgian sheep dog and the other was a chestnut-colored retriever. The dogs were barking and snapping at the front wheels of the vehicle.

Old Man Elk was standing in the yard. He called the dogs off and they obediently ran over to his side. He talked to them softly and stroked their backs until they both lay down at his feet.

Agent Pike and Hotaru got out of the car and walked toward the old Indian.

"Hanicara haipi!" Agent Pike called out.

Elk looked at him and seemed not to understand.

"Hanicara haipi!" Agent Pike called out again, this time with a

slightly different pronunciation.

"Good morning," Elk said.

The old man continued to pet his two dogs so they would not become excited and start barking again.

"I thought I'd better meet you outside," Elk explained. "Didn't want that piece of pipe to scare you so bad that you'd start shooting again."

"Thank you for agreeing to talk to us," Agent Pike said.

"You know," Elk whispered, "the three of us meeting today is a real multicultural happening. Just think about it. Here we are, an old American Indian artist, an African-American federal investigator, and an Asian-American scientist. And we're all meeting in one place. This little gathering would scare the living daylights out of a lot of people around here. We're probably being watched right now."

The old man chuckled and the two visitors laughed as well.

"Mr. Elk," Agent Pike said, trying to set a more serious tone. "I have to admit that I don't know much about your people. But I did a little background research last night and I tried to learn what I could."

The old man seemed pleased. "Tell me some of what you found out. Maybe I'll learn something as well."

"Well," Agent Pike began, "I learned that the Winnebago call themselves the *'Ho-Chunkara.'* And the Winnebago originally came from up in Wisconsin, near Green Bay and Lake Winnebago."

The old Indian listened intently and seemed to be hearing all of it for the very first time, so keen was his interest.

"Oh," Agent Pike continued, "and I discovered that Winnebago is not an easy language to master. I must have really messed up that greeting. You seemed not to understand me at all when I greeted you a few minutes ago."

Elk smiled broadly. "So that was Winnebago you were speaking to me?"

"Okay, okay," Agent Pike said. "My accent was off."

The old Indian doubled over with laughter and had to steady himself between his two dogs. "Oh, you have no idea. You were way off. I'm not Winnebago. I'm Pawnee!"

Agent Pike looked very surprised. "But we were under the impression that you were Winnebago."

The old man kept laughing until there were tears in the corners of his eyes. "Winnebago?" he kept asking. "Winnebago?"

"I need to sit down," the old man said, still laughing. "Come on, let's go inside. I have some coffee brewing."

The two visitors followed the old Indian and his two dogs into the house. As they walked into the kitchen, Agent Pike stopped Elk and offered an apology.

"Forgive me for the confusion. I meant no offense."

"That's alright," the old man said. "It feels good to laugh. Just don't throw anymore of that Winnebago lingo at me. I thought my ears were failing me when you said that stuff!"

"So you are Pawnee," Agent Pike stated, in a tone that indicated he wanted to set the record straight.

"Yes," the old man said, as he peered into a large coffee pot that was dark blue in color. He motioned for his two guests to sit down at the kitchen table. The kitchen had tall wooden cabinets with broad geometric designs running down each panel. The designs looked Indian and appeared to have been done by hand. On the opposite wall of the kitchen hung a large framed drawing of the famous comic strip character Dick Tracy. The picture was an original, and in one corner of the picture there was handwriting by the illustrator. Agent Pike wanted to look at the picture more closely to read the inscription, but he refrained from doing so. He remained seated and watched the old man move about in the kitchen. The smell of strong coffee filled the room.

"Ah, you noticed my autographed picture of Dick Tracy," Elk said as he looked at Agent Pike. "The guy who created Dick Tracy was Chester Gould and he came from Pawnee, Oklahoma. He kinda inspired me. I figured if someone from my hometown could make a living as an artist, maybe I could, too. But I didn't want to draw pictures of cops and police detectives. I chose to carve animals instead. After all, I'm kind of a rare bird myself.

"You see, I'm a full-blooded Native American," the old man continued. "I am mostly Pawnee, but one of my grandmas was an Arikara who came from way up in North Dakota. I was raised in Oklahoma by my Pawnee relatives, so I think of myself as Pawnee. We Pawnee refer to ourselves as *'Chatiks si Chatiks.'* Now a lot of writers have translated that to mean 'Men of Men.' But that's not quite right. And it's rather unfair to all our Pawnee grandmothers, mothers, wives, daughters, and sisters. *'Chatiks si Chatiks'* means 'People of People.' Or maybe a better way to phrase it would be 'People of Renown.' There is an intense desire on the part of many of our tribal members to really challenge themselves and to do great things. Our Pawnee nation includes men and women who have excelled in sports, business, education, law, music, the military—even the interstellar space program. In only about a century and a half, our people have gone from tracking herds of buffalo to tracking new galaxies.

"*Ahu!* Yes, I am Pawnee. And more and more, I realize that I am Pawnee from the crown of my head to the creases in my feet. But most folks around here, they don't know my tribal affiliation. I'm just an old Indian to them. From what I hear, they refer to me as 'Old Man Elk.' Well, I'm an elder now, so that name does not offend me. You can call me 'Old Man Elk' or just 'Elk.' I go by both names.

"'Elk' is the name I use as an artist. But it is a shortened version of my full name, 'Edward Lawrence Keeps Ahead.' It would be difficult for me to sign my pieces with such a long name. So I just sign them 'Elk.' I started using the name 'Elk' a long time ago. With us Pawnee, a name is not such a permanent thing. Sometimes, we go by several names during our lifetime. The old Indian agents used to complain that the Pawnee changed their names all the time. It made it very hard for the agents to keep accurate records. But that was their problem, not ours.

"Names are funny things," the old man said, laughing to himself. "I have an Indian friend whose name is Sidney Rubbing Sky. He told me he had an ancestor who was so tall he seemed to rub up against the sky. Well, when Sidney enlisted in the Army, they combined the two words in his family name so that it would be just a little shorter. That's when he became Sidney Rubbingsky. After that, when the other soldiers saw his name on his uniform, they pronounced his name 'Rubinsky.' They all thought he was Polish or Russian! Yes, names are funny things."

Dr. Hotaru, whose eyes were red from laughing, pulled up her chair. "Were the Pawnee a warrior people like so many other tribes of the Great Plains?"

"Yes, we had a strong warrior tradition. In the early days the Pawnee fought the Lakota people, the Sioux. And the Cheyenne and the Arapaho. And certain other tribes as well. But that was a long time ago. Today we all get along pretty well. We may tease each other now and then, but we get along.

"It seems a lot of people still get most of their information about Indians from movies. But Hollywood hasn't been very fair to the Pawnee. We always seem to be at one end of two extremes. We're portrayed as 'good Indians' who wore the blue jackets of the U.S. Cavalry and who helped hunt down all the 'bad Indians.' But we're also portrayed as painted devils who had Mohawk haircuts and who would swoop down on unsuspecting White settlers for no reason at all. Young people are really influenced by that stuff and that includes our own young people. The images in those movies are very powerful—maybe more powerful than most of us realize."

Old Man Elk closed his eyes for a few moments and fell silent. He seemed to be replaying some of the movie images in his mind.

"You know," the old man said as he opened his eyes again, "the Pawnee people were once a mighty nation. We had a good life. We hunted buffalo and we grew corn and our villages were the centers of a lot of trade and commerce. Our enemies feared us because we were so strong. We numbered more than ten thousand people and we were one of the largest tribes of the Great Plains. We were organized into four bands: the Chaui, the Kitkahahki, the Pitahawirata, and the Skidi. This was our home, here in what is now Nebraska and extending south into Kansas and even west into Colorado. We had big earth lodge villages along rivers like the Platte and the Loup and the Republican. And all this land was ours.

"Yes, we had a good life. Our people stored up enough dried corn and dried meat so that no Pawnee was ever hungry after the first snow fell. In those days, during the long months of winter, the Pawnee gathered in their earth lodges and they told stories. Oh, did they tell stories! Like the ancient Greeks, we Pawnee liked to hear about heroes and we never grew tired of hearing about all their adventures and their great deeds.

"One of the best-known of our heroes was a Skidi Pawnee named Pahukatawa. Like Achilles, he was a renowned and powerful warrior. Yet he learned the hard way that he was not invincible. One day, while Pahukatawa was out on the prairie hunting, the enemy suddenly surprised him. They surrounded him and they let fly arrows from all directions. The great Pahukatawa kept fighting until his body was pierced with more arrows than anyone could count. Then the enemy warriors rushed in and killed Pahukatawa. They feared him so much that they cut his body into small pieces to make sure that he was dead and that he would never fight again.

"But the '*Nahúraki*,' the powerful spirit animals, watched all this. They felt sorry for Pahukatawa. They had always loved him and they admired his courage. So the *Nahúraki* came together and decided to do something. In the days that followed, they searched the whole countryside so that they could find all of the pieces of Pahukatawa. The remains of the great warrior seemed to be everywhere. When the *Nahúraki* finally gathered them all together in one place, it was like a big jigsaw puzzle of little bone fragments and bits of decaying flesh. But all things are possible with the *Nahúraki*. They have great power.

They can revive even those who are long dead and whose remains have been scattered to the winds. And so Pahukatawa was brought back to life and he returned to fight again. When his old enemies saw this, they trembled at the sight of him.

"You see that picture over on the wall?" Elk asked.

There were many objects and pictures hanging in the old man's kitchen, but Elk directed his guests' attention to a large framed photograph on the far wall. The black and white picture was that of a broad-faced, Plains Indian man who was standing on the prairie and looking straight ahead. The photograph appeared to be very old, yet the detail in the picture was striking. The man was wrapped in a large buffalo robe, the skin side of which was decorated with dozens of painted stars. Despite the grainy quality of the old photograph, the man's eyes and each of the five-pointed stars on his robe seemed to glow with intensity.

"That man was a Pawnee and his name also was Pahukatawa," Elk explained. "Historians say he just happened to bear the name of the legendary Pawnee hero. But an old Pawnee woman once told me that the man in the picture was Pahukatawa. Historians may not like to hear stuff like that because it would mean that Pahukatawa was kind of like an immortal being or a ghost. And I have yet to meet a White historian who believes in ghosts!"

Everyone laughed, but Agent Pike's laughter was more subdued. It was obvious he was growing impatient and that he wanted to ask some questions. Just as Agent Pike tried to change the direction of the discussion, the old Indian started up again.

"History is interesting, especially when you look back and think about how everything turned out. The soldiers of the Spanish Empire conquered the great civilizations of the Aztec and the Inca. But when Commander Pedro de Villasur and his Spanish soldiers marched on the Pawnee Nation back in 1720, our people and our Otoe Indian allies stood up to them. We stopped the invasion, in a great battle that occurred on the River Platte only a few miles from here. Villasur and many of his soldiers died at the hands of Pawnee warriors. So this was as far north as the Spanish ever got into the interior of North America.

"You know, it was José Naranjo, 'the Black Indian,' who had given the Platte its old Spanish name. He had both African and Pueblo Indian ancestry. Naranjo was an early guide for the Spanish soldiers, and he named the Platte in honor of the Christian son of God and his mother. That's why the Spanish called the Platte 'Río de Jesús María.' But after Villasur's defeat, that old Spanish name for the river didn't last. It was washed away with blood. José Naranjo died alongside Villasur and many others on the sands of the Platte. Just think about it: The Pawnee Nation defeated the soldiers of the mighty Spanish Empire right here on these prairies. We changed the whole course of world history. Yes, the *Chatiks si Chatiks* have a proud history. No Pawnee youngster should ever hang down his head or feel ashamed.

"After the Spanish retreated, it wasn't long before the French and many other White people came into the land of the Pawnee. Their diseases killed more of us than French muskets or American Winchesters ever did. And as more and more White people arrived, our population became much smaller. And our homeland became smaller as well.

"Everything changed, even the names that we had given these rivers and streams centuries before. When the White people established towns, they gave them European-sounding names like Columbus, Ferdinand, Isabella, and Genoa. The names were meant to remind us that the land was slipping away from us and would no longer be ours.

"Soon even the little reservation we had left here in Nebraska was desired by the Whites as well. Again and again, our old tribal enemies raided us. And our White neighbors made us feel as if we were no longer welcome in our own homeland. So the Pawnee left Nebraska and went to Oklahoma. It was known as Indian Territory then. My great grandparents were little children when they made that long, long journey with wagons and horses. And once they got to Oklahoma, many of our people died of malaria and other diseases. But they always remembered Nebraska, especially the fertile lands along the

Platte and the Loup. Yes, I was born and raised in Oklahoma, but I always heard the elders talk about Nebraska. And so I returned here to the old, old homeland of my people."

Elk now held up the backs of both his hands, so that the tattoos on his fingers could be seen. Beneath each knuckle of each outstretched finger was a number.

"On my left hand is the date 1873, the year when the first Pawnee group left Nebraska," Old Man Elk explained. "And on my right hand is the date 1875, the year when the last of my people went down to Oklahoma. The re-settlement in Indian Territory took three long years, from 1873 to 1875. These are dates no fair-minded person should ever forget."

Both Agent Pike and Dr. Hotaru wanted to discuss other matters. They glanced at each other nervously but kept restraining themselves. In light of all the confusion and misunderstanding of the past two days, they felt they owed the old Indian this opportunity to tell them something about himself and his people.

Old Man Elk, who had been laughing hard only a few minutes before, now seemed very serious and even sad. His eyes and lips quivered occasionally as he talked about his people's history, but there were no tears. The old man sat upright, still showing the backs of his hands. He held them up for a long time, in a manner that was as awkward as it was defiant. It was evident he wanted his two visitors not only to see those two dates, but to etch them in their minds as well.

CHAPTER
17

"It's my special egg coffee," Elk explained, as he poured the steaming brownish liquid into three large mugs. "I don't use instant coffee or strainers. I just add a raw egg and the coffee grounds stick to that egg. If the taste doesn't suit you, just add as much sugar as you want. Not sure where I learned how to make this egg coffee. Maybe from some old Swedish chicken farmer who had a lot of eggs."

The old Indian looked into his coffee mug and continued talking.

"In Pawnee, we call coffee *'dakits katit'*—the dark brew. I have several notebooks full of Pawnee words and phrases. But I don't do like the anthropologists, who run all the sounds together and create these mile-long words that even an old Pawnee like myself can't pronounce. For example, the Skidi Pawnee word for a 'waitress' is twenty-seven letters long. Twenty-seven letters! It sounds something like this: *'iriiraraakaaruurarikaawarii.'* If a hungry trucker had to spell that word correctly before getting any food, he'd starve for sure! Me, I just write down the Pawnee words the way they sound. And sometimes I space them apart a bit so they don't get so long. That way our young people will be able to read and remember our ancestral language. So, whenever an old Pawnee word comes to mind, I jot it down in one of my notebooks and then I say it out loud several times to Apollo and Artemis. By now, they probably understand as much Pawnee as they do English. And of course they know their own dog language. So I guess you could say that Apollo and Artemis are trilingual."

Agent Pike and Dr. Hotaru slowly sipped their egg coffee, but they did not say anything until Elk emptied his own mug. From inside the kitchen, the two visitors could see numerous carvings of animals in the next room.

Noticing their interest, the old Pawnee seemed pleased. He encouraged them to step into a large sunlit room that was filled with carvings of all kinds. Likenesses of deer, beaver, bison, eagles, grouse, and countless other animals and birds could be seen. Some of the carvings hung on walls, but the larger pieces stood upright. In the northeast corner of the room, there was a high stack of dusty volumes and notebooks that nearly reached the ceiling. Dr. Hotaru noticed a whole shelf of books dealing with astronomy and the ancient Greeks and classical mythology. Several different editions of Homer's *The Odyssey* stood side by side.

In the southeast corner of the large room was an expensive-looking tan and silver telescope mounted on a tripod. Behind it was a detailed map of the various star constellations that included handwritten notations and dates. A few yellowed newspaper clippings also were attached to the map.

Directly in front of a large picture window that faced east was a rough-hewn workbench and chair and an array of carving tools. Fragrant wood shavings covered the floor and the curled shavings crunched under their feet as the agent and the scientist walked over by the workbench.

"Here's where I do my work," Elk said, as he gently touched each of the tools on the table. "I work with all kinds of wood, mostly basswood, chinaberry, and rosewood. I also work with woods that are native to this area, like Plains cottonwood and Nebraska cedar. I carve every day until I get tired. Then I take a little nap and go back to work again. When my arms get tired, I give them a break and do some reading. But then my eyes get tired. So I go back and forth between my carving and my reading. I don't have a television set. To relax, I wait for a really good night and then I look at the stars through my telescope. It's better than TV. There are no commercials, no bad Westerns, and none of those so-called reality shows."

Dr. Hotaru smiled but then raised her eyebrows when she looked up and saw what appeared to be a huge pair of elk antlers mounted on the wall. The trophy seemed strangely out of place. As the scientist stood under the antlers to view them more closely, she realized that they were actually two matching tree branches that had been polished and joined together. Dr. Hotaru was not sure if the object was intended to be artistic or humorous. When she looked at the old man to provide some kind of explanation, he coughed a little but otherwise remained very quiet. Elk seemed to be thoroughly enjoying the reactions of his guests.

The scientist also noticed an unusual carving of a jackrabbit. The animal was hunched down and appeared to be hiding. Its extremely long ears were tilted back at an odd angle. The jackrabbit's exceptionally large eyes reflected fear and even terror. As Dr. Hotaru examined the piece, she noticed that there was a small brass plate at the base that identified the sculpture as "Witness at Massacre Canyon." Again, the scientist looked over at the artist, but he did not offer any interpretation.

Agent Pike slowly walked all around the room. He looked at each of the carvings and then stopped at one showing two large cranes with extremely long, thin legs and graceful, curved necks. The two birds were walking side by side. One of them was hunched down a bit and appeared to be looking up at the other. The head of each bird was tipped with a small cap of inlaid wood that was a deep scarlet color. The agent gently ran his fingers along the curved necks of the two cranes, feeling the delicateness and the smoothness of the grayish wood. He did this repeatedly, as if he could not believe the sensation that he felt under his fingers.

"That one is called 'Mates for Life,'" Elk said, finally breaking the silence. "Sandhill cranes come to the Platte Valley of Nebraska every spring. They've been doing that for millions of years. They like to travel in pairs and they have their courtship rituals. When they dance with each other, they bow and they are able to jump six feet off the ground. Those sandhill cranes mate for life. Did you know that?"

"No," Agent Pike replied. "I didn't know that." He continued running his fingers along the necks of the two cranes.

Dr. Hotaru also was studying each of the carvings. Occasionally she reached out and touched one of them. "They're so lifelike," she murmured. "They look as if they'll dart off at any moment. I am very, very impressed."

Elk stood in the light of the room and seemed to blend in with his creations. He looked around the room as if he were seeing all of his carvings for the first time.

"You truly know wild animals," Dr. Hotaru commented. "It's evident from the way you carve each one. Do you work from sketches or photographs?"

"Neither," the old Indian answered. "I spend a lot of time on the River Platte. Sometimes I walk, but now that I am older, I prefer going down the river very slowly in a canoe. That way I don't disturb the animals. They see me, but they don't run off. I watch them for a long time. Then I come back here and carve a likeness of them. I never know ahead of time how it will turn out. Each animal is different and each carving is different as well."

"You have any idea what's going on with all these wild animal attacks?" Agent Pike suddenly asked, changing the subject completely. His tone was serious and very business-like.

Instead of answering, Elk pushed some large tree stump chairs to the middle of the room, where there was space for the three of them to sit and talk. The chairs were more comfortable to sit on than they looked.

Elk took a couple of minutes to arrange himself on the chair. But he did not say anything or look at his visitors. He seemed to be deep in thought.

Now Dr. Hotaru tried. "Because of your knowledge of the wild animals in this area, we thought you might be able to help us understand what is going on. Can you shed any light on the wild animal attacks that are occurring in this area?"

The old Indian was silent for a few more moments, but then, gazing at his animal creations that surrounded him on all sides, he began to speak.

"People who buy these carvings of mine often ask me: 'How do you make them so lifelike? How on earth do you do it?' I tell them this: 'There is no blueprint. There is no secret. And there is no answer that can fully explain it. My eyes and my heart and my hands work together. They all work as one. You see, all the living things in this world share something. We are all travelers on the great pathway.' "

Agent Pike and Dr. Hotaru both looked at the old Indian as if they were still waiting for an answer to their questions. The two visitors then looked at each other as if they were not sure how to proceed.

"Ah," Elk said with a deep sigh. "I see that look in your eyes. I know it all too well. You seem kinda lost and maybe there is just no way of reaching you. This is very sad. But I do not blame you for this. I blame Thales of Miletus."

Dr. Hotaru was taken aback. "Thales? You blame Thales of Miletus?"

"Thales?" Agent Pike echoed, also sounding very surprised.

"Thales," Dr. Hotaru said, now realizing she and the old Indian were referring to the same person. "Thales of Miletus, the ancient Greek philosopher who emphasized objectivity and scientific proof. Rational thought versus mythical thought. Right?"

"Yes," Elk said, as he looked out the window. "The human mind pitted against the natural world. It seems to be a constant struggle for so many people. We Indians belong to many different nations, but despite our tribal differences we all have a deep respect for nature.

"You see, many of us also believe in the great pathway. On this circular pathway are plants and trees and birds and animals—and humans. We are all fellow travelers on the great pathway. And we are all equals.

"But the White people, the Europeans, they were influenced by Thales of Miletus and by other philosophers who followed him. These men thought they could take humans off the great pathway and move humans to the center. These men did this out of arrogance and in the name of science. And they forgot that humans are supposed to be on the great pathway and not at the center of everything.

"You ask me about these so-called attacks. You make it sound like something totally unexpected. You make it sound like something completely new. And you make it sound like a problem for which there must be a rational answer and some kind of scientific explanation."

The disappointment in Agent Pike's face was evident. He frowned but then formed his lips as if he were trying to whistle. Instead, he simply blew a little air out as if to cool himself down.

"I'm not sure I understand what you're getting at," Agent Pike admitted. "You're losing us."

"Yes," Old Man Elk answered. "That is always the dilemma, isn't it? Every time Indians talk, non-Indians seem to get very confused and they say 'you're losing us.' Well, it is not we who are confused or lost."

"Elk," Dr. Hotaru said, holding out the palms of her hands as if she expected the old Indian to grasp them and help her across the invisible divide that separated them. "We mean no disrespect. And we are listening. But we don't quite understand what you are saying. For this I am truly sorry."

"I don't blame you," the old Indian said, shaking his head. "I blame Thales of Miletus. He rejected the ancient ways and the mythology of his own people. And then he did a mind job on a whole lot of other people. When you get back on the highway that takes you to Columbus, look around you. You will see the legacy of Thales of

Miletus. It is all very sad."

An entire minute of silence passed. Pike and Hotaru looked at each other, trying to anticipate who should talk next and who would be more successful in getting the information they wanted. But before either of them was able to ask another question, the old man started up again. He spoke very slowly and he was careful to enunciate each word. As he talked, he occasionally would moisten his lips with his tongue, as if he were tasting some of the words that slowly left his mouth.

"You know," Elk said, "I was listening to the radio the other day. A fellow was talking about how this summer has been one of the hottest and driest in the whole history of Nebraska. That fellow went on to say something else. He said, 'We thought we'd suffered through just about everything this summer. And then the animals turned.'

"I am not sure what he meant by those words," the old man continued. "'And then the animals turned.' It sure leaves me wondering. Is this supposed to be the summer when animals turned against humans? Or is it just a matter of something good that turns bad, like milk that turns sour? Did that fellow on the radio mean to say that the animals have turned from gentle, timid creatures into vicious, dangerous beasts? Ah, words in the English language can be very hard to understand, even tricky. Maybe that is why I don't always trust them."

Agent Pike suddenly stood up and went over to a large carving of a buffalo. He placed his hand on the buffalo, as if taking a solemn oath.

"Dr. Hotaru and I were there on the scene, right after those three bison were killed. But we got there too late. We weren't able to save them from being shot to death. We don't want to see any more animals or people get killed. And surely you don't either."

Elk stared at Agent Pike a long time. "Yes," the old man said, "I heard about what happened to those three buffalo out by Isabella. But the radio reports were rather confusing. Several of the eyewitnesses said it was only the buffalo bull that charged, not all three animals."

Agent Pike had a puzzled look on his face. "I'm not sure if any of that makes a difference. The end result was that all three animals were killed: the bull, the cow, and even the calf."

"Ahu," the old man agreed. "Yes, all three were killed. But it sounds like it was only the bull that charged. That does not sound like a wild animal attack to me. It sounds more like one buffalo making his stand. Buffalo bulls do that, you know. It is not out of character for them. My elders who told stories about the old buffalo-hunting days often spoke of buffalo bulls that would leave the main herd and make a stand. Those bulls chose to face the hunters and die bravely. It is the way of buffalo. And it is a way my people understood and respected."

"Elk," Dr. Hotaru said, as she rearranged herself on the log chair. "You seem to doubt any attacks by wild animals have taken place. Do you feel these acts of aggression are merely the way certain animals behave and thus are nothing out of the ordinary?"

The old Pawnee rose from his chair. Then he looked at Dr. Hotaru and answered.

"You are a scientist. I should not have to tell you how important it is to consider every possibility. Maybe these things are hard for you to understand, but they are not too hard for an old Indian artist like myself to understand."

Elk shook his head as if he had suddenly grown tired and was not going to say anymore. But then he looked at both Agent Pike and Dr. Hotaru and continued talking.

"At various times in this country's history, the original inhabitants of this continent have been seen as trusted friends or even admirable figures. But when Indians suddenly were viewed as treacherous enemies or bloodthirsty savages, things always went very badly for us. We were hated and massacred and nearly exterminated. But know this: It was not us who changed. Yet every time the mental perceptions of the White man changed, it affected us. And these mental perceptions still affect us. We Indians have learned the hard way that the White man's perception is not all that different from the White man's reality."

Agent Pike's cell phone rang and he excused himself to take the call outside. Dr. Hotaru and Elk continued to converse in the center of the room.

"I'm an old man," he continued, "and I remember many things during my lifetime. Back when I was a boy, I heard about something on the radio. And I never forgot it. It seems a few people in a big city out west became very frightened when they noticed these little pits in their windshields. Others who heard about the little pits checked their cars and, sure enough, they found little pits in their windshields as well. The pits were real hard to see, but if you looked close enough, you could find at least one or two of them. Folks worried that some awful force was at work, maybe millions of tiny meteors were showering down from outer space.

"After those little pits got noticed, things sure changed. People wouldn't take their cars out as much and a lot of folks just stayed at home because they thought it was safer. Everyone got real scared. But you know, they just scared themselves. Sometimes people think too much. And the perception of a few becomes the reality of everyone."

Dr. Hotaru was not sure how to respond. She was a native of Seattle, the city to which Elk was referring, and she remembered hearing about the windshield scare from her grandparents. They even had their own theory at first, that the pitted windshields resulted from the atomic bombings of Hiroshima and Nagasaki. Her grandparents felt it was the kind of slow, divine vengeance that would be visited on the perpetrators for generations.

As Susan Hotaru contemplated what Elk had just told her, Agent Pike rushed into the room and said they had to leave immediately.

The old Indian watched his two visitors hurry out of the house. As they got into the car, he saw Dr. Hotaru glance at the windshield of the vehicle before she got in. The scientist looked at it quickly but deliberately, as if examining it for any tiny imperfections.

CHAPTER
18

The morning sun burned hotter than usual, and the dusty car that Agent Pike was driving already felt like the inside of a bread oven. It took several minutes to cool the car down with air conditioning and yet the vehicle still reeked of overheated plastic and hot-to-the-touch upholstery.

As Agent Pike sped back toward Columbus, he told Susan Hotaru about the message he received on his cell phone.

"It was Jake Vogel. There's been another incident and a bad one. A big-horned buck that was being pursued by hunters went through the picture window of a child care center over in River Junction, which is just to the southeast of Columbus. The kids were sitting by the window having a snack when the deer crashed in. Vogel said the day care provider, a Mrs. Snow, took the brunt of it. She was able to dial for help, but she bled to death before the ambulance got there. At least four of the children were injured and the rest are pretty shook up. It happened about half an hour ago."

Hotaru fell silent. Despite the cold air circulating in the car, she felt unable to breathe.

"If you think things have been getting hot," the agent continued, "they've just been turned up to the boiling point. It's a whole new ball game now and it's going to get real ugly. And yet Mr. Elk wants us to think these incidents are nothing out of the ordinary? Who is he trying to fool?"

"Zeph," Hotaru said, speaking very slowly, as if she were still unable to breathe normally. "I agree that this latest incident is going to change things, and for the worse. But Elk is just providing another perspective. We still don't know exactly what is going on. And we do need to assess the whole situation before we rush to any conclusions. We can't let our emotions overly influence us."

Zephaniah Pike did not answer. He drove as fast as he could toward Columbus. Hotaru noticed that he seemed unnerved by the latest report about the child care center. The scientist remembered that Agent Pike also had a young daughter and that her name was Twila.

"Elk is very eloquent and very perceptive," Dr. Hotaru continued. "At first, I was a little turned off by all of his talk about some kind of 'great pathway.' It seemed so corny and stereotypical, listening to an old Indian man talk about how people and animals are all related. But the more I listened, the more I realized how sincere he sounded. You can tell that he reads a lot and that he thinks deeply about things. I found it very interesting when he told us how he believes all living things are interconnected. Most of my scientific education resists that kind of perspective. But the funny thing is that when my colleagues and I talk about the possibility of a 'jumper' virus, we are arguing something very similar to what Elk is saying. Humans and animals share so much in common that it may be possible for them to infect one another. Maybe we're all connected in ways we still don't realize. It really makes one think, doesn't it?"

The agent simply looked at the scientist in a way that told her he was listening but was not in the mood to talk about philosophy or science.

As Agent Pike and Dr. Hotaru pulled into the parking lot of their hotel in Columbus, they could see a crowd of more than a hundred people. Many individuals were shouting and carrying large hand-lettered signs. One of the signs declared "ANIMALS HAVE RIGHTS,

BUT WHAT ABOUT HUMANS?" Another sign carried the message "PROTECT OUR CITIZENS, PROTECT OUR CITY." Still another sign proclaimed "ENDANGERED SPECIES!" The sign had a massive arrow that pointed down to the middle-aged man who carried it.

In another area of the parking lot, two groups were loudly shouting at each other. Several policemen wearing riot gear stood in the middle and struggled to keep the two groups apart. A large number of environmentalists stood arm in arm under a banner emblazoned with bright green letters: "HAVE SOME GUTS. STAND UP TO THE ENEMIES OF OUR EARTH!" Only a few yards away, a group of sportsmen, many of them wearing camouflage clothing, raised a hurriedly-made sign of their own: "WE DO HAVE GUTS. AND GUNS!"

Off to the side of the parking lot stood a lone woman in a rainbow-colored gown. She also wore wrap-around sunglasses and a wide-brimmed sun hat decorated with ribbons and silk flowers. The woman held a poster that seemed as incongruous as the sign-carrier herself. The poster was completely black, except for white letters that spelled out a message which made nearly everyone turn and look at it a second time: "NOT EVERY ISSUE IS BLACK AND WHITE."

Jake Vogel, who was waiting outside the front of the hotel, hurried toward Agent Pike's car as soon as he saw it. A group of TV reporters and journalists followed closely behind.

As Agent Pike and Dr. Hotaru got out of the car, Vogel ran up to Zephaniah and tried to be heard above the noise of the crowd.

"Sir," Vogel explained, "the press people have been bugging us all morning. Maybe you should tell them something."

Agent Pike straightened his tie and walked up to the reporters. He cleared his throat and motioned for everyone to calm down. He did not speak until everyone was quiet.

"Good morning. My name is Zephaniah Pike and I am an agent with the Federal Special Projects Division in Washington, D.C. I have been here in Nebraska the past couple of days, investigating reports of wild animal attacks. Our investigation is ongoing and it is thorough. I beg your cooperation as we try to do our work here in Nebraska.

"This afternoon, the FSPD will be meeting with city, state, and federal officials to discuss possible courses of action and emergency measures. Please know that your safety and welfare are foremost in our minds. Thank you."

As Agent Pike and Dr. Hotaru walked toward the hotel, several reporters ran alongside them and asked them questions. But Agent Pike waved them away and indicated he had nothing more to say.

* * * *

At two o'clock that afternoon, Agents Pike and Vogel, along with Dr. Hotaru, joined about eighty other people in the large conference room of the hotel. Microphones were set up on the conference table, but only a few members of the press were allowed inside. Although there was air conditioning in the room, a large electric floor fan was set up in a corner of the room and several of the people arranged themselves so that they could feel the slight breeze that it generated. The meeting was conducted by Roland R. Rawlins, a former Nebraska state senator and the owner of Triple R Aviation.

As the meeting began, Senator Rawlins asked if Reverend Gordon Hillman was in the room. When the minister indicated that he was present, the senator gestured for him to stand and to give an invocation.

The tall, distinguished-looking clergyman cleared his throat and began by asking everyone to bow their heads and to pray with him.

"Heavenly Father, our hearts are heavy today due to the death of someone who was very dear to many of us. Velma Mae Snow was a kind and gentle Christian woman who loved children and who loved this community."

The minister's voice broke, but he kept his eyes tightly closed and he paused for a few seconds. Then he cleared his throat again and continued.

"Heavenly Father, we ask you to bless and watch over Mrs. Snow. Comfort the grieving members of her family. And bring healing to all those innocent little children who were injured or traumatized today. Dry their tears and comfort them in this very difficult time. Heavenly Father, we also ask you to look down upon this gathering and to imbue our leaders with wisdom so that they know how to exercise good judgment. Fill their hearts with compassion and love so that they know how to act and to do whatever must be done. We ask these things in your holy name. Amen."

Senator Rawlins now turned to Miriam Tyler, the mayor of Columbus, and asked her to say just a few words. The mayor, who was very tall and looked rather young, seemed nervous. As she began talking and establishing eye contact with her listeners, she gradually sounded more confident.

"Good afternoon, everyone. As the mayor of Columbus, I welcome a lot of different groups to this city, but usually I do so under much happier and far different circumstances. I must apologize for a couple of things that unfortunately seem outside my control. First, the terrible and oppressive heat. And second, the strange and baffling situation in which so many of us now find ourselves. It is unprecedented."

As the mayor spoke, she looked over at Senator Rawlins and noticed that the senator already was giving her a little finger spin to indicate he wanted the mayor to keep her words to a minimum and to wrap up things quickly.

Mayor Tyler nodded and took a deep breath. "I want you all to know something. This is a very friendly and progressive community, filled with hardworking families, caring neighbors, and good citizens. But we need your expertise. We appreciate your coming here today and trying to help us out. We really do. The people of Columbus need your assistance and insofar as we can be of any help to you, we stand ready and willing. On behalf of all the residents of Columbus and the surrounding area, we thank you."

Following the mayor's remarks, everyone introduced themselves in a courteous fashion. But within twenty minutes, the mood in the conference room suddenly changed. Even Senator Rawlins seemed surprised by the lively and heated debate that ensued. Federal officials and city and state administrators argued over matters of jurisdiction. Health officials and human service advocates expressed their concerns. Several members of the California-based organization NAASER, the North American Alliance for Safeguarding Environmental Resources, indicated that they had traveled a great distance and demanded to be heard. When they were given the opportunity to speak, some of their comments were met with smirks and even groans. Representatives of several sportsmen's organizations challenged the views of NAASER and also the U.S. Fish and Wildlife Service. Senator Rawlins allowed those present to vent their frustration and to question one another's views. But then he noticed that Zephaniah Pike was motioning that he also wished to speak.

The FSPD agent stood up and tried to look all around the table as he spoke. "We're not going to get anywhere if we keep pointing fingers and keep tearing at each other's throats. I've been encouraging everyone to stay calm and that includes us.

"It is clear that we have a lot of issues before us, but from what I've already heard this afternoon, there are two basic problems that need to be addressed and dealt with. First, how do we stop more animal attacks from happening? Second, what do we do about the groups of armed citizens that are mobilizing even as we bicker and argue? Or the carloads of college-aged environmentalists from Lincoln and Omaha who are pouring into this area every day? Make no mistake about it, we not only have dangerous animals to deal with, we have very angry citizens on both sides of the issue and they can prove just as dangerous and unpredictable. Now, regarding the first problem, I would like Dr. Hotaru to update us on what she and the other scientists have learned about the animals that were involved in the attacks of the past few days."

Agent Pike sat down and Dr. Hotaru also looked all around the room before she began. She remained sitting as she spoke.

"Most of the lab tests we need to run require many days of analysis. Our scientists are working around the clock. The greatest difficulty we face is the variety of animals we're dealing with: badgers, bison, bobcats, coyotes, white-tailed deer, red foxes, red-tailed hawks. Altogether, we have only a dozen carcasses of animals directly involved in these attacks that are available to us for study. And we have called in specialists that are intimately familiar with each of the species that have been involved thus far.

"All of our wildlife experts agree that we need to capture the wild animals that exhibit unusual aggressive behavior. We need to take them alive so that we can observe and analyze them more closely. If they are suffering from some kind of disease, we need to identify that disease as soon as possible."

A stern-faced woman raised her hand and interrupted Dr. Hotaru.

"We have reports that there are large numbers of dead animals all along the river. How can there be any doubt that some kind of disease is already at work and is taking a heavy toll?"

"Many of the dead animals along the river are not dead due to disease," Dr. Hotaru replied. "Most of the animal carcasses that my colleagues and I have examined are dead due to shooting, spearing, poisoning, and even the use of explosives. The numbers of animal carcasses are growing at such a rate that we cannot keep track of which ones were killed and which ones may have died as a result of disease or dehydration. Only upon close examination can we ascertain the exact cause of death."

A man with large, dark-rimmed glasses spoke up at this point. "But Doctor, if certain wild animals are suffering from an unidentified and possibly contagious disease, isn't there the danger of this thing eventually spreading to humans?"

Dr. Hotaru nodded, but she put up both her hands as if to block any more interruptions. "Yes, there is that danger. We refer to it as 'jumping' across the species barrier. If indeed we're dealing with a contagious disease, we could be seeing evidence of this 'jumping' by virtue of the range of wild animals involved in the attacks. But thus far there is no hard evidence."

The people around the table began talking among themselves, but the man in the large, dark-rimmed glasses spoke up again.

"Yet we may be dealing with something that endangers human beings and may soon be of epidemic-like proportions! Surely you're aware of the fact that our hospitals are filled with hundreds of people who are delirious and running extremely high fevers. Some doctors say it is heatstroke or sunstroke. But several of our health officials fear it is something else that may be very serious and prove to be contagious and even deadly.

"Dr. Hotaru, we've all seen the pictures of you in our newspapers, pictures that show you in a protective mask and gloves as you go about inspecting the carcasses of dead animals. So I repeat, might we be dealing with a deadly disease that could endanger human beings? Please, Doctor, just answer my question."

Dr. Hotaru looked over at Agent Pike and paused before answering. "Yes, there is that danger, but once again, we have no hard evidence that humans might—"

A white-haired man in a neatly pressed suit interrupted. His red face made his hair look even whiter.

"Just read the newspapers, Doctor! People have been killing each other for thousands of years. They kill each other every day. They do it for money, they do it in the name of war, they even do it out of passion. Some of them do it for kicks. But my own question is this: Because humans seem so violence-prone, how would we ever know for certain if there is a direct connection between some sick animals who display aggression and some sick humans who display aggression? How would we ever know?"

Many of those seated around the table nodded and began talking to each other. Senator Rawlins allowed for a few moments of mumbling before calling the meeting back to order.

"Please! Let's give everyone a chance to be heard. There is someone we haven't heard from, and due to his position I think we should listen to him. Harold Dawson is the Director of the Nebraska Fish and Wildlife Division. Mr. Dawson, you have been very quiet this afternoon. We'd like to hear your thoughts."

Everyone grew quiet as Harold Dawson pushed his chair back and stood up at the table. He was a tall, slender man with bushy gray eyebrows and a moustache that was much darker in color. He walked over to a large map showing the Platte River Valley in eastern Nebraska.

"Yes," he began. "I have been very quiet and I have listened closely to everything that was said today. But what I have to say, what I have to contribute, is difficult for me."

He pointed to the map as he continued. "We looked at this map earlier and we know that these wild animal attacks have occurred within about a hundred-and-forty-mile stretch of land running on both sides of the Platte River. Thus far, the problem seems confined to this portion of the valley. And unless we act quickly, the problem will become much, much bigger.

"Some of the wildlife in this valley, such as several species of waterfowl, migrate to other areas. Certain birds travel as far north as Siberia and as far south as Mexico. We even have Swainson's Hawks, which often migrate to the southern tip of South America. So what we decide here may have implications far beyond the borders of Nebraska and even the United States. What we do, or fail to do, may well have international ramifications—and we in Nebraska will have to answer for that.

"It's my responsibility to oversee the care of the fish and wildlife in this state. And I take that responsibility seriously. But I don't want this problem to spread to other parts of the state or to other regions or even to other countries. No matter what the cause, there is obviously a big problem. We must contain it. And we must do so as soon as possible."

Everyone in the room grew silent. No one spoke, no one coughed, no one even moved. Everyone simply waited.

Senator Rawlins looked at Harold Dawson and urged him to continue. But the man with bushy eyebrows seemed to stare at something that no one else could see.

"Mr. Dawson," the senator said, "we are listening. What do you propose?"

Harold Dawson stopped staring into space and looked at all those sitting around the table. "I think we have only one plan of action that will contain the situation. We must eliminate all the wildlife in this portion of the Platte River Valley."

Again, the whole room grew uncomfortably silent.

"How would one go about eliminating all the wildlife in such a large area?" the white-haired man with the red face and neatly pressed suit asked. "Is such a plan even feasible?"

Harold Dawson nodded. "Something like this has been done before. A number of years ago in Wisconsin, approximately 25,000 deer were hunted down in a 400-square-mile area where cases of chronic wasting disease had been reported. It was not pretty. But despite public outcries and protests, it was done and it proved successful. What makes our own situation so different, however, is the fact that we will not be singling out one animal species, but all wild animal species. That will be a massive undertaking."

A female legislator sitting toward the back of the room suddenly raised her voice. "But how could such a thing ever be accomplished? Could you please be more specific? Please?"

Harold Dawson went back to his chair and sat down. He first looked at the legislator and then looked at some of the others as he answered. "In Wisconsin, hunters were recruited and paid to eliminate all the deer. The head of each animal was severed and sent to a lab for testing. A number of the animals did prove positive for chronic wasting disease."

A middle-aged man at the opposite end of the table now spoke. "I guess that takes care of the other problem that was mentioned earlier. Instead of arresting or trying to control those who are already hunting down animals, we simply pay them for carrying out Mr. Dawson's plan. They'll actually get paid for hunting out of season and for killing all the wild animals that they come across. The plan certainly sounds feasible to me. We need to do something. And if our Nebraska Fish and Wildlife Office gives its seal of approval, that's good enough for me."

Senator Rawlins thanked Harold Dawson for his comments and then recognized a young woman in square-shaped glasses who was patiently holding up her hand.

"Thank you, Senator Rawlins. My name is LaRita Anderson-Kiley and I am here representing the local branch of Social Services. But I must admit that I am also here as a concerned Columbus citizen who loves this community and its people. Among the things that a lot of us appreciate is the natural beauty of this area and especially its wildlife. Now don't get me wrong. I'm not a tree-hugger and I don't throw rotten tomatoes at those who wear furs or leather jackets. I just don't want to see this part of Nebraska—my Nebraska—resorting to any extreme measures. And I know I don't stand alone. I simply can't imagine this area with all of its wildlife destroyed. Can any of you imagine such a terrible thing? No wildlife? It would be a nightmare for our many bird-watchers and nature lovers. Ironically, it also would be the worst possible thing for our many hunters and sportsmen. Surely there's another way, one that is more reasonable and less damaging. There must be an alternative."

Several of the people sitting around the table now raised their hands to speak, but Senator Rawlins indicated that he wished to take the floor and propose something.

"As I listened to Mr. Dawson speak a few minutes ago, I could not help but think there may be yet another alternative—one that will do what Mr. Dawson proposes, but do it in a less bloody and yet in a more comprehensive and timely fashion.

"Now just hear me out, for what I have to say may seem a bit extreme. But let's face it: We're in an extremely difficult situation, possibly one that calls for extreme measures. Trying to track down and shoot every diseased wild animal could take many weeks and even months. And there is no guarantee that every diseased animal will be found. We also need to think about the safety of our citizens. A lot of people live fairly close to the river and we run the risk of endangering a lot of lives with so much shooting and so many guns involved.

"I think we should consider evacuating portions of the Platte Valley. Once everyone is safely evacuated, planes could fly over the valley and eliminate the wildlife along the river with a lethal spray. I personally feel this would prove faster and far more effective than hunting down individual wild animals."

The female legislator raised her voice yet again.

"Senator Rawlins, in response to your own plan I have two questions. First, is such a lethal spray available to aviation centers such as your own? And second, how long after it is administered would it take for the environment to be completely safe and for people to return to their homes?"

The senator nodded and answered almost immediately.

"Yes, Triple R Aviation is but one of many companies that can acquire a lethal spray of the type that I speak. So yes, it is available. We would have to do some checking, but maybe we could use something that does not linger much beyond the first few moments of its application. People probably could return to their homes in a day or two. And we would take every measure to ensure human safety, of course."

The white-haired man with the unusually red face now raised his hand and asked a question.

"Could we really evacuate a whole river valley such as ours, and if so, how would we do it?"

Senator Rawlins turned to Colonel Grayton, the main representative from the Nebraska National Guard, and asked him to respond.

"It would be difficult," Colonel Grayton answered. "But yes, we could coordinate a mass evacuation of at least a portion of the Lower Platte Valley. It probably would take a few days until completion.

The governor would have to authorize this, and it would need to be a mandatory evacuation."

A well-dressed woman who had remained silent up to this time now asked to be recognized. She was very soft-spoken, but she stood up as if to be sure everyone heard what she had to say.

"It seems like we have two plans before us. That of Mr. Dawson and that of Senator Rawlins. Personally, I favor the latter because it sounds more feasible and more expedient."

Dr. Hotaru raised her hand, and stared directly at Harold Dawson and then Senator Rawlins. "I certainly respect your positions and your views. But I cannot support either plan. Eliminating all forms of wildlife in order to control a yet unidentified problem is simply too drastic. And what of the impact on the entire Platte River Valley? The ecological balance will be completely upset, the ramifications to the natural environment may—"

The well-dressed woman again rose up from her chair and motioned with both her hands as she spoke. "What other option do we have, Doctor? Do we wait for weeks, maybe months, until you scientists tell us something definite? Earlier today, a kind and wonderful woman was killed by a crazed animal over in River Junction. And several little toddlers who were in her care were seriously injured. How many more human lives must be lost? How many more blood-covered children must suffer and cry out for us to do something? I fully support Senator Rawlins' plan, and I urge others to do so as well. But we must act soon. The sooner the better. Something must be done."

The majority of those sitting around the table nodded their heads and voiced agreement. There was even applause from one corner of the room.

A barrel-chested police officer entered the conference area, looked all around, and hurriedly approached Senator Rawlins. Without excusing himself for the interruption, the officer handed the senator a piece of paper and remained standing at the senator's side.

Everyone in the room became silent, which made the sound of shouting outside the room all the more audible and unsettling.

"I have just received an urgent message," Senator Rawlins said. "We must bring this meeting to a close because the hotel here has gotten a bomb threat. So we need to vacate this building. Please, everyone, try not to be alarmed. We must follow protocol. We will inform the governor about this afternoon's meeting, and it is our governor who then will have the final word. Now please make your way out of this hotel and do so carefully and calmly. Thank you, everyone. And God help us all."

As the doors of the conference room swung open, people immediately streamed out and began making their way outside. Agent Vogel escorted Senator Rawlins and several other officials down the long hallway. A few members of the press called out for comments and reactions, but there was no response from anyone.

Agent Pike grinned at Dr. Hotaru and slowly shook his head as if to indicate he did not take the bomb threat seriously. He and the scientist were among the last ones to leave the conference room. As they made their exit, they both turned and looked behind them. A strange noise was coming from a far corner of the room. The sides of the large map of the Platte River Valley flapped and fluttered with each whirling movement of the electric fan.

CHAPTER 19

When Dr. Hotaru saw Agent Pike in the hotel lobby later that evening, she found him standing near the life-size painting of Christopher Columbus. Dr. Hotaru actually had to give the agent's arm a nudge to get his attention. She suggested that they walk to the small park that ran between the hotel and the river. Although the sun was slipping in the west, it still felt as hot as it had hours before.

"Your instincts were right," Dr. Hotaru said as they walked to the park. "There was nothing to that bomb scare. But at least I got a chance this afternoon to talk on the phone to some of my colleagues. They voiced the same objections to the Dawson and Rawlins plans that I did. It's madness."

"Maybe you haven't heard everything," Agent Pike said. "When we got outside, one of Senator Rawlins' aides gave me a printed version of his plan. It's all spelled out, even though he discussed only a few of his ideas at this afternoon's meeting."

"There's more to his plan?" Dr. Hotaru asked, incredulous.

"Yes," Agent Pike said. "He also proposes that it might be wise if all domestic animals—house pets, horses, cattle—be rounded up and quarantined. After that's done, every person in this portion of the valley would be evacuated and quarantined as well. Then planes would fly over this area and spray everything thoroughly. Only if the area tests clean in a few days would people and domestic animals be allowed to return."

"Tests clean?" Dr. Hotaru asked. "Clean of what? We still don't know what we're up against. There is no evidence of any specific disease."

"Chances are," Agent Pike mused, "that Rawlins is betting that the governor and other state officials will endorse his plan. I think a couple of the people who kept asking Rawlins questions in the meeting were some of his cronies. I wouldn't even be surprised if they are the ones who orchestrated this afternoon's bomb scare. Did you notice when Rawlins made that announcement during the meeting and how it brought such an abrupt end to the discussion? There seem to be a lot of forces at work here. Regardless of what happens, it is all shaping up to be pretty ugly. And everything is moving very fast."

Dr. Hotaru stopped walking and looked at Agent Pike as she spoke. "Zeph, ever since today's meeting I've been trying to come up with an alternative plan. I even ran it past a few of the locals who seem supportive. What if we were to get a team together and go down the river, collecting live specimens? Thousands of animal carcasses won't help us. We need to observe and capture a few of the animals that are behaving strangely and run tests. I am confident that would yield the kind of information we're seeking."

"Are you thinking of netting or trapping wild animals?"

"No, not necessarily. Maybe we could use tranquilizer guns. We could capture animals that are behaving strangely, as well as others that act normal. That way, we would have animals of the same species to observe and compare."

"And how will we know which animals are acting the way they should and which ones are acting strangely? Won't every animal act a little odd once they see us aiming a tranquilizer gun at them?"

Dr. Hotaru nodded. "Perhaps we could get Elk to help. You heard him this morning. He is intimately familiar with the animals on this river. He'll know which animals are not behaving like they usually do. Maybe Elk will help us."

At the mention of Elk's name, Agent Pike stopped walking. He frowned in a way that made Dr. Hotaru realize something was very wrong.

"I don't think we should involve him in any way," Agent Pike stated. "The file on 'Mr. Elk' came in and it is not a thin one. He's an ex-con and he did quite a bit of time in prison. He killed a woman."

Susan Hotaru's face reflected both shock and disbelief.

"The whole thing is kind of sick," Agent Pike continued. "The woman he killed was Indian as well. He turned himself in and admitted shooting her. He claimed that it was an accident. But her body was never found. He was in the Oklahoma State Penitentiary for about twenty years. After he got out, he changed his name and moved out to that place near Calico Creek."

Dr. Hotaru listened to the agent's every word, but her expression of horror slowly turned to one of concern and sympathy. "I guess that would explain why he lives all by himself the way that he does. But it sounds like he owned up to the crime and paid his debt. And he certainly has tried to make the rest of his life count for something. Is his real name the same one that he told us this morning?"

"Yes," Agent Pike said. "He's been going by the name of Elk for years. Back when he was convicted, he was known as Eddie Keeps Ahead. Keeps Ahead. Well, he learned he couldn't keep ahead of the law. It all caught up with him and—"

"Zeph," Hotaru interrupted as she grabbed Agent Pike by the arm to stop him from going on. "He told us his real name this morning. He didn't hold back. Has his record been clean since he was released?"

"Seems so," Agent Pike answered. "Other than an occasional letter to the editor about the environment or Native Americans, he seems to be fairly law-abiding. And he's been living by Calico Creek for over thirty years. There hasn't been any real trouble to speak of until these animal attacks started."

"Surely you don't think Elk has anything to do with the animal attacks? Zeph, it just doesn't make any sense. He's a gifted artist. I don't think he's an environmental terrorist who trains animals to attack and kill."

"But we do know he is capable of murder," Agent Pike countered. "I was a bit suspicious of him before and I'm even more suspicious now. Instead of involving him, we might want to keep a close eye on him. A very close eye."

CHAPTER
20

"Have you had breakfast?" Agent Pike called out early the next morning. He was behind the wheel and parked in front of the Christopher Columbus Hotel and Convention Center. The car windows were down and the engine was running.

Although it was shortly after sunrise, Susan Hotaru nodded. She held high a small plastic cup of hot tea as if offering an early morning toast.

"So what's going on?" the scientist asked, as she drank the last of the tea before getting into Agent Pike's car.

"First, a quick little trip to the public library here in Columbus. Then we'll head out to Calico Creek and meet with Edward Lawrence Keeps Ahead."

"What made you change your mind about seeing Elk?"

"My boss," Zephaniah Pike answered. "Last night, I talked to Kerrington and told him about your alternative plan. He thought it had merit. He agreed to talk to some people and see if Rawlins' plan could be postponed a few days. He's pretty sure they'll buy it, because it will take a few days to complete a mass evacuation. I reckon Kerrington doesn't want the FSPD to get involved in something that reeks of overkill. Our office tries to manage crises, not exacerbate them. So he told us to do what we can today and he would do what he could by talking to the governor and other officials. If things don't work out, well then, at least we tried."

"Wait a minute," Hotaru said, "last night you sounded like you didn't want to work with Elk, and now you've set up an early morning meeting with him. What are you not telling me?"

Agent Pike was silent for a moment before he answered. "I'm leveling with you. I still think we should keep a close eye on Elk and maybe this is the best way to do it. Besides, my boss told me to give your plan a try. You go ahead and ask Elk to help us. And I'll go ahead and ask him some questions that I have.

"But before going to Calico Creek, we need to stop at the public library here in town. I had a couple of phone calls last night from a Justin Wright. He's a reference librarian there. He said he had something we should see and that he would meet us at seven this morning."

"What could he possibly have that's so important?" Susan Hotaru asked.

"We'll soon find out," Pike murmured. "Justin Wright said that because of all the talk about a planned evacuation, the library will close down for a few days. He's the one who urged that we meet early this morning. We may not get another chance."

As Pike parked in front of the library, a pleasant-looking man in a short-sleeved shirt and a paisley tie stood at the front door. He wore a large diver's wristwatch on his right arm and he waved for the two visitors to enter.

"Thanks for coming," the librarian said, as he looked at his watch. "I know you must be very busy and pressed for time. So am I. Please come this way."

Pike and Hotaru followed Justin Wright into a spacious, well-lit reading room. On the wall hung a brightly colored mural that was about fifteen feet in length. The painting was positioned on the upper portion of the wall, so that one had to stand back to get a good look at the entire piece.

"There it is," the librarian proudly announced. "A full-size copy of

Segesser II. It's an amazing example of early folk art from the Great American West. The original was painted on pieces of tanned bison hide way back in the 1700s, most likely by Indian artists. There are a couple of Segesser hide paintings in existence, so everyone refers to this one as Segesser II. The paintings were preserved for generations by the Segesser family. But our Segesser II is just a copy. The original hide painting is housed down in Santa Fe, New Mexico, and it—"

"Please, Mr. Wright!" Agent Pike interrupted. "Just tell us why you think we need to see this. We have a full day ahead of us."

"Well," Justin Wright began, "I heard that the doctor here and maybe some others might be going on an expedition down the Platte. Yes, word gets around real fast in a town the size of Columbus. A lot of people are talking about it. So if any of you do go on such an expedition, it won't be the first. This painting is of the Platte River Expedition of 1720. It did not go the way the organizers anticipated and this old mural tells the story. It shows Pedro de Villasur and his soldiers and their Pueblo Indian allies when they were overcome by a combined force of Pawnee and Otoe tribesmen. The actual battle happened only a few miles southeast of here, near where the Loup River empties into the Platte. My grandparents used to farm in that area. We kids were always out in the fields looking for arrowheads and Spanish musket balls. As you can see in Segesser II, the battle was not a little skirmish. It was quite a big one—and a bloody one."

"This is that battle between the Pawnee and the Spanish that Elk told us about yesterday," Hotaru remembered.

"Are you referring to Mr. Elk?" the librarian asked.

"Yes," Pike answered. "Do you know him?"

"Of course," Justin Wright responded. "We don't see him too much in the summer. But Mr. Elk does come in here during the winter months. He's quite an avid reader. And his interests are wide-ranging: art, astronomy, history, philosophy, zoology, just about anything and everything. Sometimes, Mr. Elk will pull up a chair and just stare at Segesser II for hours. He said he finds something different every time

144 • TIMOTHY J. KLOBERDANZ

he studies it. There's an awful lot going on in the painting. One needs quite a while to take it all in."

"We don't have quite a while," Pike tried to explain. But even as the agent spoke, his eyes were riveted on the incredibly detailed battle scene. There appeared to be about two hundred figures in the painting. Pawnee warriors and Spanish soldiers were locked in fierce hand-to-hand combat. Nearly all of the Indian attackers were naked, while the soldiers wore leather armor and wide-brimmed dark hats. At the center of the huge mural, the fallen military commander lay bleeding to death as more and more Indians closed in on the outnumbered Spanish troops. A Catholic monk with a large cross seemed strangely out of place in the picture. The friar had pulled up the lower half of his blue robe over his tonsured head, as if to shield himself from all the arrows and tomahawk blows. But the monk had been hit by at least three arrows, one in the back, another in the hip, and a third in the left leg.

"That monk there looks to be in a heap of trouble," Pike said, pointing to the figure in blue. "He's trying to flee, but there is no escape for him."

"Actually," Justin Wright responded, "if you look more closely, you will see that the padre is running into the thick of the battle. Despite his wounds, he is trying to get to the dying Pedro de Villasur and administer last rites.

"A professor-priest from Creighton University stopped here a couple of years ago," the librarian continued. "He spent the whole afternoon examining the painting and making extensive notes. Before he left, he took me aside and shared some of his findings. The professor explained that in the early 1700s, a Catholic chaplain was an essential member of every Spanish military campaign or expedition. Besides saying daily Mass and hearing confessions, one of the chaplain's main responsibilities was to carry on his person a small round container called a 'viaticum pyx.' It was made of gold or silver and it held the consecrated hosts. So the priest in this painting was not trying to merely shield himself. He was on a mission. He was trying to protect the Holy Eucharist and get it to Villasur before the commander died. From the Catholic point of view, receiving communion in the final moments of one's life assured bodily resurrection and eternal salvation. Now I'm just a reference librarian, but I think the actions of that padre were rather courageous and even heroic."

Zephaniah Pike listened to every word but did not take his eyes off the painting. He noticed that in still another part of the mural, two Indians in full body paint held down a blond-haired soldier. One of the attackers grabbed the soldier's wrists, while the other held him by the ankles. A third Indian ran up and drove his lance into the soldier's chest. Still another Spanish soldier lay sprawled on his back, blood gushing out of his nose and mouth. The crotch of the soldier's pants was torn open and his genitals were exposed for all to see.

"The painting has sparked some debate and it has proven to be rather controversial at times," the librarian whispered. "Several of the elementary school teachers have insisted that we take it down due to the nudity and the various acts of violence that are depicted. They claim the painting is in very poor taste. But some of us feel differently and we want it preserved and displayed. After all, Segesser II is an important part of our area's history and heritage."

"What's going on there with the wounded soldier whose privates are visible?" asked Agent Pike. "That does seem excessive."

Justin Wright slipped his left index finger under his necktie as if to readjust it and make it easier for him to speak.

"Yes," the librarian agreed. "There's been a lot of speculation about that part of the painting. Everyone who studies it seems to have his or her own theory. Most people think it indicates that the soldiers who fell later were stripped and sexually mutilated by the Indians. I always wanted to ask Mr. Elk about it and see if he could shed some light on the matter."

"You never asked?" Agent Pike interjected, sounding somewhat surprised.

"Oh no," the librarian responded. "I didn't think it would be appropriate. Not with him being an Indian and all. You know what I mean."

As Agent Pike studied the painting, he noticed something else in the upper right-hand corner of the mural. Dr. Hotaru's eyes also were fixed on the same part of the painting. One of the figures in the battle scene was that of a small, dog-like creature with a bushy tail. The animal ran along the margins of the battle. It did not appear fearful or distracted in any way. It looked rather content and had a strange half-smile. The animal was a coyote.

"I'm still not sure why you wanted us to come here and see this painting," Agent Pike said.

Justin Wright's disappointment was obvious. The librarian furled his brow and stared at both the agent and the scientist.

"I think anyone planning an expedition down the Platte should know about Segesser II," the librarian responded. "We can always learn something from history."

"But this incident happened some three hundred years ago," Dr. Hotaru countered. "Times have changed. And the challenges we face today are very different."

"Yes," Justin Wright agreed. "Times have changed. But you know, my Grandma Wright told us kids something on her deathbed. She said: 'Life's tough and dying is no picnic. We can't change things that can't be changed. God is God, the Platte is the Platte, and that is that.'"

As the librarian said this, he looked up at Segesser II in an almost reverential fashion, as if the mural corroborated his grandmother's last words. Then he glanced down at the diver's watch on his right arm to check the time.

* * * *

On the highway leading west to Calico Creek, Pike and Hotaru noticed the bodies of freshly killed foxes, hawks, and rabbits that were strewn all along the road. At one point, they slowed down and counted more than fifty animal carcasses that hung limply from a makeshift, barbed wire fence. At another spot along the highway, there was a pile of dead animals and large birds, including a bald eagle that had been shot repeatedly.

As Pike and Hotaru drove into Elk's yard, the two dogs came running and snapped at the front tires. Elk, who was sitting outside, yelled for the dogs to stop and to come to him.

The early morning rays cast a strange golden light on everything in the yard. Old Man Elk had a hand axe and was removing pieces from a long piece of wood. He was wearing a sleeveless T-shirt and old pants. Sweat ran down his face and back as he hacked away at the wood.

"Nawa!" Elk called out in Pawnee. But even as he spoke, he continued to work.

"Morning," the two visitors said as they watched Elk shaping the wood.

"I see your window is fixed," Agent Pike observed. "So someone did come out and take care of it."

"Yes," Elk answered, putting down the axe and wiping the sweat off his face with the back of his hand. "He seemed kind of nervous after I told him a bunch of federal agents shot out that window. But he managed to get the job done without wetting his pants. Real nice man. And a really fast worker."

"The drive out here wasn't so pleasant this time," Dr. Hotaru said. "But here at your place it does seem peaceful."

"Yes," Elk agreed. "This is the way I like it. Especially in the stillness of a summer morning. It's very quiet and peaceful."

Almost at the same time as Elk spoke, gunshots could be heard in the distance. One, two, then more shots. Elk seemed to sense the irony of what he had said and the sounds that everyone now was hearing.

Zephaniah Pike approached the old Indian and looked him in the eyes as he spoke. "Would you say your whole life has been peaceful?"

The old man met his eyes and then turned away. It was not his habit to stare at another person directly.

"Agent Pike, it seems like something is troubling you so early in the morning. I have a feeling you've got something on your mind."

"I'm not one to beat around the bush," Agent Pike said. "And I'm not one to ignore an individual's history."

"Ah," Elk answered. "So you want to delve into history this morning? Oh, this old Indian can talk about history. Where should we begin? Ten thousand years ago? Five hundred years ago? How about the year 1492?"

"Let's speed it up a little. How about the year 1720 and the massacre that is depicted in the Segesser II painting?"

"I'm impressed, Agent Pike. You've been doing a little research and maybe you even spent some time in the library in Columbus. But that Villasur affair was no massacre. It was a real battle. There were no women and children involved on either side. It was a battle that pitted armed defenders against armed aggressors. And like I told you before, it was an important encounter that changed the whole course of history. But that event took place long, long before I was born. You can't hang that one on me."

"Okay," Zephaniah Pike responded. "How about an event that you were very much a part of, like the time that you shot and killed a young woman? You did twenty years in prison for that crime."

"Yes," Elk admitted. "I was in the big house for twenty years. But it seemed a whole lot longer to me. . . ."

"That's the idea," Agent Pike said. "A long, long time for a terrible crime. The punishment for killing someone is not supposed to be easy."

Old Man Elk looked at Agent Pike and realized the agent was not going to be quiet until he heard more.

"It was a long time ago," Elk remembered. "More than fifty years ago. I was only twenty then. And Gina was eighteen. Her given name was Regina, but I always called her Gina. I told her I wanted to show her how our people used to hunt and fend for themselves. So the two of us camped along a river, just like in the old days. I hunted and I wanted Gina to taste wild game that was prepared over an open fire. It was a nice, sunny afternoon. But then it all happened fast, too fast. Our elders told me many times that alcohol and guns do not mix. Instead of impressing my Gina for being a great hunter, I fumbled with my gun and killed her. I never touched alcohol after that. But I do not blame the alcohol. I blame myself. I lost my Gina. I lost the love of my life. Can you imagine what that is like, Agent Pike?"

Hearing this, Zephaniah Pike turned his back to the old man and looked away.

Dr. Hotaru stared at the two men and sensed they were both uncomfortable, but still she remained silent.

"The other day," Elk started up again, "one of your men shot into the front door of my home. Not just once, but twice. If I had been killed, would your agent have wound up in prison for twenty years? Or would the whole thing have been dismissed as merely an unfortunate accident—a sad but understandable mistake? This is a White man's country with White man's justice. I have a feeling that maybe the two of you can understand that better than most."

Agent Pike turned around and faced Elk again.

"You admitted you killed your girlfriend," he stammered. "But you refused to help the police recover the body."

Elk looked down at his feet as he spoke. "There are some things non-Indians would never understand. Even other Indians might not understand. Maybe only a Pawnee can understand another Pawnee."

Agent Pike continued to ask questions. "If you and your people understand each other so well, then why do you live so far away from the rest of your tribe? They're all in Oklahoma and you're here in Nebraska. You seem to be the only Pawnee Indian around here."

"You are mistaken," Elk answered. "I am not 'the only Pawnee Indian around here.' Look closely at what is left of these prairies. Here and there you will see a cedar tree. Think of each one as the spirit of a Pawnee who once lived here. You will not be able to count all of the cedar trees, they are that great in number. So you see, I am not alone. The spirits of the Pawnee dead are close by and they are everywhere. Only a few miles to the northwest, there are nearly a thousand Pawnee who are buried in one big grave on the east end of the Genoa Cemetery. For many years, the remains of those Pawnee were scattered in museums and laboratories all across the country. And then all those Pawnee came back home. At long last, they were reburied here in Nebraska, in the land of our ancestors. So I am not 'the only Pawnee Indian around here.'

"But," Elk continued in a voice edged with anger and deep emotion, "if you want to think of me as a *'kitsa hudiksu,'* a loner or an old man in self-imposed exile, then think what you will. Do not blame my people back in Oklahoma. And do not think they shun me. My Pawnee relatives and even my Arikara cousins from North Dakota have come here a number of times and asked me to live out the rest of my days with them. But I told them I prefer to die here, close to the Platte and the Loup, in the old, old homeland of the Pawnee."

"You took a young woman's life," Agent Pike said. "And that is not something that is easy for us to ignore or overlook. It just isn't that easy."

"Do you think it is easy for me?" the old Indian asked. "Yesterday I showed you those dates that are tattooed on my fingers. Those dates are for others to see and to ponder.

"But these tattoos are for me to see and to ponder," Elk said as he extended his bare arms. On the inside of his right arm, in dark blue letters that were at least two inches high, was the name "REGINA TWIN CHIEF." On the inside of his left arm, in blue markings of similar size, were the words "DIED APRIL THE 27TH."

Agent Pike and Dr. Hotaru grew silent and remained quiet for a long time. Finally, Elk lowered his tattooed arms and petted the two dogs that brushed up against his legs.

"Elk," Dr. Hotaru said as she approached him. She was moved by what he had said and her lips quivered as she spoke.

"I did not come here to dredge up the past. What is in the past cannot be undone. And I am truly sorry. I came here this morning to seek your help. If you decide not to help us, I will understand. But I want to give you a chance to help prevent a terrible, terrible thing that is about to happen."

Dr. Hotaru looked at Zephaniah Pike and wondered how much she should say. When she saw the agent nod, she realized she could say the things she needed to in order to help Elk understand the gravity of the situation.

"Animals are being killed and piled up all along the highway even as we speak," Dr. Hotaru explained. "But there are even bigger plans to destroy all the wildlife in this portion of the valley, from Grand Island to possibly as far east as Fremont. There are those who feel all the wild animals in this area must die in order to destroy those responsible for the attacks."

Dr. Hotaru could see the disbelief in Elk's eyes. But she continued anyway.

"Despite what others propose, we have an alternative plan. Maybe we can go down the river, and with your help we can single out the animals that are behaving strangely. We will not kill them. We'll stun them with tranquilizers and bring them in alive to see what is making them sick. We will also bring in animals that appear to be normal, so that we can compare their blood and run comparative tests. The animals that appear healthy will be released back into the wild. If there is no way to help them, those that are behaving strangely will have to be euthanized. But destroying a few animals may be better than destroying all the wildlife here in the valley. I am being honest with you, Elk. And I'm telling you what we might do to avert a much greater catastrophe."

The old man listened closely and was quiet for a long time before he spoke. "And what do you want from me?"

"Elk," Dr. Hotaru said, "you work closely with animals and you know their behavior. But I don't know the ways of the animals of this valley the way you do. You could help us identify the animals that

152 • TIMOTHY J. KLOBERDANZ

look and act normal, and those that do not. You will serve as our guide and our wildlife interpreter."

"Ah," Elk answered in a rather disgusted tone of voice. "You want me to point out the animals who need to be brought down. It will fall on me to decide which animals will be captured and analyzed for your research.

"You know," the old man continued, "the Pawnee served as army scouts for the U.S. Cavalry back in the 1860s and 1870s. But after the Indian Wars ended, our cooperation was forgotten and we were treated worse than the hostile Indians whom we scouted against. Will that be my fate as well if I serve as your guide?"

"I hope not," Dr. Hotaru answered. "But to be honest, I do not know how any of this will work out. Maybe you'll get nothing for your efforts. Maybe Agent Pike and I will lose our jobs if this alternative plan backfires. I'm afraid I can't offer any guarantees."

Elk listened but showed no outward sign of how he was inclined to respond. "How much time will there be for this little outing?"

"Only two or three days," Agent Pike answered, "maybe even less. We don't have much time before the killing begins. And let's face it, we most likely won't stop the slaughter that is sure to come. There are folks who already are taking things into their own hands and hunting down animals. It's unauthorized, but a lot of killing already has begun. So this plan of ours could prove dangerous. You need to know that."

Dr. Hotaru nodded in agreement. "Whether you help us or not is up to you, Elk. But we have only a short time to prepare. There's a lot of equipment to gather up and we need to be ready to go in only a day or so."

The old Pawnee stood straight, still showing no outward sign of which way he was leaning. More gunshots could be heard in the distance. Finally the old man spoke.

"This is what I say. I need to consider all that has been said here this morning. And I need to decide what is best for our animal brothers and sisters. Give me until later today. Then call me. If I pick up the phone and talk, it will mean I want to cooperate and maybe be like one of those old-time Pawnee scouts. But if you call and I do not even pick up the phone, it means I do not want to be involved in any way. And you must respect my wishes. And you must leave me alone."

Elk looked at Agent Pike and Dr. Hotaru for a long time. Then the two visitors walked toward the car and the old man sat down and gently petted his dogs. During all this time, not another word was said.

PART THREE

KINGFISHER, KINGFISHER

*A*ll that day, Ahwa heard the Two-Leggeds. They traveled in packs, and as they noisily made their way through the wooded river bottoms that lined the Great Flat Water, they would point their long thunder-sticks and slay whatever creature happened to be in their path.

Even a small killdeer with two black bands around her neck became a target. The bird tried to divert the Two-Leggeds away from her nest by pretending to have an injured wing. As she scurried about, she cried out with a loud sound that echoed through the dry grasses and the tall trees. In the high-pitched language of the killdeer, the frightened mother screamed: "Kiiilll jeeer, kiiilll jeeer." The shore-bird sacrificed herself and died bravely. Her piercing cries hung in the air, much like the puffs of blue smoke that were made by the long thunder-sticks of the Two-Leggeds.

One pack of Two-Leggeds was very determined and continued to seek out larger prey. But they were startled when a white-tailed stag with velvet-covered antlers bounded out in front of them. The thunder-sticks of the Two-Leggeds made much noise and smoke, but the deer leapt away without injury.

The Two-Leggeds angrily waved their thunder-sticks back and forth, as they ran through the grass in pursuit. But the white-tailed stag was too fast for them. It knew the area well and raced ahead. It stopped only briefly near an old cottonwood tree. As the deer did so, its antlers seemed to become a part of the great cottonwood itself.

Each time the thunder-sticks of the Two-Leggeds went off, the deer would dart away, and as it did so, other animals could be seen hurrying about or seeking a hiding place. Every so often, the deer would *look up to watch a red-tailed hawk. It observed the hawk's circling motions, and by these it could tell that the hawk was letting the animals down below know about the movements of the Two-Leggeds.*

Now, as the Two-Leggeds moved among them, creatures of all kinds felt a new bond with one another. Ancient grudges and rivalries were forgotten as the bobcat and the red fox ran together. The blood of the long-tailed weasel and the long-necked sandpiper mixed and stained the same earth. And the white-tailed deer and the red-tailed hawk worked in tandem.

Ahwa watched all of this and took a deep breath. The stench of rotting flesh already was in the wind. Blood was in the air. And everything, everything smelled of war.

CHAPTER
21

The old man sat in the fading light of the window and watched the wood in his hands take on a different shape. He always looked forward to the moment when a piece of wood assumed a life of its own and spoke to him. It was a rare moment, and when it happened the old man felt like he had released something that had always resided there in the wood. Often, after he put the finishing touches on a piece, he held the carving in his hands for a long time. In every single piece that he carved, he sensed a small spot in the wood where it was warm to the touch. When he felt it, the old man knew that he had found its heart. Sometimes, he held the finished carving close to his own heart, as if to draw in some of its warmth.

All day Old Man Elk tried to focus on his carvings, but he could hear the constant gunshots. His two dogs usually stretched out and slept in the big room as the old Indian did his carving. But today they got very little rest. With the sound of each gunshot, their ears perked up and the dogs whined softly. The old man repeatedly told them to quiet down and go to sleep. But the dogs continued to whine and they grew more restless.

At one point, Elk turned on the radio and hoped to find a station with music that Apollo and Artemis might find soothing. But nearly every station carried news reports and commentaries about recent events in the Platte River Valley. Elk found it very hard to work under such conditions. By evening, he managed to finish one carving. It was that of a black-billed magpie with an unusually long tail. He searched for the warm spot that was its heart and felt better when he found it. On this day, he closed his eyes and held the carving of the magpie to his chest for a long, long time.

Nearly every hour, the telephone in Elk's home rang. But he did not personally answer any of the calls. The message on his answering machine simply stated: "Calico Creek Art Studio. Elk is not able to come to the phone right now. So leave your name and number and he will call you when he can. Please be patient. And stay well."

Most of the incoming calls were from art dealers or customers who expressed interest in purchasing some of Elk's work. The old man was in no hurry to return any of the calls, for he knew that he could never carve all of the pieces that everyone requested. He had the luxury of taking each day as it came and working on only those carvings that he really wanted to complete. Money had ceased to be a central concern many years ago. The only limitation was time. There was so much he still wanted to do.

Around nine p.m. the telephone rang. It was Dr. Hotaru and she waited a few moments before leaving a message. Her voice sounded strained and tense. Elk simply looked at the answering machine and made no effort to go to the phone.

"Elk," the voice began, "this is Susan Hotaru. I don't want to pressure you. I just want you to know that we do need your help. You may have heard that the governor and other Nebraska officials have called for a mandatory evacuation of this portion of the valley. Everyone will have to pack a few basic items and then leave. All pets and livestock will need to be quarantined in separate facilities. So it doesn't look good for the wildlife that remains behind, Elk. I know—"

The voice suddenly was cut off by the timing mechanism in the answering machine. Elk stared at the telephone, as if he expected Dr. Hotaru to call again. But she did not. And Elk felt relieved.

The old Pawnee looked at Apollo and Artemis and spoke to them: "My friends, it looks like we may all have to go away for a while. But do not worry. I will not let us get separated. We'll stay together."

Apollo and Artemis seemed to understand the old man, for their heads bobbed up and down and their tails wagged. They stayed close to Elk and they took turns brushing up against him.

Gunshots could be heard again, but this time they were much closer. The two dogs began howling and running around in tight little circles.

The old man looked out the window and then gestured for the dogs to quiet down and to remain inside. Elk nudged the door open and stepped outside. He slowly made his way down the steps.

Besides hearing the gunshots, he could sense something else. He feared that hunters might be trespassing nearby, so he went to the wood pile and picked up an axe.

Elk cautiously walked all around his yard, looking for anything that might be out of the ordinary. He carried the axe in his right hand and clenched it more firmly as he came across fresh tracks. He also detected movement behind an old shed. As Elk approached the building and peered around the corner, two large eyes met his.

A white-tailed deer stood before him and stared directly at the old man. But the large-antlered deer did not move. It looked at the old Indian for a long time. The two simply stared at each other, as if trying to see beyond the shiny darkness of each other's eyes.

The eyes of the deer seemed to plead with the old man, asking that he not shout out or reveal the animal's whereabouts. The eyes of the old man seemed to plead as well, pleading that the deer not do anything foolish to endanger the safety of both of them.

The deer held its head erect and its velvet-covered antlers did not move in the slightest. The old man gripped the double-headed axe close to him, so that it looked like an antler-like extension of himself.

A distant gunshot suddenly pierced the evening air and faintly echoed through the yard. The deer shivered a bit, but it did not stop staring at the old man. Ever so slowly, the deer spread its rear legs and urinated. The animal peed for a long time and did not stop until a large foamy puddle had formed. Elk figured that the deer had been running most of the day and had not taken time to relieve itself.

The old man waited a moment and then backed up very slowly without making any sound. He continued to do this until he had taken several steps backwards. Then he gently lowered the axe that was in his right hand.

The deer lowered its head as if to reveal the full breadth of its antlers. Then it quickly looked to the right and leapt in that direction. The deer easily scaled an old wooden fence at the end of the yard. As it hurried away, its bright white tail was clearly visible.

Elk watched the white tail grow smaller and smaller in the darkness. A few minutes later, as the old man walked back into the house, it was not the white tail that continued to loom before him; it was the look of the deer's eyes as they peered into his own.

CHAPTER
22

After telephoning Elk and being cut off by the answering machine, Susan Hotaru let out a deep, audible sigh. She had agreed to leave him alone if he chose not to pick up the phone and answer. Now she had to confer with Agent Pike and discuss new plans. But first, she needed to take a few minutes and think about options.

Although there was air conditioning in the hotel in Columbus, the room felt muggy and stifling. Dr. Hotaru decided to go outside and take a walk. The evening air was hot and the intense heat of the day still could be felt on the pavement.

She saw reporters and federal agents and state officials who were in small groups talking among themselves. So she deliberately walked back and forth in an empty corner of the well-lit parking lot.

"Susan!" Agent Pike called out, as he headed out of the hotel. He was carrying several files. "Susan!"

Dr. Hotaru was afraid to face the agent and tell him the bad news, but finally she turned completely around.

"I take it the news is not good," Agent Pike said as he stood before the scientist. "Elk did not answer his phone. Right?"

Susan Hotaru nodded to indicate the agent correctly guessed how things stood. She had the kind of face that enabled people to size up a tense situation almost immediately.

"But I'm thinking of what else we might do," Hotaru responded. "I know I can count on some of my colleagues. But we still don't know what we're up against. All I know is that we have to save whatever animals we can. If Rawlins and his group decide to spray a powerful toxin here in the valley that destroys all of the wildlife, we may never know what caused the problem to begin with. And then where will we be?"

Agent Pike thought over her words for a few moments.

"You're the wildlife expert here," the agent began, "and so I trust your judgment. It's too bad Elk won't help us. But I am not at all surprised. Besides, he's an old man who may not be up to the task. Perhaps it's just as well. So tell me, what can I do, Doctor Hotaru?"

He emphasized the word "Doctor" to try to get a laugh out of the scientist and it almost worked. She smiled a bit before answering.

"Okay, we need to find living animals of various species. We could sedate and tag them. We can't have too many people on the river at one time or it will scare away all the animals. I'm thinking of two boats, with two individuals in each one. Out east of here a lot of people use those everglades-style airboats on the Platte, but the airboats make an awful lot of noise and will be too disruptive. Canoes are quiet, but boats with small, muffled motors might work best for us. That way we don't have to worry about rowing or tipping over. One person in each boat can point out the animals to be sedated and the other one can use the tranquilizer gun. There are some new, high-powered tranquilizer rifles that are very effective."

Agent Pike wrinkled his eyebrows to indicate he wasn't sure of something. "Once the animals are sedated, how do you keep the 'problem ones' separated from the ones that appear to be normal? And how do we retrieve the animals and transport them back to a lab for study?"

"I've thought about that," Hotaru answered. "We could use tranquilizer darts of three kinds. Red ones for animals that are acting unusually aggressive or abnormal. Yellow darts for animals that we are unsure of. And green darts for animals that appear to be normal. Once we have located and sedated an animal, we will radio a recovery team that will come in right behind us. They could retrieve the animal, tag it, and place it in a transport carrier. Since the members of the backup team actually will handle the animal, they may need to take special precautions. They could wear masks and gloves, maybe even full-body protective suits."

"How many individuals do you think we'll need in the backup team?" Agent Pike asked.

"About eight to ten," Hotaru replied. "As many as we can manage. If the mass evacuation of this valley goes through, there won't be nearly enough health personnel on hand for all that needs to be done. But if push comes to shove, I'm confident I can count on my academic colleagues."

"And you can count on some additional federal assistance," Pike added. "We have a special animal disease facility out in New York. I've been in touch with them and they are willing to help us. But I guess my real concern is the safety of whoever is out on the river. What if it is a contagious disease that can be spread from animals to humans? Won't that be dangerous for those individuals actually handling and tagging the animals that we tranquilize?"

"Maybe," Hotaru said. "But they'll be the ones in the masks and protective suits."

"And what about those of us who are on the river doing all of the finger-pointing and the shooting?" asked Agent Pike.

"Us? Are you sure you still want to be a part of all this?" Hotaru asked.

Agent Pike nodded even before he uttered a single word.

"Yes, I do want to be involved. I really do. But part of the reason may be kind of selfish on my part. For years, I've hunted down and confronted the absolute worst dregs of humanity. I've seen the disgusting things they've done and I tried hard to understand why they did it. Sometimes, after an assignment, all I could do was shake my head. I felt like I needed to be in a scalding hot shower for a week just to rid myself of all that I had seen. I think I've rubbed up real close against the essence of human evil, something that is as foul as it is indescribable. Time and time again, I told myself that wild animals never could sink as low as some of the cold-blooded characters I've come across. I still want to believe that there's a basic goodness about animals, a basic goodness somewhere out there, something uncorrupt and unspoiled. It may sound odd, but I think seeing that would help restore my faith in people and in life itself."

The agent seemed to realize he was sounding overly philosophical. The tone of his voice shifted almost immediately to one that was more light-hearted and whimsical.

"Besides," Zephaniah Pike continued, "I've seen it all, remember? And my boss expects Vogel and me to be there to assist you. I would much rather be out on the river rounding up some wild animals than helping manage a mass evacuation. It sounds like the Platte River is where the real action will be."

"Yes," Hotaru agreed. "It may well be the scene of some real action. But it may also pose the greatest risk. Zeph, we still don't know what we're up against."

"Whatever it is, I think we've all been exposed already. You and Vogel and I have been crouching over dead bodies and dead animals during the past few days. So if we are up against that 'Jumper' you warned us about, we may all be walking time bombs. And I have a feeling that those little masks you sometimes wear won't afford much protection either."

Even in the darkness of the hotel parking lot, Agent Pike knew that Susan Hotaru's face betrayed uncertainty. Yet she did not say anything to allay the agent's concerns. Together, the two slowly walked, back and forth, as the loose gravel in the parking lot crunched beneath their feet.

CHAPTER
23

Her cell phone rang even before a single ray of sunlight crept into the hotel room. Susan Hotaru glanced at her watch but was unable to read the time. When she finally answered the phone, she heard an old man's voice as he said "good morning."

At first, the caller sounded like her grandfather, but he had been dead for many years. Grandpa Hirosaku Hotaru used to call her early in the morning, when she was away at college. Even though he had to call long distance, he wanted to be sure she did not miss her first class of the day. She often thought about her grandparents. It was only rarely that she thought of her parents because the memories were too painful. She preferred to think about her grandparents and especially her Grandpa Hotaru. For a few seconds, she was transported back to a less crowded time of her life and the feeling was as overwhelming as it was brief.

"Dr. Hotaru?" the caller asked.

It was Old Man Elk.

"Good morning" she replied, trying to sound very awake.

"Just want you to know I've been considering what you asked of me. I would be willing to help, but I want you to agree to some things first. Are you listening?"

"Yes. Please go ahead, Elk. Tell me what's on your mind." Dr.

Hotaru searched for a pen and some paper as Elk cleared his throat. She could not find her notebook, but she did locate a few sheets of hotel stationery in the drawer of the nightstand. She wrote quickly as Elk talked.

"I heard that the governor approved Senator Rawlins' plan that calls for a complete evacuation of this part of the valley. Then they're going to spray and kill off all the wildlife. Is that right?"

"Yes. That's the plan. I don't support it, but at this point the officials are more concerned about people than wild animals. While I don't endorse the senator's plan, I understand why the governor feels it is necessary. His chief responsibility is to the people."

"Of course," Elk replied. "People vote. Animals don't. It's political."

Dr. Hotaru was silent. She wanted to voice objections to what Elk was saying. But she did not.

"Elk," she said, "I'm relieved that you changed your mind and that you want to help us. But what do you want in return?"

He was quiet for a few seconds and then answered.

"I want you and Agent Pike to promise me that the animals we bring in will be treated with respect and will not be harmed. If I go with you, I want you to promise me that my place near the river will be safe and that my studio will not be disturbed in any way. And I want my dogs Apollo and Artemis to go with me. I don't want them caged up and quarantined while I'm out on the river helping you."

Dr. Hotaru wrote everything down and numbered each of Elk's conditions.

"Anything else?" she asked.

"Yes," Elk answered. "There's one more thing. But I don't want you to mention it to Agent Pike or anyone else. It'll be an understanding between just the two of us."

"Go ahead," Hotaru urged. As she waited, she gripped the pen tightly in her hand but did not write anything down.

"You must do all you can to watch my back," Elk said. "I don't trust the Fizz-Pidds or any kind of federal agents. They tend to be a little too trigger-happy. And I don't like being outnumbered."

Dr. Hotaru was surprised by Elk's concern. Thoughts raced through her mind, but she decided not to ask for an explanation.

"I'll do what I can," Dr. Hotaru promised. "And I'll discuss those first three requests with Agent Pike and see what we can do. Taking your dogs along may prove to be the biggest obstacle. It'll be awkward. Are you sure your dogs won't scare away the wild animals that we see?"

"No," Elk replied. "Apollo and Artemis go with me all the time and behave themselves when we go in a canoe out on the river. They often spot the other animals before I do. They won't be any trouble and they will be a big help to us."

"Alright," Dr. Hotaru said. "Let me run these things past Agent Pike and we'll see what happens. Okay? I can't make any promises. We still haven't been given the official go-ahead to make this little trip down the river. If we do get the green light, will you be able to be gone for two or three days? And can you be ready to go tomorrow morning?"

"Apollo and Artemis and I will be packed and waiting," Elk answered. "But remember, we all go or I will not be able to help you."

"I understand," Dr. Hotaru responded.

Just as she was saying goodbye, she noticed on her cell phone that Agent Pike had tried to reach her early that morning. But she was not ready to talk to him yet. She needed some time to think about Elk's list of conditions and how to present them to Pike.

Susan Hotaru turned on the television and switched from channel to channel. As she brushed her teeth, she learned that the mandatory evacuation in Nebraska was the primary topic of morning discussion, not only on the national networks but on the international news as well.

A well-known commentator indicated that there would be no further travel to or from the state of Nebraska. Massive numbers of the

National Guard were being called into active duty. Gymnasiums, schools, and other large buildings in central and northeastern Nebraska were being prepared for thousands of evacuees from the Lower Platte River Valley. And, for the first time in U.S. history, an entire state was under quarantine.

CHAPTER 24

"We have a big day ahead of us," Agent Pike announced as he faced a group of FSPD agents. They all stood in a large meeting room of the hotel.

"This is the kind of thing all of us have trained for and thus we must do what we can to make sure everything goes smoothly. Some of the people we encounter today are going to be edgy—and maybe even downright ugly. So it is up to us to remain cool and calm. We need to set an example for everyone. Do you hear me? No matter how hot it gets today, the words for today are 'cool and calm.'"

Agent Pike handed out sheets of paper to each of the agents with detailed sets of individual assignments. More agents from other FSPD offices in the state were entering the hotel as well. Pike was very surprised when he saw his boss, Douglas Kerrington, come through the front door accompanied by several officials.

"Douglas!" Agent Pike called out. "How in the world were you able to get here?"

"Connections," Kerrington answered with his characteristic wink. "It wasn't easy, but I made it through just as the doors into Nebraska were closing. Where can you and I talk?"

Zephaniah Pike gestured for him to follow. Kerrington made apologies and indicated to the other officials that he wished to be alone with Agent Pike.

The two men found a corner of a large conference room where they were able to sit down. Cell phones were ringing and people were hurrying back and forth with maps and reports. Pike asked one of the staff members to make sure the two men were not disturbed as they conversed.

"First, how are you doing?" Kerrington began.

"I'm alright. This thing is getting pretty big, but I think I can manage it."

"You sure?" Kerrington asked.

Pike could not tell if he detected concern or doubt in his boss's eyes.

"Yes, I'm fine. But if you're thinking this is all too much for me to handle—"

"It's too much for you or any one man to handle! But hell, I'm not here to check up on you. I'm here to help shoulder the burden. Seems like the eyes of the whole world are now on the state of Nebraska. The burden shouldn't fall just on your shoulders. And if there's any glory to come of all this, well, maybe I'll share some of that, too."

Agent Pike nodded, even though he did not fully understand.

"So what's the latest?" Kerrington asked.

Zephaniah Pike pointed to a large map that was tacked to a wall of the conference room. The map was of the eastern half of Nebraska and showed the Lower Platte River Valley in great detail.

"The governor has called for a mandatory mass evacuation of everyone who lives within five miles of either side of the Platte River, from just outside the city of Grand Island east to Fremont. That's a distance of roughly a hundred and forty miles. Folks who live along the Loup River northwest of here also will be evacuated. The number of people to be affected will be in the tens of thousands. A total of 120,000 people may not be unrealistic. Three of the largest population centers are Columbus, Central City, and Schuyler. Columbus has about 25,000 residents, Central City 3,000, and Schuyler about 6,000.

We're trying to contain this thing so that it does not directly affect the much larger population centers of Grand Island and Fremont."

"Or Omaha and Lincoln," Kerrington added. "If the two largest metropolitan areas of this state are affected, it will be nearly impossible to evacuate everyone to safety."

Pike went over to the map and pointed to the areas where evacuees would be detained.

"All the details are being worked out, but we expect that people will be temporarily housed in schools and auditoriums and makeshift shelters north of the Lower Platte Valley. Food and water and medical services will be provided. Nearly three hundred people have been diagnosed with heatstroke, but just to be safe they will be housed and cared for in a special facility near Norfolk, which is about fifty miles north of Columbus. The National Guard, FEMA, city and rural fire departments, and local officials all will be involved in the mandatory evacuation."

"What about looting?" asked Kerrington.

"People in the endangered area have been told that they must leave their homes by the deadline and that anyone who remains behind will be suspect and treated accordingly. Folks in this part of the Midwest seem fairly law-abiding, but we will need to take every precaution, just in case."

"What are the plans for people's pets and livestock?"

"Everyone will need to register their pets and lodge them separately. Cattle and other livestock will have to be rounded up and transported to temporary holding pens north of the river until the critical period has passed."

"And when will the evacuation be completed?"

"Within the next three days. On the morning of the fourth day, planes equipped with ISE-41T will spray a hundred-and-forty-mile stretch of the valley. The effects will be almost immediate. All vertebrates will sicken and die. We are not sure how the toxin will affect other wildlife forms. But at the present, Senator Rawlins and his aides assure us that ISE-41T is the best thing they have available. After a twenty-four-hour period has passed, National Guardsmen in masks and protective clothing will seek out all the dead animals they can find and inventory them. Then they will burn or bury the remains. When each area is cleared of the carcasses and disinfected, people will be allowed to move back into their homes and hopefully things will return to normal."

Kerrington was unusually quiet before responding.

"The key word in that last sentence of yours is 'hopefully'?"

"Yes," Pike said, "we need to hope for the best." As he said this, he saw Dr. Hotaru on the other side of the room talking to Agent Vogel. When she realized that Pike had seen her, she held up a white tablet. On it she had written three words with a black felt pen: "ELK SAID YES."

Dr. Hotaru's timing seemed perfect, for Kerrington's next comment dealt with the plan Pike had discussed with him on the phone.

"Are you still concerned that vital information will be lost if all the wild animals are destroyed?"

"Absolutely," Pike answered. "Once all the animals are dead, we won't have much to work with. Chances are there may be affected animals or birds that already have migrated elsewhere. And so the same problem may crop up in a few weeks in another place or in another state. We need to know what we're dealing with here in Nebraska so that we are prepared if we must confront it again."

"You have a plan to remedy that, right?"

Pike nodded.

"Well, that's one of the main reasons why I'm in Columbus," Kerrington admitted. "If you have something in mind that allows for the collection of living specimens, I can support that. Meanwhile, I could work with state and federal officials and direct things from here. Let's go over that plan of yours in detail."

"Of course," Agent Pike agreed. "But first, there is someone I want you to meet—the wildlife scientist who came up with this plan.

Her name is Dr. Susan Hotaru."

Pike motioned for Hotaru to approach them and to join in the discussion. As she made her way across the room, Agent Pike gave her a confident nod and a Kerrington-style wink.

CHAPTER
25

The Director of the FSPD listened to the plan that Dr. Hotaru and Agent Pike presented without interrupting them even once. When they both had finished, Douglas Kerrington said he supported the general outline, but he expressed deep concerns for the safety of those participating. Kerrington thought it might be best if the two boats were accompanied by a third boat in which there were more special agents or armed National Guardsmen.

Pike argued that both boats would be equipped with tranquilizer guns and that they would remain in frequent contact with the recovery team only a short distance behind them.

Kerrington also voiced concern regarding the inclusion of a civilian who was well past retirement age. But Hotaru stood her ground and argued that Elk was one of the most knowledgeable wildlife observers in the valley. She insisted that his intimate familiarity with all forms of wildlife perhaps made him the most valuable member of the team.

"There is something else you need to know," Agent Pike told Kerrington. "The Indian who is known as Elk, or Old Man Elk, did time in prison." When he said this, Dr. Hotaru blinked hard and then kept her eyes shut for a couple of seconds.

"But for more than thirty years," Agent Pike went on, "Elk has been clean and has worked as a wildlife artist. He knows animals and he has agreed to help us. Although he is in his early seventies, Elk appears to be strong and healthy. He moves around like a man who is much younger."

Douglas Kerrington frowned and shook his head.

"The more I think about all of this, the less I like it. But we don't have the time to be overly critical or too choosy, do we? If you all plan to go on this animal recovery mission, you had better hop to it. And I will need frequent updates from you, Zeph. If it gets too dangerous out there, I want you to call the whole thing off and come in. While you are all cavorting about on boats, I'll do what I can by coordinating things here and working with other officials and the press."

"Thank you, Mr. Kerrington," Dr. Hotaru said, "but there is something else. As you no doubt know, there's been a drought here for the last few years. In some parts of the valley, the Platte is completely dry. Perhaps you could talk to the governor and ask that any available irrigation water be diverted into the main river channel. Water will attract the wild animals and make our job easier. And it also will simplify things when it comes time to spray the river valley. The animals and birds will go to the river once it is flowing with water again."

Kerrington raised his eyebrows. "Water is not my speciality. But if there's a way to divert some more water into the river, I'll see what can be done. I dare not linger here much longer or you'll make me wish I had never set foot in the state of Nebraska."

He laughed a little to indicate he was only half-joking. The minute he left Agent Pike and Dr. Hotaru, several agents surrounded him and each one of them handed him reports and other sheets of paper.

"So what made Elk change his mind?" Pike asked.

"A number of things," Dr. Hotaru explained. "He's concerned about the safety of his art studio and his two dogs. I assured him that we could have someone keep an eye on his place. And I do think it would be okay if he brought along both his dogs."

"That's crazy!" Agent Pike exclaimed. "There's no way we can do that. No way."

"Elk claims his dogs can spot wild animals quickly and they are accustomed to doing that. If they get in the way and are a problem, we can always send them back."

"I think it's crazy," Agent Pike said. "But everything seems a little crazy around here."

Zephaniah Pike looked at Susan Hotaru for a long time. He moved closer so that he could talk to her and not be overheard.

"After we've both finished our chores for today, maybe we could have a nice relaxed dinner later tonight. It might do us both some good."

Hotaru looked away and laughed nervously.

"I'm not sure what to make of such an invitation," she said with even more intermixed laughter. "Especially the tone."

"Did I miss something?" Pike asked.

"No, I'm sorry. I didn't mean to laugh. I was thinking of how I had taped a picture of you on the ceiling of my dorm room when I was in college. It was a full-page picture of you from some sports magazine. You were running and you had such an incredibly sexy look on your face. I went to sleep looking at that picture many a night. If only I would have known then that you would ask me out to dinner one day."

"Well, guess what," Pike replied. "He may be a few years late, but the Zephyr's standing right in front of you. And he's asking."

Susan Hotaru stepped back and faced the agent squarely.

"You're very considerate, but I don't think it's a good idea. I enjoy working with you. But I don't think we should let any personal feelings get in the way. Besides, you're married, Zeph."

"My wife and I are separated. So it's not dishonest or anything."

"No," Hotaru agreed. "It's not dishonest. I know that. But I just don't think it's a good idea. When I get back to my room, I'm sure I'll replay this conversation back and forth in my mind a thousand times. But I'd rather have it that way than allow any personal feelings to suddenly complicate everything. Don't you think?"

Zephaniah Pike stared into Hotaru's eyes and finally nodded.

When the two parted, each immediately went to work making arrangements for the next few days. Both were so busy making phone calls and running errands that they hardly noticed when the sun began its descent into the west.

The onset of evening especially surprised Agent Pike. He hurried to his hotel room, took off his jacket and tie, and made a phone call. It rang a long time before a woman answered.

"Hello."

"Hello, Darla. It's Zeph. How are things there?"

"Alright."

"This time I managed to call before it got too late."

"Yes."

"Is Twila there?"

"No. She's at a baseball game."

Zephaniah twisted the telephone cord in his fingers and felt its rubbery thickness.

"What time will she be getting back?"

"I'm not sure what time she'll be home."

"Would you tell Twila I called?"

"Yes."

"Darla?"

"Yes."

"I'm heading out on an assignment tomorrow. I'm not sure when I'll get a chance to call again."

There was silence on the other end.

"Darla, can you hear me?"

"Yes."

"I'm still in Nebraska, working on that wild animals case. Maybe you've heard about it?"

"Yes."

"God, Darla. I wish we could talk in person. I know it would be easier for us. It's so hard to talk on the phone."

"Yes."

"I want you to know how sorry I am. I've had a lot of time to think about everything. I'm really sorry."

As Zephaniah Pike spoke, tears welled up in his eyes. It was hard for him to talk, but he went on.

"Darla, I miss what we had together. And . . . and I miss. . . ."

Zephaniah let out an anguished cry. Then he pounded his fist on the night stand again and again. For a long time, he could hardly speak.

When he was finally able to talk, he worried that the person on the other end of the line might not be there. But then he heard Darla's voice, for she was sobbing and crying out as well.

CHAPTER 26

"Nawa!" Old Man Elk called out to the little group that entered his yard. Apollo and Artemis also barked and appeared to follow the old man's lead. The sun had just come up, and there was a slight breeze that made the leaves on the nearby cottonwoods rustle softly.

"Nawa," the old Indian called out again. He was dressed in old, loose-fitting clothing, but on his feet were sneakers that looked very new. The shoes were black and white high tops, a type of canvas sneaker that had been very popular among young people in earlier years. As Elk approached the group, he seemed to have a slight spring in his step. In the dawning light of morning, the high top shoes seemed to rejuvenate and transform the old man.

The assembled group included Agents Pike and Vogel, Susan Hotaru, and another FSPD agent. Everyone was dressed in visored caps and casual clothes, except for the new agent who wore a suit jacket and tie.

"This is Agent Brian McKenney," Pike said, pointing to the lone man in formal attire. "He'll keep an eye on your place here while we're gone. If there's any sign of trouble, he'll let our other agents know. So I hope this puts your mind at ease."

Elk nodded and looked at the young agent squarely.

"Go ahead and make yourself at home. I don't have a TV, but the radio and the toilet both work. Just don't mess with any of my carvings. Look all you want, but don't bother them. Oh, and you need to kick at the front door just a little when you go out. I always used a piece of lead pipe to push it open, but one day I got shot at for doing that."

As Elk spoke, he eyed Agent Pike and laughed a little.

"Yes, sometimes government agents shoot up your house and a few days later they invite you to go boating with them. Life is like that, you know. It's all kinda funny if you stop and think about it."

Even as he spoke, gunshots could be heard up and down the river.

"I do believe a lot of people are hunting out of season," Elk said.

"Yes," Agent Pike explained. "The Dawson plan was never approved. Those that are hunting down animals are doing so illegally. Seems that a few people want to kill whatever animals they can before everyone is forced to leave the valley."

Elk nodded but just as quickly shook his head. "I don't like any of it. The Rawlins plan doesn't sound any better. There won't be much to come back to after the spraying. The whole valley will reek of death for a long time."

"Maybe what we do will make a difference," Dr. Hotaru interjected. "We'll save whatever animals we can during the next couple of days. But you're right. The ecosystem may be impacted in ways that will affect the various species for a long, long time to come."

"Especially those of us who live here," Elk answered. "This valley is our home."

"Could I examine Apollo and Artemis?" Dr. Hotaru asked. "I just want to take a good look at them and make sure everything's normal." She leaned down and petted them as she peered into their eyes and ran her hands over their entire bodies.

"Not sure what you mean by 'normal,'" Elk replied. "They are dogs, and they are a bit spoiled. But that's my fault. They eat an awful lot. I brought along a few days' worth of dog food just for them."

"No need to worry," Dr. Hotaru said. "We'll be taking along

sufficient food and bottled water for all of us. So we should have everything."

"Elk," Agent Pike said. "I do need to ask you to submit to a body search and we need to go through your supplies. It's standard procedure."

"Ah yes," Elk answered. "First, Dr. Hotaru checks Apollo and Artemis. Now you frisk me. Will I be allowed the same courtesy to see if any of you are armed?"

Agent Pike frowned and then motioned for Vogel and McKenney to search Elk's person. Then they examined everything that Elk planned to take along. When they were finished, they showed Pike a small hand axe, a hunting knife, and several small knives and pointed objects that they had found.

"You've got about a dozen weapons here," Agent Pike stated, in a very disappointed tone of voice.

"Didn't know we were boarding an airplane," Elk quipped. "I thought we were going down the river in a boat. None of those things are weapons. I use the axe and the knife when I camp out. The other things are carving tools. I always take them with me."

Agent Pike paused for a long time. He closed his eyes and then slowly opened them again.

"Alright," Agent Pike agreed. "I'll allow them, but I want them kept in a separate backpack. Again, it's standard procedure. We need to ensure everyone's safety."

"I hope that includes my safety as well," Elk said.

"Yes," Pike shot back. "It does indeed."

"We also found this," Jake Vogel said, as he handed Agent Pike an Army bugle that he found in one of the old man's backpacks. The bugle was dented in several places and looked as if it had been carried into every single military engagement during the Indian Wars. A long strand of reddish-brown hair hung from the curved handle of the instrument.

Zephaniah Pike inspected the old bugle and let out a slight groan as he ran the long strand of reddish-brown hair through his fingers.

"It's not what you think," Elk said with a smile. "It's horsehair. Belonged to one of my grandpa's favorite horses. My grandpa often told us stories about that horse. He was a dandy."

"You really feel you need to bring this along?" Agent Pike asked as he inspected the bugle more closely. "Are you planning to sound reveille for us each morning?"

"No," Elk answered. "A little revelry maybe. But there will be no reveille."

Agent Pike rolled his eyes as he handed the Army bugle to the old man. Everyone was smiling except Zephaniah Pike. Susan Hotaru had to turn away and pretend to cough so that she did not burst out laughing.

"So what's the plan?" Elk innocently asked as he stuffed the old Army bugle into one of his backpacks.

Agent Pike pushed up the bill of his cap so that the seriousness in his face could be seen. As Pike spoke, he made a point of briefly looking at everyone, including Elk's two dogs. Dr. Hotaru had attached a long leash to each animal.

"Okay," Zephaniah began. "Agent McKenney will remain here and watch Mr. Elk's residence. Agent Vogel and Dr. Hotaru will take one vehicle, and Mr. Elk and his two dogs and I will head out in the other. We'll drive down to the river bridge that is south of Central City and then take two boats down the river. A recovery team comprising ten people will follow us at a distance of about half a mile or more. They will collect and tag any animals that we come across. We will need to be in constant contact with the recovery team. We'll have special two-way radios, cell phones, and tranquilizer rifles in each boat. Elk and Dr. Hotaru will do most of the observing and will point out the animals to be brought in. Agent Vogel and I will operate the boats and do the shooting and the tranquilizing. We need to be careful that none of the animals that we tranquilize fall into the water and drown. We want them to be recovered on land, not in the water. It may all be a little disorganized at first, but we'll develop a system and we'll have to give it our best shot. I think that's everything."

"Yes, Agent Pike," Dr. Hotaru said. "But I think we need to focus on only those forms of wildlife that are close to shore. Once they're shot and tranquilized, they'll probably turn away from the shore and head for the trees to try to escape. But they shouldn't get more than a few feet. The tranquilizer darts we will be using are very effective and very fast-acting. You've heard of 'shooting the rapids,' right? Well, we don't expect to encounter any rapids or white water on the Platte River. But we will be 'shooting the colors.' And here is how it will work. Each of the tranquilizer darts are brightly colored. Red is for animals that definitely appear to be acting strangely. Yellow is for those about whom we're uncertain, and the green darts are for those animals that appear to be healthy and normal. It will all have to be done very quickly, and at times it'll be somewhat subjective. But the different color codes will help the recovery team organize the animals into three initial groupings. Subsequent laboratory tests and observation may lead to very different judgment calls.

"Make no mistake about it," the scientist continued, "what we will be doing out on the river is very important. Yet due to time constraints, we will be facing tremendous odds. The odds are that our little group won't make much of a difference in the grand scheme of things. We need to be realistic about that. But we also need to give this plan all we've got. We need to try. We need to at least try."

"What about using our FSPD camera drones?" asked Jake Vogel. "Having some visuals high above us could help pinpoint the location of the animals well before we even reach them."

"No," Dr. Hotaru countered. "We've already considered that. Even small surveillance drones may be too noisy and intrusive. We need things to be as quiet and normal as possible. So we'll have to depend on our own eyes and our own good judgment."

"Everyone ready and everyone know what to do?" Agent Pike asked as he looked at each member of the team. Then the agent looked down at the two dogs who appeared to be very uncomfortable with the new leashes Dr. Hotaru had attached to them. "Personally, I think taking dogs along is not very wise. But we'll see if you two can behave yourselves.

"Oh, there's one more thing," Agent Pike added. He walked over to the trunk of one of the cars, unlocked it, and handed out neatly folded jackets to Agent Vogel, Agent McKenny, Dr. Hotaru, and Old Man Elk. The jackets were dark blue in color and had the letters "FSPD" emblazoned in bright yellow on the back.

"It's a little gift from the federal government," Zephaniah Pike explained. "In this heat, I doubt if we will need jackets, but I think we had better bring them along just in case."

Elk looked down at the blue and yellow jacket and grimaced, as if he were examining a piece of contaminated clothing. Everyone could tell by his reaction that the old man had little intention of ever wearing such a jacket.

"Okay," Agent Pike said. "Let's get going and meet up by the Platte River bridge that is south of Central City."

Agent McKenney helped Elk pack his things into one of the vehicles. The two large dogs excitedly jumped into the back seat and waited for Elk to join them. But before getting into the automobile, Elk walked over to his house and flattened his right hand against the weathered side of the building. He closed his eyes and stood there for a few moments. Then he picked up a carved wooden stick that stood near the front door. He did not ask Agent Pike's permission to bring the long stick along. He simply placed it in back of the car, directly behind the front seat. Agent Pike, who had already started up the car, did not ask any questions. He was busy watching Apollo and Artemis in the rearview mirror.

The two cars headed down the narrow road, and although they did not go very fast, clouds of dust rose up behind them. Agent Pike, who was driving the first car, approached the highway, but he had to stop and wait there for a long time. Highway 30, which normally was not very busy at that time of the day, now was choked with a long, long line of slow-moving traffic.

Without explanation, Old Man Elk got out of Pike's car and stood near the highway to get a closer look at all the vehicles that were crawling along. There were automobiles and pickup trucks filled with family members, suitcases, pillows, and other bedding. School buses and vans loaded with boxes of supplies were making their way eastward. And the sounds of cattle in several huge semi-trucks could be heard, even above the sounds of crying children and distant sirens.

When Elk got back into the car, he talked as they waited their turn to get on the highway.

"I've seen a lot in my lifetime," Elk began, as he watched the cars and trucks slowly moving on the highway. "But I never thought I would see an exodus like this one. Everyone is being moved out of the valley. Part of me wants to shout out for joy because now these White people finally know what it is like to have to leave their homes and all that they hold dear. This is exactly what happened to us Pawnee back in the 1870s. We had to pack up and load all our belongings and make the long trip to Indian Territory in Oklahoma. I often wondered what it must have been like. And now, these many years later, I see it happening before my eyes. But no matter how bad all this looks, it was even worse for my people. We did not leave with the knowledge that we would be returning to our homes in a few days. We left knowing that we had to leave this place forever. That was a hard, hard thing."

As Elk spoke, Agent Pike was silent. And the two dogs in the back seat were quiet as well, as they watched the seemingly endless caravan pass by before them.

"You know," Elk continued, "we Pawnee had a leader at the time of our exodus from Nebraska. He was from the Chaui band and his name was Petalesharo, or Man Chief. He was very much against the move to Oklahoma. But all his efforts were in vain. On the first day of the long journey to Oklahoma, Petalesharo suffered a gunshot wound. The history books claim that a White neighbor shot at him and his family as they prepared to leave. But there are others who say that the wound was self-inflicted. After he was wounded, Petalesharo remained behind and he died here in Nebraska only a few days later. So he never had to part from his homeland.

"Yes," Elk went on, "seeing all of this makes the bitter side of me feel kind of happy. All these White people are getting a little taste of what my Pawnee people had to endure so long ago. But there is another side of me that just feels very sad. After all, we Pawnee went through all of this and so it hurts to see it happen all over again. Just look at the little children in those cars. And look at their parents and grandparents who already seem so tired and sad. And their ordeal is only beginning. My heart wants to leap for joy. But instead it goes out to them and it aches. Oh, the poor people!"

CHAPTER
27

It took much longer to get to Central City than Agent Pike had planned. The highway was crowded with traffic for the entire forty-mile stretch. Near the small town of Clarks, two dust-covered fire trucks managed to squeeze by, with sirens going and lights flashing. Many of the other vehicles on the highway had to pull off the road or into the ditch to give the rural fire trucks sufficient room. As the fire trucks headed west, the long caravan on Highway 30 came to a complete stop. Tired of waiting, Agent Pike and Old Man Elk got out of the car and stood on an elevated rise on the right side of the road. Using a pair of binoculars, the agent could see a prairie fire that was burning close to the highway. A cloud of white and gray smoke billowed up and hung over the highway like a menacing thunderhead.

"Some fool probably tossed a lit cigarette," Agent Pike scoffed as he looked at his watch. "You would think people would be more careful. It's like a powder keg around here." He angrily kicked at the dust under his feet to drive home the point.

A short while later, the smoke started to dissipate and the caravan of vehicles inched westward. When the two government cars finally reached the outskirts of Central City, they were unable to turn south due to the non-stop traffic. They had to wait for several minutes until a military vehicle slowed down and allowed them to turn off the highway.

As they waited, the two men studied a large mural on the east side of an old mercantile building. Dozens of freshly painted American flags framed a proclamation-type message that took up more than half the wall. Each of the words had capital letters that appeared to be at least a foot in height:

> WHEN DROUGHT ENGULFS THE LAND,
> WE COWER NOT IN WIND OR SAND.
>
> WHEN FEAR DIVIDES THE LAND,
> WE JOIN TOGETHER HAND IN HAND.
>
> WHEN TERROR STALKS THE LAND,
> WE NEBRASKANS TAKE A STAND.

"Ah, our tax dollars at work," Old Man Elk quipped. "It appears the war on terror already has begun here in Central City."

"Doubt that mural was funded with any tax dollars," Pike replied "Besides, with your penchant for painting signs, I thought you might be a bit more appreciative of roadside art."

* * * *

A large group of individuals was waiting on the banks of the Platte River south of Central City. The group included local wildlife officials, environmentalists, journalists, and members of the recovery team. There were seven boats, two of which were equipped with small outboard motors and supplies. The other five crafts were aluminum pontoon boats that carried a surprisingly large number of metal cages of various sizes.

Agent Pike and Dr. Hotaru introduced themselves and shook hands with all the members of the recovery team, which included six men and four women. After briefly reviewing the work to be done, Agent Pike gave the signal and everyone began getting in the boats. A couple of local townspeople who had leased the boats discussed boat safety with Pike and Vogel. They also showed where the fuel was stored and talked about potential problems. One of the recovery team members showed the two agents how to use the new locational devices that were in each boat.

It was now mid-morning and the sun burned bright. There was not a cloud in the sky. More supplies were loaded onto the two boats, including the tranquilizer guns and several boxes of colored darts. Vogel and Hotaru took their seats in one boat, while Pike and Elk and his two dogs situated themselves in the lead boat. Elk sat at the front of the boat, holding a wooden stick that had an intricate carved head. He held it in his right hand, as if it were a flag or a ceremonial staff. In the other hand, he held a small dark rattle that looked ancient.

Just as they were about to set off, Old Man Elk stood up in the boat and motioned for everyone to be still. Even the members of the recovery team and the others who were watching grew silent. Elk patiently waited until every single person had stopped talking.

He then held the stick even higher so that everyone could see its carved head. The likeness was that of a bird with an unusually long, thin bill and with feathers on its head that stood out and formed a ragged crest.

"This bird," Elk called out, "is the kingfisher. He is a real little fellow, but he is very brave and very special to us Pawnee. He is an old, old resident of the River Platte. He is the messenger bird and so I want to sing this song to him. I will sing most of the words in English. The kingfisher is a wise little fellow and maybe he can understand us, no matter what language we use. He knows many languages and carries messages back and forth all the time. So I sing this song for him. And I sing this song for all of us who are gathered here this morning:

> 'Kingfisher, Kingfisher,
> Little Brother, hear us!
> Carry our message far.

> The pitiful ones are here.
> But we only mean to help,
> We do not mean to harm.
> Kingfisher, Kingfisher,
> Little Brother, hear us!
> *Kacii-kaha'!*
> *Kacii-kaha'!*'"

As Elk sang the last words in Pawnee, he shook the small gourd rattle vigorously to imitate the high-pitched rattling call of the belted kingfisher.

After Elk finished singing, he put the rattle down and took a small leather pouch out of his pants pocket. The pouch had a thick fringe at its base, and like the rattle it appeared to be very old. Elk untied the bag and removed a pinch of dried tobacco. He let the tobacco fall on the waters of the Platte. Then he repeated the same action three more times. Apollo and Artemis were as quiet as everyone else. The dogs watched the dried tobacco leaves float down the river as they were carried eastward.

Jake Vogel moved closer to Zephaniah Pike, so that he faced him and could say something in confidence.

"I sure hope that's tobacco the old man is using," Vogel whispered. "What if it's some of that you-know-what that grows along the road to the old man's house?"

Agent Vogel grinned to himself, but Zephaniah Pike kept a straight face and did not say anything in response. He was more surprised by the reaction of the people on the shore. Their faces and eyes reflected a mixture of curiosity and awe as Elk performed his ritual. Through it all, everyone was very quiet and a few people even removed their hats and reverently bowed their heads.

When Elk was done, he took the carved wooden staff and placed it into the river as if it were a dipstick. The stick only went down about three feet until it appeared to touch the sandy bottom.

"There's almost enough water here to make some coffee," Elk proclaimed. Hearing this, everyone laughed heartily and this was followed by a spontaneous round of applause. They realized Elk's solemn ritual had ended and that the time to embark had come.

As Elk sat down, Agent Pike eyed him for a long time. He wanted Elk to know that the FSPD did not appreciate the old Indian taking on the self-appointed role of high priest. But this was not the time for a reprimand.

Zephaniah Pike started his outboard motor and the boat began to move. He was surprised at how quiet the engine was and how effortlessly the boat moved across the water.

"Get over into the main channel of the river," Elk instructed, "or we'll get hung up on a submerged sandbar. Always try to keep the boat in deep water. If we get hung up, it'll cost us a lot of time."

Pike looked behind him and could see Vogel and Hotaru following in their boat. He could also see the recovery team members preparing to launch their pontoon boats. They would be out of sight most of the time and would remain behind at a distance of about two thousand feet.

Several times, Pike tried to increase the speed of the boat, but it appeared to go only a few miles an hour. As Pike became familiar with operating the boat, Elk and the two dogs watched the shores for signs of wildlife.

For the first time in days, Zephaniah Pike felt a bit more relaxed. The feel of the sun and the gentle humming of the boat helped put his mind at ease. He looked back and could see Vogel and Hotaru smiling broadly. Both were wearing sunglasses. The sun and the fresh air seemed to agree with them as well.

Judging from the information in Jake Vogel's file, Pike expected Agent Vogel to be the primary shooter. His full name was Jacob Alexander Vogel and he had worked for several years as a FSPD sniper and firearms expert. He had participated in numerous special operations and had been decorated for most of them. Jake Vogel was the kind of experienced professional that the government clearly wanted on its side.

The group had embarked only about fifteen minutes when Elk's dogs became restless. They both looked to the left and growled a little as if they spotted something. Elk watched the two dogs and then pointed in the direction they were looking.

"Over there," Elk whispered. "Head over to the north bank, but stay in the main channel."

Agent Pike decreased speed and the boat behind them also slowed down as they made their way to the left.

As they neared the shore, Elk pointed at a large white-tailed deer that was partially submerged in the water. It was a doe and she appeared to have been shot several times. Only a few feet away, sitting in some grass, was a fawn. It looked dazed and did not even stand up and try to run away.

"What color?" Pike asked. But there was no response from Elk. "What color of dart?" he asked again.

The agent turned around and looked at Hotaru. He mouthed the words "What color?" and hoped that she could understand him. She finally nodded and held up a yellow dart. Vogel had his own gun ready, but he grinned in a way that told Pike it was up to the group's leader to make the first "kill." Zephaniah Pike loaded his rifle with a yellow dart and aimed in the fawn's direction. There was a scope on the rifle, and when Pike looked through it he could see the fawn looking all around as if it were waiting. The white spots on its reddish-brown body were clearly visible. Although the day was hot and dry, the fawn was shivering.

Pike closed one eye and pulled the trigger, but he completely missed his target. The yellow dart went flying past, far to the left. He took out another yellow dart, loaded it, aimed, and fired. Again, he missed. He could feel Elk and even the dogs tense up as he shot a third time. This time, the dart hit the fawn in the neck. The frightened fawn quickly got up, but it keeled over within only a few seconds. The dogs whined and Elk, who had his back turned, said nothing.

Zephaniah Pike looked into the screen of the locational device. Then he took out a two-way radio and gave the locational reading to one of the recovery team members. He also described their first target of the day: "A fawn. About five feet from shore. Its mother's body lies nearby. Not sure if the fawn was sick or just disoriented. Code: Yellow."

After completing the call, Pike started up the motor and headed downriver. He was upset and wanted to say something to Old Man Elk. But he was not sure what to tell Elk, other than that he had wanted the old man to decide what color of dart and to do so quickly. As he thought about all of this, Elk's black Belgian sheepdog turned to Agent Pike and whined softly. Apollo looked at the agent with its sad eyes and just stared at him. Pike put out his free hand and rubbed the dog's head. The animal kept its eyes open and seemed to enjoy the sensation. When Pike finished, Apollo crouched down and reciprocated. He slowly licked the agent's entire hand, one finger at a time.

CHAPTER
28

"There!" Elk shouted, as he pointed to a small sandbar on the right half of the river. Only Elk and his two dogs seemed to see something. As hard as Pike tried, he could see nothing but sand and weeds and large pieces of driftwood.

Hotaru and Vogel, who were close behind in the other boat, removed their sunglasses and also studied the sandbar for signs of life. As Hotaru and Vogel drew closer, a large long-necked bird with equally long legs began to fly off.

"A great blue heron!" Hotaru excitedly called out. "Green dart!" As she spoke, she grabbed a rifle, loaded it, and fired. But the tranquilizer missed its target and Pike, who was not able to load his own gun fast enough, watched the huge bird fly out of range.

"Don't worry," Pike said. "This is going to take some getting used to before we are comfortable with these guns. Maybe we should practice a little before we go on. Otherwise, we're going to use up all our darts and the recovery team won't have much to collect."

The two boats headed to the sandbar. As they inched closer, the two dogs jumped off and began to explore the island.

"It's time for a break anyway," Pike said as he beached the boat. Then he called a member of the recovery team to let them know they were stopping and that he would call them back when they were ready to set off again.

Old Man Elk walked over to the far side of the island and stood there for a long time. The two dogs followed him, but they paused to sniff pieces of driftwood as they ran across the sandbar.

"Elk and his dogs work well as a team," Dr. Hotaru said. "It's amazing just to watch them. They seem to anticipate one another's every move."

"Give us time," Pike urged. "When we've been on this river for a few more hours, we'll find our groove. It just takes a little time."

Vogel reached into a cooler and called out for everyone to come and get a bottle of half-ice. When Elk took his bottle, he warmed the water in the palms of his hands before giving any to Apollo and Artemis. By the time he was done, only the frozen bottom half of the spring water remained. He stood the bottle on the sand in front of him so that it was in direct sunlight and would melt faster.

"You like your water warm?" Vogel asked the old Indian as he sat down beside him. While they talked, Pike and Hotaru were doing target practice with the tranquilizer guns and an old log.

"No," Elk stated. "I don't like warm water. I just don't like to drink ice-cold water on a hot day. It's not good for you."

"But it tastes good," Vogel replied as he took huge gulps from his own bottle of ice water.

"Yes," Elk agreed. "A lot of things that taste good are not good for you."

"You sound like my old man," Vogel said. "He used to tell me 'All that glistens is not gold. Sometimes it's snot.'"

Elk laughed. "I never heard that one. But I like it. It's very down-to-earth."

"Oh, my old man was down-to-earth alright," Jake Vogel admitted. "He used to take me hunting on this river. Been thinking about it all morning. This little outing of ours sure brings back a whole grunt-load of memories."

"I take it your father is no longer living?" Elk asked.

"No. He died quite a few years ago. My father was a poor German-Russian kid from the North Bottoms of Lincoln. He and his folks came to this country as 'displaced persons' after the Second World War. Seems they had lost everything over in Russia. They sure had a lot of really depressing stories to tell. You name it, they talked about it—mass executions, deportations, starvation, even cannibalism. Dad spoke some kind of German dialect and he could talk that stuff better than English. Sometimes, the old man would just sit there and say *'alles geht rum.'* Guess that meant something like 'what goes around, comes around.' My dad was a railroad man and an occasional hunter. He even had these old clothes and this crumpled old hat that he wore only when he hunted. God, he loved to go on this river and hunt. Maybe it reminded him of the Volga back in Russia. Yeah, he was quite the avid hunter. But the thing Dad really excelled at was pessimism. To him, a glass of water wasn't half empty. He'd argue with you and convince you there wasn't even a glass or any water at all. The old man would say, 'We didn't have any drinking glasses when I was a kid. All we had was an old pail with a rusty dipper in it. Each of us kids had to drink out of that same dipper. And sometimes there wasn't any water left in the pail and we had to go to bed thirsty and miserable.' That's just how my old man talked. No wonder he always murmured *'alles geht rum'* and went on and on. God, he was something."

Jake Vogel took another drink of the ice-cold water and continued talking.

"After I left home, the first thing the old man would ask me when he saw me was, 'Yah-kob, did you hear about that bad train wreck in North Platte?' or 'Yah-kob, did you hear about those two kids who drowned over by Ogallala?' That sort of thing. He didn't ask how I was or how my work was going. Well, I learned to be even more negative and to beat the old man to the punch. Whenever I saw him, I'd say something like, 'Hey Dad, did you know that there was an earthquake over in Iran that killed 5,000 people?' I always went for the big numbers. That way he couldn't top any of my bad news.

"Well, one Sunday after church the old man told my mother he had to go do something. He put on his old hunting clothes and hunting hat and went into the garage. Then he shot himself. I think the shock of it killed my mother as well, for she died within a few months. I was just married and it sort of put a damper on things. Geez, I reckon my 'ex' kept thinking I might do the same thing to myself someday."

Jake Vogel looked directly at Elk and then gestured as if he had a pistol in his right hand. The agent pointed a finger at his temple and closed one eye. He held his finger against the side of his head for a few seconds and then slowly raised another finger to form a strange-looking "V" sign. As he did so, he smiled in a sad and distant kind of way.

"What did you and your father hunt on this river?" Elk asked.

"Mostly ducks and geese. We'd get up real early and drive up here from Lincoln and we'd hunt all day. And we always came back with something, even if the old man had to buy a duck or two from another hunter."

Elk laughed a little.

"There is no shame in coming home empty-handed," the old Indian said. "That is the way of hunting. Sometimes the animals and the birds allow you to take them, and at other times they decide you should go home with nothing."

"You really believe that? That they allow you to take them?"

Old Man Elk did not answer. He was watching Pike and Hotaru practice with the tranquilizer guns.

"It's my turn!" Vogel called out as he got up and brushed off the sand on his trousers. Hotaru handed him the rifle she had been using.

"Elk," Pike called out, "do you want to give this thing a try?" The agent extended the rifle to him, as well as a couple of colored darts.

The old Indian waved the gun away as if he did not even want it near him.

"No," Elk said, as he looked up at the agent. "I'm not your dragoon or your foot soldier, Commander Villasur. I'm just an old Pawnee scout who happens to be on this little expedition. Ah, but I never thought I would be scouting for the Fizz-Pidds. Uhhhh!"

He made a face and shook his shoulders as he again made the "Uhhhh!" sound. It was evident that he was having second thoughts and was quite unhappy with himself.

"This is no expedition," Agent Pike said, as he stood directly in front of the old man and looked down at him. The agent's voice had a different tone and he enunciated each and every word. "This is a recovery mission. You know that. And I don't appreciate being referred to as 'Commander Villasur.' "

The old man nodded. But then, just as the agent was about to turn away, Elk tilted his head and cleared his throat to indicate he had something more to say.

"Are you telling me you are not in command here, Agent Pike? If so, do the rest of us get to exercise our full democratic rights while we're on this 'recovery mission'?"

The agent stiffened and again looked down at the old man, who remained in a sitting position. But this time, Zephaniah Pike stood so that the bright sun was directly behind him. In so doing, the federal agent now seemed much taller and even twice his size.

"You always have something to say, don't you?" Pike responded. "Now I will admit that some of what you say is clever and even funny. But then again, I think a lot of what you say is sarcastic and bitter. You have such a big chip on your shoulder that I'm surprised you've been able to walk upright as long as you have. Sometimes a chip on the shoulder has a way of eating its way into the heart of a man and crippling him."

"That may be," Elk said, as he stood up so that he faced the federal agent. "But I think what you say tells me something about yourself as well. Perhaps you are also among the crippled ones?"

Zephaniah Pike glared at Old Man Elk. Then the agent reached for the radio and told the recovery team that they were preparing to continue down the river. He called for Hotaru and Vogel to follow in the boat behind.

For the next six hours, they went down the river in search of more animals. Elk and the two dogs spotted various kinds of wildlife, many of which hurried off or flew away before a single shot was fired. The team tranquilized thirteen animals and birds, including the fawn that had been their first target. But all of these specimens had been brought down with a yellow or a green dart. The red darts in the boxes of both boats remained untouched.

CHAPTER 29

"How's everyone doing?" Zephaniah Pike asked as the four team members made their way down the river. The sun was going down, but it was still light enough to see.

Old Man Elk sat in the front portion of the boat and keenly studied both sides of the river. He did not answer. Instead, he gestured for the agent not to talk so loud.

Pike turned around and saw Hotaru and Vogel nod and give him a thumbs-up sign, as if to indicate they were both alert and not overly tired. Both of them had removed their sunglasses, and by doing so had revealed the full extent of the sunburn on their faces. Their foreheads and cheeks were bright red and the sunburn only accentuated the pale skin around their eyes. Pike's face and hands stung as well. During the day, the members of the team already had devised a simple but effective system of sign language. By the way that Elk gestured, the others could tell if the next target was a bird or an animal and if it was small or large. Elk also was able to sign for all three colors. Red was a thumb up with clenched fist, yellow was a hand that waved two upraised fingers, and green was a horizontal hand that slowly moved from side to side.

More dead animals could be seen on both sides of the river. At times their carcasses could be seen draped over tree limbs or floating in the river. Most of the dead animals appeared to have been shot and sometimes they were beheaded or disemboweled.

"Iditaku," Elk whispered in Pawnee. "There, there on the left." Apollo and Artemis stared in the same direction, and Pike heard them make a strange growling sound deep in their throats. Pike got a rifle ready but was not sure what dart to choose. He was disappointed when Elk signed that it was another "green."

Agent Pike loaded the gun and prepared to shoot, but he still did not see anything.

"Wait 'til he goes ashore," Elk cautioned. "It's a beaver and he's a big one." He gestured dramatically as he whispered the words.

Pike positioned the rifle stock on his shoulder, peered through the scope, and shot the green dart at the beaver as it began to crawl up on the riverbank. The animal was indeed large and thus a fairly easy target. After the dart hit it in the rump, the beaver struggled for a few moments and then slumped down.

After shooting the beaver, Pike laid his rifle down and radioed the recovery team to give them a locational reading. He also told them that everyone should be prepared to stay out on the river for a few more hours. The agent explained that it felt much better to work in twilight and to finally be out of the fierce heat of the summer sun.

Only about fifteen minutes later, Elk pointed to a small side channel and a tiny island. He motioned for everyone to be very quiet as they drifted closer. Lying in the water were four raccoons, one of them fairly large and the other three much smaller. They appeared to be hot and tired as they allowed their bodies to remain half-submerged in the water.

"Color?" Pike whispered as he readied his rifle.

Elk gave the flat hand sign for green, but then he quickly changed to another signal. The old man waved a hand with two upraised fingers repeatedly. Pike was so busy watching Elk's hands that he missed what was going on in the side channel to the left. He glanced over and saw the large raccoon hissing at the team members and making a valiant stand as the younger raccoons made their escape. The large raccoon not only made a stand, but the animal continued to hiss so loudly that the birds in the nearby trees became silent.

Zephaniah Pike loaded a yellow dart in his rifle and prepared to shoot. But Elk gestured for him to wait. The raccoon grew silent and then began to advance toward the boat.

Pike quickly removed the yellow dart from the rifle and substituted a red one. But when he prepared to take aim, the raccoon dove into the water. As Pike lowered his rifle, he saw the submerged raccoon heading straight toward the boat. Apollo and Artemis were barking loudly now and acted as if they were about to dive into the water themselves. But Elk held them back. The raccoon struck the underside of the boat, loudly scratching it with its extended claws. Then, just as quickly, the raccoon swam away. A few seconds later, it surfaced in the same spot where they had seen it earlier.

The raccoon shook itself off as it emerged from the water, its long striped tail dragging behind. Agent Pike took aim and fired the red dart. The raccoon let out a piercing cry and in a few seconds, the animal lay quiet.

Pike wasted no time in calling the recovery team to report a "code red" specimen. He gave the locational reading and urged them to approach quickly before it grew too dark to retrieve the raccoon.

As the team members made their way down the river, they passed a large island that was carpeted with tall plants sprouting clusters of purple blossoms.

"Now there's a sight," Pike said approvingly. "Wildflowers like those help make this old river a bit more pleasing to the eye."

"Appearances are deceiving," Elk countered. He turned completely around, so that everyone could hear what he had to say.

"See those tall plants over there? That's purple loosestrife. But more and more people now refer to those plants as 'marsh monsters' or 'the purple plague.' You see, when purple loosestrife comes into an area, it chokes out all the native vegetation. And that eventually affects the whole environment, especially the wildlife that feeds off the native plants. Purple loosestrife may look kinda pretty. But it quickly takes over and dominates everything. It's an invader that shows no mercy."

"So where'd it come from?" Jake Vogel asked.

"Europe," the old man sternly answered. And he stared directly at the blond-haired, blue-eyed agent.

"Geez Louise," Vogel muttered as he looked again at the island covered with purple loosestrife. It was an odd thing to say, but the others were very quiet and seemed deep in thought.

Old Man Elk's eyes softened a bit as he looked at the young agent. Then the old man turned around and again faced the river.

"We need to find a place where we can spend the night," Pike announced. But instead of looking for a campsite, Elk and his two dogs had spotted something on the right side of the river.

Apollo and Artemis became very excited and they both began to produce a steady growling sound, as if they were trying to sing with their throats.

"It's Coyote," Elk softly said. "And he's seen us. Go over to the right, but stay in deep water and go as fast as you can. Coyote is running."

Agent Pike waved for the second boat to follow and to do so quickly. Only now and then did Pike even get a glimpse of the coyote. At times, the animal would stop and look back, as if challenging the team members to keep up with it.

For about ten minutes they kept up the chase and then it grew too dark to navigate. The water was much lower at this point on the river and Elk suggested they camp on the right bank where there was a small clearing.

"Coyote has led us to a campsite," Elk announced. "I bet we'll find a bunch of his droppings here."

"Can't imagine that's a good thing," Pike said as he steered the boat toward land. "I'd prefer a four-star hotel myself."

After they all had come ashore, Pike called the recovery team and gave them the location of the campsite. He advised the recovery team members to stay out of sight and to be prepared to head off again at sunrise. By camping apart, the two teams would not make as much noise or appear too intrusive.

"I'm not sure about all of you," Pike said into the two-way radio, "but we are sunburned and hungry and bone-tired. Take care and good night. Over and out."

The three members of the team began to set up small pup tents for everyone and to roll out sleeping bags. Elk sought out large pieces of wood to build a campfire. At one point, the old Indian called out to the others to inspect some fresh coyote tracks.

"They look just like dog prints," Vogel said.

"Not quite," Elk countered. "Look again. The toes of a coyote are more pointed than a dog's. The front four toes and claws have a broad pad at the base that looks like a rounded triangle. And look here, these are the tracks made by the hind paws. The pads at the base are a lot smaller and the sides are more pointed. See?"

Dr. Hotaru and Jake Vogel studied the tracks closely, but Zephaniah Pike seemed uninterested.

Soon everyone was busy taking care of a variety of tasks. Elk tended the fire. Vogel prepared something to eat for everyone. Hotaru took notes on the day's activities and the number of animals tranquilized. She even made sketches of coyote tracks, based on Elk's observations. Pike phoned Kerrington to give a full report and to find out how things were going in Columbus.

"Come and get it!" Vogel called out. "We have an outdoor gourmet meal courtesy of the federal government. Beans and wieners. Crackers and cheese. Instant coffee. And some crunchy Nebraska trail mix for dessert."

"Not sure I even want to know what's in a Nebraska trail mix," groaned Pike. "Let me be surprised."

As everyone sat down to eat, Elk picked the wiener slices out of his portion of beans and gave them to Apollo and Artemis. He also fed them some dried beef that he had brought along. The two dogs quickly ate all their food and then sat and stared at everyone, hoping to get more.

"Not another train," Dr. Hotaru groaned. Everyone could hear a freight train in the distance, sounding its horn as it approached one crossing after another. All that day, the group had heard the sounds of different trains, for a major railway ran along the northern edge of the Platte River.

"You'll hear the trains at night, too," Elk said. "So you best get used to it. Ah, but it's the sound of civilization."

"I had thought it would be real quiet along the river," Dr. Hotaru mused.

"Oh, it gets quiet out here," Elk said. "In between all the different trains that go by."

Dr. Hotaru laughed, even as she contemplated her first night on the river.

When everyone finished eating, Elk removed his black and white sneakers and stretched out his feet near the fire. He flexed his toes repeatedly. Seeing this, Dr. Hotaru and Agent Vogel both removed their shoes and also tried to get comfortable.

"All in all," Dr. Hotaru said, "I think it went pretty well today. We came across a lot of animals. And the behavior of that raccoon was unbelievable."

"Have you ever seen a raccoon act that way before?" the scientist asked Elk, who was still flexing his toes near the fire.

"No," Elk said. "And I am not sure she deserved a red designation. She may have been feeling the effects of today's heat or just being overly protective of her young. But I guess you all needed at least one red designation."

"Well," Vogel said as he looked directly at Elk, "I think that raccoon gave itself to us so we wouldn't be empty-handed today." He chuckled as he said this, but Elk did not even smile.

"I am sure she did," Elk finally said. "She was very brave and self-sacrificing. I hope even Dr. Hotaru would agree."

"Yes," the scientist responded. "But Elk, you need not keep calling me 'Dr. Hotaru.' Calling me Susan is perfectly fine."

"Ah," Elk said. "I like the name 'Hotaru.' It sounds Pawnee. You see, when we speak of a wind that blows across the prairie, we use the word 'hutawi'u'.' It sounds similar to your name. So you should be proud. You have a good name, a strong-sounding name."

"Actually, my name means 'firefly' in Japanese," Hotaru explained. "I never thought much about it except once. When I was about six or seven, my parents took me to stay with my Grandma and Grandpa Hotaru one summer. They were very old-fashioned and very frugal. When they left Japan and came to the United States, they worked as farm laborers in Washington and Wisconsin. They sure knew how to pick cherries. Even after they were retired and living comfortably, they would always go out to some cherry orchard and pick at least a pailful of cherries for their own use. I loved helping them and they made me feel like I was a big help to them. But I think I always ate more than I picked. The cherries were delicious when they came right off the tree."

As the scientist spoke, Old Man Elk listened intently and occasionally made a slight *"ahu"* sound to show he was enjoying the story.

"One evening after we had picked cherries," Hotaru continued, "we drove past a meadow and my grandfather parked on the side of the road and we just sat there and waited. As it grew darker, the meadow suddenly was lit up with thousands of fireflies. My grandparents and I caught several of them in a small glass jar and we brought them home with us. My grandma cooked up a mixture of sweet rice and fresh cherries, and while the smell of that food filled their home my Grandpa Hotaru showed me how to make a small paper lantern. After he finished it, he took the jar of fireflies and placed it in the middle of the little lantern. And so we sat there in the darkness, eating the wonderful cherry and rice mixture with the firefly lantern in the middle of the kitchen table. My grandparents didn't say a single word. We just sat there and enjoyed the food and the little firefly lantern. I guess they wanted me to appreciate my name and they found a delightful way to show it. I think of that special evening all the time."

Elk again made the *"ahu"* sound and closed his eyes as if he were picturing everything in his mind.

"You honor your grandparents by telling that story," he said, after opening his eyes. "They knew who they were. And they wanted you to know who you were. One doesn't always need to use words to do this. I don't think my grandparents ever said 'I love you' to me even once. They didn't need to. Just being with them made me feel special and real good inside. Such is the way of the elders."

Now Dr. Hotaru nodded as well, for she realized that Elk understood what she was trying to say.

"My name means 'bird' in German," Agent Vogel interjected. "All the kids in the North Bottoms of Lincoln called me 'The Bird Man.'"

"You were called that because of your last name?" Susan Hotaru asked.

"No, not really," Jake Vogel laughed. "When I was a kid, I used to catch these little brown sparrows and I got pretty good at it. I'd wait for Saturdays because that's when the German-Russian families in our neighborhood would clean up their houses real good. The whole house had to be spic-and-span before they attended church services on Sunday morning. So, as soon as it got dark on Saturday, I would take a sparrow and slip it in between the screen door and the front door of someone's home. Then I would ring the doorbell and hide and watch all the commotion. It never failed. Someone would open the door and the frightened sparrow would fly into the house. Everybody in the household would run after the sparrow and chase it with brooms and mop handles and anything else they could find. The old timers would scream and shout out things in German that were really funny. They'd huff and puff and wring their hands as if the world were coming to an end. Sometimes, it took all the members of the family a couple of hours to chase that little bird out of the house. Yeah, that's how I spent my Saturday nights in the North Bottoms. It sure livened up things and it kept everybody on their toes."

"Did you ever get caught?" Dr. Hotaru asked. She looked directly at Jake Vogel, but the scientist could not help smiling.

"Nope."

"And your parents never suspected anything?"

"I don't think so," the agent answered. "Because our name was Vogel, it kinda made sense for the other kids to call me 'The Bird Man.' Whenever my dad heard about sparrows being released into the neighbors' homes, he just figured it was some dumb-ass kid who did it. To avoid suspicion, I even let a sparrow fly into our house one time. It flew right into my bedroom and crapped all over my pillow."

"Now that's karma!" Hotaru exclaimed. She laughed and pretended to clap her hands to show her approval. But as she did so, the scientist looked over at Agent Pike and noticed that he was very quiet. He seemed disinterested by so much personal talk and reminiscing.

"What about that coyote we saw today?" Dr. Hotaru asked, in a tone of voice that indicated she wanted to change the subject. "It was odd the way the coyote would stop running and look back at us, as if it wanted us to chase it."

Although Dr. Hotaru intended her comments to open the conversation to everyone, Pike and Vogel both looked at Elk for a response of some kind.

Instead of answering, the old man rose up and went over to one of the boats. He rummaged through his backpacks until he returned with the old Army bugle that had the long strand of hair hanging from its handle.

Standing close to the campfire and at mock attention, Elk took a deep breath and blew with all his might into the old bugle. He blew with such force that his cheeks swelled to the size of tennis balls. Soon he produced a strange sound that seemed more like a discordant, high-pitched cry than a bugle call. Again and again, he blew into the bugle. Then the old man, who was nearly out of breath, slowly sat down and gestured for everyone to be very quiet.

Within only moments, an eerie howl could be heard coming from somewhere in the west. The lonely cry seemed to mimic the sounds that the old man had made with his Army bugle. Soon other howls could be heard farther off in the distance.

"Works every time," Elk said softly as he rested the old horn against his chin. "There's more than one coyote out there and it seems they're eager for some choral arrangements and maybe even a little jamming tonight."

Old Man Elk put the bugle to his lips once again and sounded still another high-pitched call, this time from a sitting position.

Soon the darkness beyond the camp area was punctuated with the howling of even more coyotes. Their cries filled the nighttime sky and made the travelers realize that their every movement was being watched. The outlying blackness did not shield them from the wilderness; it merely draped everything in an elusive cloak of darkness.

Apollo and Artemis sat up and with their ears fully erect and pointed to the stars, the two dogs listened intently to the howling of the coyotes. The dogs continually moved their heads to different positions, as if trying to pinpoint the right frequency for deciphering the signals. At times, the ever-changing head movements of the two dogs were completely synchronized, as they each tilted to the right and then to the left. But Apollo and Artemis did not make even the slightest sound themselves. They were all ears.

One of the coyote howls sounded especially close and seemed to come from only a couple of hundred feet away. The howl started out clear and strong and then faded into an almost sweet-sounding and soothing echo of itself.

"It's beautiful," Dr. Hotaru whispered. "I can feel that coyote's call go right through me. It gives me goose bumps."

"Yes," Elk said. "But you need to be careful. A hunter who camps out here by himself can get confused and disoriented if he listens to their singing too much. The experienced hunter who does not want that to happen stuffs a little beeswax into his ears and then waits for the first light of morning. The singing of the coyotes is very powerful."

Eventually the howling of the coyotes died down and it grew strangely quiet again.

"I didn't know Indians knew how to play the bugle," Vogel said in a teasing tone of voice.

"Ahu!" Elk exclaimed. "But most folks have no idea. Over a hundred years ago there was a great Kiowa warrior named Satanta who fought the U.S. Cavalry down on the Southern Plains. He noticed that the soldiers would advance or retreat or draw their sabers each time one of the troopers blew on his bugle. So Satanta told his men to do everything they could to capture the young soldier with the bugle. They managed to do so, and when they brought him into camp Satanta treated that bugler real good. He was just a young kid and Satanta treated him better than the kid's officers ever did. As a Kiowa captive, he got lots to eat and he didn't have to march or wear those tight-fitting boots that always hurt his feet. That young bugler taught Satanta how to use the bugle and to make all the various military calls.

"Well the next time the Kiowa faced the U.S. Cavalry on the field of battle, it was mass confusion. The army's replacement bugler sounded 'charge' but Satanta, who was hiding in the grass only a short distance away, sounded the command for 'dismount.' After all the soldiers got off their horses and were on foot, Satanta sounded 'retreat' and all those soldiers turned and took off running as fast as they could. Satanta's warriors charged in and they rounded up all of the soldiers' horses and even the Army mules that were loaded down with supplies. Not a single shot was fired. It was a glorious day for the Kiowa!"

As Elk told the story of Satanta, he gestured with the old bugle as if it were a conductor's wand. The light of the campfire was reflected in the old man's dark eyes and wrinkled face.

"But how did *you* learn to play the bugle?" Jake Vogel asked. The agent seemed intrigued by the old man's stories, yet he always looked over at Zephaniah Pike each time he questioned the old man.

"Not really sure I do play the bugle," Elk admitted. "But I manage to make a lot of noise with this old horn. Besides, every elk can bugle."

Jake Vogel and Susan Hotaru chuckled, for they understood the old man's pun.

"Every elk can bugle," Vogel repeated. "That's good. That's good." He looked again in Zephaniah Pike's direction to make sure the humor was appreciated by everyone. But Pike stared blankly into the fire, giving no clue that he was even listening.

"So what about the coyote we saw earlier today?" Dr. Hotaru asked again. She prided herself in her persistence, even when she was amused or distracted. "Did that coyote seem to be behaving normal?"

Old Man Elk laughed, and as he did so the bugle that was resting on his chest shook as well. "When it comes to Coyote, nothing is normal. Coyote always does what you least expect. Coyote keeps everything interesting. And Coyote always breaks the rules."

"What do you mean?" Dr. Hotaru asked, trying to get the old man to say more. "Are you saying every coyote is indeed a trickster?"

Elk nodded. "Sometimes Coyote is a trickster. Sometimes he is just Coyote. Like I said, he is unpredictable and he keeps everything interesting.

"You know," Elk continued, "our old people told a lot of stories about Coyote. When I was a boy, I used to think they were true. Then, when I got older, I thought the stories were all made up. But now that I am an elder and have observed coyotes for so many years, I think there is much wisdom in those stories, maybe even great truth.

"For example, the way we saw Coyote running along the river this evening. He often seems to be running and looking behind him. *Kutaruhu'*. Yes, it is his way, Coyote's way.

"A long time ago, Coyote was going along the River Platte. Yes, along this very river. He came to a high hill, and when he got to the top there was a big rock that was on the top of that hill. The rock was so ancient that everyone called it 'Grandfather.' We Pawnee would leave food or other offerings by that rock to show our respect. But Coyote, he often broke the rules. Or maybe he followed only his own rules. So he went to that rock and he left an offering. But then he quickly turned around and took the offering back again. Grandfather Rock was very angry to be treated in that fashion. So as Coyote went on his way, the big rock pulled itself out of the ground and began to roll after Coyote.

"A short time later, Coyote looked back and saw a dust cloud behind him. He felt the earth shaking beneath his feet. He looked back again and now he saw that big rock coming after him. So Coyote ran as fast as he could. When he got tired, he would stop and look back, but that rock just kept coming.

"This went on for a whole day and a whole night. Coyote was not able to eat or to rest. He would ask other animals to help him, but when they saw Grandfather Rock coming after him the animals told him that Coyote was on his own. They did not want to anger Grandfather Rock and have to run away in fear.

"As Coyote was running, he came to a little cave in the side of a hill. The opening was real small, but Coyote was so skinny from running so much that he was able to squeeze inside. But there were bats in the cave and they asked Coyote why he had barged into their home.

"Coyote told the bats that a big rock was coming after him and he begged the bats to help him. The bats did not trust Coyote, but they felt sorry for him. He looked so pitiful. So the bats gave him some food and told him they would help him.

"When Grandfather Rock rolled up to the opening of the cave, he kept hitting at the entrance, trying to get in. Grandfather Rock knew that Coyote was inside. He demanded that Coyote come out. The rock called out and threatened to hit against the cave until it was destroyed.

"Now Coyote was very worried. But the bats told him to watch what they could do. Each of those little bats went over to the entrance.

One by one, they flew up close to the big rock and let off these little bat farts. And they kept this up. Soon all those little bat farts began to make that big rock crack and break into little pieces. Yes, that's just what happened.

"When Coyote saw that the rock was no longer a threat, he laughed a long time. Then he prepared to leave. As he slipped out of the cave, he made fun of the bats that had saved him. He told them they all looked funny and that they smelled funny. Then Coyote went on his way.

"The bats who had helped him became very angry. You see, those little bats were not ordinary bats. They were *Nahúraki*—powerful spirit animals. 'What has been destroyed, can be made whole again,' the leader of the bats declared. 'It is within our power.'

"And so all those *Nahúraki* bats sang a very powerful song and they went to work and quickly put every little piece of the big rock back together. Then they rolled it back on the prairie and pointed it in the direction that Coyote had been going.

"Now Grandfather Rock went rolling after Coyote again. Even today, Grandfather Rock sometimes gets mad at Coyote and decides to roll after him. That is why Coyote is always running and that is why he always stops to look behind him. Yes. *Kutaruhu'*. It is his way. It is the way of Coyote."

"That's a great story," Hotaru said. "And hearing it out here, by a fire along the Platte and with coyotes howling in the distance, makes it even more special. Elk, you managed to transport me and that's the mark of a really good storyteller. Bravo!"

The old man looked away, as if he were embarrassed by the scientist's praise.

"My grandpa told me that story," Elk said softly. "He didn't have many teeth, so he was kinda hard to understand. But he could sure tell a story. Once, we were walking on the prairie and we came across this big rock. Under one end of the rock was this long coyote tail sticking out. I'm still not sure if my grandpa put the tail by the rock as a joke or if there really was a squashed coyote under that big rock. But it sure made an impact—the story, I mean."

Elk laughed for a long time and then tilted his head back and looked up at the stars. The old Army bugle was still on his chest and he held onto it as he laughed.

"Is there a message in the story about Coyote and the rolling rock?" Hotaru asked.

Old Man Elk was very quiet. He placed the bugle at his side and then reached down to pet each of the two dogs that were now sleeping at his feet.

"I'm not sure about the message of the story," Vogel said in a very serious tone of voice, "but one thing that I got out of it was that a little farting isn't always a bad thing. Considering that we ate beans tonight, I think we all should remember that."

Jake Vogel laughed, and even Pike had to laugh. Dr. Hotaru, who was trying very hard to keep a straight face, felt better when she saw Elk shake his head and chuckle as well.

"Vogel," Elk finally said, "there is more of Coyote in you than I expected to find in a man with blond hair and blue eyes. Ah, but that is the way of Coyote. He always turns up where you least expect it. He always breaks the rules. And Coyote is always full of surprises."

CHAPTER 30

It was still dark when the sounds of two gunshot blasts filled the morning air. The second shot was followed by a high-pitched howling sound that ended as abruptly as it began.

The campfire had died down and Agents Pike and Vogel searched for flashlights.

"Elk!" Pike called out when he saw the old man run into camp and grab a handful of darts and a rifle from one of the boats. Armed with the gun, Elk ran toward a stand of trees to the south of their campsite. The old man did not look like himself, for his long gray hair was not tied back. In the darkness, he had a more youthful and wild look.

"Elk!" Pike called out again. "Elk!"

Dr. Hotaru also had awakened and she helped the two agents find the flashlights. Vogel already had the other rifle and the box of tranquilizer darts. Pike drew a firearm out of a holster that was tucked under his sleeping bag. He looked at Vogel and pointed in the direction that Elk had gone.

"Susan, stay here and watch things. We need to find Elk and see what's going on."

The two agents ran toward the trees and finally picked up Elk's tracks in the sand of the river bottom. They pointed the two flashlights in the direction of the tracks. But they were slowed down by overhanging branches and old logs that lay in their path. At one point, Vogel tripped and fell on his side in the sand. But as he fell, he kept the rifle away from him and high over his head.

After Vogel got up, the two agents continued running through the trees.

"There!" Pike called out, as he saw two eyes in the glare of the flashlight. It was Artemis and she was shaking. Although she was not tied down, the dog acted like it was unable to move. Its eyes shone wildly. Only a few feet away was Apollo. The large sheepdog lay on its side, softly whimpering. He had been shot and dark blood stained the sand beneath him.

"Damn!" Pike said, as he stopped to observe the wounded animal. He wanted to do something, but he was worried about Elk.

"Elk!" Pike called out, this time much louder. "Elk!"

In the darkness, the two agents searched the ground for tracks and finally picked up Elk's trail. But they worried when they suddenly saw more footprints.

The sun was just beginning to come up, and in the faintness of early twilight the two agents finally spotted Old Man Elk.

He was walking toward them with the rifle. He held the gun in an awkward sort of way, as if he resented having to carry it.

"Elk!" Pike called. "Are you alright?"

"They shot Apollo," Elk said as he handed over the rifle and a handful of darts to Agent Pike. "And so I ran after them and shot them. Now you have two real 'code reds.' They're over there." Elk pointed to a clump of small cedar trees.

As the old man tended to his dog, Pike and Vogel searched the area that Elk had pointed out and found the bodies. They were those of two young White men who appeared to be in their early twenties. Both were lying on their stomachs and were about fifteen feet apart. One man had a red dart in his shoulder, the other in his right buttock. The man who was lying farthest away was wearing a headlamp with a small halogen bulb. The beam of the headlamp created a single, thin line of light that trailed away from the man's body. The shotguns and an upturned nylon knapsack littered the ground near the outstretched youths. The red dart in each man seemed to give off a strange, luminous glow in the first light of early morning.

"Are these tranquilizers even safe for humans?" Vogel asked.

"Let's hope so," Pike answered. "At least it looks like Elk shot them only once. Not sure what two or three darts would have done."

Pike looked down at the two men and shook his head, as if he were trying to awaken from a bad dream. The scent of whiskey and barbecue-flavored chips hung in the early morning air. The mixed smell was not a pleasant one.

"Vogel," he finally said, "keep an eye on these guys. When they come out of it, bring them back to camp. But don't let them get anywhere near their guns. We've had enough excitement this morning."

Pike hurried back to where he remembered seeing the two dogs. He found the spot, but the two animals and Elk were not there. He looked down at the large bloody stain in the sand and again shook his head.

When Zephaniah Pike reached their campsite along the river, he could hear Apollo whimpering. Elk and Hotaru were bent over the dog and Artemis looked on and whimpered a little as well.

"I'm sorry," Dr. Hotaru said, "Apollo's in bad shape and he's in pain. If you want, I can use one of the tranquilizers to make his last moments painless."

"No," Elk said. "I want him to know that Artemis and I are here. Apollo needs to know we will be with him when he dies."

Old Man Elk gently picked up Apollo and carried him over to the river and sat down with him. Elk cradled Apollo in his arms and began to sing a song that sounded sad but soothing. The old man rocked back and forth as he sang, his long gray hair hanging loosely on both sides of his face. Artemis sat close to Elk and did not make a sound. When Elk finished singing, everyone knew that Apollo was dead. But Elk continued to hold him, and to gently rock back and forth even after the sun had begun its slow journey across the eastern sky.

Agent Pike radioed the recovery team and informed them of the early morning's events. He also used his cell phone to call the FSPD agents in Columbus so that they could take the two hunters into custody.

"We may run into other hunters farther down the river," Pike warned Kerrington after he reached him on the cell phone. "Maybe this animal recovery mission wasn't such a good idea. It could have been one of us who got shot by those hunters. We thought everyone was being evacuated out of the valley."

"There's been some resistance," Kerrington answered, "especially by families that live directly on the river. Evidently, some of them are trying to carry out the Dawson plan even before the Rawlins plan is set into motion. I guess it's to be expected. But I think you and the others should continue on and complete your work. I could have security helicopters or small surveillance drones do sweeps over the river to make sure you won't encounter any more lawbreakers."

"No," Pike responded. "Dr. Hotaru thinks the noise of the helicopters and drones might scare away the wildlife. Maybe you just need to get the word out that anyone hunting along the river during the next couple of days will face stiff penalties."

"Alright," Kerrington agreed. "We could try to do that. But I'm not sure it will deter everyone. In the meantime, why not send the old Indian and his other dog home?"

"Yes," Pike answered. "I think that might be best. I could have one of the recovery team members fill in for him."

"Keep me posted," Kerrington concluded. "And be careful."

* * * *

By seven o'clock that morning, the two hunters finally awakened and were taken into custody by the FSPD. The boats were packed and the team members watched as Elk dug a grave up on a grassy slope overlooking the campsite. The old Indian declined Vogel's and Hotaru's offers to help him dig the grave. He wanted to do it himself. As Elk was still digging, Pike approached him.

"Elk," the agent began, "I'm real sorry about Apollo. We all feel bad about what happened. I was on the phone with my boss and we decided that it's time for you and Artemis to go home."

The old Indian, whose hair still hung loosely down both sides of his face, was sweating. He stopped digging and looked up at the FSPD agent.

"Do we go home?" Elk asked. "Or do Artemis and I just join the big exodus and then become separated?"

"I'm not sure what will happen," Pike said as he squatted down beside Elk. "But I'm relieving you. You're free to go. I'll call and make arrangements."

As Pike got up and turned away, the old Indian became angry.

"No!" he cried out. "Apollo went out early this morning because he heard something. He heard the noise long before I did, so I let him run ahead. While the rest of you slept, Apollo was the one who was wide awake and who tried to protect the camp. And now he lies here dead. Don't let the loss of his life be for nothing."

"Zeph," Hotaru said as she approached the two men. "I don't want to get in the way, but if we continue on I think it's important that Elk and Artemis go with us. We owe that to them, especially to Apollo."

As she spoke, the scientist was looking down at the body of the dead dog that was lying on the grass.

Pike stared at Jake Vogel as if he wanted him to back him up and refute what Susan Hotaru had just said. But Vogel just looked down at the body of the animal that Elk was preparing to bury.

"Are you really up to it?" Pike finally asked Elk. "Do you want to continue on with us?"

The old Indian nodded.

"The portion of the river that lies ahead to the east is the part that Artemis and I know best. So yes, we will help you. But first, let's put

Apollo in the lap of *'Atida,'* our Holy Mother Earth."

Old Man Elk rose up from digging the grave and walked over to where his dead companion lay. He gently lifted the limp body of Apollo. He carried it reverently and then bent down and placed the dog in the grave. Nearby, the old Indian had placed some pieces of food, a handful of wild sage, and a sprig of cedar. He placed these on top of Apollo's body and then he spoke some words in Pawnee. He repeated them over and over. As he spoke, he stroked Apollo's long black neck hair.

Elk then rose up and faced the sun in the east. As he did so, his long gray hair and wrinkled face radiated a soft golden light. When the old man spoke, he turned to look in all directions, as if he were addressing every living thing around him.

"Apollo was brave. And smart. And most of all, he was a true friend, not only to me but to Artemis here. Sometimes, in the winter when it was too cold to go outside, I would sit and read *The Odyssey* out loud. Apollo liked that, he really did. And so I want to recite these lines. They are from Apollo's favorite part of the book, when Odysseus and his companions showed great courage by confronting the Cyclops. But that encounter was not without bloodshed and sacrifice:

'When dawn's scarlet fingers
brushed across the morning sky
I awakened all my shipmates
for the time to sail was nigh. . . .
As we set out for our destination
we felt grateful just to be alive.
But our hearts grew heavy when we thought
of mates who never would arrive.' "

Artemis sat nearby and quietly listened. The chestnut-colored retriever did not make a sound, even when Elk dropped down and placed the first handful of earth into the grave. Susan Hotaru moved forward and also put several handfuls of soil on the dog's body. Jake Vogel crouched down and joined in as well.

Zephaniah Pike stood nearby for a long time, but soon he got down on his knees and took his place beside the others. He grabbed large handfuls of earth and scooped them into Apollo's grave. As everyone helped cover the grave, Old Man Elk rocked back and forth and keened. Earlier that morning, the song had helped soothe the suffering of one who was dying. Now this same song helped soothe the suffering of the living ones as well.

PART FOUR

BLOOD ON THE
MOON SHELL

She had been up most of the night and now she rested behind a thick stand of weeds. She positioned herself carefully, so that she could watch everything. Every now and then she turned and looked behind her.

Earlier this same morning, Ahwa had heard the booming sounds of the thunder-sticks. She crouched down and waited. Later, when she went to investigate, she smelled fresh blood. She followed its scent to the edge of the Great Flat Water. It took her to the campsite of a small war party.

Ahwa had seen these same noisy Two-Leggeds the day before. They seemed more quiet today. She watched and she listened as the Two-Leggeds moved about. A small group of them huddled close together, for they were burying something on a grassy knoll close to their camp.

She then watched the Two-Leggeds take their large pointed containers and push them closer to the river. Ahwa saw that they carried long thunder-sticks that looked different from those of the other Two-Leggeds. The thunder-sticks of these four hardly could be heard, except for the arrow-like objects that they sent flying through the air. Small as they were, the arrows seemed much more powerful than they looked, for no matter what creatures they struck, the miniature arrows seemed to work a deadly kind of magic.

Although their thunder-sticks were not as deafening, this group of Two-Leggeds made much noise as they handled things of many different shapes and sizes. She watched as they put all of these things into the large pointed containers that bobbed up and down in the water.

As Ahwa watched them, she was very surprised to see them do something she did not expect. They stood by the water's edge and were quiet for a few minutes. And then the long-haired one among them raised his voice in song.

But the song was hard to understand because of its unusual sounds. It did not sound like a typical war song that challenged the enemy to do battle. Nor did it sound like a teasing song that mocked the ways of those who were afraid.

She listened closely and strained to hear each of the song's strong sounds. Although she could not understand the words, the song seemed vaguely familiar.

Ahwa did not know what to make of all this. The singing bothered her, but it intrigued her even more. She crept a little closer but still stayed hidden. Now she heard the song with renewed interest. Ahwa let the sound of the singing fill her ears and to pass into that other place, the place of ancient memory and ancient recognition.

CHAPTER 31

After burying Apollo, Old Man Elk and the others stood up and stared down at the mound of earth. Without saying a word, Elk turned and headed into the trees as if he had forgotten something.

When he returned, he carried an armful of cedar branches. These he carefully spread out over the grave. Then he went back into the woods and brought back a large cottonwood branch. It was so dry the leaves rustled as Elk placed it on top of the carpet of cedar that covered the grave. By now, there was little trace of the burial and the outlines of Apollo's grave could not be seen. It was very quiet, except for the occasional cawing of a crow or the whirling of a dragonfly.

Old Man Elk turned and went back to the campsite. He began packing and the others followed his lead. They put their sleeping bags and other things into the two boats. They dowsed the campfire with river water and pushed the front portions of the two boats into the river.

Zephaniah Pike radioed the recovery team and informed them that they should be ready to follow behind, as they had done the day before.

Before they set off, Elk raised his staff with the carved head of the long-billed bird and pointed it to the east. Then he sang the same song that everyone remembered hearing when they first went down the river:

"Kingfisher, Kingfisher,
Little Brother, hear us!
Carry our message far.
The pitiful ones are here.
But we only mean to help,
We do not mean to harm.
Kingfisher, Kingfisher,
Little Brother, hear us!
Kacii-kaha'!
Kacii-kaha'!"

Elk sang the song three more times, and with each singing his voice grew more shrill. By the time he sang it a fourth time, the others were surprised by the power of the old man's voice. He loudly shook the gourd rattle whenever he sang the Pawnee words. When he finished singing, it was absolutely still. The crows and the dragonflies were silent. Even the waters of the Platte seemed to slip by without making much sound.

The old Pawnee took out his leather pouch and dropped tobacco into the water of the Platte. Then he dipped his kingfisher staff into the river, as he had done the previous morning. The river level was even lower than it was when they first began. But this morning there were no humorous remarks.

Old Man Elk turned and looked back at the spot where Apollo was buried. Then he climbed into the boat and called for Artemis to join him as he sat in front. Zephaniah Pike sat in the back and operated the motor. Hotaru and Vogel, whose faces still showed signs of sunburn, followed in the second boat. The tranquilizer rifles and darts were placed on top of the baggage in each boat so that the guns could be easily loaded and fired.

As they headed down the river, the two boats stayed in the main channel. The river was very wide, but was comprised mostly of sandbars and small, weed-covered islands. Elk and Artemis did most of the observation, since the two agents and Hotaru had to spend nearly all of their time navigating the narrow channel to avoid the sandbars. After a few minutes, the main channel widened a bit and the two agents breathed sighs of relief.

At one point, a flock of ducks flew up, and Jake Vogel was able to bring down a duck that straggled behind. Hotaru had signed "green" and Vogel responded quickly. But the duck landed in the river. Vogel steered the boat in the floating bird's direction. Hotaru retrieved it and placed it on a sandbar so that it could be easily seen. Then she took the locational reading and radioed the recovery team.

The group soon spotted more wildfowl of many different kinds. Pheasants and quail suddenly would fly up on either side of the river, but due to their size and speed they proved to be difficult targets. Nonetheless, Hotaru continued to make the sign for "green" and to point to the pheasants and quail.

Shortly after noon, Elk drew everyone's attention to a great horned owl that was in the upper branches of a tree. Artemis had spotted the bird first and Elk petted the dog in appreciation. The old man made the sign for "green" and pointed to the owl's location in the tree. Agent Pike fired, but he missed by only a couple of inches. The great bird flew off, and the bright green dart remained embedded in the tree trunk.

The sun blazed directly overhead, stinging the eyes and skin with equal intensity. The sunlight reflected off the river water and made surveying the riverbanks extremely difficult.

The two boats approached a large concrete bridge that was jammed with traffic. As the boats slowly passed beneath the bridge, Elk and the others saw several flatbed trucks on the bridge that were heading north toward one of the evacuation centers. Hundreds of metal cages rested on top of one another on the back of the trucks, and in each of the cages were pets of various types and sizes. There were beagles, cocker spaniels, collies, poodles, and various dogs and cats of every color. Many of the animals ran back and forth inside the cages. Most cried out frantically, while a few others appeared to be totally lifeless. Large blue and white tags with numbers were wired to each cage. When the caged animals saw Artemis and the people going by below them in the boats, they became even more excited and made so much noise that the truck drivers began honking their horns as if to try to drown out the animals' cries. The whole scene was so disturbing that Elk pulled Artemis close to him. The old man talked to his dog and tried to distract Artemis from seeing so many other animals in distress.

After passing under the bridge, it took everyone a few minutes to shake off what they had just witnessed. Elk continued to talk to Artemis, but the dog whimpered, and at times she tried to turn her head to catch another glimpse of the caged animals on the bridge. But Elk held Artemis close to him and he continued to reassure her.

When the two boats passed under the bridge, Zephaniah Pike noticed writing on one of the concrete pillars. The words were familiar and unmistakable: MISERERE NOBIS. Again, they appeared to be written with a brownish, rust-colored substance that looked like dried blood. But this time, directly beneath the Latin phrase, was a name that also was rust-colored: JUAN MÍNGUEZ. Pike quickly jotted down the name and the location of the river bridge. The Latin phrase was identical to the one that appeared on a cement pillar near the place where the body of Muskie Perkins was recovered.

"Elk," Agent Pike called out. "I want to ask you something. Elk?"

The old man, who was still comforting Artemis, turned his head a little to the right so that he could hear better.

"Was your friend Muskie a Catholic?"

Elk shrugged his shoulders. "Don't know. Muskie and me, we never talked about his religion. And he never tried to convert me."

"Did Muskie know any Latin?"

Old Man Elk turned completely around and looked at Pike as if he suspected the agent had suffered heatstroke. And then, without saying a word, he turned around again and faced forward.

"Okay," Zephaniah Pike admitted, "I know that was a long shot.

But let me try something else. Does the name Juan Mínguez mean anything to you?"

Even though Elk did not answer or turn around, Pike could see the old man's back straighten and stiffen.

After a couple of minutes passed, Old Man Elk turned to the right and shot the federal agent a quick and uncertain glance. But then he spoke.

"Juan Mínguez? There was a Spanish missionary by that name. He was with Villasur in that big battle here on the Platte."

"You mean the priest who pulled his blue robe over his head?"

"Yes," Elk answered. "He's the one. But that blue robe didn't do him much good. He got killed."

"Why would his name show up on one of the pillars of that bridge back there?"

The old man was silent and seemed to ignore the question. But then he turned and answered.

"I'm not sure. But I heard there's a group who wants to see that missionary declared a saint. They meet in the public library in Columbus. Guess they feel Juan Mínguez was a martyr. At least those folks know their history. And maybe some of them really care."

Zephaniah Pike nodded, but not in a knowing kind of way. He nodded to indicate he had heard Elk's words and was weighing them very carefully.

＊ ＊ ＊ ＊

The summer sun seemed especially hot and intense. Everyone was sweating profusely and wiping their brows. As the occupants in the two boats approached a bend in the river, they felt a slight breeze and it helped alleviate the effects of the suffocating heat. As they drew closer to the other side of the river, they saw something. A white-tailed deer with large, velvet-covered antlers stood on a sandbar, looking directly at them. The buck was extremely skinny, which made the antlers on its head look all the more enormous. The animal showed no signs of preparing to make its escape. It watched as the two boats slowly made their way down the river.

Elk made the sign for "green" as he pointed in the direction of the big buck. But when the animal defiantly moved towards them, Elk signed "yellow" and turned to look at Zephaniah Pike. The agent disagreed with Elk's call when the deer suddenly charged in their direction. Vogel loaded his rifle with a red dart and was waiting.

As the deer moved toward them, Pike fired but missed and the dart went whizzing past the animal. As Pike quickly reloaded, Vogel fired at the deer's midsection and hit it. The deer continued on for a few more steps, wobbling, and then went down. Its eyes were open and it seemed to be looking at the two boats as they quietly sailed past.

Hotaru radioed in the location of the tranquilized deer and repeated that the color designation was red. Elk whispered to Pike that the deer appeared to be sick and that may have explained its strange behavior.

★ ★ ★ ★

At around two o'clock in the afternoon, Pike called for the group to stop. The water level had dropped even more at this point. The four individuals rested briefly along the river and ate some crackers and canned tuna. After eating her own portion, Artemis eagerly licked clean all of the other tuna cans.

A helicopter flew directly overhead as the group rested. Pike waved at the aircraft and a few seconds later received a call on his cell phone. It was Douglas Kerrington.

"Zeph," he said. "Can you hear me down there?"

"Just barely," Zeph said. "It's hard to hear with the noise of the helicopter."

"We're doing a fly-over of the river this afternoon. Want you to know that you are going to run into some problems up ahead."

"What kind of problems?"

"The river is completely dry for the next twenty miles or so. There's not a drop of water and there is nothing anyone can do about that.

You'll have to go ashore and resume farther down the river. There is more water downstream. Just go ashore before the river runs dry. You and the recovery team will be taken to another location. There will be transport vehicles waiting."

"Is the mass evacuation completed?"

"Not yet. It's still underway and that's one of the things we're checking out this afternoon."

"Have there been any other developments?"

"There have been all kinds of developments, including some pretty heated protests from animal rights advocates and environmental groups all across the country. There's an awful lot of resistance to the Rawlins plan. But Nebraska is still under quarantine and the governor isn't budging. He fears for the safety of the state's two largest metropolitan areas. So the Rawlins plan is set to go."

"I'm not surprised."

"How's your work going?"

"We made some more hits today. But a long stretch of dry river is going to cost us some precious time."

"I understand. The transport team will get you to your new destination as soon as they can. It may take a little while. You four and all your gear will have to be inspected closely when you come ashore. We're still not sure what we're up against. Are you all feeling okay?"

"We're hot and tired. But yes, we're okay."

"Is Mr. Elk alright?"

"Yes. He seems to be holding up pretty well."

"Good. I'll let you get back to work. Later."

"Yeah. Later."

After taking their break, Agent Pike and the others continued down the river. They were only able to go about three and a half miles before coming to a place where the river narrowed to a shallow stream. The river level was so low that the boats were unable to go any farther. And the sun burned more furiously than it had the day before. Everyone got out of the boats, but they moved more slowly than usual because of the heat.

Agent Pike tried to radio the recovery team, but he was unsuccessful. Due to the intense heat in the river bottom, radio and even cell phone communication was spotty at times. The agent advised everyone to rest until he again tried making radio contact.

All four individuals sought a bit of shade on one of the sandbars closest to the riverbank. But even in the partial shade, the ground beneath them felt steaming hot and clouds of sand fleas and buzzing flies swarmed in on all sides. It was almost impossible to remain sitting in one spot for more than a few minutes.

The pungent smell of death hung heavy in the hot summer air. Much of the stench came from the bloated carcasses of mule deer and white-tailed deer. But some of the acrid smell was that of carp, catfish, shiners, and other decaying fish that could be seen in greasy clumps all along the dried-up side channels of the river. At times, the combined stench of so much death was close to suffocating.

"Geez, what a stink," Vogel groaned, as he rapidly fanned his face with both hands. "This drought thing really packs a wallop. Geez!"

Old Man Elk rose from his sitting position, brushed the sand off the back of his pants, and looked over at Jake Vogel. Before speaking, the old Indian cleared his throat and moistened his lips with his tongue.

"You know, this 'drought thing' is actually a female giant. I have seen her in my dreams. She sleeps in a deep cave and she awakens every few years or so. *Atika,* Grandmother Drought, is very old and she gets kinda cranky. If she chooses, she can start a fire with the hotness of her breath. In some ways, she is like the Chimaera of the ancient Greeks.

"Yes, *Atika* is very powerful. Wherever she goes, she leaves behind the signs of her passing: bones and skulls, blackened prairie, dead trees, dry streambeds. *Atika* can get down on all fours and when she does that, she laps up all the water in the ponds and the rivers and the streams. Due to the hotness of her breath, she has an insatiable thirst.

"Sometimes, *Atika* really shakes things up. It is within her power to turn the world on its side. She can even turn the world upside down. It happens for only a brief moment in time. But when it happens, everything seems different. Nothing is the same."

Susan Hotaru stared at Elk with a mixture of amazement and disbelief. As the scientist listened, she remembered what some of the hospital patients in the surrounding area had told the doctors. The patients were being treated for heatstroke and they indicated they felt confused and disoriented. Several complained, saying "the world's topsy-turvy and things just aren't the same." But how, Susan Hotaru wondered, would Elk know about this? She had not discussed any of the heatstroke cases with the old man. The scientist had spoken only to the FSPD agents about the contents of the medical reports.

"Grandmother Drought," Old Man Elk continued, "she can be relentless and very cruel. But we need to remember something: like it or not, *Atika* is a part of this land. And she is as old as the land itself. We may fear and even despise her, but she is an elder. So *Atika* demands our attention. And our respect.

"As I look around us here, I see that Grandmother Drought has passed by this place. She may be near us yet."

The old man looked at Jake Vogel without blinking and then reached down to knead the ears of Artemis.

"If you're saying we see the effects of the drought here," Vogel responded, "I think we can all agree on that. No problem. And yes, it certainly does seem like that fire-breathing old grandma of yours paid this place a little visit."

Dr. Hotaru busied herself by trying to get her cell phone to work. She wanted to check the phone for messages and updates. At one point, she sat in an odd, hunched-over position so that she could create ample shade for herself. In the bright sunlight, the small screen in her phone proved extremely difficult to read.

"A number of cities had record-high temperatures yesterday," the scientist finally announced. "Lincoln hit one hundred and fifteen degrees and Omaha was only one degree shy of that. But the weather bureau claims a storm system appears to be moving out of Colorado and into Nebraska. Maybe some rain will come our way and cool us off. Wouldn't that be something?"

"Yeah, right," Vogel said, still fanning himself and wrinkling his nose. "Won't hold my breath. Then again, maybe I should. Feels like I've been inhaling fumes of sulfuric acid or something equally nasty. There's just no letup with this stench."

Zephaniah Pike was listening to Vogel and the others, but he also was deep in thought. He had to use both hands to shield his eyes from the blinding sun as he looked up and down the full length of the river. There were numerous dry streambeds that ran close together. Here and there, an elongated sandbar lay between the remains of the old channels. The sight of so much sand and so little water gave the impression that one was in a barren desert instead of a riverbed. The wide stretches of white and tan-colored sand seemed endless.

A dust devil danced across a nearby sandbar, spinning and whirling like a knee-high dervish. Despite its frenzied movements, the dust devil managed to stir up only a few dead leaves and bits of sand. The miniature whirlwind seemed to come out of nowhere and then slip back into the same void from which it had escaped.

"What a godforsaken river," Pike murmured.

Elk turned and looked at the federal agent to make sure he had heard right. The old man seemed surprised that Zephaniah Pike would say such a thing.

"This is not a godforsaken river," Elk said in response.

The old man bent down and scooped up a handful of river sand. He slowly opened his right hand, letting the fine grains of sand escape between the widening spaces of his outstretched fingers.

"If God were a river, God would be the Platte," Old Man Elk said. And as he said these words, he patted the riverbed beneath him with his other hand.

Zephaniah Pike shook his head and looked down at the old man. Sweat dripped off the agent's forehead and nose as he spoke.

"You sure about that?" the agent asked. "With real rivers out there like the Amazon and the Nile and the Mississippi, there's a whole lot more in the world to choose from than this so-called river."

"Yes," Elk replied. He rose to his feet and faced Zephaniah Pike. "Those rivers are great rivers. And yes, they are well-known to everyone and they carry a lot of water. But the Platte has many faces and it has more mystery than water. God is the Great Mystery. And the Great Mystery is drawn to that which is most like itself. So if God were a river, God would be the Platte."

Pike glared at Old Man Elk and started to say something, but then he stopped. In the heat of the moment and in the heat of an incredibly hot and taxing summer day, the agent had lost his cool. Instead of apologizing or seeking a shady spot along the river to sit and rest, he walked over to a large sandbar and stood by himself in the blazing August sun.

Zephaniah Pike could not help but think about Elk's strange and perplexing words, words that equated the greatness of God with a largely unknown river that stunk and lacked sufficient water. The agent remembered other strange and perplexing words. They were quoted by the librarian back in Columbus: "God is God, the Platte is the Platte, and that is that."

Agent Pike shook his head and pursed his dry lips as if he wanted to blow such utterances far, far away. He was not a deeply religious man, but he believed that if someone did recognize the greatness of a supreme being, one needed to at least be deferential. It was beyond Zephaniah Pike how anyone could use words like "God" and the "Platte" in the same sentence. What was he missing? Was it him? Was it the stench? Or was it the heat? Why, he wondered, did he not see anything mystical or supernatural in a nearly dry riverbed and the endless channels of shifting sand? The agent closed his eyes for a few seconds, as if to give his surroundings a second chance. But when he opened his eyes, everything seemed even more dismal than before and the whole scene now burned with new and raw intensity. Nonetheless, he continued to look all around him, as if he were really trying to find something.

The others watched Zephaniah Pike, who continued to stand all by himself on the sandbar. They were waiting for him to make a move or to say something. At one point, Dr. Hotaru began to approach the agent with a cold bottle of water, but Vogel stopped her and gestured for her to wait a little longer.

Meanwhile, Old Man Elk sat and gently petted Artemis. The dog was panting and salivating, but she remained at Elk's side. As he stroked her chestnut-colored hair, he also whispered Pawnee words to her. Each time the old man did so, the dog closed her eyes and wagged her tail as if she understood. Despite the heat, the two of them seemed rather content and in their own little world.

Tired of looking all around, Zephaniah Pike now lowered his gaze. As he did so, something on the sandbar caught his attention. There were faint traces of linear tracks. It looked as if a giant metal rake had descended on the river and left behind its massive imprint.

The agent walked over to still another large sandbar and crouched down to study more of the linear tracks. They seemed to be everywhere.

"You know what those are?" asked Jake Vogel, as he casually strolled over and bent down beside Agent Pike. He asked the question in a tone of voice that revealed he knew exactly what the marks were and how they got there.

"They're from dirt bikes, motorcycles, and four-wheelers," Vogel said. "There must be a town close by. When the river gets dry like this, some of the kids from town get together and have a little fun. There aren't any speed limits or stop signs down here. And so they make the most of it. They'll spend the whole day down here, racing up and down these sandbars. After it starts to get dark, there are so many bikers and riders that the kids sometimes run into each other and even hurt themselves. Nearly everyone sees this dry weather as a terrible thing. But not kids. They always seem to find a way to entertain themselves, no matter how bad things get. And why not? Who can blame them for trying to enjoy life a little?"

Pike stood up and finally was able to radio the recovery team. He informed them that they were at a standstill due to the water level. As they waited for the recovery team and the transport team to meet up with them, Artemis spotted an opossum on the river's left bank. The animal seemed blind and disoriented as it struggled to make its way to the narrow stream of river water. Elk made the sign for "yellow" and waited for one of the agents to do something.

Susan Hotaru stepped forward and shot the opossum with a yellow dart. She waited for the animal to stop moving and then approached it slowly. The scientist was reluctant to get too close. As she stared at the animal, she wondered if it was sick or simply suffering from the effects of the excessive summer heat. She noticed that the opossum had extended its right foreleg ahead of itself, as if trying to reach the dwindling water of the river.

CHAPTER
32

It was already evening when Agent Pike and the other members of the team were able to get their boats back into the river. The move had taken much longer than anticipated, primarily because of the many cars and trucks that packed the highway. The great exodus was still underway, and there were potholes in the highway that had been caused by the constant traffic over the past couple of days.

Even near the city of Columbus the river bottom was completely dry. So the team had to travel many more miles eastward until they were opposite the town of Schuyler. Here the Platte River once again was deep enough for the boats to float. As Pike and the team prepared to set off, they were given additional food provisions and drinking water. Each of them had been checked thoroughly by two medical experts. Blood and urine samples were taken soon after they came ashore. Their temperature and blood pressure were recorded and they each had to disrobe and submit to a physical exam in case they carried parasites. Each team member checked out clean, except for Jake Vogel, who had a wood tick extracted from under his left arm.

Pike and Hotaru were told that they had elevated body temperatures, but the medical personnel conferred and decided that these were due to the summer heat. Vogel's body temperature was normal, but he was treated for his sunburn. Although Elk was the oldest member of the team, his vital signs appeared to be surprisingly good. Even his body temperature appeared to be normal, despite the heat and the fact that he did not wear a hat.

Artemis also was checked and found to be in good physical condition. Blood and saliva samples were taken from the dog and sent to Omaha for testing. Hotaru explained to Elk that all of this was being done merely as a precaution.

As everyone waited to get in the boats and continue their journey, Zephaniah Pike stared at the river.

"It's really good to see some water in the Platte again," the agent said. "No offense, Elk, but a river's just not a real river without some water."

"It's not the Platte's fault," Old Man Elk said. "Besides the moodiness of Grandmother Drought, there are many dams and diversions all up and down the river. The Platte has undergone a lot of change. One only wonders what the future will bring. This is one of the last wild areas that is left in eastern Nebraska. But all of this will look very different in the future. People will reduce the Platte to a filtered stream. The whole river will be walled off and artificially lighted. And of course it will be climate-controlled, so that it never gets too hot or too cold or too dry or too wet. Tropical orchids and South American songbirds will line the banks of this river. The Platte of the future will be perfect in every way. The people who stroll along this river will be able to connect with the river on their terms, not nature's. Yes, everything will be just perfect. But when all that happens, this wild river will no longer be the Platte. They will destroy it in order to save it. And then this river will be just another thing that has been re-made and re-shaped to the White man's liking."

"Maybe things will turn out differently," Agent Pike countered. "Let's hope the people of the future will have some sense and leave this river alone."

"Ah, you know better than that," Elk answered. "In less than two days all of the animals along the Platte will be killed off. It will be but the beginning of many more changes to come. So as we go down the river today and tomorrow, we need to remember something. We are seeing the Platte in a way that future generations will never know it. Behold, behold the River Platte."

"Let's get moving," Pike announced. "We've got work to do. And time's a wasting."

Everyone climbed into their boats and took up their positions. Artemis nudged up close to Elk, as if the dog were the only one who understood human words and took them to heart.

Now, as Pike and the other team members went down the river, they noticed that the water was indeed deeper and this made for easier navigation. They still remained in the main channel of the river and they were all amazed at the great width of the Platte. Sandbars could be seen everywhere, a few of which seemed to stretch on for hundreds of feet.

Old Man Elk pointed to a bald eagle that was circling overhead. Its great size and wingspan impressed Pike and he stared at the huge bird for a long time. The eagle's wingspan looked like it was at least six feet. Everyone realized that the eagle was well out of range and Elk turned around and smiled. The old man seemed pleased that the eagle was determined to keep its distance and to go untouched.

Artemis began to growl a little and Elk finally realized what had caught the dog's attention. Elk pointed to a small animal that was scurrying about on a sandbar.

"Iditaku," Elk said softly. "Over there. It's a muskrat." Then he quickly made the sign for "green."

Hotaru took aim and hit the muskrat on the first try. The animal showed amazing stamina and struggled for a long time before it finally went down.

Shortly after shooting the muskrat, Elk pointed at a coyote on the opposite side of the river. He kept his eye on the animal but did not give a color designation. Pike steered the boat out of the main channel and into the direction where the coyote was running. Every so often, the big-eared coyote turned around and watched the two boats following behind. Agent Pike was so intent on getting closer that he misjudged the depth and got hung up on a sandbar. Pike waved Hotaru and Vogel ahead and gestured for them to get as close to the coyote as they could.

Hotaru loaded a rifle with a green tranquilizer dart and did not let the coyote out of her sight. She took out a pair of binoculars to get a closer look at the animal. Whenever it turned to gaze behind, Hotaru was able to get a good look at its long snout and pointed ears. She was even able to see the amber color of its eyes.

Meanwhile, Vogel operated the boat and tried to keep it afloat. But only a few minutes after Pike had grounded, Vogel ran the second boat onto a sandbar as well.

The four individuals removed their shoes and rolled up their pants legs. Elk tied the long strings of his black and white high tops together and draped the shoes around his neck. Everyone got out of the two boats and went to work trying to get the boats back into the water. They kept this up for some time, and Pike had to laugh as Hotaru and Vogel freed the boat but almost failed to hold onto it. They fell and splashed each other and fell again. But they were able to finally grab hold of the boat.

After much pushing, Pike and Elk also were able to free their boat. Artemis seemed to enjoy jumping in and out of the craft, as the two men struggled to keep a firm hold on the boat and yet crawl into it at the same time.

A few minutes later, as the two boats made their way back into the main channel of the river, Elk pointed at a coyote on the opposite side of the river. This one looked darker and skinnier than the one they had been pursuing.

"It's the same coyote," Elk explained. "He saw the fun we were having and decided to go for a little swim as well. He crossed the river and now he wants us to resume the chase. He's in a playful mood."

"Let's not disappoint him," Pike called out. As he said this, he loaded the rifle with a green dart and placed it directly in front of him.

When the coyote saw that the two boats were coming towards it, the animal began running. As the speed of the two boats increased, the coyote ran faster. When the boats slowed down, the coyote would stop and look behind, panting.

The chase continued for nearly an hour, and then the coyote was no longer in sight. Pike said the animal crawled into some weeds and was hiding. Hotaru argued that it had gone into a nearby corn field. Vogel swore that he saw the coyote abruptly turn and go north.

Elk laughed and said nothing. Although Pike was disappointed that they were not able to tranquilize the coyote, he felt relieved to hear Elk laugh. Pike's relief was such that he laughed out loud. Soon Hotaru and Vogel joined in as well, especially when they saw Artemis wagging her tail in response to everyone's laughter.

For the next hour or so, the two boats continued down the river. Despite the drought, there were patches of brilliant green on both sides of them. The sun no longer burned as hot, and as everything cooled down there was a subtle explosion of sound and color. The river took on new life and it became difficult for everyone to focus on their task. The water depth now was becoming much greater, and as a result the river seemed to take on more of its natural character. Small birds called to each other and every now and then a jumping fish or croaking frog could be heard.

Near the water's edge, a flock of wild turkeys had gathered and several of them were exhibiting their colorful plumage. Elk pointed at the turkeys and made the sign for "green." Pike and Vogel almost were reluctant to load their rifles. But they did so, took aim, and fired. Both men seemed surprised when each hit their target. The other turkeys scattered, but the two birds that had been hit collapsed in a heap of feathers, the bright green dart in each clearly visible.

As they continued on, Old Man Elk pointed and held his nose shut with his fingers. Pike wondered what this meant until he saw a large striped skunk on a small island. The animal had its back turned to them and was chewing on something. Elk signed "green" and watched as Pike shot the dart at the animal. The dart nicked the animal, slightly clipping one of its ears. The skunk turned around and seemed furious. Seeing the animal's angry reaction, Hotaru reloaded her rifle with a yellow dart, but she missed as well. By the time Vogel was ready, the skunk was so agitated that Hotaru could not decide if the color should be yellow or red, so Vogel finally decided on yellow. He took careful aim, but the skunk lunged forward and Vogel missed. Pike tried a second time, this time with a yellow dart, and finally hit the angry animal.

By the time the team members set up camp that evening, they had brought down nearly forty animals and birds of various kinds. But only one of these, the white-tailed deer, was given a red designation.

The group's campsite was on a large island in the river, where there were patches of weeds and plentiful supplies of driftwood. Elk built a fire and Vogel heated up some canned beef stew and biscuits.

After it grew dark, the river bottom remained visible due to a full moon that loomed overhead. Traces of rust-colored clouds could be seen drifting across the moon's brightness. At times, the moon changed from a pale cinnamon to an almost crimson color.

"That's a red coyote moon," Old Man Elk said when he saw that the others were staring at the strange color of the moon. "You don't see that too often."

"Probably just another prairie fire somewhere," Vogel commented. "A big grassland fire would make the evening sky kinda red like that."

"Is a red coyote moon a good sign?" Hotaru asked.

"Depends," Elk answered.

"On what?"

"Mostly, it depends on whether you're a coyote or not."

Hotaru laughed but was very persistent. She looked at Elk and did not look away until he told her more.

"When you see a red coyote moon," Elk explained, "it means Coyote is talking to Moon. Maybe Coyote is asking Moon for something. If so, Moon will ask for something in return. Coyote and Moon are creatures of the night and thus they are old, old friends. I don't think they trust each other completely. But they do understand each other. Sometimes, that is enough.

"Coyote is very powerful. He can cloud your judgment and he can change himself into just about anything he wants. Many times, a hunter will chase down a coyote and corner it in a canyon. But the hunter often finds no sign of a coyote at the back of the canyon. Well, if the hunter looks real close, he will see a hawk or an owl fly out of that same canyon. Oh, Coyote is very powerful."

"Sounds like Elk is getting ready to tell us another coyote story," Vogel said with a smile.

"Not really," the old man answered. "I'm sure you're all very tired and want to sleep."

"But with that red moon overhead, it's a perfect setting for a story," Hotaru said.

Old Man Elk looked at Agent Pike as if to ask if it would be alright to tell a story or two. But Pike kept a straight face and expressed no preference. Instead, he changed the subject completely.

"We need to take turns keeping watch tonight," Pike said. "I'll take the first watch, and when I get tired I'll wake someone else. Sound alright?"

Vogel and Hotaru nodded, but Elk remained quiet and simply stroked the hair of Artemis.

"Are there stories about the Platte River?" Hotaru asked Elk.

"Yes," the old Pawnee answered. "There are many stories about this river. The whole state of Nebraska owes its name to the Platte. You see, the Otoe and the Omaha peoples called the river something like the 'Ni-Braska,' which meant the 'Spread-Out Water' or the 'Flat Water.' We Pawnee, we call this river 'Kits Katus.' In our language, we say the word 'River' first and then we speak its name. That's why I prefer to say the 'River Platte.' It may sound a little odd to some people, but to me it's more respectful. 'Kits Katus' means the 'River

Flat Water' and you can see why we call it that. When the French explorers came, they, too, were amazed by how broad and flat this river seemed, so they called it *'Rivière Platte.'* And then when the Americans came, the name 'Platte River' was used. So that was one thing the French and the Americans and the Otoe and the Omaha and the Pawnee all agreed on—the flatness of this great river. They did not agree on everything, but it seems those five nations saw the Platte in pretty much the same way.

"This river was always very special to the Pawnee. Its banks hold the remains of our ancient ones. But this river is special for many other reasons. Only a few miles east of here is a very sacred place on the river that we call *'Pa'u' Ckadahkat'* or 'Hill in the Clouds.' It looks like a big earth lodge and it is covered with cedars and other trees. Because of its size, the White people call it 'High Point.'

"There are always many animals and birds all around Hill in the Clouds. There are even families of kingfishers who make their homes there. Lots of kingfishers can be found over on the Loup to the northwest. Maybe that is why the Lakota always referred to the Loup as the River Kingfisher in their language. But most of the kingfishers I have seen make their homes near Hill in the Clouds on the Platte. You see, kingfishers do not nest high in the trees like so many other birds. They make tunnels in the sides of hills or in riverbanks. And they burrow in real deep, maybe five or six feet. They prefer to make a home using the earth itself. And so it is there in the hillside that those kingfishers rear their little ones and it is there they spend most of the cold winter months.

"The kingfisher is very special to us Pawnee. And it was special to the ancient Greeks as well. Maybe you all remember the story of Halcyone, the daughter of the Wind God. Halcyone married Ceyx, the son of the Morning Star. Now those two were quite a couple! They knew how to enjoy life and have a lot of fun. They loved each other so much that when Ceyx drowned at sea, Halcyone could not bear her loss. She took it hard and she nearly cried her eyes out. Her body

250 • TIMOTHY J. KLOBERDANZ

began to weaken and wither away. So the gods took pity on Halcyone and they turned her into a kingfisher. As soon as she had wings, she flew off and found her husband's body, which had washed up on shore. She touched the decaying body of her husband and, because her love was so great, Ceyx came back to life and he also turned into a kingfisher. So they were both given a second chance and they lived as kingfishers after that. Surely one of you remembers this story?"

When Elk posed the question, all three of his listeners looked down as if they were back in school and were afraid to admit they had not done their homework. The old Indian smiled in an understanding sort of way and looked up at the red moon. Then he began again.

"You know, when I first went to the big house, they didn't have much of a library there. But they had some old books on Greek mythology. I wasn't interested at first, but I could see similarities between the ancient Greeks and the old Pawnee. That was a real eye-opener for me.

"I came to realize that the ancient Greeks believed that nearly everything around them had special meaning and special power: the wind, the sun, the moon, and the stars. The Greeks even believed in the power of little creatures like the kingfisher. And those Greeks had their powerful and sacred places, places that made the mortals tremble, places like Mount Olympus. We Pawnee have such places as well. Hill in the Clouds is our Mount Olympus.

"You see, Hill in the Clouds is very special. It is not just a big hill that overlooks the Platte. Hill in the Clouds is the great council lodge of the *Nahúraki,* spirit animals who have very special power. They all meet there. It is where representatives of all the animal nations gather and make important decisions. The place is kind of like their United Nations building."

"Have you been there?" Hotaru asked, sounding very intrigued.

"Yes," Elk said. "The first time I went there was when I was just a boy. I was at home back in Oklahoma and staying with my grandparents. I was very ill and burning up with a high fever. That went on for a couple of days and nights. I was so hot I kept crying out for water. Suddenly I felt a cool sensation and I found myself inside this huge lodge. All the *Nahúraki* were looking down at me. Then I saw two tall sandhill cranes and two large golden eagles come towards me. They were all dressed real nice, real fancy. They sang and then they danced back and forth, back and forth. And the more they sang and danced, the better I felt. When I woke up, I was back home and my fever broke. I told my grandparents about it and they told me that my spirit had gone all the way to a special place up in Nebraska, to Hill in the Clouds. I got better after that. My grandma and grandpa were so happy they threw a big feast for me and invited lots of our relatives."

"But have you been to the actual place?" Vogel asked. "You dreamt you went there while you had a high fever. But have you been to the actual place here on the Platte?"

"For us Pawnee," Old Man Elk tried to explain, "dreams can be very real. I do not think that my grandparents doubted my spirit had gone to Hill in the Clouds.

"Ah, but I know what you are asking, Vogel. I was always kind of scared to go there because the place is so powerful. Some of our old people used to tell me that the underwater entrance is guarded by *Tawakiks,* a giant water serpent that spits out fire. He is a half-fish, half-snake creature. When he comes out of the water and dances in the sky, the opening to the council lodge becomes visible. The opening is a cave that is in the side of the hill, but it is under the water. That cave is known as 'The-Place-That-Slips-Out-Of-Sight.' When the great serpent goes back into the river, the cave opening closes. It completely slips out of sight."

"No wonder you were scared," Hotaru said.

"Yes," Elk said. "But I have been there many times and I never saw the water serpent that spits out fire. It makes me wonder what our old people were talking about. Maybe they just told us about that serpent so we would kinda fear the place, as well as respect it. Hill in the Clouds does feel very *'waruksti,'* very special. It is hard to explain, but we Pawnee heard stories about that holy place from the time that we were very small.

"Sometimes, when I visited Hill in the Clouds, especially after it started to get dark, I could sense something beneath my feet. It felt like a big drum that was beating deep down in the earth. And the sound of it kinda went through my whole body, from the soles of my feet to the top of my head. It was like electricity. I really felt it. But now, these many years later, I no longer think it is a drum. No, it is something else. The River Platte has a beating heart. And Hill in the Clouds is a place where you can feel the beating of that heart."

The old man paused. He noticed that Hotaru and Vogel were looking up at the moon, which was still an eerie crimson color. Agent Pike seemed deep in thought, but he appeared to be listening.

"The old ones," Elk continued, "they said that a long time ago there was a Pawnee man who desired great power and wisdom. He felt that if he sacrificed something that was very dear to him, it would help him gain the kind of power that he wanted. So one day the man took his young son hunting on the Platte. When the man saw that he and his son were all alone, the man took out his knife and he stabbed the boy. *Ahu!* Yes, the father killed his own son and he watched the boy's body grow lifeless in his arms.

"Because they were on the banks of the Platte, the father placed the body of his dead son in the river. He watched as the blood from his son's body mixed with the waters of the great river. The man knew that the river would carry his sacrificial offering to the *Nahúraki* at Hill in the Clouds.

"Later that day, the father returned to his people, but he said nothing to his wife or to anyone else. Of course they all wanted to know what happened to the boy. But the father never said a word about what he had done. The man waited and waited. Yet he received no great power and no great wisdom. He had killed his own son and now he had to live with that horrible deed for the remainder of his life.

"Meanwhile, the body of the murdered boy floated and floated down the Platte. Finally, the body of the boy washed up on a sandbar near Hill in the Clouds. Now Kingfisher was flying by and he saw the body of the dead boy down on the sandbar. He took pity on that poor little boy.

"Kingfisher was the messenger bird, so he dove deep into the water. Because of Kingfisher's diving ability and small size, the giant water serpent was not able to see him. It took Kingfisher four tries, but he found the entrance to 'The-Place-That-Slips-Out-Of-Sight.' Because he was so small, he was able to slip inside. There he begged all the spirit animals who were gathered in the great lodge to restore the dead boy back to life.

"The *Nahúraki* argued among themselves, but Kingfisher was very persuasive. So they agreed to help the boy. The body was carried into the great lodge and all the spirit animals used their power to bring the boy back to life. They restored the boy's body and made it good again. And they taught the boy many secret and wonderful things before he returned to his people. He became a powerful Pawnee medicine man and a great healer among our people. But he never said anything about what his father had done to him. He did not need to. You see, he was not only able to heal and do wonderful things. He was able to forgive. *Ahu!* And so he achieved the kind of great power and great understanding that his father had sought.

"Yes, the *Nahúraki* who dwell in Hill in the Clouds have much power. They can heal the sick and they can even restore life to those who have been dead for a long time. It is all within their power."

Old Man Elk paused and looked into the faces of Hotaru and Vogel. They were no longer looking at the moon but looking at Elk and listening. Pike also was looking at Elk, but the agent did so in a way that conveyed obvious discomfort. Nonetheless, the old man continued talking.

"As we have been going down the river the past couple of days, I have been thinking of the spirit animals who dwell in Hill in the Clouds. Maybe they are already meeting and deciding whether or not to sanction a great war that will be waged against the humans. Perhaps they feel the animal nations have suffered too much at the hands of humans. The *Nahúraki,* they look around their lodge and they must see many empty places. The elk and the grizzly bear and the gray wolf and the wolverine are all gone from this portion of the Platte Valley. The *Nahúraki* must worry that many more animal nations will be killed off or driven away. But I do not think the animals at Hill in the Clouds have agreed to go to war just yet. Perhaps the animals and birds that have been troublesome so far are more like renegades. They are like the fighter bees that appear before the big swarm. I'm just not sure.

"But this I do know: If war is ever declared at the great animal lodge and news of this war goes out to all the animal nations, it will not consist of little skirmishes here and there. It will be all-out war. It will be a war like no other. They will come from all directions and all at once. They will come out of the sky and from out of the earth.

"When they unite, theirs will be a fighting force like nothing ever known. Besides their great numbers, they have something else on their side, something very powerful."

Old Man Elk paused and was very quiet. Everyone could tell he was going to say something more. But he seemed to hold back before speaking again.

"They have the most powerful and the most terrible weapon of all," Elk finally said. He spoke very slowly and very earnestly.

"They have time. Yes. They have all the time in the world."

CHAPTER
33

When Zephaniah Pike assumed first watch, he loaded his rifle with a red dart. He also placed a flashlight beside him. Hotaru and Vogel were in their sleeping bags and appeared to have fallen asleep right after retiring. Elk sat in front of the fire, carving a piece of driftwood. Artemis lay sleeping beside him. Every so often, the old man picked up some shavings and tossed them into the flames. Small sparks arose whenever he did this.

Pike stared at the old man, but the agent said nothing for a long time. He wanted to be sure that Hotaru and Vogel were asleep before he engaged the old man in conversation.

"So what was the point of that story?" Pike asked. He tried to whisper, but he could not conceal the anger in his voice. "Why are you always trying to stir things up?"

Old Man Elk was silent and continued to carve. He did not even look at the agent. Instead, the old man looked down at his axe and other carving tools that were within easy reach.

"What was the point?" Pike repeated, his voice still sounding angry. He held the rifle in his lap in such a way that the barrel pointed away from him, yet made the red dart clearly visible.

"I seem to have touched a nerve," Elk said. "Stories can do that, you know."

"You're trying to mess with me," the agent shot back, "and I don't appreciate it. In fact, I resent it. Tonight you crossed the line."

Elk nodded, but not in a way that indicated he understood. He stared at Zephaniah Pike and waited for the agent to say more.

"If you continue to undermine me," Pike warned, "you will be sent packing. And if you and Artemis become separated, then that will be the way it has to be."

On hearing her name uttered, Artemis opened her eyes and stared at Agent Pike.

"I am not undermining you," Elk answered. "I just told a story because Dr. Hotaru asked me to. But I did not try to undermine you."

"You did!" Pike shouted. He no longer tried to keep his voice down.

As Elk stared at the agent, he saw the eyes of Zephaniah Pike turn from eyes filled with anger to eyes that were filled with pain. And soon the eyes of the man glistened with tears.

The old Indian simply looked at the federal agent and then he gazed into the fire. He was not sure what to do or what to say. He stopped carving and tried to show that he was listening and trying to understand.

Pike wiped the tears from his eyes with the back of his hand, but he kept a firm grasp of the rifle with his other one.

"Yeah," Pike said in an accusing and mocking tone, "you just had to tell that goddamned story about the father who killed his son."

Elk did not apologize or say anything. He just stared into the flames of the fire. When he did look up every so often, he could see that the agent's eyes still shone with tears.

"Twila was our first born," Zephaniah Pike said as he took a deep breath. "Hers was a normal birth and she was healthy. But when Travis was born two years later, he was premature. He had a lot of problems at first, but we loved that little guy so much and we took care of him and he always pulled through. Twila did her part as well. She was the big sister and she grew up to be very protective of Travis. But I kept telling my wife and Twila not to overdo it. I wanted Travis to be tough because life is tough. I wanted him to be strong because you gotta be strong. But I pushed him too hard. I just pushed too goddamned hard.

"I never told Travis he had to go out for track. But I know he felt that I wanted him to run because I had been a big track star. I was 'The Zephyr' and he wanted to make me proud. He competed in a big meet last spring and he ran as fast as he could. He ran until he couldn't run anymore. His heart and lungs just weren't strong enough. He did it for me, I know it. It killed him and it's my fault. He was only a freshman in high school and he had his whole life ahead of him. And he threw it all away because of me.

"I killed him, just like the father in that goddamned story of yours. I killed Travis. I killed my own son."

The tears continued to wash down Zephaniah Pike's face and they shone in the light of the fire. Elk had heard every word and bowed his head. Hotaru had awakened and heard the conversation as well, but she kept her eyes closed and pretended to sleep. She wanted to get up and comfort Zephaniah Pike, but she was not sure if she should let on that she had heard so much.

"So who told you?" Agent Pike asked Elk. "Who told you about Travis?"

The old man looked very surprised and did not respond right away.

Finally, Elk said: "No one told me about your son. I have no television or computer. I do not keep up with everything. I spend nearly every day carving. And at night I look at the stars through my telescope. So believe me, I did not know. But losing a child must be very hard. I am truly sorry."

"You have no idea," Pike said. "You have no idea what it is like to see your son literally run his heart out and then collapse and die in the middle of a bunch of gawking spectators. And you want to know the shitty, shitty irony of it all? I hadn't been able to go to any of his other track meets. Oh, but I had to be at that one. I wanted to be the good father and so I took off work and I surprised him. Travis saw me right before he started off. He saw me there on the sidelines. I smiled at him, but he didn't smile back. He had this strange look in his eyes, this strange look that told me 'I'm gonna show you, Dad. I'm gonna show the Great Zephyr what I'm made of. And I don't care what it takes.' Oh, he showed me alright. Oh God, he showed me! I should have just stayed the goddamned hell away. If I had done that, Travis would still be alive. But I was there, and because I was there, I killed him."

It was not Elk's way to stare at someone, but he looked directly at Pike and tried to convey how sorry he felt. The old Indian slowly spread out all the fingers of his right hand and placed them over his heart. It was a traditional gesture meant to show that he understood and that he felt great sympathy.

"Why did you tell that story?" Pike asked. "It was no coincidence. You were rubbing my nose in something that has already caused me and my family a whole lot of hurt. In my book, that's unforgivable."

The old man remained quiet. But after a couple of minutes, he unbuttoned his long-sleeved flannel shirt and removed the garment completely. He again showed Agent Pike the insides of his arms, with the large tattoos showing the name of his dead girlfriend and the date of her death.

"Yes," Elk admitted, "telling that story about a man who kills a loved one can cause pain. But the pain is usually mine. Every time I tell that story or even think of it, I feel that man's pain. And each time I work in the yard or get ready for bed, I look at these arms and I remember. And I am in pain. These tattoos don't weigh very much, but they feel heavy, for they are a constant reminder of what I did and what I lost. More than fifty years haven't made these tattoos feel any lighter. As I get older, I feel myself getting weaker. But these tattoos just get heavier and heavier."

The old man, who had bared his arms, now watched as a couple of buzzing mosquitoes tried to land on him. He reached into his pants pocket and pulled out his leather tobacco pouch, along with a book of matches and a small rectangular packet of cigarette papers.

Pike watched the old man roll a cigarette. He did so deftly, without spilling even a bit of tobacco. When the old man finished, he inspected his work and nodded. Then he reached around the fire and offered the freshly rolled cigarette to the federal agent.

"I don't smoke," Pike grumbled.

"Of course you don't," Old Man Elk said. But he continued to point the cigarette at the agent until the object was accepted.

The old man rolled a second cigarette in even less time than it took to make the first one. He struck a match, lit the cigarette and inhaled deeply. Then he blew big puffs of smoke to his right and left.

"A lot of folks hate smoking," Elk said, "but nobody hates it more than mosquitoes." The old man blew smoke all along the length of both his bare arms. He sat in such a way that the large tattoos on his inner arms were clearly visible.

"I don't have any tattoos," Pike said, "but I have this."

He reached into his pants pocket and took out a medal that was attached to a worn ribbon.

"This is the medal Travis won on the day that he died," Pike said. "His coach gave it to me and my wife at Travis's funeral. I've carried it in my pocket ever since. Each time I go to bed, I empty my pockets and lay everything out on the nightstand and there it is. And then I try to go to sleep, but I can't."

Zephaniah Pike's eyes began to shine with tears again, as he held the medal and looked down at it.

"So I know what you mean," Pike said, "about carrying something that doesn't look all that heavy. To everyone else it looks light. Sometimes the weight of a thing is so great that it can't even be measured on any scale. And when you carry something like that, it's a heavy load."

Elk nodded, for at last the two men seemed to understand each other. Both individuals shouldered a great burden and now it was as if the crushing weight of each man's burden had shifted a bit.

"You know," the old man said, "I have read *The Odyssey* many times. After all, it is the story of a man who has been through a lot and he just wants to go back to his homeland. I could relate to that. When I was in the big house, I even played around with parts of *The Odyssey* and turned some of the words into rhymed verses of my own. It was a way for me to pass the time and to improve my English. And it helped me in other ways, too.

"There is one passage in that great epic that always speaks to me. It is when Odysseus says:

> 'Of all the many creatures
> who live and breathe on Mother Earth,
> none is so helpless or pitiful
> as a man full-grown or a man at birth.'"

Old Man Elk paused and took a final drag from his cigarette, which was now but a smoldering stub. When he exhaled the smoke, he and Zephaniah Pike watched the little cloud drift up and up until it disappeared into the vastness of the night.

CHAPTER
34

"It's your turn to keep watch," Jake Vogel said as he gently shook Hotaru. She was only half asleep and was still thinking of the conversation she had heard between Elk and Pike only a few hours before.

"What time is it?" Hotaru asked as she sat up.

"A little after four o'clock," Vogel said as he put more wood on the campfire. "If you're too tired, you can go back to sleep and I'll stay on watch."

"No," Hotaru answered. "I'll be alright." She looked around the campfire and could see that Elk and Pike were both lying down on opposite sides of the fire, but she could not tell if they were awake or sleeping.

A heavy fog covered nearly everything and there was an unexpected chill in the air.

"Jake," Hotaru whispered to Agent Vogel. "Did you hear what Elk and Pike were talking about last night?"

Vogel shook his head. "No, not a word. I was so tired I fell asleep the minute I crawled into my sleeping bag. Why?"

"I'm worried about Pike," Hotaru whispered.

"Pike?" Vogel repeated, sounding very surprised.

They walked about thirty feet from the campsite.

"He sounded so different," Hotaru said. "And he was so emotional.

I'm really worried about Pike. I don't know if it's pent-up anger or if it is something else. We just don't know what we're up against out here. Whatever it is, it may be affecting some of us already."

Vogel did not say anything. He just stared at Hotaru and tried to convey that he shared her concern.

"I can stay up with you," Vogel said. "And we can talk."

"No," Hotaru said. "You need to get some more rest. But you could keep watch for a few minutes longer until I get back."

"Where are you going?" Vogel asked.

Hotaru frowned as if she did not care to spell everything out in detail.

Jake Vogel finally nodded and turned away. He sat near the fire with his back turned to Hotaru so that she could have a little more privacy.

With rifle in hand, Hotaru walked to some high weeds, but then she decided to go on to a stand of cottonwoods. Due to the early morning darkness and heavy fog, it was hard to see clearly and the scientist had to walk slowly and reach out at times to feel what was ahead of her. Finally, she came to a clump of bushes that were growing near an extremely large cottonwood. She leaned the rifle against the tree and then relieved herself. As she finished, she heard something to her right. She quickly pulled up her jeans and looked in the direction of the strange sound. Seeing nothing out of the ordinary, she turned and was shocked to see a shadowy figure standing between herself and the rifle.

Hotaru wanted to cry out, but she felt she needed to get to the rifle even more. The figure stepped toward her, but in a very innocent way, not in a menacing fashion.

"Are you with the group that is going down the river?" the stranger asked. The voice was that of an older woman with a distinctive accent that Hotaru had never heard before. It was hard to see the woman clearly in the fog, but she looked as if she were wearing a long trench coat and a man's fedora.

"Who are you?" Hotaru asked, trying to sound very calm but very firm.

"I don't live far from here. I saw the light of your fire. Was wondering if you are with that group."

"You shouldn't be here," Hotaru warned. "Everyone is being evacuated out of the valley. Haven't you heard about the mass evacuation?"

As Hotaru talked, she tried to move in such a way that she could step past the figure and quickly get to the tranquilizer rifle.

"Why are you shooting the animals and why are others picking up their bodies?" the stranger asked. The hat that the stranger wore suddenly looked more like a battered military helmet than a fedora.

"We're just trying to help," Hotaru replied, her eyes still riveted on the rifle. She noticed that the figure had both her hands in her pockets, as if she were having a casual conversation with someone.

The stranger seemed to be well aware of the scientist's plan, and so the figure would step in front of Hotaru each time she tried to get to the rifle.

"How are you trying to help?" the stranger asked. Now her headgear resembled an old-style nurse's cap with a faded red cross.

"We will run tests and see if the animals are sick in any way," Hotaru explained. She spoke a little louder, hoping that Vogel would hear voices and come to investigate. "And if any of the animals are sick, we'll help them get better. That's what we're doing."

"Are you sure that's what you're doing?" the stranger asked, and she tilted her head in an odd sort of way as if trying to see from a different angle. This time she was wearing a light-colored pillbox hat that was splattered with blood.

"Are you sure that's what you're doing?" the stranger in the long trench coat repeated. But now the words all ran together and sounded more like *"Aryushurthatzwhutchyurdewin?"*

The scientist seemed completely taken aback by the stranger's choice of words. They had a sharp, mocking tone.

"Vogel!" Hotaru shouted as loud as she could. "Vogel!"

As she cried out, the stranger turned and began to run away. Hotaru grabbed the rifle, but it was difficult to see in the fog.

"Vogel!" Hotaru called out again.

Within seconds, Jake Vogel was at her side and asking what was the matter.

"It was a woman and she was standing right here. She went running off in that direction!" Hotaru said excitedly, pointing to the south. "She may have something concealed under her coat. Jake, be careful!"

Vogel ran in the direction that Hotaru had pointed. He carried his rifle in both hands, but it was hard for him to see. At times, the fog was very dense, but then there would be a small clearing.

Pike and Elk had awakened and also came running. The agent carried a rifle and Elk had a flashlight. When they reached Hotaru, Artemis circled all around them, her nose close to the ground and sniffing.

"Where's Vogel?" Pike asked.

"He went after this woman who approached me," Hotaru explained. The scientist was talking unusually fast and trying to breathe in with her mouth at the same time. "She was dressed in a long trench coat and her hats kept changing every time I looked at her. She wanted to know what we were doing here on the river."

Hotaru could tell by the look on Pike's face that he doubted her.

"Come back to camp," Pike urged. "It's hard to see clearly out here."

As Pike and Hotaru headed toward their campsite, Elk crouched down and watched Artemis, who was still circling and sniffing. Elk shone the flashlight on the ground and studied the footprints closely. He also shone the flashlight in all directions. The old man then shone the flashlight up into the nearby trees, checking out even the highest branches.

* * * *

More than half an hour later, Jake Vogel stumbled into camp. He was out of breath and sweating heavily. He dropped the rifle and gestured for something to drink. Pike quickly gave him a bottle of water. Vogel was so exhausted he had to bend over and put his head between his knees. Then he raised his head up and took a long drink of water before saying anything.

"I ran after her as fast as I could," Vogel said, still trying to breathe normally. "But it was hard to see and she ran awfully fast. I was going to shoot her with a tranquilizer, but I wasn't able to. At one point, she just stopped and turned around and looked straight at me."

"So you got a look at her face?" Pike asked.

"Only for a few seconds," Vogel said. "This is going to sound crazier than hell, but for a split second there I thought I was looking at my old man. He was just standing there in his old hunting clothes and hunting hat. It was the weirdest damn thing I ever saw. I guess I wasn't getting enough air and my eyes were playing tricks on me."

"It's all so strange," Hotaru said in an excited tone of voice. "She just seemed to come out of nowhere. And she had this really odd accent that I just can't place. And believe me, the hat on her head kept changing from one different type to another. It was all so odd. How else can I describe it?"

"I'll call the backup team," Pike said, "and I'll alert them. Sounds like this woman was just some wacko from outside the area. Then again, she may have been armed and determined to do some real damage. Either way, we need to be cautious and to keep our eyes open."

As the agents and Hotaru talked, Old Man Elk was very quiet. He sat near the campfire and stared into the flames.

"Elk," Hotaru said as she went over beside him. Her hands were still shaking, and so she locked them together in an attempt to keep them from trembling. "Do you have any idea who that woman was?"

The old Indian looked up at Dr. Hotaru but remained very quiet. He picked up a twig and held it in the flames of the campfire, watching the twig catch fire and then fall into the flames, one small piece at a time. Artemis also watched as the twig disintegrated in the heat of the fire.

"I find it interesting," Elk finally answered, "that she chose to talk to another woman. Maybe she thought that a man wouldn't listen. And maybe, just maybe, she was trying to give us a warning or some kind of sign."

"A sign?" Hotaru exclaimed, finally realizing what Elk might be getting at. "You don't really think she was a spirit or something like that? Even Vogel saw her. She was real."

"Yes," Elk agreed. "She was real. Both you and Vogel saw her. But we are now nearing a place where the real and the unreal are not so distinct. They kinda blend in and at times they make it real hard for even smart people like yourself to see how things are."

"I don't think I understand," Hotaru apologized. "I want to, but I just don't."

"Yes," Elk said. "As I told you once before, you don't understand. But I don't blame you. I blame Thales of Miletus."

CHAPTER
35

After Hotaru's early morning encounter with the mysterious woman, no one was able to go back to sleep or get any rest. The camp became a center of heightened activity. Elk made coffee and oatmeal while Pike radioed the backup team. Susan Hotaru talked on her cell phone and jotted down notes. Vogel seemed especially unnerved by the early morning's events. He carefully examined and cleaned his side arm. Then he holstered the gun on his hip so that it would be within easy reach.

As the sun came up, two different helicopters flew directly overhead, going from west to east. Only a few minutes later, a small plane flew over the river and it also was heading east.

Dr. Hotaru went to the river's edge to wash her hands. For some reason, she felt compelled to do so several times. As she crouched down and dipped her hands in the river yet again, she saw something that looked like blood in the water. Her eyes widened and she did a double take. She remembered the story that Elk had told the previous evening about the Pawnee father who had sacrificed his young son. When the father placed the lifeless body of his son into the Platte, he had seen his son's blood in the water.

The scientist rigorously splashed at the river water with both her hands until she noticed that the strange, bloody color was no longer visible. Then Susan Hotaru took a small packet out of her pocket, tore it open, and used the lemon-scented towelette to thoroughly scrub her hands.

Thick fog continued to hang in certain places all along the river. The morning was cooler than the previous ones, and Agents Pike and Vogel were wearing their blue and yellow FSPD jackets when they sat down to eat. The sky was beginning to fill with clouds, and even though the sun had risen in the east it could not be seen.

"The fog is clearing from the top down," Elk murmured. "That means we may actually see some rain today."

"I spoke with the recovery team," Pike said as he sipped some of Elk's coffee, "and I told them to be watching for that woman. I also called Kerrington and told him about it. The helicopters that just went over were piloted by the FSPD and they're doing an aerial sweep of the whole valley. Maybe they'll come up with something. Kerrington said that they did arrest a couple of men yesterday who were carrying explosives. They were apprehended outside the main hangar of Rawlins' aviation business in Columbus. Kerrington is afraid there might be other extremists to deal with. So we need to be alert and ready for anything."

"Will the mass evacuation be completed today?" Vogel asked.

"It should be," Pike replied. "Kerrington said that the absolute deadline for everyone to be out of the valley is eight o'clock tonight. The sun sets around 8:45. So we need to conclude our work here on the river well before that. The spraying will take place about this time tomorrow. If all goes according to plan, people can move back into their homes a couple of days afterwards."

"I checked with our agents in Omaha," Vogel added, "and it sounds like there have been protests from one end of the state to the other, mostly animal rights groups and environmentalists. One of the biggest demonstrations is taking place today in Washington, D.C."

"It's to be expected," Pike said. "This sort of thing hasn't been done before. But at least the four of us are doing something to offset the ultimate impact and to save some of the wildlife."

"I have some news, too," Hotaru offered. "I talked to several of the lab analysts from Omaha and from Lincoln. Most of the animals we've recovered seem to be weak and dehydrated but otherwise okay. Unusual chemical readings have come to light in at least a couple of the animals. So our lab analysts may be on to something."

"What kind of chemical readings?" Pike asked.

"They're not sure," Hotaru said. "The problem is that wildlife in this part of the country are subjected to so many chemicals that it may take a while to isolate the elements that could be causing behavioral changes. Chemical fertilizers and insecticides are used regularly and crop dusting occurs all along the river. Then there are the pollutants that can be found in nearly every drop of river water.

"So there's something else we need to do today," Hotaru continued, "we need to take some samples of water from any standing ponds or natural springs that we come across. These might yield information that is different from our ongoing analysis of the actual river water."

Agent Pike threw the rest of his coffee into the smouldering ashes of the campfire. Everyone knew this indicated that they needed to pack up and be on their way.

"Elk," Hotaru asked as she put her hand on his arm, "could you point out any ponds or springs where we might take a few samples?"

"Yes," Elk answered. "There's a spring along the river that is a few miles ahead. But we will need to walk in a ways. The water from that spring flows into the Platte."

"That sounds perfect," Hotaru agreed. "Once they spray tomorrow it will be impossible to get a sample of any natural waters in this area."

"It's crazy," Elk said, "trying to treat chemical poisoning by using more chemicals. Where does all of this stop? It's all crazy."

"Our lab analysts will know more by the time we complete our work today. Then we'll have a better idea of how to proceed."

Old Man Elk shrugged his shoulders as if he did not share Hotaru's optimism.

The team members hurried as they packed the two boats and prepared to head down the river. The sky was still cloudy and the morning air was cool, so the two agents kept their FSPD jackets on as they pushed the boats into the river. Elk wore his old flannel jacket and Dr. Hotaru had draped a lightweight sweater around her neck.

At the river's edge, the old man had started a small fire. Everyone watched as he dropped a handful of dried cedar into the orange flames. Smoke immediately rose up from the tiny fire and the old man cupped both his hands and quickly fanned the smoke toward himself. Then he fanned the smoke from the burning cedar in the direction of Artemis and the two agents and Dr. Hotaru. As the old man waved the smoke in their direction, he spoke very softly and appeared to be praying.

Old Man Elk now brought out his kingfisher staff and asked everyone to be patient as he held the carved stick and sang the kingfisher song. In only two days' time, the singing of the song had become a regular morning ritual. But at the start of this day, as the four humans and Artemis paused at the river's edge, the song took on new meaning. Everyone had heard Elk's story the night before and now they could relate a bit more to the little bird known as the kingfisher. Elk sang the song four times, and as he sang it a final time he shook the small gourd rattle and sang with a voice that was choked with emotion:

> "Kingfisher, Kingfisher,
> Little Brother, hear us!
> Carry our message far.
> The pitiful ones are here.
> But we only mean to help,
> We do not mean to harm.
> Kingfisher, Kingfisher,
> Little Brother, hear us!
> *Kacii-kaha'!*
> *Kacii-kaha'!*"

When Elk was finished singing, he stood in silence on the edge of the river. The stark black and white colors of his high tops seemed even bolder. Then he appeared to wave to the river by making a huge, full circle with his extended right arm. He did so very slowly, as if he were executing an intricate t'ai chi movement. Elk did not explain what the strange circular wave meant. But he had done so in a way that made everyone take notice. The old man reached into his pocket and took out the leather tobacco pouch. He removed a pinch of tobacco and offered it to the Platte. Then he emptied the entire contents of the bag. Everyone watched the little clumps of dried tobacco float down the river. A few moments later, Artemis jumped into the boat and watched as all the others climbed in and took their places.

Hotaru and Vogel had looked closely at Elk and saw that his eyes were filled with pain. And they detected pain in the eyes of Zephaniah Pike as well. Both Hotaru and Vogel wanted to say something to dispel the pain and to offer words of comfort. Instead, they looked at each other to acknowledge a mutual feeling of helplessness.

During their first two hours on the river, there were no sightings of birds or animals that were large enough to shoot. The team members went down the river very slowly, enjoying the unusually cool summer weather and looking closely at everything. Here and there were islands with clusters of small wildflowers. Butterflies of various shapes and colors circled the blossoms, as if doing a strange little dance. Everyone seemed to realize that the tranquil scene would be very different tomorrow and that the river might not be the same for a long, long time to come.

Not a single train could be heard in the distance. As the day of the mass evacuation drew closer, the freight trains had stopped running. An eerie, uncommon silence descended upon the entire Platte Valley.

Artemis sighted the first animal and it was an adult red fox that had raided a nest on one of the islands. Elk gave the sign for "green," but since the second boat was closest to the target, Vogel shot the fox and Hotaru radioed in the location.

Around ten o'clock in the morning, Pike called out for everyone to go ashore. The group took a short break on a side island of the river, where there was ample room to dock both boats and let Artemis run free. Agent Pike called the recovery team to let them know they were stopping for a few minutes. As he spoke, he spotted something half-buried in the sand near where he stood. It was a small round object.

Pike brushed the sand off the disk and noticed that it was light brown in color and had a tiny hole drilled near the edge. It looked very old and so the agent showed it to Elk.

The Pawnee elder held the object in his hand and nodded, as if he had been shown a button from a favorite old coat. For a long time, he ran his fingers over the object and kept nodding.

"Ahu," Elk said, "this is very old. It's a shell pendant and probably was worn by one of my people. Last night, I told you that the River Platte was known by many names. We Pawnee always called this river the 'Flat Water' in our language. But many other Indian nations referred to the Platte as the 'Shell' or the 'Moon Shell' because they would come here and trade for shell necklaces and other ornaments. The moon shell was carried in all the way from the East Coast, over many hundreds of miles. Yes, the ancient ones are with us today. Finding this old moon shell is a sign. *Idiwe tudaahe*—It is good."

Zephaniah Pike looked down at the round object in the old man's hand and then stood very close to Elk as he spoke.

"I think it's a sign for both of us, Elk. It connects you to your people and it connects me to mine. You see, I know all about moon shell. Every summer, my wife Darla and the kids and I would vacation on the eastern shore, just south of Ocean City. It was an easy drive from our home in Washington, D.C. And it was a place where we could really get away. We would go to Assateague Island and pick up moon shells along the beach that were this same color. And the place where we stayed was a little bed and breakfast resort called the 'Moon Shell Inn.' "

The agent looked at the old man with eyes that betrayed a wide range of emotions.

"What are the chances?" Zephaniah Pike excitedly asked. "What are the chances of finding this same kind of moon shell here on the Platte River of Nebraska?"

The old man smiled. "Well, I can tell you this: I am a great skeptic when it comes to 'coincidence.'"

Elk handed back the moon shell pendant to Zephaniah Pike, but the agent motioned for the old man to keep it.

"It may have come from my part of the country," Pike said. "But it wound up here in Nebraska for a reason. Maybe we all wound up here for a reason."

"Yes," Elk said. "I was thinking the same thing before I prayed at the river's edge this morning. We are four humans who are going down this river. Four is a sacred number of the Pawnee. And we four humans are members of the four ancient groups: the Red, the Black, the Yellow, and the White. Such things do not all come together and happen by accident. There is more at work here. We are all here on the River Platte for a reason. Each and every one of us."

The old man looked down at the moon shell pendant and then gently slid it into his shirt pocket.

"Okay," Pike shouted. But he raised his voice in an upbeat and encouraging kind of way. "Let's finish what we set out to do."

In the hours that followed, the team members successfully tranquilized more wild animals, including two beavers, three raccoons, a screech owl, and a rare spotted skunk. All of the animals were given a green or yellow designation, except for the spotted skunk. It was defiant and feisty enough to be finally brought down with a red dart.

Instead of camping to make lunch, everyone snacked while they worked. The team members were well aware of their deadline, which was now only a few hours away.

The weather remained cool and big clouds began to gather in the west. Some of the clouds moved swiftly across the sky, and as they moved past, other clouds followed. Due to the cloud-filled sky, the sun no longer shone so bright and even the river water felt cold to the touch.

"Up ahead is the spring," Elk said, loud enough for even Hotaru to hear. She followed behind with Vogel in the second boat. Elk gestured for Pike to make his way to a large island near the right bank of the river.

When they reached the island, they tied down their boats and everyone went ashore. Pike and Vogel carried rifles, as well as a number of tranquilizer darts. Hotaru also carried a rifle, along with a small case for taking water samples. Elk brought along only his carved kingfisher staff and at times used it as a walking stick. Artemis ran ahead, sniffing the ground nearly everywhere she went.

Hawks could be seen in the nearby trees as the four people and the dog approached a small stream that ran into the Platte.

"This is the water from the spring," Old Man Elk explained. "The spring itself is just a little ways up ahead."

As they neared the natural spring, rotting animal carcasses of many different kinds could be seen on the sandbar. Flies buzzed around and the stench of decaying flesh became worse as they got closer to the spring.

Most of the bodies were those of crows and large, brownish-colored hawks. Many of the carcasses appeared to have been there only a short time. Even more dead animals and birds littered the area adjacent to the spring.

"The spring may have been poisoned," Hotaru said as she knelt down to take several water samples.

"Maybe," Elk said. "Either that or the animals were killed as they came up to the spring to drink." He held out his hand and showed Hotaru several shotgun shells and cartridges that he had picked up while walking to the spring.

The hawks in the nearby cottonwood trees cried out and at times the sound of so many large birds was deafening. Suddenly, the hawks grew completely still.

From out of the distant corn fields that lay ahead of them, large numbers of white-tailed deer emerged. They included mostly full-grown bucks and does, along with a much smaller number of younger deer. All of the animals ran close together, so close that one could hear their velvet-covered antlers making dull, muffled sounds as so many branched horns collided. The white-tailed deer kept running until they had formed two large groups, one on each side of the spring. Finally, they came to a running stop and stared at the group of humans and the dog. The dark intensity of so many deer eyes grouped so close together seemed unusually threatening. Each of the animals stared directly ahead as if they were waiting for a signal.

"Geez, Louise. There . . . there must be more than a hundred of them," Vogel stammered. "If they come at us, we won't have enough darts."

As everyone in the group braced for a frontal assault, a high-pitched growl suddenly echoed in all directions at once. The two groups of white-tailed deer immediately turned and ran into the fields. Soon not a single deer was anywhere in sight.

"What happened?" Pike asked.

"Quiet," Elk whispered. "Be very, very quiet."

Everyone drew in a deep breath and tried not to make even the slightest sound. As they paused, they could hear the sound of distant thunder rumbling in the west. But they also heard something else that was much closer: It was another loud and menacing growl. The cry made Artemis lower her head until it nearly touched the ground. The growling sound grew louder and louder and seemed to ricochet off every tree within earshot.

A large, tawny-brown creature came into sight. It growled as it slowly made its way toward the spring.

"Tell me that is not what I think it is," Pike said softly. "Tell me that is just a wild tomcat with a glandular problem. Susan?"

Hotaru was almost speechless as she stared at the animal. It was nearly seven feet long and probably weighed one hundred and fifty pounds or more.

"It's *Felis concolor* alright," she whispered. "I can hardly believe it—an honest-to-God mountain lion. But I'm not sure if our tranquilizers can bring him down if he comes this way."

As Hotaru spoke, she slowly set down her water samples and then loaded her tranquilizer gun. Without hesitation, Pike and Vogel raised their rifles and took aim.

The animal growled again and now faced the group. It was unafraid and showed absolutely no inclination to run away.

"Artemis and I will draw it closer," Elk said. "If it attacks, all three of you must shoot. Maybe one of you will get lucky."

Pike began to protest, but Elk had already stepped forward. He repeatedly called out the animal's name in Pawnee: *"Pakstit kukits!"* Then he began singing and doing a strange little dance as he took steps toward the mountain lion. The sight of the old man dancing in his black and white sneakers seemed surreal. Artemis kept her head down, but she stayed right at Elk's side. The hair on the dog's back rose so much that Artemis suddenly seemed to have sprouted a hump-like growth.

The mountain lion watched the old man and the dog approach and then the cougar let out a tremendous growl. It opened its mouth wide and bared all of its teeth as it did so.

Everyone in the group took a step back when they heard the mountain lion's growl. The animal walked over to the spring. The cougar lapped up water as it watched the four humans and the dog. When the mountain lion was finished, it turned and walked away as if it had absolutely nothing to worry about.

Old Man Elk kept singing and he waved his carved staff as the mountain lion disappeared into the trees. The hump on Artemis's back continued to grow, but the dog did not leave Elk's side.

"Amazing!" Dr. Hotaru said. "We had no idea that there were any mountain lions left in eastern Nebraska. And they almost never make an appearance during the day. Amazing!"

Only a few minutes after the cougar went into the trees, a much smaller animal emerged from the same shaded area. It was a yellowish-brown coyote that appeared to be going toward the spring, but suddenly the animal changed direction and ran in front of Elk and the others. The coyote moved in a bizarre, zigzag pattern. Artemis barked and Pike and Vogel shot several darts in the coyote's direction. But because of the animal's quick movements, it was able to dodge all of the colored darts. The coyote turned, then backtracked and again ran in a zigzag fashion that was almost comical. Again, several darts went flying past the animal.

"Wait!" Elk shouted. "Coyote is just playing with you and trying to make you look foolish. Don't shoot again unless you have a clear shot."

The coyote now ran back and forth very fast. Pike and Hotaru and Vogel all reached for the red darts. Each took aim, but it was difficult to follow the coyote's swift movements.

"The next time it gets close to us," Pike whispered, "everyone take a shot."

The coyote again moved in a zigzag fashion and then ran toward a stand of willows. As it did so, the three individuals fired.

"I think I hit him," yelled Vogel. He sounded ecstatic.

But it was difficult to tell how close Vogel had come, for the coyote already had made its way into the willows and was out of sight.

As everyone slowly walked toward the willows, the hawks in the nearby cottonwoods could be heard. More and more of the birds alighted on the branches and their crying grew louder and louder. Then, as if on cue, all the hawks stopped crying out. Their heads turned toward something in the sky.

A dark blue drone soon appeared overhead and tiny red lights on the drone flashed erratically. The object seemed to come out of nowhere, and it emitted a high-pitched, whirling sound.

"That's one of our surveillance drones," Pike shouted. "But it shouldn't be here. It's acting odd and it doesn't sound right. Oh shit, look! There's something coming up right behind it. And it's coming fast. Oh shit!"

A large red-tailed hawk with outstretched wings and massive talons body-slammed the lightweight FSPD drone and hit the spider-like object so hard that the whirling sound immediately stopped. The surveillance drone plunged out of the sky and the air was filled with dust and feathers and metal parts. The attacker also went down and the large hawk appeared to be injured or stunned.

"Let's go!" Elk shouted, as he pointed at other hawks that were now circling and flying low all around them.

"Wis!" Elk called out in Pawnee. "Hurry!" The old man grabbed the case of water samples and motioned for Hotaru to hold onto her rifle with both hands and to run back toward the river. Vogel ran ahead so that he could begin untying the boats.

More and more large hawks were flying directly overhead, sounding very excited and making shrill cries.

As the team members hurried toward the boats, they could see Vogel aiming a rifle above their heads. Jake Vogel's eyes were so full of fear everyone knew something was very wrong.

Vogel fired the rifle and, when he did so, the sky exploded with even more cries. The red-tailed hawks descended on the team members with extended talons and open beaks. The birds made a piercing "keeeeer" cry as they swooped down in greater and greater numbers. Each hawk cry sounded like a small rocket cruising toward its mark. "Keeeeer," the huge birds cried. "Keeeeer!"

The hawks attacked the team members with ferocity, and there was hardly a chance to fire the tranquilizers. Artemis barked and tried to fight off the birds by snapping at them. Elk threw the water samples into the boat and then used his kingfisher stick to wave the attackers away. Due to all the commotion, Pike and Hotaru simply could not get any clear shots. Vogel, who was unable to reload, was using the rifle as a club and swinging at the red-tailed hawks.

The shrill "keeeeer" cries of the attacking hawks were matched by the shouting of the team members and Artemis's frantic barking. At times, the "keeeeer" cries were very abrupt and sounded like "kiiilll!"

Pike helped Hotaru into the second boat, but he fell in the attempt. Elk pulled off the hawks that were attacking Pike and pushed the agent into the first boat. The old man was able to get into the boat as well, but only because Artemis was barking and diverting their attention. Elk called to Artemis to get in the boat, but the dog was too busy trying to defend itself to hear.

"We've got to get out of here!" Pike shouted as he tried to start the boat. But more red-tailed hawks descended and attacked, this time even more furiously than before. In an attempt to either divert the hawks' attention or simply to outrun them, Artemis began to run along the sandbar toward the trees. A half-dozen red-tailed hawks flew behind the dog and were in close pursuit.

Vogel screamed out as several hawks clawed at his face and arms. One of them buried its talons deep in his neck and shoulders. The agent reached down and drew his side arm. He fired into the air, hoping to scare the hawks away.

Hearing the sound of gunfire, Pike turned and screamed, "No!"

Hotaru, hearing Pike's cries, tried to restrain Jake Vogel and keep him from shooting. But she was able only to pull his arm down, and as she did so Vogel fired two more shots.

As Agent Pike shouted "No!" once more, he swung the tranquilizer rifle all around him, trying to beat off the red-tailed hawks. The birds continued to fill the air with their piercing "keeeeer" cries as, one by one, they descended.

The attacking hawks kept growing in such numbers that now they flew into one another as they tried to attack. Only when large raindrops and marble-sized hailstones began falling did the red-tailed hawks finally pull away and withdraw.

Soon the hailstones had become much larger and several of those that fell were the size of golf balls. The hailstones noisily bounced off the boats and thousands of the hailstones bounced up and down on the sandbar as if doing a wild dance. The hailstones struck the members of the group repeatedly and with tremendous force, but the stinging pain of the hailstones did not hurt so much as the wounds they had all just suffered.

As the pounding hailstones began to dwindle, the sky above them crashed with thunder and more rain began to fall.

Pike, whose head and back had been badly clawed, saw that there was blood all over the boat. But Elk remained in a sitting position toward the front and was calling out for Artemis.

The agent turned around and saw Hotaru holding Vogel in her lap. She was scratched almost beyond recognition and their boat also was covered in blood. The sight of huge white hailstones lying in so much blood was something Agent Pike had never seen before. Even the edge of the river now was red with blood. Zephaniah Pike was momentarily angry with himself for having so often said "I've seen it all." He had never witnessed a scene anything like this one.

"How are you?" Pike asked Hotaru, shouting. "And how's Vogel?"

"I'm okay," Hotaru bravely answered. Framed by so much fresh blood, her teeth seemed excruciatingly white. "But Jake is hurt bad. He's got a deep neck wound and is bleeding a lot. I'm applying pressure, but I'm not sure I can stop it. We need to get help."

Pike tried to radio the recovery team, but there was only static. He looked behind him and could see that much heavier rain was falling in the west, in the direction of the recovery team. Pike tried his cell phone but he could not get a signal.

"We have to head downriver," Elk said, his words somewhat strained. "When this rain stops, the hawks will regroup and attack again."

"Hotaru!" Pike called out. "Can you operate that boat?"

"Yes," she said with great effort, as she tried to move out a bit from under the weight of Vogel's body. "I can reach the controls. Go ahead and I'll follow you."

Pike started up the motor and headed downriver. He looked behind him to make sure Hotaru had gotten the boat started and was following.

"We need to find Artemis," Elk called out. "She should be up by those trees."

"We have to get Vogel to a doctor," Pike said. "We don't have time to look for your dog."

"Then I'll look for her," Elk said. "She's all I got. So when we get up to those trees, let me off."

As they approached the grove of trees along the river, Elk studied the shoreline. But there was no sign of Artemis.

Suddenly, there was another crash of thunder overhead. As the thunder boomed up and down the length of the river, Artemis made her appearance. She was bloody and shivering.

Old Man Elk called out in Pawnee to Artemis. *"Siksa!* Come here! *Siksa!"*

Agent Pike steered the boat close to shore and the excited dog jumped into the boat. Artemis was whimpering as Elk pulled the dog close to him. But the dog slipped and slid back and forth on a pool of blood in the front of the boat.

Zephaniah Pike looked at the huge amount of dark blood and then noticed a spreading stain on the back of Elk's flannel jacket.

"Elk, are you okay?" the agent called out. "Elk! Were you hit? Just hang on! We need to get to some higher ground so I can call for help."

"Hill in the Clouds is up ahead," the old man said weakly. "You will see why the White people call it High Point. You should be able to call from that place."

The rain was falling, but they were still keeping ahead of a much bigger storm that was moving in close behind them.

Soon High Point came into view. It looked like a huge, tree-covered dome that loomed above the waters of the river. Pike was amazed at its massive size and its strange, shadow-like appearance. There was a long grayish cloud directly above High Point. And big flashes of lightning could be seen at one end of the cloud.

As they headed down the river, Old Man Elk clung to Artemis and stared straight ahead. But Elk did not see a long grayish cloud with flashes of lightning. He saw an enormous creature writhing in the dark stormy sky and the great serpent was spitting out fire.

CHAPTER
36

The rain was falling hard as Pike steered the boat to a sandbar near the base of High Point. One channel of the river flowed right beneath the huge hill. Pike intentionally ran the boat ashore and looked behind to make sure Hotaru was not far away. She grounded the boat about sixty feet behind the first boat. Pike ran to Hotaru and helped pull out a tarp in order to cover both her and Vogel in the pouring rain.

"Remain here with Vogel and stay under this tarp!" Pike shouted. "How's he doing?"

As Pike peered under the tarp, he was surprised to see a tranquilizer dart in the agent's leg.

"The bleeding has let up, but I still worry about that neck wound," Hotaru said. "I was afraid he'd go into shock. So I tranquilized him. We need to get help right away."

"I know," answered Pike. "Elk is hurt real bad, too. I think Vogel hit him when he was firing his handgun. Elk's lost an awful lot of blood."

"Oh no!" Hotaru cried. "Do you want me to check on him?"

"No," Pike replied. "Stay here with Vogel. I'm going to try to climb up High Point and see if I can get a call through for emergency assistance. Stay put and wait here for help."

Agent Pike ran back to the first boat and helped cover Elk and

Artemis with the tarp that they had used to cover their supplies. Elk was hunched over and holding on to the dog. Both were wet and shivering. It was raining so hard that Pike crawled under the tarp as well.

"Elk," Pike shouted. "Elk!"

The agent had to grab hold of Elk and shake him a little to get his attention.

"I don't have much strength left," Elk said as he gestured for Pike to draw closer. "We need to talk."

"Save your strength," Pike advised. "I'm going up that hill and I'll call for help. So don't talk. Just take it easy and hang on."

"You won't be able to call in this rain," Elk said. "You need to wait until it lets up."

"Where did you get hit?" Pike asked.

"In the back," the old Indian said weakly. "Imagine that."

Old Man Elk was shivering and his teeth were chattering as well. Artemis sat nearby and was quiet.

Pike got closer to the old man and tried to warm him with the heat of his own body. The agent dug deep into one of his pockets and took out the homemade cigarette that Elk had made the night before. The cigarette was bent and damp but Pike managed to light it and place it in Elk's mouth. The agent would puff on the cigarette to keep it lit and then put it between Elk's lips for a few seconds.

"Maybe this cigarette will help keep us warm," Pike murmured. "At least the smoke will keep the mosquitoes away." But Elk did not laugh or say anything in response.

As the two men smoked and waited for the pouring rain to lessen, Elk closed his eyes and seemed to fall asleep for a few minutes. The old man let the weight of his body nudge up against Zephaniah's own.

"Elk," Pike said in a very soft tone, "I'm sorry how I've acted at times toward you. My wife Darla often told me I can be arrogant and that I've got a real smart-ass side to me. I'm afraid you saw some of that the past few days. And for that I'm truly sorry."

The old man moved a little, so Agent Pike knew he was awake.

Then Elk spoke, but he did so haltingly.

"At least you have a loved one who cares for you and looks out for you. I have no wife to tease me about my shortcomings. But this I know: I've become a little stubborn in my old age. And it seems I always have to have the last word. Even other Indians tell me I talk too much. They say it is very un-Indian."

"Yes," Pike said, chuckling. "Sometimes you do talk too much. And you shouldn't be talking so much now. Just try to rest and take it easy. Okay?"

Old Man Elk took a deep breath, but then he began coughing and shaking. The agent held him in his arms and steadied him so that he would not fall forward.

"Elk," the agent whispered, "hold on. You'll be alright. When we get out of here, I want you to come out to the East Coast and visit me. I'll show you Assateague Island and I'll be your guide. There are moon shells all along the beach, so many you can pick them up by the handful. And there are herds of wild horses at Assateague. They are a sight, especially when they run along the beach with their manes and their tails flying. You gotta see them, Elk. You just gotta."

Pike was not sure the old man could hear what he was saying. But the agent continued to talk and for some reason his thoughts returned again and again to Assateague Island.

The old man moved slightly and it seemed as if he were going to cry out or moan. But then he formed his mouth in such a way that he could speak while holding the rest of his body very still. When he finally spoke, his breathing was labored and the words trickled out slowly.

"Remember the story that I told last night?" Old Man Elk asked. "The one that made you so angry?"

Pike nodded in such a way that Elk could feel the agent's head brushing up against him.

"We are at that place," Elk continued. He swallowed hard and he spoke slowly and with difficulty. "This is the place where Kingfisher dove into the water to find the entrance to the great animal lodge. Under the water here is the entrance. And *Tawakiks,* the great water serpent, he is up in the sky. So the entrance is open and all the spirit animals are waiting."

Zephaniah Pike nodded again, not because he believed what the old man was saying, but because he wanted him to stop talking and conserve his strength.

"This is the place," Old Man Elk whispered. "This is the place where I put my Gina so many years ago. We were not in Oklahoma when the accident happened. We were camping here on the River Platte. This is where I put my Gina's body. Right here."

Pike pulled away and stared at the old Indian, The agent did not want to hear any more.

"Yes, I placed her body here. And I waited for the *Nahúraki,* the spirit animals, to come and bring her back to life. I waited a long time, but nothing happened. Now I know why. I had not seen the great water serpent that spits out fire. But I saw that serpent in the sky today. Now I believe all that was told to me as a boy. It's all true. All true.

"I need to go down and talk to the Great Animal Council. I'm an elder now, so maybe the *Nahúraki* will listen to me. I will ask them to forgive the heat-crazy humans who have hurt them. And I will warn them about all the killing that will take place tomorrow. Maybe this hard rain that is falling will cool everyone off and wash away the blood that already has been shed. Maybe there is still time for the Great Council to make everything good and to make all things new."

Old Man Elk's voice was sounding weaker. It was still raining hard, but Pike decided to go up the hill and try to make the call for help. He made sure he had the cell phone and he rustled around for the rifle and the tranquilizer darts. When he had found everything, he turned to Elk and spoke directly into the old man's ear.

"Elk, you stay right here with Artemis and don't do anything. I'll make my call for help and then I'll come back down here and we'll get out of this. Just sit tight, okay?"

The old man moaned a little but he turned to Pike and faced him.

"Leave your gun behind," Elk advised. "This is one of the most sacred places in the whole world. Here is where you can feel this river's beating heart. So don't take your gun. When you get to the top of the hill, you will see a big rock. Offer that rock something and show your respect. You must address the rock as *'Atipat.'* That's Pawnee for 'Grandfather.' Then make your call."

As Pike listened, he tried to remember the word *"Atipat—A-ti-pat."* He sounded it out and envisioned a porcelain teapot to help him commit the Pawnee word to memory.

"There's something else," Elk continued. "I'm sorry about your son. But you still have a wife and a daughter. When your daughter marries, she'll bring a new son into your family. And when they have children, they will give you and your wife more little ones to love as well. You've got to have hope. All is not lost. Everything can be made good again. Everything."

"Just sit tight, Elk. I'll make that call and then I'll come back and take care of you. You hear me? So just hold on. Hold on!"

Zephaniah Pike took the rifle and tranquilizer darts, but as he waded into the river it was chest-deep. So he flung the rifle and the darts to the other side of the channel. Then he took out his cell phone and held it above his head as he swam to the other side. The water was cold and the current was more powerful than it had looked on the surface. As he neared the middle portion of the channel, his feet could not touch the bottom and he was surprised at the depth and the strong current.

Once on the other side, he gathered up the darts and the rifle and started up the hill. The rain was still coming down hard and the side of the hill was slick and muddy. Each time he tried to climb up the steep banks of the hill, he would slide back down. After several tries, he threw the tranquilizer darts down and used the barrel of the rifle to dig into the side of the hill as he climbed up. But still he slid down again.

On the next try, Zephaniah Pike threw the rifle down as well. He took off his shoes and socks and again started up the hill. With his bare hands, he dug into the slippery soil and left big enough holes so that he could use them to dig his feet into the hillside as he climbed higher. At one point he was eye-level to a small hole in the side of the hill that looked deep and was dripping with mud. He heard strange rattling sounds and feared the hole might be a rattlesnake den. But then he remembered that Elk had told them that kingfishers made their homes in the side of the great hill. The coarse rattling sound reminded him of how Elk would shake his rattle as he called out the name of the kingfisher when he sang each morning.

Despite the heavy rain and muddy slopes, Pike was able to finally pull himself up to a place on the hill where there were trees. He used the trees to support himself as he went from one to another. He would grab hold of a tree, take a couple of breaths, then reach out and try to grasp a branch that enabled him to reach another tree. He kept this up until he was near the top of the hill.

Peering down, he could see both boats in the river bottom below. He could even see the tarps in both boats. He was amazed at how far up he had climbed and at how small the boats looked from the top of High Point.

Zephaniah Pike took out his cell phone, and as he did so he saw a large boulder on top of the hill. For a few seconds, he struggled with himself. He wanted to make the call right away, but there was another part of him that drove him toward the rock.

He went over to the large boulder, looked down at it, and saw a rather ordinary-looking rock. But he remembered what Elk told him, so he said "a teapot," and then gave those two words a slightly differ-ent pronunciation so that it sounded more like *"Atipat."* He quickly went through his pockets and could feel coins, keys, and an old money clip. In his back pockets, he had a wallet and a comb and a hand-kerchief. In his right pants pocket, he had something else. He took out Travis's track medal and looked at it for a long time. He ran his fingers over the surface of the medal, as if memorizing every detail before pressing it into the grassy soil at the foot of the rock. Then the agent placed both his hands on the rock and took a deep breath. He remained in that position for a few seconds before getting up.

Now the agent turned and faced the west. It was still raining but not as hard. He took out his cell phone, opened it, and dialed the FSPD office in Columbus. It took a few moments, but he heard a voice on the other end. It was barely audible. Pike spoke into the cell phone, saying every word slowly and deliberately.

"Agent Pike here. We have an emergency situation. Two individuals are down and two others are hurt. We are in two boats at the base of a large hill on the south side of the Platte River known as High Point. Send a medical team immediately. We have an emergency situation here. Do you read me?"

It continued to thunder even as Pike talked into his cell phone. He had to repeat his entire message, due to the amount of static and other interference.

Finally, an agent in the Columbus FSPD office replied: "We read you, Agent Pike. We have to wait for the storm to let up. Two medical helicopters will be en route shortly. If you have emergency flares, be sure to set them off when you hear the helicopters."

Pike felt relieved and prepared to go back down the hill. But the rain was coming down again, even harder. He had never before experienced a storm such as this one. It seemed to go in successive waves, sending one torrential downpour after another.

As the agent made his way down Hill in the Clouds, he saw a white-tailed deer standing between two cedar trees. The animal was wet, but it had an almost regal look because the raindrops that clung to its velvet-covered antlers glistened like jewels. The deer paid the agent scant attention. The animal had its tongue out and was trying to lap up some of the falling rain.

CHAPTER
37

It was difficult going down the steep and muddy slopes of High Point. At times, Zephaniah Pike crouched down and let himself slide, but each time that he did so he tried to grab hold of a tree or even a clump of grass to keep him from going down too fast. About midway down the hill, he stopped briefly to rest. He could see the two boats. The agent was relieved to see a hunched-over figure under the tarp of the first boat. He worried that Elk might try to do something foolish.

More thunder could be heard and it was even louder now. And the rain poured down with fresh intensity.

As Pike let himself slide down again, he lost his balance and slid all the way into the river. The current was even stronger now, and the agent struggled as he tried to get to the other side of the channel. As he swam and tried to keep himself afloat, he remembered something from his college days. He was competing in the 1,500 meter event and it was raining hard. He just closed his eyes and ran as fast as his legs could carry him. And before he knew it, he had finished and won. Now, when Zephaniah Pike opened his eyes, he was almost on the other side. He got out of the water and dragged himself over to the first boat to check on Elk. He could see a figure under the tarp in the boat, but it was very still.

Pike shook himself off and quickly climbed into the boat. He peered under the tarp, but he could not find Elk. The old man's king-fisher staff was propped up in the front of the boat, holding up the tarp. Only Artemis was there. The dog looked up at Pike but barely wagged its tail. Pike pulled back the tarp so that he could see more clearly and spotted Elk's jacket and shoes. The black and white high tops looked completely different, for they were now discolored and caked with blood. The moon shell pendant that Pike had given Elk lay near the old man's shoes. There was blood on the moon shell. The agent also saw a trail of blood that led from the boat to the river's edge.

"Elk!" Pike called out. "Elk!"

Now Pike ran to the second boat.

"Hotaru! Did you see Elk?"

Dr. Hotaru lifted the tarp and shook her head. She was still cra-dling Vogel in her arms.

"I think Elk dove into the river," Pike shouted. "He told me he buried his girlfriend's body here and that this is where the underwater animal lodge is. He really sounded out of it. But listen, help is on the way. Until then, I've got to find Elk. Stay here and see if you can set off a flare after this rain lets up. But don't do it 'til you hear the chop-pers. Okay?"

Hotaru nodded and began searching the boat's supplies with her free hand.

"Zeph!" she shouted. "Wait 'til help gets here. Zeph!"

The agent ran back to the boat and hoped that maybe Elk had re-turned. But only Artemis was in the boat. Pike made sure the dog was completely covered by the tarp. Then he removed his shirt and pants and threw the sopping clothes into the boat.

Zephaniah Pike looked at the water that flowed directly beneath High Point. The water was brown and murky and here and there he could see a small whirlpool. He looked up to the top of the high hill and then looked back down at the water.

Without hesitating another second, the agent took a deep breath and dove into the river. The water felt cold at first, and then became strangely warm. There was a strong undercurrent, but he managed to make his way to the other side. He was amazed at how quiet it was under the water, in contrast to the crashing thunder and falling rain that could be heard above the surface.

The water turned darker again as he felt for the sides of the riverbank and dislodged some of the soil. There were numerous dead branches and tree roots that protruded out of the base of High Point, and he tried to dodge these or brush them away as he looked for an opening. He was running out of air, so he quickly swam up toward the surface. But as he did so, he hit a large branch and it nearly knocked him unconscious.

He took in water as he struggled to get away and swim to the surface. Every now and then he felt a hailstone in the water. Suddenly, the current took him back toward the riverbank and into a clump of tree roots. As he fought to free himself, he felt himself swept in still a different direction.

When he finally was able to get air, it was not on the surface but in a place deep beneath the water. He had found a breathing hole, but it was completely dark and he hardly had space to turn around. He held onto some tree roots as he coughed up water and tried to clear his throat and lungs. He coughed for a long time, and each time he did so he could hear a faint echo. The side of his head throbbed from having hit the tree branch and he could taste his own blood. The agent rested for a few moments and tried to decide what to do. The pain in the side of his head was excruciating, and he felt like the small space that he was in was closing in on him.

"Elk!" Zephaniah Pike called out. "Elk!" Again he could hear his voice echo, but it was a strange-sounding echo. It seemed to go in all directions at once.

"Elk!" he called out again. "Elk!"

Pike could still feel the hailstones as he splashed about and tried to free himself. And he continued to taste blood. All of this seemed oddly familiar. Then it came to him. He remembered a dream that he had shortly before coming to Nebraska. He was running in the darkness and fell into a pool of blood and ice. In his dream, he struggled to get away and now, in the stormy and bloody waters of the Platte, he tried to extricate himself as well.

Zephaniah felt increasingly weak and disoriented. He took in several deep breaths. The throbbing in his head felt like drumming. His heart was beating fast and he could feel every single beat. The sound of his heart seemed amplified in the dark breathing hole, as if his heart was beating in rhythm with something that was even larger and more powerful.

Then he saw his wife Darla Ann. She was nodding in an exasperated kind of way and smiling. At her side stood their daughter Twila. They were clowning around on the beach and laughing at each other.

"Darla!" Pike called out. "Darla!"

He struggled and again tried to free himself, but still he could barely move.

"Twila!" the agent cried. "Twila!"

The faces of his wife and daughter faded. But now he saw his son Travis. They were playing basketball at a park in Ocean City. Travis kept running up close, trying to take away the ball. He was nose to nose with his father and he was smiling.

"Travis," he said. But he did not shout the name. He said it very softly: "Travis."

The face of his dead son soon faded into darkness as well. The agent saw a trickle of water that ran into the clay-lined banks of tiny Calico Creek. He watched as the creek water rose and then merged with the wide waters of the Platte.

Now the agent saw himself standing on a sandbar in the river, directly in front of several tall concrete pillars. On the first pillar was the figure of a diamond, surrounded by orange and red flames of fire. On the second concrete pillar was a faded image of Christopher Columbus. The famous explorer was looking up and reaching out with hands that were extremely delicate and pale. On the third pillar a Spanish friar could be seen. The tonsured priest carried a cross and he was running. Arrows protruded from his body. As the priest ran, he pulled up his blue robe and used it as a shield. On the fourth pillar there were words written on the concrete column, and the words were written in blood. With each beat of his heart, Zephaniah Pike could feel the words pulsate and drip with fresh blood. The agent now repeated the words over and over.

"Miserére nobis. Miserére nobis. Miserére nobis!"

Suddenly the fourth concrete pillar changed into the trunk of a great tree and the tree slowly shriveled into a tall, slender stick. At the top of the stick was a long-billed bird with a ragged crest of feathers on its head.

Zephaniah Pike smiled to himself, for he recognized the odd-looking bird. It was the kingfisher.

The agent could feel a warm sensation. The pain in his head no longer felt so unbearable. Even though he was still unable to get out of the air hole and free himself, he suddenly felt better. He could barely feel his arms or his legs.

He began to sing, very softly at first, but then louder. And as he sang, his breathing and the rapid beating of his heart slowed. The darkness no longer seemed so terrifying. And the hole in which he found himself no longer seemed to be closing in on him. He felt like he was being embraced and the sensation was soothing.

The song that Zephaniah Pike sang comforted him. He listened to the words echo, and they went back and forth, like the slow movements of a graceful but determined little bird:

> "Kingfisher, Kingfisher,
> Little Brother, hear us!
> Carry our message far.
> The pitiful ones are here. . . ."

CHAPTER
38

Dr. Hotaru lifted the tarp and looked in the direction where she last saw Agent Pike. The rain was still falling and she worried that if the torrential downpour continued, both boats might be swept away.

She had found two flares in the boat but was careful not to get them wet. She kept peering out from under the tarp, hoping to get a glimpse of Pike or Elk.

Dr. Hotaru held onto Jake Vogel, and as she did so she felt a strange sensation whenever she pulled the agent's body close to hers. The heat of his body felt comforting, but she kept wondering about many things as she waited for the rain to let up.

When family members or friends asked why Susan Hotaru was still single, she would tell them: "I don't want a personal relationship. I prefer to depend on myself. And I don't want children. My articles and books will be my pride and joy." She had wanted to be independent and go in a completely different direction than that of her parents and grandparents. Family and tradition would not dominate her life. Any gaps left by shirking family and tradition would be filled by scholarship and the academic community.

Dr. Hotaru's decision to devote her life to science had caused problems between her and both of her parents. She loved them and had tried, in her own way, to make them proud. Susan was an only child and at first her parents had encouraged her in nearly every academic undertaking. But after she earned her Ph.D., her parents could not understand Susan's decision to take a job in far-off Nebraska and to live the rest of her life as a single woman.

The last time Susan Hotaru saw her parents was five years before, when they made the long drive from Seattle to Lincoln. They stayed with her for a week, and during that time they attended some of her lectures and met some of her colleagues at the university. But each evening seemed to end on the same discordant note. She and her parents would talk about her future and they would argue. Susan would stand her ground and assert her independence. Night after night, her father would shake his head and give his daughter a hurtful look before going to bed. Susan's mother would cry and plead with her to find a university job closer to Seattle and to try to have both a career and a family.

"I'm making a good life for myself here," Susan would counter. But her mother, with reddened eyes and a crumpled ball of wet tissue in each hand, stood in front of her only child and kept asking, "Are you sure that's what you're doing?"

The last night of her parents' week-long visit had been the worst. Her father said he was tired and disgusted and so he went to bed early. Susan and her mother argued until well past midnight. It ended with a kitchen table covered with crumpled balls of tissue. The next morning, Susan Hotaru was actually relieved to see her parents put their suitcases in their car and head west. But less than three hours later, she was called out of class and informed that her mother and father had been killed in a car-truck accident near Kearney, Nebraska. In the months following, Susan Hotaru felt numb. After her parents' estate was settled, she threw herself into her work as never before. During the past five years, she tried not to think of the words her mother so often had repeated: "Are you sure that's what you're doing?"

Yet only the night before, Susan Hotaru had heard those same words again. And she did not hear them in her mind. She heard them when the mysterious woman with the constantly changing hats had asked Dr. Hotaru: "Are you sure that's what you're doing?" Why, the scientist wondered, did the mysterious woman choose these same words? Susan Hotaru tried to put the haunting words out of her mind, but she could not. What was it about this river that seemed to summon and draw forth the restless spirits of the dead?

As Hotaru clutched Vogel's body close to hers, she alternated between feeling extremely warm and extremely cold. The sudden, ever-changing sensations confused and disoriented her. Horrible thoughts with hawk-like wings and talons swooped down on her and seemed to dig their way deep into her scalp. Try as she might, she could not shake them off.

The scientist's clothes and hands were covered with Jake Vogel's blood and her own. But her real concern was that there might be other blood on her hands, the kind of blood that could not be washed away. When she tried to stop Vogel from discharging his gun during the hawk attack, she may have been responsible for shooting Elk. Vogel had his arm raised high in the air, but it was Hotaru who pulled the agent's arm down as he fired his gun.

Yes, Hotaru told herself, it was Vogel who took out his firearm and did the shooting. But the scientist feared that it was she who had inadvertently aimed the weapon in Elk's direction and caused him serious injury. What if Elk were dying or had already died? The mere thought of this possibility caused Hotaru to become nauseous and to groan and cry out. But, sick as she was, she could not vomit any more than she could expel the terrible thoughts that tormented her.

As Hotaru agonized and waited, she thought of Elk and Pike and Vogel. And she thought of the events of the past few days. All these things swirled around in her mind like the little whirlpools of leaves and broken twigs that churned past her in the rising waters of the river.

The rain was drizzling now and Vogel was murmuring in his sleep. The effects of the tranquilizer were wearing off. Hotaru held up the tarp and could see the rain coming straight down. After years of drought, the Platte Valley was now getting an unbelievable amount of moisture.

Peering through the rain, Susan Hotaru saw some movement over by the first boat. The vertical sheets of rain made everything look fuzzy and shadow-like, but she watched as two dark figures carried a body out of the river and then placed it in the boat. The two youthful figures appeared to be naked and each had black, waist-length hair. She could not see their faces, but she was able to tell that one was male and the other was female. Hotaru looked on as the figures lifted Artemis out of the boat. Then the shadowy figures hurried away, with Artemis running behind them.

The scientist was almost too stunned to utter even a word of protest. It took several moments, but finally she lifted the tarp higher and called out: "Hey! Hey there! We need help!"

A few minutes passed, and as the rain finally began to let up Hotaru pushed Vogel up into a half-sitting position. She made sure the flares were nearby and that they were dry and ready to go.

Then Hotaru climbed out of the boat. She was stiff and barely could walk. But she limped over to the other boat and looked inside. To her relief, she saw the body of Agent Pike. His eyes were closed and his body was wet and completely still. She tried to take his pulse, but her hands were cold and trembling. So she leaned down and put her right ear to his chest. His body felt extremely cold, but at last she heard the beating of his heart.

As the scientist stood up, she heard something else. She was not sure at first, but then she recognized it: the distant sound of approaching helicopters.

CHAPTER 39

It took a long time for him to open his eyes. When he finally did so, he opened them very slowly, allowing in only a tiny amount of light.

"Zeph!" a voice called out. The force of that voice compelled Pike to close his eyes again, even though he now could see light through both of his eyelids.

"Zeph!" the voice called out again. The agent finally recognized the voice. It was that of Douglas Kerrington.

Pike slowly opened his eyes and he could see the round, bald head of his boss.

"Welcome back, Zeph!" Kerrington said with a wink and a smile.

Zephaniah Pike opened his eyes wider and tried to adjust to all the light. He was groggy and his mouth was extremely dry. He motioned for water and a nurse who was standing nearby held a straw and a glass of ice water up to his mouth.

The agent took in a few drops of water and, as he did so, he noticed that it was light outside and that rows of raindrops clung to the window like strands of transparent pearls.

"You're in the hospital in Norfolk, Nebraska," Kerrington said, his voice no longer sounding so distant or so loud.

"You took quite a blow to your head and you look like you were at the center of a pretty vicious cock fight. But you're going to be okay.

So just lay there and try to rest."

Kerrington looked on and motioned for his agent not to try to speak.

"How's everyone?" Pike asked, but getting out those two words was harder than he had anticipated.

"You better rest," Kerrington urged. "We'll talk later."

"Tell me," Pike persisted. "How is everyone?"

Douglas Kerrington asked the nurse to leave so that he and his agent could talk alone. As soon as Kerrington heard the heavy hospital door close, he faced the other agent and spoke to him in a very formal tone of voice.

"Agent Pike, you've been involved in a special project of the FSPD. What is the name and number of this project?"

Zephaniah Pike closed his eyes and then spoke very slowly, so that he would not have to repeat the words again. To repeat the code name of a special project was never done.

"Fire Diamond eight-two-zero," Zephaniah said. As he uttered each of the words and numbers, he continued to close his eyes and he briefly saw the image of a diamond surrounded by orange and red flames of fire.

"Yes," Douglas Kerrington answered. "That's correct. Now I'll give you a quick update. Agent Vogel is in another room recuperating from surgery. It was touch and go for awhile, but the doctors say he should be alright. Dr. Hotaru needed a few stitches, but she's already on her feet. She's waiting to talk to you."

"What about Elk?" Pike asked. "How is Elk?"

Kerrington's expression changed as he answered.

"We couldn't find him, Zeph. According to Dr. Hotaru, Mr. Elk may have been accidentally shot during the hawk attack, but it's pretty clear the cause of his death was drowning and that his body was swept away during the storm. None of you is responsible. Accidents happen and fair-minded people understand that. But in any case, our agents are on it and they are still looking."

"Did you search the base of High Point?"

"Yes," Kerrington replied. "We sent several divers in, but they could find no trace of him. With all the broken branches and tree roots it was like an obstacle course down there. But no, they couldn't find him. I'm sorry."

"Did the divers find anything? Did they find any bodies at all?"

Douglas Kerrington was completely thrown by Pike's last question, but he raised his eyebrows slightly and then let it pass without seeking additional clarification.

"They didn't find anything," Kerrington answered. "Dr. Hotaru said there was supposed to be some kind of underwater cave at the base of High Point. But other than a few nooks and crannies, the divers could locate no cave. By the way, one of the local divers was a man by the name of Wright—Justin Wright. He said he knew Mr. Elk and that he had met both you and Dr. Hotaru a few days ago in Columbus. Quite a coincidence, don't you think?"

Pike did not respond, but he blinked his eyes to indicate he was thinking about everything he was hearing.

Douglas Kerrington stiffened and then reached into the pocket of his suit jacket.

"Our investigative team went over the whole area and even searched the top of High Point. They did find this," Kerrington said, and he held out a small medal with a ribbon.

"You must have dropped it when you made that call for help," Kerrington explained. "It belongs to you, doesn't it?"

Zephaniah Pike took the medal in his hand and his fingers slowly closed around it. But he did not look at it. He simply held the medal tight and nodded.

"What's happening out there?" Pike asked as he looked at the rain-covered hospital window.

"They were supposed to spray the valley today. But the spraying has been postponed. Our scientists tell us this series of successive rainstorms happens only once or twice in a century. Undoubtedly, it is yet another sign of 'climatic crisis.' The experts claim that sudden downpours like this one sometimes occur in areas that have been experiencing a long and serious drought. The rainfall has been so great in some areas of the valley that there has been lowland flooding. So the mass evacuation turned out to be quite fortuitous. It probably saved a lot of lives. And most of those people who were hospitalized with high fevers are improving. Seems they were suffering from a very extreme form of heatstroke. The medical researchers here in Nebraska have even given this disorder a name—TDTT. That's the new acronym for 'Triple-Digit Temperature Trauma.' But now things are cooling off and everything is slowly getting back to normal."

"What about the rest of the recovery team?" Pike asked, still clutching his son's medal.

"They're fine. The sudden storm forced them to stop their work, but they were able to collect quite a few specimens of wildlife. But none of that would have been possible without your group's efforts, of course."

Douglas Kerrington stared at Agent Pike for a long time.

"We got real worried about you and your team, Zeph. Right before that storm moved in, I sent out one of our surveillance drones to make sure you all were okay. But that drone must have gotten off course due to the storm. We lost track of it and we're still unsure what happened to it."

"It was a hawk," Pike muttered. "A hawk took it out."

Kerrington raised his eyebrows and then stroked his chin in a slow downward motion. "A hawk, you say? A single hawk?"

There was a light knocking at the door and Kerrington immediately went over to send the visitor away. But when Pike heard Hotaru's voice, he asked that she be allowed to enter.

"Don't you think you should get some rest?" Kerrington asked Pike.

"I'll rest better once I know how everyone is," the agent answered.

When Susan Hotaru entered the room, she carried a floral arrangement of daisies and miniature sunflowers. She placed the flowers beside the hospital bed and smiled at Pike.

"You're a sight for sore eyes," Hotaru said.

Pike had to laugh a little, for there were numerous scratches near Hotaru's eyes and all across her face and neck.

"Sore eyes, indeed," Pike said softly. "But don't tell me I look worse than you do."

"Well, you're the one who is bandaged up and lying in a hospital bed," she teased. "So just imagine! But I'm relieved you're awake and talking. How are you, Zeph?"

The agent nodded, yet he did not know what to say. But there was something on his mind.

"They can't find Elk," he finally said.

"Yes, I know," Hotaru replied. "But try not to worry. Everything that Elk helped us with was not in vain. I've been going over the initial lab reports from the animals we helped bring in. There is no evidence for any kind of contagious disease. But the animals that were so aggressive may have been suffering from chemical poisoning."

"Chemical poisoning?" Pike asked.

"Yes," Dr. Hotaru repeated. "Silver iodide." But as she said the two words, she looked directly at Agent Pike and gave him a slight Kerrington-style wink, so that only Zeph could see it. Then she continued her explanation in a very detached and academic-sounding voice.

"It appears local officials have been using massive amounts of silver iodide up and down the Platte Valley the past couple of years to seed clouds and artificially try to produce rainfall. The silver iodide also included some suspicious additives. And guess who has been behind most of the cloud seeding?"

Agent Pike shook his head slightly to indicate he had no idea.

"Senator Rawlins. And he just happens to be the major owner of Triple R Aviation. It's the same company that was scheduled to spray the valley and kill all the wildlife today. So this new information has been causing an awful lot of debate and discussion. The EPA and various other environmental groups are demanding a full investigation. I think Elk would be very pleased to see everything that has come to light."

"If only Elk were here to see it," Pike said. "I don't think he would have been too surprised to hear about Rawlins and his financial interests. It always seems to boil down to that. Money trumps everything."

"Not everything," Dr. Hotaru answered. And she sounded like she meant it.

Susan Hotaru looked at Zephaniah Pike for a long time without saying another word. Despite the scratches on her face, her eyes had a new and strangely different look.

"Zeph," the scientist finally said as she leaned closer. Her voice was only a whisper now. "I really need to tell you something else, something that I saw—"

"I think we should talk later," Kerrington interrupted. "This is all a bit much for Agent Pike. He needs to get more rest."

"No," Pike answered, and he did not care if he sounded obstinate. "Tell me what you saw, Susan. Please. I want to know."

Hotaru looked at Kerrington, but he turned away and went over to the window, as if he wanted nothing to do with the conversation.

"After you dove into the river looking for Elk," Hotaru began, "I waited for you to come back. It continued to rain and rain. I waited a long time. Then, as the rain let up, I saw two figures carrying something out of the river and put it into your boat. That 'something' was you, Zeph. After that, the two individuals both turned away and left. And Artemis followed them, with her tail wagging."

Zephaniah Pike blinked several times and looked at Hotaru with disbelief. She was smiling and her eyes were filled with light.

"Who were they?" he asked.

"A young man and a young woman," Hotaru answered. "They were wet and naked. They looked Indian, but I couldn't really tell. After they put you in the boat, they just ran off in the rain. I called out to them, but they didn't turn around and they didn't answer. They just ran off like it was all so natural and they were the only two people in the world."

"But who were they?" Zeph asked again.

"Do you remember anything that happened when you dove into the water?" Hotaru asked.

"I got trapped and I couldn't get out," Zeph answered. "That's the last thing I remember."

"But you were under the water for such a long time. I never saw you come up for air even once."

"I couldn't get to the surface," the agent said. "I was trapped down there and everything started closing in on me. That's all I remember."

"A sudden crisis has a strange way of playing tricks on a person," Kerrington interrupted. "In a crisis situation, a few seconds can seem like minutes and a few minutes can seem like hours. You both know that." He faced the window as he spoke.

The scientist was silent. But she was staring at Zephaniah Pike and did not even turn around to look at the FSPD director, who was still facing the window as he continued speaking.

"Dr. Hotaru, in terms of the two figures that you saw, maybe you did see them and maybe they did pull Agent Pike out of harm's way. They may have been two Mexican kids who were out skinny-dipping. But our investigative team found no evidence of such individuals. The four of you went through a lot. It will take time, but you'll be able to sort everything out in a rational way. And we'll be here to help you do just that. In fact. . . ."

Susan Hotaru did not say anything in response as the director continued speaking. She simply put her hand over Zephaniah Pike's clenched fist, as if to try to put him at ease. But he was not bracing for a fight. He was deep in thought.

As Agent Pike tried to remember everything, he gripped his dead son's medal tighter and tighter. As he did so, he did not listen to his boss, who was still talking to the window. Zephaniah Pike was trying to hear another sound, the sound of something that had been away for a long time and now was trying very hard to make itself heard. It was the sound of rain.

CHAPTER
40

After several days in the hospital, it felt good to get behind the wheel of a car and just drive. Once he got out of Norfolk, the traffic was light and the driving helped clear his head. Zephaniah Pike took his time and headed south on Highway 81.

Earlier that morning he had stopped in to visit Jake Vogel, who was still recovering in the hospital. There was a floral arrangement of bright purple flowers beside his bed and tucked in the colorful blossoms was a bird ornament and a large, hand-lettered note that proclaimed: "To the Bird Man. Geez Louise!" Vogel was unable to talk much, but before Pike left, the wounded "Bird Man" raised two fingers and flashed his characteristic "V" sign. Outside the hospital entrance, Pike saw Susan Hotaru and she showed him a draft of the preliminary report she had prepared for the Nebraska governor and other officials. She urged that no conclusions be drawn until a lengthy investigation be conducted. Because there had been no animal attacks since the recent deluge, the quarantine had been lifted and Douglas Kerrington already was back in Washington, D.C.

Although it had transpired only minutes before, Zephaniah Pike kept thinking about the conversation he had had with Susan Hotaru near the hospital entrance in Norfolk. He went over every single word, committing each one to memory.

"Do you still think it all boils down to silver iodide and some suspicious additives?" the agent asked.

Instead of answering one way or another, the scientist raised her eyebrows and posed a question of her own.

"Do you still think you pulled yourself out of the river?"

The agent and the scientist faced one another for a long time, searching each other's eyes for the smallest trace of doubt or disbelief.

"No matter what Kerrington or the whole FSPD thinks," Susan Hotaru said, "I know what I saw in that storm. I witnessed it with my own eyes. And things haven't been the same since. Zeph, do you remember what Elk told us that day on the river when he was talking about Grandmother Drought? Do you? Elk said she had the power to turn the whole world upside down so that nothing is ever quite the same again. Well, my worldview has been shaken to its core and now everything looks different. And for me it's a good thing, a really good thing. My life as a scientist is in for quite a change, maybe even a classic paradigm shift. But it's okay. I welcome it. And I feel better now than I have for a long, long time."

Agent Pike smiled, for he indeed could detect a change in Susan Hotaru's eyes and in the sound of her voice.

"Zeph, you really need to go out to Calico Creek and stop at Elk's place. Don't go back to D.C. until you've done that. Promise?"

The agent shrugged his shoulders and extended his right hand. But Susan Hotaru ignored the gesture. She used his outstretched arm to balance herself as she stood on tiptoes and kissed him on the cheek.

Several moments of awkward and prolonged silence followed as the two individuals stood outside the hospital, facing each other and the bright light of day.

"Hang in there," Pike finally said. "No matter how much guff anyone gives you, just stick to your guns and hang in there."

"Come hell or high water?"

"Yep. Come hell or high water."

At the mention of "high water," the agent and the scientist both laughed. It seemed the perfect way to say goodbye.

★ ★ ★ ★

As Zephaniah approached Columbus, he could see people moving back into their homes. Clothes and blankets hung from wash lines and front porches. Puddles of water still could be seen everywhere and the fields along the river looked more alive and much greener.

The agent stopped only briefly at the FSPD office in the hotel in Columbus. Zephaniah Pike talked to some of the agents there and then picked up the last of his reports. Before he left, he stood in the main lobby of the hotel and stared once again at the life-size painting of Christopher Columbus. But as he turned to leave, he glanced back and once again his eyes met those of the dark figures crouching in the background of the picture.

As the agent drove west toward Calico Creek, he could still see the eyes of the dark figures in the Columbus painting. Only as he drove farther and farther west did the eyes gradually fade out of sight. Even though he could not see them so distinctly, he could feel them.

There were many new potholes in the highway, but Zephaniah drove slow enough so that he was able to avoid them. He passed through the tiny town of Calico Creek and then turned down a narrow country road that led toward the river. The wild hemp plants lining the road were no longer dust-covered. They appeared to shine in the sunlight.

The agent smiled to himself as he passed a number of signs that warned against trespassers, hunters, solicitors and proselytizers. He stopped the car when he saw the boldly lettered sign that declared: "ABSOLUTELY NO VISITORS WITHOUT PRIOR APPOINTMENT. CALL FIRST."

Zephaniah Pike took out his cell phone and dialed a number. It rang for a long time and the agent was almost ready to end his call when he finally heard a voice. It sounded like that of a young man.

"Yeah?"

"Is this Elk's Art Studio?"

"Yeah."

"This is Zephaniah Pike. I am a friend of Elk's. Can I stop by for a couple of minutes?"

"Yeah."

Zephaniah drove on and slowly pulled into the yard. A large reddish dog jumped up and began barking. It ran toward the vehicle and snapped at the front tires of the agent's car.

"Artemis!" the agent called out, and as he did so the dog looked up and stopped barking. "Is that you, Artemis? Come here, come here."

The dog wagged its tail as Pike stroked the animal's fur. But he had to do so carefully, for he saw many clumps of dried blood and matted hair that marked wounds on the dog's body.

"We all had quite a time out there, didn't we?" the agent said as he lightly stroked the dog's fur. "Didn't we?" Artemis now lay on her side, so that the agent could scratch her underbelly, which was free of injuries.

The front door of the farmhouse suddenly popped open. Agent Pike jumped at the sound and instinctively reached for his firearm. But the outstretched fingers of his right hand froze in midair.

"Sorry," said a young Indian man with long black hair and intensely dark eyes. "It's just a door opener." He stood on the front steps holding a long piece of lead pipe. "Didn't mean to scare you."

The agent looked at the young man and at the piece of lead pipe in his hands.

"Oh, you must be a relative of Elk's," Zephaniah said.

But the young man did not answer right away. He just looked at the agent for a long time.

"A bunch of Fizz-Pidds and some other suits have been here already," the young man said. "And I answered a lot of questions. I told them that I'm Teddy, a nephew of Elk's. And I told them I'm here to look after my uncle's things."

Zephaniah nodded and then pointed to the car. "I brought some of

Elk's stuff, mostly his camping gear and some carving tools. And his old Army bugle. And the kingfisher staff that he made."

The agent went to the car, took out the items and arranged everything at the feet of the young man.

Zephaniah Pike reached into his pants pocket and took out something else that had been recovered in one of the boats on the river.

"I also want to give you this. I found it on the Platte and gave it to Elk. He told me it was a moon shell pendant and that it was very old. I'm sure you'll know the best place for it. Maybe give it back to the tribe or put it in a museum or something."

As Pike handed over the object, the young man looked down at it and nodded.

"I'm sorry about Elk," the agent said. "He was a good man. And a good teacher. He taught us Fizz-Pidds a lot."

The young Indian man remained quiet and continued to look at the moon shell pendant in his hand.

"You didn't get any flooding out here?" Pike asked.

"No, the house is on fairly high ground. So things stayed pretty dry."

"Are you going to keep the Art Studio going?" the agent inquired.

"*Ahu!* Yeah, we plan to expand this place and invite other Pawnee to come here, so we can reconnect to our old homeland here on the River Platte. It's been a long, long time. Maybe someday the Pawnee people will sing and dance again in Nebraska. And maybe we can teach our White neighbors something, too."

Zephaniah nodded to show he liked what he was hearing.

"You want to come inside?" the young man asked.

"Okay," Zephaniah answered. "But I can't stay too long."

The agent followed the young man into the house. As he walked through the kitchen, Zephaniah Pike noticed the picture of Dick Tracy and also that of the Pawnee man wrapped in a buffalo robe decorated with five-pointed stars. Soon the agent stood in a large sunlit room filled with Elk's carvings and books and the telescope. As the agent looked around, he caught a glimpse of a young woman with long black hair folding clothes in a bedroom. He smiled at her, but she seemed very shy and disappeared from sight.

Pike walked around the room, looking at the various carvings. He paused beside a large carving of two long-legged cranes with small inlaid pieces of scarlet-colored wood. The one crane was hunched down a bit and appeared to be looking up at the other. Pike ran his fingers up and down the piece and simply could not resist touching it.

"That one is called 'Mates for Life,'" the young man said. "Sandhill cranes come to the Platte Valley of Nebraska every spring. They've been doing that for millions of years. They like to travel in pairs and they have their courtship rituals. When they dance with each other, they bow and they are able to jump six feet off the ground. Those sandhill cranes mate for life. But maybe you knew that?"

"Yes," Pike said. "Yes, I do remember hearing that."

The agent felt his fingers twitch as he continued to run them all along the thin necks and long legs of the two cranes. Traces of his sweat could be seen on the grayish wood. Pike did not even notice when the young man went into another room of the house. He could hear him and the young woman talking, but he could not make out what they were saying.

Zephaniah Pike waited for the young man to return, but then the agent decided to go. Before he left the room, he looked at all the carved animals. Each one reminded him of Elk and their recent journey down the Platte.

Outside, Pike petted Artemis again and then the agent got into his car and started it up. As he prepared to drive off, the young man appeared. He went to the agent's automobile, slowly opened the door on the passenger side, and placed the carving of the two sandhill cranes on the car seat.

"This is for you," the young man with the intensely dark eyes said. "Maybe the next time you come here, you'll bring your family? Okay?"

The agent nodded and extended his hand. The young man grasped it and held it for a few moments. Then he stepped back and watched the agent drive away.

As Zephaniah Pike drove eastward, he looked down at the carving of the sandhill cranes. Then he leaned forward a bit and turned off the car's navigational system.

He continued going east and crossed to the south side of the Platte River. He took one country road after another until at last he saw a large hill in the distance.

It took him more than an hour, but he finally found a road that led to the back side of High Point. The road became rough and extremely narrow, but he continued on. Large mud puddles made the driving even more difficult.

When Zephaniah could not drive any farther, he stopped the car and opted to walk in the rest of the way. He took off his gun and holster and placed them under the car seat. Due to the firearm, he decided to lock the vehicle. Then he loosened his tie and removed his suit jacket. He carried the jacket over his left arm as he walked.

At last the agent reached the grassy summit of Hill in the Clouds. From the top of the bluff, he could see for many miles in nearly every direction. He was surprised by the incredible vistas, for the last time he had climbed this same high hill it was during a storm that had blurred and darkened everything around him. Now, in the bright daylight, the lay of the land looked different. But he could still feel the special power of this place.

He looked around and soon spotted the boulder. Finding it was like coming upon an old friend who had been waiting for him. Zephaniah Pike crouched down and placed both his hands on the rock. He felt its craggy shape and ancient scars, but he also felt its warmth. *"Atipat,"* the agent said. "Hello, Grandfather."

The agent reached into his pants pocket and took out his son's track medal. He held the medal in his hand, kissed it, and then buried it in the damp soil beside the rock.

"I gave this to you a few days ago," the agent explained. "I'm sorry it disappeared for a while. The Fizz-Pidds had it. But now I give it back to you. It's yours. Okay? A gift is a gift. See, I do remember that story Elk told us about you, Grandfather. So I don't want you to get upset over my poor manners and come after me. You probably don't need any trouble and I sure don't want any. Besides, it wouldn't be easy explaining to everyone why a big rock is on my tail and chasing me. Right?"

Zephaniah Pike laughed to himself. He was sitting on the ground and conversing with a rock. But he also had to laugh because he remembered the humor in Elk's story about a mischievous coyote being pursued by Grandfather Rock.

The agent marveled at how good it felt to laugh at something that was genuinely funny, and not just in response to what someone else expected. But as he laughed, tears filled his eyes. And then the laughter turned to weeping. Some of his tears fell upon the boulder, spotting and streaking the rough, time-weathered exterior of Grandfather Rock. For a long time, the man sat beside his old friend and wept.

In the midst of his anguish, the birds in the nearby trees became very quiet. But when the agent dried the last of his tears with the back of his hand, the birds began to sing again.

Zephaniah stood up and brushed off the loose soil from his hands and clothes. He was still carrying his suit jacket and wished he had left it in the car.

The agent felt a shadow pass over him, and so he shielded his eyes from the sun and looked up into the sky. High overhead was a bald eagle. Despite its great size and the events of the past few days, Zephaniah Pike was not afraid of the magnificent bird.

The eagle glided through the sky, its outstretched wings reflecting the brilliance of the summer sun. The man watched the eagle until it became a small dot in the great blue wall of the western sky.

Zephaniah looked down at the rock and at a big bur oak that stood nearby. A few catalpa trees also could be seen, with their broad, heart-shaped leaves. Cedar trees of various sizes seemed to be growing everywhere, and some of them still glistened with the moisture of the recent storm. The fragrance of the cedars drew the man closer, and so he grasped the prickly ends of their branches and made his way to the north end of the bluff.

Peering through the trees, Zephaniah caught a glimpse of the rejuvenated river down below. He remembered what Elk had said only a few days before, that if God were a river, God would be the Platte. Zephaniah nodded appreciatively, for the sprawling Platte now seemed a whole half-mile wide and it had a majestic and even omnipotent appearance. Despite its legendary shallowness, he knew the river harbored more than its share of ancient mysteries and secrets.

For a long time, Zephaniah Pike stood on the great hill overlooking the Platte. He gazed down at the resplendent, slow-moving waters of the river. His eyes also took in the vegetation that blanketed the hill. There was a radiance about the foliage, an almost youthful glow and a new exuberance. Everything, from the tallest tree to the tiniest stem of prairie grass, seemed to quiver and pulse with life.

Before he left High Point, the agent went to the far edge of the bluff and waved to the Platte. He remembered how Elk had done this only a few days before, and so Zephaniah extended his right arm and made a slow, complete circle as he outlined its shape with the tips of his fingers.

When Zephaniah started down Hill in the Clouds, he sensed a lightness in his every step. Yet he knew it was not because he was heading downhill. As he took each step, he became keenly aware that he was on a different kind of assignment. This one was more like a mission, a true recovery mission. Zephaniah Pike was going home.

WAITING

Down by the river, peering through the tall grass, she waited.

She prided herself in her ability to wait, even if this meant waiting for many days and nights. During such times, Ahwa did not eat or sleep. Sometimes, she barely even moved.

As she waited, she watched everything around her with keen interest. Nothing escaped her attention: the twirling-down of a cottonwood leaf, the dance of a swallowtail butterfly, the meanderings of a young muskrat.

But it was the Two-Leggeds that aroused her curiosity the most, for they were the hardest to understand.

She listened intently to the harsh sounds the Two-Leggeds made. Ahwa knew that some of them would cry out "Kai-yoht!" At least that was the excited sound they made whenever they saw her: "Kai-yoht!" But that strange cry was as alien to her as the Two-Leggeds themselves. She knew who she was. She was Awakened by the Thunder, a member of the Star Singer Nation of First Prophetess. Theirs was among the oldest groups that inhabited the land of the Great Flat Water. Their nation included many renowned hunters, shape-shifters, and warriors.

Ahwa and many of her relatives had been in battles that involved the Two-Leggeds. Only a few days previous, she had shown herself to one of their war parties. The Two-Leggeds were armed with miniature poison arrows. She ran out before them in an attempt to confuse them, so that they would use up all their arrows.

Despite her agile movements, Ahwa was struck by one of the small poison arrows. The arrow landed close to her backbone and thus she was unable to reach back and remove the wicked-looking thing with her teeth.

After Ahwa was hit, she crept into the willows and it was there on the parched banks of the Great Flat Water that she died.

Later that same day, in the midst of a ferocious storm, she was reborn. When Ahwa came back to life, she opened her eyes to a world filled with thunder and lightning and hailstones and rain.

It seemed like a strange dream, but she knew it had not been a dream. The small, red-colored arrow was still embedded in her back and now it marked her as a warrior who had returned from battle. But the arrow also marked her as one who had returned from the dead. Perhaps more than anything, the arrow was a sign that her power was stronger than that of the Two-Leggeds.

One of her grandmothers and teachers, Many Hats Changing, had bestowed the name "Awakened by the Thunder" shortly after Ahwa came into the world. She often wondered about that name. But now she knew the name was a prophetic one. She had awakened from the dead during a great thunderstorm. And today, she never felt more awake or more alive. Ahwa closed her eyes and gave thanks. The Gods of the Wild be praised!

Ahwa did not know if she would ever have to face the Two-Leggeds again. But she knew if she did, she would be willing to fight and to give up her life a hundred times over.

For now, things were quiet in the valley of the Great Flat Water. The recent rainstorm had helped cool the hearts of those who wanted to avenge their dead. The rising floodwaters had washed over the blood-stained banks of the river and even swept away many of the decaying bodies.

Ahwa doubted that the peace would last. A great war still might come. And thus the Star Singer Nation of First Prophetess had to be strong-hearted and ready.

Perhaps, Ahwa thought, the Two-Leggeds were so blinded by hate that they did not realize every one of the earth's creatures had a soul.

The Two-Leggeds were indeed crafty and clever. But were they wise? What if they lacked the concept of a soul? Were the Two-Leggeds then to be pitied? Ahwa was certain of only one thing: A time would come when there would be a calling forth, a gathering of all the souls, and a day of reckoning.

As Ahwa peered through the tall grass, she remembered an old, old song. It was a song that gave her much comfort and strength. She could hear the song whenever she closed her amber eyes and listened to the sound of the river.

> *"A new day is coming!"*
> *Sings the Painted Turtle Nation.*
> *"A new day is coming!"*
> *Sings the Great Blue Heron.*
> *"A new day is coming!"*
> *Sings the Red Fox Nation.*
> *"A new day is coming!"*
> *Sings the Spotted Sandpiper.*
>
> *"Ahhh," sings the great river,*
> *"I hear you, my children.*
> *A new day is coming!*
> *Then let us wait and see.*
> *Yes, let us wait and see*
> *Just when, just when,*
> *This new day will be.*
> *Sha-ya-loh!"*

NOTES &
ACKNOWLEDGMENTS

O*nce Upon the River Platte* is a work of fiction, filled with imaginary characters and events. The book was inspired by the Platte River country of central and eastern Nebraska. Riverine towns like Central City, Clarks, Columbus, and Fremont do exist; but others, like Calico Creek, Ferdinand, Isabella, and River Junction, are fictional.

Large numbers of Pawnee Indians did live along the Platte and Loup Rivers for many generations. As the fictional character Elk relates, the Pawnee were pressured to leave their small Nebraska reservation and move to Oklahoma in the mid-1870s.

While living in their ancestral homeland, the Pawnee people believed that there were sacred animal lodges that were located along the Platte and other rivers. "Hill in the Clouds" (or High Point) is fictional, but it was inspired by traditional beliefs and stories relating to *"Pahaku"* and other sacred animal lodges. Important background information about these sites can be found in the article "Pawnee Geography: Historical and Sacred," by Douglas R. Parks and Waldo R. Wedel (*Great Plains Quarterly 5* [Summer 1985], pp. 143-178) and Peter Nabokov's book *Where the Lightning Strikes: The Lives of American Indian Sacred Places* (New York: Viking, 2006), pp. 169-187.

There really is a huge mural in the public library in Columbus, Nebraska, that depicts the historic Villasur battle between the Spanish and the Pawnee that occurred in August 1720. The original bison hide painting is even more impressive and can be viewed in the Palace of the Governors in Santa Fe, New Mexico. For more information about the Segesser II hide painting and the Villasur battle, see the book *Indian Skin Paintings from the American Southwest* (1970) by the Swiss scholar Gottfried Hotz.

Several of the narratives told by Elk in *Once Upon the River Platte* are adaptations of stories recorded by early anthropologists and other writers. A version of "Coyote and the Rolling Stone," for example, was related by the Pawnee storyteller Leading-Sun and was recorded by George A. Dorsey in his book, *The Pawnee: Mythology* (1906). Dorsey also included a lengthy version of the story about the Pawnee man who kills his own son. Different tellings of this important story and additional background information appear in Melvin R. Gilmore's *Prairie Smoke* (1929), George Bird Grinnell's *Pawnee Hero Stories and Folk-Tales* (1899), James R. Murie's *Ceremonies of the Pawnee* (1981), and Gene Weltfish's *The Lost Universe: Pawnee Life and Culture* (1965). The story of the Pawnee warrior Pahukatawa is recounted in Grinnell's *Pawnee Hero Stories and Folk-Tales* and also in George E. Hyde's *The Pawnee Indians* (1974).

Pawnee source words and phrases are based on Murie (1981), Weltfish (1965), Douglas R. Parks' *A Grammar of Pawnee* (1976), Douglas R. Parks and Lula Nora Pratt's *A Dictionary of Skiri Pawnee* (2008), the AISRI South Band Pawnee online dictionary (Indiana University), and the recent Pawnee linguistic work done by Taylor D. Moore and Zachary J. Rice. Both Taylor and Zachary reviewed my working list of Pawnee words and expressions, making many helpful suggestions. In the interest of readability, however, I spelled and spaced apart some of the Pawnee words (as Elk might have done). I also sought to use mainly South Band Pawnee words and phrases that would enhance the conversational portions of the book, and the larger Platte River story.

A multi-talented individual who contributed greatly to this work is Warren ("Jr.") Pratt, a member of the Pawnee Nasharo/Resaru Chiefs Council. Warren has taught for many years at Pawnee Nation College in Pawnee, Oklahoma. His intimate familiarity with Pawnee culture and language, including the two main Pawnee dialects (Skidi and South Band), is truly impressive. I feel very fortunate to have benefitted from Warren's guidance, knowledge, and wisdom. In appreciation, a portion of the profits from the sale of this book will go toward Pawnee language and culture programs that are aimed at youth and are sponsored by the Pawnee Nation of Oklahoma. The future of the *"Chatiks si Chatiks"* clearly is dependent on its young people and the Pawnee generations that will follow.

In June 2009, a hope expressed by one of my fictional Pawnee characters was partially realized. Head Chief Pat Leading Fox, Sr., and a large delegation of Pawnee people from Oklahoma visited Nebraska and participated in a grand celebration at the Great Platte River Road Archway near Kearney. My wife Rosalinda and I were fortunate to witness the 2009 Pawnee "homecoming." There was dancing, singing, storytelling, handshakes, hugs, laughter, and tears. The day following the historic event, it was our privilege to host Warren Pratt and several young Pawnee and show them sites of tribal significance along Nebraska's Platte and Loup Rivers. Members of the group included: Adam, Anna, Ben, Berwin, Cassie, Christa, Christina, Cora, Jennae, Joseph, Julia, Randall, and Stephanie. The interest and good-naturedness of the young people impressed us immensely.

I also want to acknowledge Marshall R. Gover, a past Pawnee Nation president. I first met him several years ago at the annual U.S. Indian School Reunion in Genoa, Nebraska. Marshall is viewed by many as a goodwill ambassador for the Pawnee people, since he travels widely and always seems willing to share insights about his tribe's heritage and history. It was from Marshall that I finally obtained a rare, thumb-worn copy of "the little green book," Frances Densmore's *Pawnee Music* (published in 1929 by the Bureau of American Ethnology).

The area in northeastern Colorado where I was born actually lies within the western portions of the old Pawnee homeland. Not surprisingly, the name "Pawnee" is memorialized in a number of Colorado landmarks and sites: Pawnee Buttes, Pawnee Creek, Pawnee Pass, Pawnee Hills, Pawnee Ditch, Pawnee Pioneer Trails, and the Pawnee National Grassland.

Indeed, the genesis of this book goes back more than sixty years to when I was growing up on the high plains of Colorado. Our family lived in the South Platte Valley and the river was within easy walking distance. By the time I was ten, I knew every bend and channel of the river that flowed just east of our farm.

As a youngster, I had frequent bouts of tonsillitis. Once, when I was fighting an especially high fever, I dreamt that I entered a cool, comfortable animal lodge under the nearby waters of the South Platte. There, I watched a variety of animals dance. They did so in a curious back-and-forth fashion that was both hypnotic and soothing. I experienced this unusual dream long before I ever heard anything about animal lodge sites in the Platte River Country. Now, more than six decades later, I still remember every detail of that strange and wonderful dream.

Many other personal experiences and various books, articles, and essays have impacted and shaped the writing of this novel. Homer's *The Odyssey* is but one of many formative influences. The great epic is now nearly three thousand years old, and its powerful message still reverberates today.

Perhaps every individual who writes a book, whether fiction or nonfiction, also owes a debt of gratitude to an extremely large number of people. I certainly feel this way as well, even though it is impossible to mention everyone by name. After all, this book project has been a long time in the making. The first draft was completed in the summer of 2004. Special thanks to those who read early versions of the book and offered insightful comments and suggestions, especially Dr. Michael P. Gutzmer, Dr. Loren R. Hettinger, Dr. Frances W. Kaye, Rev. Warren Pratt, Jr., Jenay, Moose, Willy, and several anonymous reviewers. Michael J. Kloberdanz edited the manuscript and provided astute, conscientious, and constructive criticism.

I also wish to express heartfelt thanks to a number of other knowledgeable and sharing people, including Geri and Lou, Cherrie C., Barbara and Linc, Bob and Kay, Cheri and Denny ("Spiderman"), Cassie W., Catherine, Cheri S., Drew, Ed, Elaine and Jon, Estevan, Fritz, Gordon, Gwen, Helen, James K., Jim, Les, Loren Y., Mario

Miguel, Mary Louise ("Gourd Woman"), Miku, Phil, Robert, Roger, Ron, Sandra, Sharon, Star, Troyd ("Tag"), and Vern.

Special acknowledgment is due my longtime friends Delbert Seminole and Lynette (Wohl) Seminole, as well as their six children: Cheyenne, Daniel ("Lone Man"), Prairie Rose, Dakota, Tashina, and Ree Hunter. Over the years, their fortitude and resilience (especially in the face of adversity and hardship) have been sources of real and sustained inspiration.

The completion of this book was not without its share of special challenges and even physical setbacks. In August 2005, while doing follow-up research for the book in eastern Nebraska, I slipped and fell off a high bluff overlooking the Platte. My youngest son Matt (then 24) was with me at the time of the mishap. Matt watched helplessly as I tumbled backwards more than sixty feet. After impact, my body went limp and rolled and rolled, right up to the edge of the river.

When I came to, I had no idea where I was or what had happened. A young stranger approached me. He was wide-eyed and out of breath. My "fight or flight" response immediately kicked in, for I surmised that the young man had assaulted me and knocked me unconscious. I reached down for a large branch and prepared to fight off my attacker. If I had to, I was determined to fully overcome him in order to survive. But then I heard the young man's frantic words: "Dad! Dad, are you alright? Dad?" I was confused. If this young fellow was calling me "Dad," might he indeed be my own son?

The amnesia lasted for only a few hours and luckily I suffered no broken bones or serious injuries. Nonetheless, the incident became a frequent topic of family conversation and the inevitable "what if" scenarios.

In the months and years that followed, my eyesight began to give me problems. Some days it was worse than others. An optometrist examined me and concluded my problems were due to cataracts. But the cataracts were not ready for surgical removal. I simply would have to wait. I was disheartened, for there were long stretches of time when

I was unable to visually focus and read the draft pages of my manuscript. In May 2010, I opted for early retirement from my academic position at the university. I greatly enjoyed teaching and working with students, but my health had deteriorated, owing to constant vision problems and lack of sleep.

With each passing year, I was losing more and more peripheral vision and when I looked at a newspaper, I read mostly the headlines. By 2016, my range of vision and mobility continued to narrow. Perhaps, I thought, getting back to the Platte River country would revitalize me. Soon a once-in-a-lifetime opportunity presented itself. Matt agreed to drive me down to Nebraska to witness the total solar eclipse of August 21, 2017. There the total eclipse would last more than two and a half minutes.

Equipped with our special eclipse glasses, Matt and I observed the great celestial event from the vantage point of *"Curaspa'ku,"* an old Pawnee site on the Platte River northeast of Grand Island. More than 700,000 travelers made their way to Nebraska to view the total solar eclipse on August 21. But Matt and I were the only two human beings who gathered on the cedar-covered summit of *"Curaspa'ku"* that day. Eagles circled above us. And then, when the blue summer sky began to darken, owls hooted and coyotes crawled out of their dens to serenade us with daytime song. The whole experience was surreal and unforgettable. Yet when I gazed up at the total solar eclipse, I beheld something quite disconcerting. Instead of seeing a dark sun illuminated by a dazzling "diamond ring," at times I saw two and even three dark suns.

One week later, back in Fargo, North Dakota, I sat and waited in a doctor's office to hear the results of my latest eye exam. Surely now I was ready for the cataract surgery. When the doctor entered, I could tell by his body language that something was wrong. He informed me that my ever-worsening vision was not due to cataracts or eye disease. My problem was very likely a tumor that was growing inside my head and wreaking havoc on my optic nerves. I asked the doctor if the nerve damage was irreparable. He admitted that he did not know.

Many medical tests soon followed, as well as four separate trips to the Mayo Clinic in Rochester, Minnesota. Early on the morning of October 17, 2017, I entered St. Mary's Hospital in Rochester and prepared to undergo surgery. The date October 17 had special significance to me, for it was the birthday of my oldest brother Jerry, who also had been diagnosed with a brain tumor and passed away in 2009. Two years before that (November 2007), my only sister Delores died suddenly from a brain aneurysm. So there was much to think about as I was wheeled through the hallways of St. Mary's Hospital en route to brain surgery.

The operation proceeded, and fortunately there were no complications. Within only a few days, my vision began to improve. By the time I got back home to Fargo, I was able to read the pages of my manuscript. And the double and triple images were gone.

Altogether, it took me nearly fifteen years to complete this book. Yet it would not have been possible without the involvement of caring family members and some beneficent guides. With deep appreciation and even deeper affection, I salute those individuals who first introduced me to the South Platte portion of the "Great Flat Water": my parents John C. and Elizabeth Helen Kloberdanz, as well as my siblings Jerry, Delores, Johnny, Stan, and our "brother" Chris Vrkljan.

While growing up on the South Platte, I somehow took for granted the fact that I had forty-four aunts and uncles. They were frequent guests in our farmhouse, and several of them, like "Albert's Mollie" and "Milky John," were superb raconteurs. With so many aunts and uncles, it should come as no surprise that I also could count more than one hundred first cousins. Sadly, an increasing number of those who peopled my early universe are now gone. Yet they loom large in the realm of recollection. There, in that magical domain, I see my kinfolk and they are gathering and waiting—on the bejeweled sands of the River Platte.

Most of all, I am grateful to the members of my immediate family

332 • TIMOTHY J. KLOBERDANZ

who have always been so encouraging and so supportive: my wife and best friend Rosalinda ("Rosi"), our sons Michael Josiah and Matthew Aaron, our daughter-in-law Paula Kay, and our grandson John Levi ("Johnny") Kloberdanz. I also want to mention Dancing Cloud ("Danci"), a direct descendant of Platte River Buddy.

Last, but certainly not least, I wish to acknowledge an intrepid little kingfisher that appeared at just the right time. There it was, with its long black bill and the characteristic ragged crest. The kingfisher was looking for a stream and a meal; I was in need of renewed strength and some inspiration. I like to think we both lucked out on that otherwise dreary day. *Idiwe tudaahe*—It is good.

ABOUT THE AUTHOR

Timothy J. Kloberdanz grew up on a farm along the South Platte River in northeastern Colorado. While still in his teens, he traveled the entire lengths of both the South Platte and North Platte Rivers, from their sources deep in the Rocky Mountains, to their eventual merging into a single wide river in Nebraska.

The author earned academic degrees at the University of Colorado (Boulder), Colorado State University (Fort Collins), and Indiana University (Bloomington). "Yet my very first school," he admits, "was the Platte River itself, and it provided a huge, interactive classroom that was equaled by no other."

When not visiting the Platte River country, Dr. Kloberdanz does research in the Northern Great Plains region and in other parts of the American West. A professor emeritus at North Dakota State University, he taught more than eight thousand students and received many awards during his academic career. He is the author or co-author of several books, and he has written numerous articles and other pieces, including a script for a prize-winning public television documentary.

Along with his wife Rosalinda, Dr. Kloberdanz makes his home in Fargo, North Dakota. "Fargo is renowned for its wicked winds and bone-numbing winters," the author writes. "But these realities are balanced by occasional gentle breezes and brilliant displays of the great northern lights."

Once Upon the River Platte is Timothy J. Kloberdanz's first full-length novel.

ABOUT THE PRESS

Clovis House is a small regional press based in Fargo, North Dakota. Our mission is to publish and promote books dealing with the Great American West (the region lying west of the Mississippi River and extending to the Pacific Ocean). We are especially interested in both non-fiction and fiction manuscripts that relate to the diverse cultures of the Great Plains and the Great American West.

We appreciate well-written, well-researched, and innovative manuscripts about indigenous groups, and also the various immigrant peoples who now call the American West their "home."

Currently, we are focusing on fictional works that would be ideal candidates for our "Legendary Rivers of the American West Series." The first book in this series dealt with the Red River of the North. The second focuses on the Platte River of the Central Plains. A third book about the Upper Mississippi River already is in progress. Clovis House is pleased to publish these works and thus bring attention to our region's "legendary rivers."

Our name, Clovis House, has both Native American and Euro-American connotations. "Clovis" is a term that describes the ancient big game hunting peoples who lived some 11-13,000 years ago, and who were among the earliest inhabitants of the American West. "Clovis" also refers to an ancient tribal leader who lived in Gaul from 466-511 AD. His cultural heirs and European descendants were among those who ventured into the Great American West some 1,300 years later.

Yet Clovis House is not merely a name; it is a place that houses and promotes creativity, innovation, literary excellence, and artistic vision.

Made in the USA
Coppell, TX
19 June 2020

28751447R00198